GOOD GIRLS NEVER RISE

SJ SYLVIS

AUTHOR'S NOTE

Good Girls Never Rise is the first book in the St. Mary's Duet. The St. Mary's Duet is a **DARK** boarding school romance intended for **MATURE** (18+) readers. This duet is labeled as dark due to the dark themes (strong language, sexual scenes, and situations) throughout. Be aware that it contains **TRIGGERS** that some readers may find bothersome. **Reader Discretion is advised.**

Good Girls Never Rise is the first book in the St. Mary's Duet and it will end on a *cliff-hanger*. **It is a romantic suspense slow-burn**. Book two, **Bad Boys Never Fall**, will be releasing December 2nd, 2021 and it is the final book in the duet.

WELCOME TO

SAINT MARY'S

BOARDING SCHOOL

WHERE

GOOD GIRLS NEVER RISE

S.J. SYLVIS

PROLOGUE

Two Months Ago

GEMMA

Branches slashed and whipped against my skin as if razor blades were being chucked at me from a short distance, but the pain the tiny sticks and leaves inflicted over my flesh was nothing more than a brief thought as fear wrapped itself around every last limb, pushing my feet farther and farther away from the place I'd called home my entire life.

The last few hours had completely spun my world upside down, and then again and again until my sketchbook was being shoved in my backpack and my shoelaces were being tied over my feet.

It was nearing dusk, the sun slowly dipping behind the thick clouds. Soon, he wouldn't be able to find me. Soon, I'd be gone, far and away from him and everything he'd ever done or said. His beliefs and corrupted plans for me would be nothing more than panic-inducing thoughts that the breeze of the ocean would whisk away.

The second the guidance counselor pulled me into the principal's office, I knew what a grave mistake I'd made. My sketchbook laid right there in the center of Principal Malcoy's desk, opened to the last sketch I'd done while waiting for the final bell to ring. I hadn't even known it was missing. How careless was I?

It was obvious that they'd flipped through the rest of the drawings, if their faces had anything to say. Slack-jawed, glassy-eyed, suspicious glances to my body, particularly my wrists.

Another branch seemed to come out of nowhere as another piece from earlier filtered into my head: *"Gemma, is there any truth to these drawings? Is someone hurting you at home?"*

My fingers slipped underneath the straps of my backpack as I continued dashing through the trees. My heart flew through my chest as Tobias' face came to the forefront of my brain, and I tried pushing that away too.

"Gemma, these are disturbing. And if this is something that is occurring, you need to let us know. We are here to help you."

Now, looking back to a couple of hours ago, I shouldn't have trusted them. I shouldn't have trusted them at all. The only person I should have listened to was Tobias. He may have been more like a ghost these days, but the venomous truth had never been more clear to me than at that moment: *Trust no one, and just survive, Gemma.*

My foot caught on a tree root as I thudded down to my knees. My jeans had holes in the front, and I knew I was bleeding by the sharp sting against my skin. I hopped back to my feet, regardless.

"I hate that it came to this, but my niece is mentally ill. It's why I've kept her home for most of her life. My mother, Anne, home-schooled her along with the girls at the group home. Once my mother had her stroke and the group home was shut down, I was forced to send Gemma to public school for the remainder of the year. The state,

no matter my stance in the judicial system, wouldn't allow for her to continue homeschooling without a parent or guardian's help, and given the fact that the state does not require homeschooled children to have educational records other than an affidavit, a social worker thought sending her to public school would be a good starting point. I've had full custody of Gemma since she was a young child, right after her mother committed suicide." My uncle's lies had shot through the closed door of the office, and fear squeezed against every inch of my body, and before I knew what I was doing, I was running.

And I was still running.

I would run for the rest of my life if it kept me away from him.

My *uncle*, Judge Stallard—one of the most sought-out judges in the entire country with more sway in this town than Jesus himself—was a bad, bad man who did things to me that I once thought to be normal but learned, very recently, were not.

Running was never my intention—not until Auntie had her stroke and the group home was shut down. Not until the social worker discovered that the judge of our quaint town had a niece no one had ever heard of. Not until I started getting curious and began snooping in his office when he was gone all day, working cases with criminals that were no worse than he was. Not until I'd found the old photos and videos that he'd taken of my mother when Tobias and I were in the same exact room as young babies. And now...now things were even worse.

Running was my only option, Tobias missing or not. I had to hope, with every last ragged breath I took in the forest beyond our manor of a home, that Tobias was somewhere safe and knew better than to come back for me.

He always promised he would.

But that was then, and this was now.

Now, my only option was to survive, just like he'd told me to.

My foot snagged on yet another firm root in the ground, but I was able to right myself and keep on running. My hands were still clenched around the straps of my backpack as the sun continued to disappear to make way for night. Brown strands of hair stuck to my sticky skin, and just as I reached up to push them away from my eyes, I tripped again, but this time, there was no root in the ground that caused me to fall.

Instead, there was a towering figure at my back, and without even looking behind me, I knew whose shadow it was.

"What did I tell you about good girls breaking rules, Gemma?" His hand clasped my ankle, and I was whooshed backward, the breath in my already tight chest seizing and clawing to be let out. "Now, you'll have to be punished."

Even through the sound of rapid heartbeats drumming in my ears, I could hear the sinister, sick pleasure in his tone.

Right then, I knew what a terrible, hasty mistake I'd made by trying to run away without a plan.

And now, I'd have to pay.

CHAPTER ONE

GEMMA

RAIN TRICKLED down the side of the window in an ingenuous manner, unknowing of all the evil in the world. It was innocent and free in ways that I would never be but so desperately wished I could. I was the good girl—naive, soft, quiet, submissive—but I was the furthest thing from pure. I wasn't shielded from the bad in the world. Instead, I was thrust head first into purgatory. Every single day was an uphill battle of wading through everything I'd ever been taught.

The moisture of the sky fell over my shoulders as Tobias' words echoed throughout my head, *"I'll come back for you. Just do as you're told, Gemma. Survive."*

In some ways, the rain pounding my skin and soaking my long chestnut hair felt like a rebirth, like I was cutting through the choppy waves and coming out stronger on the other side. St. Mary's boarding school, the strictest boarding school in the Western Hemisphere, probably terrified most. But it was like a beacon in the dark to someone like me. Even through the slanted rain, the building appeared like a haunted mansion with its cracked stone pillars and castle-like steeples. The archway was ominous, and the dark and looming clouds surrounding my new home should have scared me off.

But I wasn't afraid of the dark.

I'd looked pure evil in the eye before, and this place wasn't evil.

Creeping up the steps, my luggage bumped along the cobblestone beneath my shoes. I opened the door and stepped inside, inhaling the scent of aged, ancient books and stagnant dust. The entryway was gloomy, and a single chandelier hung above my head, casting the room in a dim light. The floor was wet below my feet as rain continued to fall off my gray jacket, and the ends of my hair looked black instead of the warm brown color they really were as they hung like ropes over my shoulders.

My head swung to the right as a tall, oak and wrought-iron door opened, and a man popped his head out. "Gemma?"

I swallowed before speaking. My voice was hesitant and hardly audible, and I hated that because, although I felt stronger here than I ever had before, I still fell back into that vulnerable, insecure version of myself that I'd been forced into since a young child. "Yes."

The man's expression changed for a slight moment. His green eyes dipped, a tight wrinkle etching itself onto his forehead. He squinted deeper before he shook his head, as if clearing his mind of something, and gave me a warm smile. "Please, come in. You can leave your bag right there. Do you have any more? I can send someone to grab them."

Shifting in my squeaky shoes, I quickly shook my head. "This is all I have."

His eyes dipped again as he glanced at my small suitcase then back to my face. "Okay, well, please come in."

The long, checkered hallway was unmoving and quiet as my shoes squeaked along the waxed floor. I wrapped my arms around my slender torso, feeling self-conscious as I brought attention to myself. The second I was through the heavy door, the man gestured over to a seat in front of his desk.

I eyed the shiny name plate on the mahogany surface: *Headmaster Tate Ellison*. Scanning the man again, and his large office, I'll admit, I was skeptical. He didn't look like a man in power. He was warm and inviting. The green in his eyes was charming, and the dark hair on his head was messy and looked in need of a haircut. In simpler terms, he was *boyish*. There was no way he was over the age of forty.

His crescent-like smile met his eyes as he sat down behind his desk. His chair screamed out a squeak when he leaned back, placing his hands behind his head. He was at least wearing a dress shirt and tie, but it was wrinkled. Richard said St. Mary's was strict, but the headmaster looked anything but. Then again, I couldn't really trust myself to judge.

"Gemma. Welcome to St. Mary's. I'm sure your..." The headmaster looked leery, eyeing me skeptically before clearing his throat and placing his elbows on his desk. "I'm sure your Uncle Richard has told you a bit about our school and our rules, yes?"

I swallowed again, unmoving in my seat. "Yes, sir."

"Do you have any questions?"

Did I have any questions? *Oh, did I ever.*

"No, sir."

He shifted uncomfortably in his seat, glancing away. "Your uncle wanted me to call him as soon as you arrived. Let's do that, yes?"

Was he asking my permission?

I flushed, likely more uncomfortable than he was. I knew why I was uncomfortable...but why was he?

The headmaster reached over and grabbed his phone, his office so quiet I could hear the dial tone on the other end. I glanced around the room, eyeing the worn books lining the shelves and the globe that sat on the very edge of his desk. There was a framed map behind him, and I zeroed in on the United States. I had no idea where I wanted to go when given the chance, but it would be somewhere sunny and near a beach. Somewhere where I could just *be*.

"Judge Stallard," Headmaster Ellison said, his voice stern —much different from the warm tone he had used when he welcomed me into his office. *And there it was—that power.* "Gemma has arrived."

Chills broke out along my arms as I heard my uncle's voice. I cringed internally at the word *uncle*, feeling a hot burn zip through my chest. Judge Richard Stallard wasn't technically my uncle, even if I—and everyone else—referred to him as that. Richard and I weren't blood related, and I took comfort in knowing that. Although, maybe if we were blood related, he wouldn't treat me the way that he did.

His voice was muffled, so I leaned forward, pretending to mess with my soggy shoe. *"Thank you for calling, Tate. I don't feel the need to remind you of the stipulations of my niece, but please remember to keep a careful eye on her. She has run away before, and I wouldn't put it past her again. I know you will follow through with your word to keep tabs on her."*

I slowly sat up in my seat and found the headmaster eyeing me stoically. His gaze never left mine as he said, "I can assure you that our school is well protected, and we watch our students very carefully." It might have been my imagination, but I swore the headmaster's lips twitched as the words left his mouth effortlessly.

Richard's voice boomed, and my stomach coiled. *"Don't forget...your family owes me this favor, so make sure you watch my niece. Call me if anything unsettling arises. She has a wild imagination."*

The headmaster continued staring at me as he assured Richard, again, that he would keep a careful eye on me. I began to sweat and quickly glanced away when he thrust the phone in my direction. "Your uncle would like to speak with you, Gemma."

I swallowed, and it felt like swallowing a bunch of bees. My hand shook as I grabbed onto the phone and placed it to my ear. "Hello, Uncle," I croaked.

"Gemma," he reprimanded. "You've made it safely. Good." *Was it, though?* "I hope this teaches you a little lesson. You have given me no other choice. I can no longer trust you." My nostrils flared with my rising anger, and for once, I didn't hold that back. I was too far away from him to feel that unyielding amount of fear. "The headmaster will be keeping an eye on you, and if I hear that you are doing things you shouldn't be doing and bringing unwanted attention to yourself or this family, well...you know what happens when you break the rules."

My throat squeezed as if his hands were back around it. "Yes, sir. I understand," I said, pushing down that anger that made me burn from the inside out. *Survive, Gemma.*

"Good girl. Now hang up and go get acclimated with your surroundings. At least now I know you're safe and tucked away somewhere, and you won't do anything foolish. And don't forget, sweetheart...I have ties with everyone."

How could I ever forget? Did he truly think the thought had escaped me after last time? Judge Richard Stallard was a very powerful man. I thought he was bluffing before, likely due to my perfectly sheltered life that he'd created for me. But I wouldn't be caught off guard again. I wouldn't make the same mistake twice—because my life truly depended on it.

Tobias told me to survive, and that was exactly what I was doing.

Surviving.

The line disconnected, and I gave the phone back to the headmaster. I eyed him a little differently now, much more hesitantly than before. Richard said that the headmaster, or at least his family, had owed him a favor, and it was never a good thing if you owed Judge Richard Stallard something.

As soon as the headmaster dropped the phone back to the receiver, he opened his mouth to say something to me, but it rang just as quickly as his lips parted. We both eyed it suspiciously, me assuming it was Richard calling back to give me another open-ended warning, because he could never just say it once, or even twice, but over and over again. My hand still ached from the last time he'd made me write my *mistake* down over and over again.

The headmaster abruptly answered the phone. "Head-master Ellison." His expression faltered for a moment as the other person spoke, but he quickly recovered. "Send him to me immediately." His voice was gravelly, a hint of anger beneath the surface. I glanced away, almost too afraid to look any longer. If the headmaster knew Richard...well, who knew what type of man he was. "And as for her," he started, his voice a little softer, "I'll be down to discuss the situation with her as soon as I talk with my nephew. Thank you, Mr. Clark."

As soon as I heard the receiver click down, I peeked up at the headmaster. His tired eyes were shut tightly as he pinched the bridge of his nose. The room felt tense, and I almost shot out of my seat to leave, but he slowly dropped his hand and gave me yet another reassuring smile.

"I'm sorry about that, Gemma. I have a situation with my..." He cleared his throat. "With another student. Do you mind sitting out in the lobby for a moment while I talk with him? Afterwards, I will take you to your room and get you settled."

"Oh, of course," I answered, climbing to my feet. I glanced down at the arms of the leather chair I was sitting in, noticing the crescent-like shapes that my nails had put there. My fists clenched. I hoped he didn't notice.

The headmaster quickly followed behind me, opening the door before ushering me to a bench that was right beside the door. "This won't take long, Gemma."

"It's no prob—"

Both of our heads turned to the sound of slow, shuffling feet down the hall and the lingering echo of a whistle. The headmaster groaned at the sight of a student slowly walking across the black-and-white checkered floor, the same checkered floor that I had stood on just minutes before in all my soaking glory. But now, there was a shift in the air. The white-and-black checkered floor seemed to be put down, tile by tile, just for this person to stride over. A flush started over my cheeks, my body suddenly feeling very hot.

The boy was very tall with broad shoulders, and he was sporting black pants that hung on his slender hips and a white dress shirt that was untucked at the bottom. Almost all of the buttons were undone, allowing a thin sliver of chest to show. A striped maroon-and-gold tie hung loosely around his neck, and then, over his shoulder, he was holding a matching maroon blazer with what seemed to be one single finger.

The closer he got, the hotter I burned. My tongue was stuck to the roof of my mouth as he continued down the hall with incredibly too much swagger, and I hoped that neither he nor the headmaster spoke to me, because I wasn't sure I could form a sentence.

I'd noticed boys like him before, at my old school, before my *uncle* had ripped me away. They were amongst the popular bunch, the ones that made my skin a little prickly. But this boy? He was downright dangerous because he was so captivating. I couldn't look away, even though I wanted to. Even though I needed to.

His chin tipped to the headmaster when he was only a few yards away. I noticed the red flush over his cheeks and neck and the mark of a purple blotch just below his ear. *Did someone hurt him? Or was that...*

"What's up, Uncle Tate?" He smirked, his chiseled cheeks lifting in that delicious bad-boy way.

I swallowed, the gulp working its way from my throat down to the very bottom of my belly. Suddenly, the boy's eyes flicked over to me, half hiding behind the headmaster. His head tilted in a predatory way, and I almost squeaked. *Almost.* The blue in his eyes matched the sky perfectly, except they glittered with something I'd only ever dreamed about.

"Get in my office right now, Isaiah." I shifted my attention between the two, and the headmaster's eyes were no bigger than slits across his face. Isaiah hissed a laugh under his breath as he swiveled swiftly on his shoe and walked into the office.

I let out a held breath when the headmaster turned toward me. "Please excuse me for a moment. This won't take long."

My lips stayed sealed as I nodded because I was honestly unable to speak. As I sat down on the bench beside the door, I waited until he shut it behind him, and then I scooted all the way up to its hinges. I could hear their voices on the other side, despite the large oak door acting as a barricade.

Isaiah's laugh lingered through the air, and something in my stomach fluttered.

I pushed my back against the hard wall behind me as I continued to eavesdrop.

Listening and observing in the shadows and behind locked doors was my only source of power. After all, it was how I began to learn the truth.

CHAPTER TWO

ISAIAH

MY UNCLE WAS ABSOLUTELY livid with me. My lips rolled together as I fought to keep the smile off my face. He slammed his hands onto his messy desk and leveled me with a stony glare.

"Isaiah. What the fuck."

A laugh was lurking in the back of my throat. "Did you just curse, Uncle Tate?"

The sound of his hand slapping against the desk again did nothing but heighten my amusement. "I'm not your uncle right now. I'm the headmaster. As much as I'd like to believe that what Mr. Clark said was a blatant lie, I know better. So go on. Start from the beginning."

Oh, this was going to be interesting. I leaned back in the leather chair and placed my forearms down on the arms, gripping them with my hands. I ran my fingers along the small divots embedded into the leather, glancing down to the tiny moon-shaped cuts into it. "Who's the girl out in the hall? We get a new student?"

My uncle's face—excuse me, *the headmaster*'s face turned a deep shade of red. "Isaiah, so help me God. The SMC is already threatening to expel you! You understand that, don't you?"

Of course I fucking understood that. SMC stood for St. Mary's Committee. In other words, they were the glue that held the school together. All school decisions were run through them, as were disciplinary actions.

"Do you *want* me to tell your father of all the havoc you've been setting forth since stepping foot into St. Mary's? If I'd told him about the fake IDs, or the fights, or the sneaking into girls' rooms," he growled, "or any of it...you'd be twenty feet underground, surrounded by nothing but stone walls and men twice your age breaking every bone in your body for the fucking fun of it. The committee is ready to throw you out on your ass, and your father will be livid."

I glanced away, my chest rumbling with animosity. "Why haven't you told him, then?" I asked, looking my uncle dead in the face. "You keep threatening it, but you have done no such thing. So why? And the SMC has been threatening to expel me for over a year."

My uncle and father were nothing alike. My father was all business, and my Uncle Tate, despite being in charge of St. Mary's, was lax. He didn't typically get angry, but if he did, he got over it quickly. He had a soft spot for troublemakers.

My uncle's eyes narrowed as he dropped his head. His hands came up, and he ran his fingers through his hair all the way to the base of his skull before giving me a look that had me wavering for a second. "Maybe I will, Isaiah. I thought..." He cleared his throat before clasping his hands together. "I thought I could help you. I've been you, Isaiah. I *was* you." His voice grew louder, and he glanced at the door behind me before lowering it again. "I know what it's like to be the black sheep. I'm trying to help you, Isaiah. That's why I sent you to

Ms. Glenburg for counseling, plus the SMC wanted something done with you. They wanted to see the potential in you that I see." He chuckled sarcastically, and I took a deep breath, watching him with a careful eye. "So tell me why."

"Why what?" I asked, sounding bored.

He leaned back in his seat, glaring at me. "Why did you seduce her? That's the only reasonable explanation. Some may blame the adult in this situation, but"—my uncle crept forward, almost in a menacing way, before leaning his arms on his desk—"I blame *you*."

I sighed, a small smile playing on my lips.

"Start talking. Or you can kiss any amount of freedom you have away this very second."

I peered up at him and saw that he was actually serious for once. *Fuck.*

"Fine," I started.

And then I spilled the dirty truth.

"ISAIAH." Ms. Glenburg grabbed onto my hands. Her skin was soft against mine, and she flushed the second I raised an eyebrow at her.

We'd been having these weekly sessions for about a month now, and each one, she got a little closer to me. Today, she even went as far as touching me. Naughty, naughty.

"Yes, Ms. Glenburg?" I asked slyly.

Her hands moved from mine, and she took a shaky breath. My gaze went to her chest as she inhaled, her breasts spilling out of her low-cut, dressy top. I couldn't help but wonder if she had worn it for me. If only she knew I was playing her. If I was a decent guy, I may have felt a little bad. She thought she was in control, but she was wrong.

"Are you going to be truthful today? Are you going to tell me why you have been so defiant? Why you've been acting out against your father? How you've ended up at St. Mary's?"

I shrugged, loosening the tie around my neck. We were alone in an empty classroom. Her classroom. Ms. Glenburg was the school counselor, but she also taught a few elective courses like psychology and sociology. It was poetic that a woman like Ms. Glenburg could be fooled by me when she actually studied the human psyche for a living.

I leaned forward into her space. She didn't move, and her dark-red lips parted as a breath escaped her. "Why don't you tell me, Ms. Glenburg? You've been studying me for weeks now. Why do you think I act out?"

God. It was so easy to toy with her. I knew it was wrong, but that was what I was known for. Why not live up to the standard, right? My uncle was foolish if he thought someone like Ms. Glenburg could change me.

"I think you act out because it's the only form of control you have."

I shifted my eyes from her tits to her eyes. "Go on."

She moved in her seat, recrossing her legs. "You have no control over your life. You were sent to a strict boarding school without your consent. From what you've told me, your college is already decided. Your major. Your job afterward to work with your father. You have no control over anything, so the only thing you can do is grab a hold of your behavior."

Fuck. My stomach tightened with her words. I didn't like that she was indicating that I didn't have any control over my life. I also didn't like that what she said made sense.

Something evil stirred inside of me at the very thought of my father treating me like I was a fucking puppet in his game. In a way, Ms. Glenburg was right. My choices have been made for me since I was born. I didn't have control in most aspects of my life, and that made me irate.

"You don't think I have control, Ms. Glenburg?" I asked, shifting closer to her. My hand fell onto her knee, and she gasped.

"I—" she stuttered, staring at my hand on her bare skin, sitting nice and still below the hem of her skirt.

"That's not true, Ms. Glenburg." I smirked, glancing at her lips. "I'm in control right now."

"Are you?" she whispered.

My hand stayed on her knee as I glanced over my shoulder. "You said my father has control over my life, but I don't see him anywhere in this room." I gave her a sheepish look. "In fact, I don't see anyone in this room..." My finger trailed over to the inside of her leg. "Except you."

She swallowed, her cheeks rising with color.

"Do you want to see me in control, Ms. Glenburg?" I would show her that she was wrong. *My father didn't have control over me.*

Or did he?

"I'm not sure," she answered breathlessly.

I smiled at her as my hand moved higher up her leg, disappearing underneath the dark fabric. I took my other hand and gently took her glasses off the bridge of her nose and placed them onto the desk beside us.

Ms. Glenburg was twice my age—somewhere in her thirties—but she was still hot in this authoritative sort of way. Either way, I still would have been in this situation, but it was to my benefit that she actually did get my dick hard.

"I thought we were telling the truth here," I said as my hand stopped moving up toward her center. "You asked me to be truthful, but are *you* being truthful, Ms. Glenburg?"

She gulped before licking her lips. Her hazel eyes held that hungry look in them, like she wanted me to fuck her.

"Do you want to see me in control?"

Her words were as rushed as her breaths. "I could get fired for this, Isaiah." Try *'you could go to jail,'* since I'm technically a minor, but that was just semantics.

"Then we better not get caught."

Her hand was wrapped around my tie within a flash, and she pulled us both to the desk as her legs parted around my waist. Her *fuck-me eyes were droopy and hooded as she peered up at me from lying back on the hard wood. I placed both hands beside her head, her blonde hair spilling out all around her.*

A jolt of blinding excitement went through me at the thought of getting caught. It was a rush. A rush I'd welcome over and over again until I no longer had the chance.

"You're wrong, Ms. Glenburg. I am in control." I dipped my head down and captured her lips with mine. My dick pushed up to meet her warm pussy as her skirt hiked its way to her hips. Her hands went to my biceps as her tongue swept in my mouth, taking every bit of my lust that I gave her.

A whimper sounded from her as I backed away and found her wet panties. A wicked smile formed its way on my mouth as I pushed the silk aside and ran my finger over her slick slit. She arched her back, one leg wrapping around my back, as her hand dove underneath the dip in her blouse to grab herself. "Already so wet," I teased, my finger rubbing over her swollen clit. "Tell me," I whispered, ready to finger-fuck her. "Have you been wanting this from the beginning?"

Ms. Glenburg was panting as I stared down at her, her eyes barely open. "I've wanted this since the second you stepped in this school, Isaiah. You're not like the others. You aren't a boy. You're jaded."

That was when I let my finger sink into her warm walls. They constricted almost immediately as she moaned loudly. So greedy. I have to admit, this was my first time fucking around with an older woman, but I was definitely enjoying it. She knew what she wanted, and she wasn't afraid to go after it.

Her hips curled as she palmed her tit. I reached my hand up and unbuttoned the rest of her top as I pumped her faster.

"I want to fuck you," I said, wondering if she'd actually agree to it. This was too easy. If my uncle saw this, he'd have a fucking aneurysm.

"You're the one in control," she moaned.

"That I am," I said as I pulled my finger out and unbuttoned my pants. She pushed herself back onto her desk, papers floating to the

ground wistfully, and spread her legs. I reached up roughly and pulled her panties down past her legs and dropped them to the floor.

Just as I had the condom on and placed myself at her entrance, the door swung open, and in came a cart full of janitorial products along with Mr. Clark who looked like he'd seen a ghost.

"Oops," I muttered as Ms. Glenburg peered back.

If only I could have been in Mr. Clark's position and see what he saw: me, a student, hovering over a teacher with my dick in my hand as Ms. Glenburg lay spread open on top of her desk with her chest on full display.

She quickly sat up and covered herself, trying to talk her way out of it. She was flustered, rushing her words out so quickly it sounded like she was speaking a foreign language.

"OKAY!" My uncle slapped the desk again and brought me back to reality. "That's enough!"

I smirked as I began buttoning the rest of my shirt, the buttons sliding into their slots effortlessly. I shrugged. "You said you wanted to know."

"Isaiah." He leveled me with a stare. "Did you truly fuck her—"

"I didn't fuck her," I interrupted him after crossing my arms over my chest. *But I would have if I hadn't been interrupted.*

He glared at me, and I rolled my lips again, trying to hold it together. I knew I was pushing his buttons, probably a little too far, but I couldn't help it. I was a little worked up.

My uncle sat back in his seat and rubbed his chin as if he were the one studying me now instead of her. I kept a hold of his stare for a few seconds as he squinted at me, analyzing me, scrutinizing me. Then, I began glancing around his stuffy, crammed office with entirely too many weird artifacts, like the fucking ancient globe at the end of his desk. Did it even have the correct continents on it?

"You felt threatened."

I shifted my attention back to him without changing my posture. "Excuse me?"

"She made sense. She saw right through you. It made you angry, so you did the only thing you could think of, and you turned on your charm to prove a point."

I clenched my jaw. "And what point would that be?"

His eyebrow lifted. "You wanted to show her, and me, and maybe even yourself that she was wrong. That you *do* have control." He chuckled, throwing his hands up with astonishment. "She was right. That's exactly why you act out."

"No, it fucking isn't." My temper was rising. My fists were clenching around the arms of the chair as I dug my nails into the same crescent-shaped marks that were already there.

My uncle took a deep steady breath, running his hands through his unkempt hair once again. "Isaiah." His green eyes wrinkled at the edges. *Fuck. This was it. He was kicking me out.* I wanted to pull my own hair out. I felt very unstable at the moment, completely unsteady in my seat, even though my feet were planted firmly on the ground.

"Spit it out, Uncle."

"This is your last chance. Do you hear me?" My hands unclenched slightly. "I want to help you. I do. Stop fucking up on purpose, because I can't keep turning my head at the big things. I'll lose this school, and that's the last thing I or anyone here needs."

I said nothing, and we stared at each other for far too long. We were having an unspoken conversation about all the things our family was mixed up in—neither one of us wanted to speak of it. He got out, but it wasn't that easy for me.

"Isaiah," he repeated

I held my hand up. "I hear you."

His stern gaze that resembled my father's all too well fell. "You do have a choice. You know that, right?"

I scoffed, pushing myself back into the chair forcefully. "You don't truly believe that, do you?"

My uncle looked away, thinking for a moment before shaking his head and standing up hastily. He walked around his desk, as I sat lazily in the chair in front of him, and propped himself on the edge. Leveling my chin, I locked onto his gaze.

"This is your last chance, and as much as I don't want to say those words to you...I have to. If the SMC finds out about this or anything else you impulsively do, they will likely expel you, and then your father will get involved." He pushed off the desk and began walking past me toward the door.

Silence filled his office as I stood up, keeping my back to him. I peered up at the large, framed map that was plastered to the wall behind his empty chair. How easy would it be for me to just walk away? To flip my father the bird and leave the family name behind like my uncle?

But it wasn't that easy for me. There were casualties to that.

Like Jack.

I wouldn't do to him what Jacobi did to me.

I wouldn't leave him in the dark to fend for himself. I didn't feel much these days, other than anger, but I knew, deep down, Jack meant the most to me.

My uncle's voice hit me from behind. "You could make the same choice I did."

I spun around quickly and glared at him. My rebellious, rule-breaking, gave-zero-fucks persona had vanished like quicksand between my fingers. "I won't do that to Jack."

His hand was on the doorknob, but before he twisted it, he sighed. "Then get it together, because the SMC will eventually get tired of my excuses for you, and they will go straight to your father to let him know you've been expelled. There will be no more chances."

I scoffed again, ready to walk out the door and push this conversation away. "So what are you saying exactly? That I should stop fucking teachers?" I laughed under my breath, trying to get back to my calmer state.

His jaw was tight. "Yeah, Isaiah. That's exactly what I'm saying. The SMC is already breathing down my neck." The green in his eyes hardened to stone. "If you are expelled, there will be nothing I can do to help you. And that's if they let me keep my job after saving your ass over and over again. You do know where your father will send you, right? He'll send you right to the Covens. Tell me you understand. If you think St. Mary's is bad, you'll be in for a rude awakening there."

I didn't think St. Mary's was all that bad, but I didn't say that. Instead, I grumbled, "I get it. I know what the Covens is."

"Good." He swung the door open and grinned. "Now, as your punishment, you're going to take our new student, Gemma, to her room—322—and give her a tour of the school while I go do damage control."

I rolled my eyes. That was it? *That* was my punishment?

Before I walked past him and into the hall, he pulled me back by my shirt and whispered, "She's a good girl. Take her to her room, show her around, and then leave her alone."

I snickered when he let go of me. "Don't worry. Good girls aren't my type, Uncle."

CHAPTER THREE

GEMMA

"Gemma!" The headmaster walked out of his office with his nephew following closely behind him.

I quickly averted my eyes away from Isaiah, although I couldn't ignore the dip in my stomach when our gazes collided. "Isaiah will be giving you a tour of the school, and then he will take you to your room to make sure you are settled." He glared at him once before giving me another warm smile. "I'll be sure to check on you later before lights out."

My lips gently tugged upward as he turned and began storming down the desolate hallway, leaving me alone with a guy my age for the first time in...ever.

Isaiah and I stood beside each other for a few painfully awkward seconds before he broke the silence with his cool voice.

"Did you enjoy the conversation?" he asked, his head tilting to the side as he scrutinized me. His blue eyes twinkled with something that should have warned me off, but surprisingly, I kept a hold of his stare.

"What?" I asked, feigning confusion.

He smirked, but it didn't quite reach his eyes. I followed the flicking of his chin to the wooden bench I was sitting on seconds ago. "When I went into my uncle's office, you were sitting wayyy over there." His gaze met the spot I was in when I had first sat down. "But when we came out, you were pushed all the way up to the door. So, I'll ask again." His eyebrows rose for a split second as he casually placed his hands in his pockets. "Did you enjoy hearing that I fucked a teacher?"

Did he really just ask me that?

My tongue was heavy in my mouth. Like if I were to speak, my words would tumble out in the wrong order.

The fluttering of my eyelashes tickled my cheek as I continued staring at him. The longer we looked at each other, the harder my heart beat. The pounding was deafening. It was so thunderous I wondered if he could hear it too.

After a few more seconds, Isaiah laughed under his breath before rolling his eyes. "My uncle was right. You are a good girl."

My fists instantly clenched with his words.

"Don't call me that," I snapped, feeling the skin of my palm split open from my nails. I gasped at my outburst and looked behind me, as if Richard was going to pop out of a hidden corner and drag me to the basement to repent for my sin of not only talking to Isaiah with such a harsh tone but for just talking to him in general.

When I turned back around and met Isaiah's face, he was grinning wildly. His white teeth glimmered behind his perfect blush-colored lips.

"Hmm," was all he muttered before reaching down and grabbing my bag. He spun around and began walking down the hall. I followed after him because I wasn't sure what else I was supposed to be doing. But I was still agitated that he had provoked me, and even more so that I had acted on it.

The hallway grew darker the farther we walked, as if we were stalking toward the pits of hell. The strangely bare walls stole my attention before I found myself standing below a large staircase that had dark, wooden, decorative handrails that seemed to go on for forever.

Isaiah glanced back at me, still sporting a smirk between his chiseled cheeks, before he began hopping up the stairs like an Olympic athlete, holding my one suitcase in tow. His long strides pulled him quickly, and I struggled to keep up, but before long, we were standing on the landing with two more sets of stairs on each side.

"To the right is the girls' wing, and to the left is the boys'." I nodded, and he continued on. "We aren't allowed to go to the other wing except for special circumstances. But some of us break the rules." My brow crinkled, and he had a hard time keeping his face straight. "As in, boys sneak into the girls' rooms, and sometimes the other way around...depending on the type of girl." He started inching toward the right set of stairs, walking backward as he smiled at me. "We won't have to worry about you doing that, though. Right, Good Girl?"

I ground my teeth and inhaled all the oxygen that I could.

He laughed, and I wasn't sure I liked the way my heart squeezed at the sound. I was naive, and I had a hard time reading people, but I knew he was making fun of me. And I didn't like that. Not one bit. It made me feel small, and I was really freaking tired of feeling small.

"Stop calling me that," I bit out, crossing my arms over my chest.

He chuckled and hastily turned around and skipped up the rest of the steps. I waited a few seconds, calming down the heat stirring in my belly before stomping up the rest of the stairs. He was all the way at the end of the hallway by the time I reached the top, but I could hardly see him through the thick darkness.

The hallway was long and deep, laid with dark-red carpet underneath my feet. It was bathed with an eerie light from the few sconces on the wall in between each set of doors, and if I believed in ghosts, I would certainly be feeling a little bit uneasy at the moment.

"Are you coming?" Isaiah shouted. "Or are you afraid of the dark?"

I didn't answer as I crept along the soft floor, running my finger along the grooved, walnut-colored wood. So far, St. Mary's seemed like an old medieval castle that was turned into a boarding school. And for all I knew, it was. Each door I'd passed was thick, dark wood with intricate carvings in the mass of them. They each had iron-clad doorknobs with chains attached at the bottom, and for the first time since setting foot in this place, a chill raced down my spine.

I was a few steps away from Isaiah, the warm glow of a lantern light shining on the side of his face, making him that much more beautiful. I gritted my teeth at the thought that came through, but it was suddenly gone as the sound of one of the chains ricocheting off another came from behind me. Panic set deep into my bones, and I ran straight into Isaiah's hard chest, bouncing off him like I'd hit a brick wall.

"Whoa," he blurted as his strong hands wrapped around my upper arms, steadying me.

I gasped at the touch. Sparks flew. Heat sourced from his palms, and when he let go, I instantly took a step back.

"Isaiah?" a girl whisper-yelled. I quickly spun around and saw a pretty girl with long lean legs step out of a door. "Sneaking into the gi—" She stopped talking when her eyes dropped over to me. "Oh. Who's this?"

Isaiah groaned, his words clipped. "New student. Go back to your room, Callie."

She huffed as she crossed her arms over her chest in a bratty manner. "Who are you? Father Isaiah? Telling me to go back to my room..." She huffed out the last part of her sentence, and Isaiah snickered.

"I remember you calling me daddy a few nights ago, so yeah, I guess you could call me that." My mouth dropped open slightly, and then she yelled, "Fuck you, Isaiah," and then swiftly turned around and slammed her door.

Wow.

"Let's go, Good Girl," Isaiah whispered in my ear, and I jumped before following after him again.

He waited until we were stopped in front of what I assumed to be my new room to say, "If you're afraid of the dark, I suggest getting a flashlight."

I gingerly peered up, still feeling a bit vulnerable that I was so spooked from the sound of chains that it had me running into him. And if I was being honest, I was a little embarrassed to admit that his and Callie's little spar distracted me enough to make me forget about the chains all together. That was very unusual. "I'm not afraid of the dark."

Isaiah studied me with an interested look before raising his hand to knock. "Then what *are* you afraid of?"

The chains were clamping around my wrists. The gag was being stuffed in my mouth. "Nothing," I answered as he rapped his knuckles on the door. "Nothing at all."

He kept his icy-blue gaze on me as the door opened up. Before I brushed past him, his hand clamped down on my elbow, and he whispered his hot breath into my ear, "And here I thought good girls didn't lie, *Gemma*."

Heat spread over my skin like I was standing in the middle of a burning room. I inched my head to the side, my neck more exposed than before. "Well, maybe I'm not a good girl, *Isaiah*." Then, I ripped my elbow out of his grasp and entered my new home.

It took him a few moments to follow after me, and I was certain it was because he was as surprised as I was at my behavior. I wasn't sure what had come over me. I had never, in my entire life, talked to someone as confidently as I had just spoken to Isaiah. I felt in control but totally out of control at the same exact time, which made absolutely no sense at all.

What I did know was that, without Richard breathing down my neck and watching me with his dirty, beady eyes, I felt at ease, and that wasn't good even in the slightest. Letting my guard down around anyone, especially Isaiah, would only bite me in the ass down the road.

I wouldn't make the same mistake twice.

My lungs burned as snippets from the last few weeks filled my head, but they quickly disappeared as I let my gaze scour around my new room. My mouth fell as I took in the beautiful, glowing fairy lights that hung from every corner, making the small area seem like some sort of fairytale instead of the dungeon that I'd expected.

"I know," a girl announced, snagging my attention. I glanced to the center of the room and saw a petite girl with shoulder-length black hair. Her smile was as bright as the pink on her lips. "It's weird coming from a creepy hallway to a room that's..."

"Beautiful," I finished for her, looking up to the ceiling that had some type of 3D paper butterflies taped to it. The room was all things light and fluffy, which were two things I wasn't really familiar with. I would be lying if I said it didn't make me feel lighter, though.

"Gemma, this is Sloane. Sloane, this is Gemma, your new roommate."

She smiled again as she walked over to me and held her hand out. "Welcome to St. Mary's."

I took it cautiously and glanced at Isaiah who was staring at me intently with an unreadable expression on his face. "Alright, I'm out," he finally said, still keeping me pinned to my spot.

"I thought I was supposed to get a tour of the school?"

"I'll give you a tour," Sloane said, dismissing Isaiah.

My shoulders immediately dropped in relief. Being around Isaiah was exhausting, even if it had been only for a few minutes. I was acting way out of character with him for some reason. It was better this way. I'd be able to keep myself in line by getting a rundown of St. Mary's from my new roommate rather than *him*.

He made me feel...something. Something I wouldn't allow myself to feel because I already knew it would be a distraction.

"Great." Isaiah slapped his hands together. "I'll see you around, Good Girl." He winked at me, and my face flamed.

As soon as he left the room, Sloane laughed. "That's Isaiah for you. He's a lot, huh?"

I thought very carefully before I spoke. "He makes me nervous," I said, and although it was true, it wasn't the first word to come to mind when answering her. Isaiah made me feel excited and maybe a bit scared. And hot. Really hot. Like, sweat-was-coating-my-back hot.

She nodded, her straight, shiny, ebony strands swaying. "He makes all the girls nervous. He's a bad boy, though. Through and through." She sighed. "You should probably stay away from him, or you'll end up in the closet."

The closet? I absolutely hated that I was so out of the loop on just about everything teenage-girl related. It only took a few days at Wellington Prep to realize that high school was not what I had expected—or what I was taught. I had learned a lot from watching others my age navigate their *normal* high school lives, and the things I'd overheard at the lunch table made me blush just being near someone who had done them. I was curious, too. Really curious.

I nodded in Sloane's direction, pretending I knew what she was referring to with the closet thing, but I really had no idea. I could only guess that it was something my dear Uncle Richard wouldn't approve of, though.

"Well, anyway," she started, shaking away the conversation. "Let's get you settled. I'm glad to have a roommate again. My last one had to..."—Sloane averted her eyes—"leave pretty abruptly."

"Why?" I asked curiously. "Did she break a rule or something?"

Sloane threw her head back and laughed as she pulled up my suitcase for me and placed it on the bed opposite of hers. "Oh, Gemma. We all break the rules here."

My stomach fell. *Then why would Richard send me here? Was it a test?*

"Is this all you have?" Sloane asked, tucking her hair behind her ear. She glanced around my body and jutted her lip out.

"Um. Yes." Seeing the confusion on her face, I quickly added, "I just wasn't sure what to bring, so I only brought the essentials. I mean, we get uniforms here, right?"

She eyed me curiously, her hazel eyes showing a lot of depth behind them. "Yeah. We do. But we don't have to wear them after classes end. You're welcome to borrow my things if you want. I have tons of clothes. My parents feel bad for sending me here, so they always send me new things."

"They feel bad?" I asked, taking a step closer to my bed.

Sloane popped back onto hers with a whoosh, her legs dangling below. She was a tiny person. She hardly reached my 5'5" frame.

"Yeah." She grabbed a small pink, sequined pillow and wrapped her arms around it. "They're both in the military, and they both deploy a lot. My grandma used to take care of me, but she got Alzheimer's, so she's in a nursing home now. There was no one else I could stay with, so they sent me to the best boarding school in the nation." She shrugged. "At least I'll get into a good college, right?"

College. Such a wistful thought.

I began to turn around to empty out my suitcase that had nothing significant in it, except for one discolored Polaroid photo of me, my mom, and my brother, when Sloane asked, "What about you? Why are you here?"

Awkwardness hung in the air like the stench of spoiled meat as I tried to come up with something that wouldn't raise too many questions and, again, something that wouldn't make me seem...different. I had a serious battle of what was considered normal and what wasn't.

"Are you one of the good ones? Or bad ones?"

My second pair of jeans were like dead weight in my hands as I pulled them out of my suitcase. "What do you mean?" I asked, looking for a place to put my clothes.

Sloane nodded to the chest of drawers pushed up against the wall next to a desk that had nothing on it but a pamphlet of some sort.

I get my own desk?

As I walked over to it, Sloane sat up a little taller. "Yeah. Are you an uber-smart student, and your parents sent you here for a better chance at a college? Or are you an orphan with a bad past?" Her last assumption was said jokingly, but it really wasn't that far off from my real life.

Clearly seeing my confusion, Sloane chuckled while giving me an incredulous look. "You don't know much about St. Mary's, do you?"

Not a single thing. That actually wasn't necessarily true.

Richard had told me all about St. Mary's, but I trusted him about as far as I could throw him, and spoiler alert: he was three times my size.

I shifted on my feet nervously. "Not really." I glanced down. "My uncle sent me here. That's who I lived with... before now."

Pity was clear on her soft expression, but it was totally unneeded. Being sent here was an upgrade. "Oh. I'm...sorry?"

My heart had a slight dent as I pushed away any sad lingering thought that involved my mom and Tobias before I put my hand up. "It's okay. But to answer your question..." I had to force the lie out. "I'm here for academics mostly. Plus, my aunt isn't well, and my uncle works a lot, so it was better for all of us for me to come here."

The lies were bitter on my tongue. Like I'd taken a mouthful of battery acid. That wasn't true at all. Richard was forced to put me in Wellington Prep a few months ago because some of the girls at the group home, who had to relocate because of Auntie's sudden debilitating stroke, talked to their social worker about *the teen who lived in the house with Judge Stallard,* thus raising too many questions. Then, I seemed to blow my chances for a normal life at a normal high school because I'd shared things with the wrong people.

I really could trust no one that Richard knew. In fact, I couldn't trust anyone but the one social worker who was relentless in figuring out who I was and why I was living with Richard in the first place. And I didn't even really trust her, either.

I quickly darted my eyes away as Sloane's began to look suspicious. I rummaged through the rest of my things, shoving them all into the empty drawers as a distraction, when she finally spoke again.

"The headmaster will love you."

"Why do you say that?" I asked, slowly turning around.

She laughed lightly, tucking her shiny hair behind her ear again. Her other hand played with the glittery sequins on the pillow.

"Because the more fucked up you are, the more he likes you. He has a soft spot for the really messed-up ones."

My mouth fell open as a knock sounded on the door.

Sloane slid her feet to the ground and patted my arm. "Don't worry, Gemma. We're all a little fucked up at St. Mary's. You'll fit right in."

Then, she bounced to the door and opened it, leaving me feeling like I had rocks in the bottom of my stomach.

CHAPTER FOUR

GEMMA

PULLING down the maroon blazer I was wearing, I shivered.
Nerves were making my skin tingle and itch like I was
standing on the edge of a cliff with someone behind me,
ready to push me below into an abyss of icy-cold water with
an uncertainty of everything I was about to crash into.

Yesterday evening, after Sloane deemed me as *fucked up*—
which was more or less a good thing because she insinuated
that it was pretty normal around here—the headmaster
walked into our room, holding a pile of new uniforms in one
hand and a cardboard box in the other.

Sloane excitedly went through the box as the headmaster
gave me my schedule and handed me a school map in case I
got lost after my tour with Isaiah, which never ended up
happening. I didn't tell him that, though, because I was more
relieved than anything.

As soon as the headmaster left our room, Sloane laughed
and said in a sing-song voice, "See?" She ushered toward the
cardboard box. "He likes you."

When she pulled me over to the box, the heavy rocks in my stomach turned to dust. Inside were school supplies, a laptop, and some twinkle lights that Sloane draped over my bed posts. It was the only thing on my side of the room that said, *"I'm loved,"* as I literally had nothing else to my name, not even a nice blanket, but that was okay. I slept better last night than I had in months, which wasn't really saying much.

Picking up my new journal on my way out the door this morning, Sloane draped her arm through mine and led me down the dark, windowless hallway with tons of other girls bustling around. I even saw a few running over the blood-red carpet with towels perched on top of their heads, yelling that they were going to be late for breakfast.

Sloane and I were right on time.

"Here," she said as she handed me a tray and nodded over to the lunch line. The cafeteria was just as medieval as the rest of the school. Large, wooden tables sat parallel to one another with seats fit for a king on both ends. On the sides were long benches, which seemed to be where mostly everyone sat.

"Wow," I whispered, pulling steaming oatmeal—which seemed to appear out of nowhere—onto my tray. The smell of cinnamon filled my senses, and I sighed wistfully.

Sloane nodded back at me. "I know. The food is pretty good here."

I said nothing as she pulled me by the elbow toward a table closest to the two French doors. We sat at the end, near no one in particular, but before long, the entire table was filled up, and everyone was whispering and staring in my direction. I pulled at my white collar underneath my scratchy maroon blazer and rubbed at the hives along my neck.

I was used to going unnoticed, pushed away into the shadows, keeping my mouth shut, and following the rules. I was submissive and quiet by nature because I knew my place, and

I knew what would happen if I stepped a toe out of line. So this? This was awful.

"Everyone..." Sloane slowly stood up, gaining everyone's attention. My face was on fire as I dipped my head down low, my dark locks swaying over my face. Part of me wanted to straighten my spine and prove to myself that I wasn't that quiet, passive girl I was bred to be, but old habits died hard. "This is Gemma. My new roommate."

The entire dining hall went quiet except for the clanking of silverware and opening of milk cartons. Sloane cleared her throat, and I peeked up to what felt like five million pairs of eyes on me. I scanned over their faces quickly, like the fast forwarding on a VCR, and felt a tiny bout of disappointment. At first, I wasn't sure why. I didn't expect—or want—to make many friends. It was too hard for me to keep up my *normalcy*, not to mention keep my story straight. And also, I had big plans that didn't involve a single person here. But when the French doors clamored open again and everyone's attention swung toward them, I realized right then why I'd felt the slight twinge of disappointment.

Isaiah. I'd been scanning the long dining table for him. I'd been searching for those icy eyes that had sparked something to life in me yesterday.

My face flamed even brighter with the thought. I was wading in unknown waters, unknowingly chasing after something so completely foreign to me that I didn't even know what to call it.

Sloane plopped back down beside me, picking up her spoon and pushing it into her gooey oatmeal. "And just like that, the attention is off of you."

I blinked several times, unable to look away from Isaiah and what looked to be his pack of friends as they slowly prowled into the dining hall with so much commanding, hot authority I actually started to sweat.

"Wh—what?" I stuttered, trailing over each of them before landing back on Isaiah. They were all flawless. Each and every last one of them. Tall...some leaner than others, but they all appeared to be in good physical strength—like Tobias. I could still see him through the darkness of my room as he did a million and one push-ups in the middle of the night when he knew I couldn't sleep. He always stayed until I fell asleep, even when I begged him to go back to his room so he didn't get in trouble.

I sighed softly, pushing away the memory. Isaiah and his friends' school blazers fit their broad shoulders tightly, and somehow they each had a type of *air* surrounding them, like they were totally unbothered by a single thing in the world. Lazily hot, with so much confidence that everyone was forced to stare. Authoritative, in a way, which was something that *wasn't* completely unknown to me.

I quickly turned my head from the pack of guys as yet another hush fell over the dining hall. Sloane dipped her head closer to mine. "I knew the Rebels were about to walk through the doors. That's why I made a quick intro of you, knowing the attention wouldn't last long when they walked in. Figured it was better to get it over with than drag it out, right?" She went back into her own personal bubble, giving me room to breathe before shrugging. "You're introverted. You're a lot like my last roommate, and she would have *hated* having attention on her."

My lip twitched at the corner. It was a nice thing that she did, whereas before, I kind of wanted to knock her chair over for putting me on the spot. "Thank you, Sloane."

Her pearly whites beamed behind her pink lips before she stuffed more oatmeal in her mouth. She was pretty when she smiled, and it was a friendly one, at that. I kind of wanted to be her friend, even though I knew the friendship wouldn't last long. But it felt like we were on that path, and I wasn't sure I had it in me to pretend that I didn't desperately want someone in my corner.

I began eating my breakfast even though my stomach was in knots. The silver spoon in my hand continued to slip through my sweaty fingers as I brought another spoonful of the cinnamon oats up to my mouth. The dining room had picked up some more chatter, and I noted a bunch of people pulling out their cell phones. I had a cell phone, but it was mostly for show, given to me by Richard before I started to attend Wellington Prep. I'd never really used it because he told me he could see everything that I did on it, so I hardly touched it. Even the mere thought of giving him even more insight to who I was caused a slight chill to blanket my skin.

Sloane laughed softly beside me as she put her phone down on the table. She shook her head and mumbled, "Jesus."

"What?" I asked, placing my spoon beside my bowl. I couldn't stomach another bite of my breakfast, even if it was delicious.

Sloane caught my eye briefly. "There's a new post on Mary's Murmurs." Seeing my confusion, she shook her head. "Sorry, I forgot you have no clue what I'm talking about. Mary's Murmurs is the gossip blog for St. Mary's." She rolled her eyes. "It's usually all about who the Rebels are fucking or their latest bad-boy drama."

The muscles along my face stayed nice and steady as she continued on, but I felt the heat rise to my cheeks.

"Today, it's about Isaiah." She laughed under her breath, and my heart slipped in my chest at the sound of his name. *Why? Why did it do that?*

My voice cracked at first before I cleared my throat. "Who writes on the blog? How do they know all the gossip?"

Sloane shrugged. "No one knows. The Rebels love the

attention, though, so they just go with it. They're so full of themselves."

She said the last part in half awe and half disgust. It was like she was annoyed but also fascinated. I had to admit, I kind of was too. Not annoyed but maybe a little intrigued. I wanted to ask more about them. Why they were called the Rebels and why everyone was so drawn to them besides the obvious reason: *because they were really, really attractive*.

Slowly, *very* slowly, and discreetly, my gaze traveled over Sloane's tray lined with an assortment of breakfast foods, to the dark wood of the dining table underneath it, to my oatmeal, and then down the long dining table, past all my new classmates. I locked onto the chair at the very end—the one fit for a king.

I gasped, my breath hitching in the back of my throat.

Sloane's voice hissed in my ear, but I hardly registered it. "Why the hell is he staring at you like that? Or should I say glaring?"

My eyes bounced between Isaiah's, the ice-blue color summoning me to submit. Submit to what? I wasn't sure. But I felt my legs shaking underneath the table. My heart skipped a beat, my stomach somersaulting to the point that it was convulsing inside my body.

A harsh ring sounded out around my ears, and it quickly took me out of the stupor. I jerked back, my head snapping back down to my oatmeal. Sloane's hand fell onto mine, "Come on. It's time for class."

My movements were jerky. I was shaky when I stood up from long bench, the sturdy wooden legs scraping slightly along the intricate tiled floor. My fingers clutched around my notebook as my paper schedule crumpled between my fingers.

"Are you okay? That was weird, right?" Sloane asked, weaving her arm back through mine like before. Relief settled in my bones as she pulled me along because I wasn't sure I could walk straight, and also, I was so glad to be out of Isaiah's grasp.

"Yeah, I'm fine," I answered after peering behind my shoulder. I braced myself for the pair of piercing blue eyes again, but Isaiah was gone.

CHAPTER FIVE

ISAIAH

MY JAW ACHED from clenching it every few seconds. I narrowed my eyes on the petite, chestnut-haired girl running her deft fingers over the drawing pencils with a laser-like fascination. The muscles along my forearms bounced as my fists squeezed tighter, hot blood soaring through my veins.

"Fuck. She is hot as hell. Who cares if she spilled the tea? We usually welcome the talk." Brantley's voice was low, a grumble almost, as he stared at Good Girl—who apparently wasn't as good as I had pegged her to be.

The little snitch.

Let's go back to two hours ago, when my uncle called me into his office at the crack of fucking dawn.

My hair was still damp from my shower as I wrapped the maroon tie around my neck, not bothering to tighten it around the collar of my white dress shirt. I knew my uncle would look at me disapprovingly, but I truly didn't care—and not just because it was well before the sun had even peeked through the gloomy clouds. In general, I just didn't give a fuck.

The hallway was silent as I swiftly made my way to his office, the door slightly open with a faint glow coming from the heirloom lamp on his desk.

His head popped up as I stepped through the threshold. I hoped he could sense the irritation coming off me in thunderous waves, but like me, he most likely didn't care about my feelings toward him.

"Isaiah."

"Uncle," I said in the same tone he used as I threw myself down into the seat I'd occupied no less than twenty-four hours ago when he'd caught me with Ms. Glenburg, who—I'd noted—had already left the premises. "Is this my real punishment for *almost* fucking a teacher? I told you I'd get my shit together. No need to drag me out of bed at six in the morning."

My uncle sighed, clearly annoyed. He leaned back in his leather chair and steepled his fingers together. "The SMC has called for a meeting."

"Okay, so?" I said, flicking my eyes down to my uncle's coffee cup that was steaming above the brim.

What would he do if I just grabbed it and downed it? Nothing?

"So," my uncle seethed. "They already fucking know you were caught with your hand up a teacher's skirt! Who did you tell about Ms. Glenburg, Isaiah?"

My mouth opened slightly in shock. There was a dip in my cool facade that I wore like a second skin. My uncle interrupted my thoughts, slapping his hands down onto his desk in his usual frustrated manner. "Did you tell the rest of your alpha pack?" His face scrunched as if he was fed up with the entire situation. *That made two of us.* "The Rebel Boys?"

"It's just the Rebels," I clarified.

The group was born long ago—before I or my uncle

attended here. It was a century-old society set within the thick, damp walls of this dark boarding school, originating from the Latin word, *Rebellis*. The history behind the group was that there needed to be order within the students. The students that came here in the far past were from two separate upbringings. Split right in half. Some were orphans—sent from an orphanage a few blocks over with no one to answer to and with no one to teach them right from wrong. The others were descendants from parents who did illegal shit but who were also prestigious in the outside world. It was still like that—with the students, I mean. I fell into the latter of the group. My last name was well-known. My family was wealthy, and we were considered high society. But that didn't mean we were good. My father was a piece of shit. He dabbled in crime behind the scenes of his business investments and charitable dues. His bad side was elusive to many.

The walls of St. Mary's were secure, though, like a completely different civilization breathed here rather than in the real world where there was true crime and death. The Rebels, at least a century ago, were the ones who ruled the school, set forth rules, and kept others in line, all while causing havoc in their own way. It wasn't like that anymore. It was more or less a myth. The group had been dormant until Brantley, Cade and I came here. Our other friend, Shiner, knew all about the Rebels and their...traditions...and that was when the elite group had started up again.

And as the story stated in the old journal that we'd found, the Rebels changed and evolved over the years with the different generations. One group was like a family evolving, branching the students together like a giant tree. But others were more like a hierarchy. I'd like to think the current group of Rebels, the one I was a part of—which consisted of me, Brantley, Cade, and Shiner—was a mix of the two. Again, we were more of a myth, a fraternity of sorts, but for some reason, students still came to us if there was a problem. And we definitely ate up the fame because with fame came perks, and the perks were always *hot*.

My uncle's voice rang out, "That's right. The Rebels. Tell me, does Nash know what you, Cade, and Brantley know?"

My jaw flexed. "You know Shiner doesn't go by Nash anymore." *He hated his first name.* "And no, he doesn't." My jaw ticked again. "And to answer your question, I didn't tell the boys."

Yet.

It wasn't that I planned to keep Ms. Glenburg a secret. I meant to tell the Rebels at some point, but if the SMC was as close to expelling me as my uncle said, then they'd likely cut me for good if they knew what had happened with me and Ms. Glenburg. I wanted to be on full lock-down when I spilled the dirty details, so there wasn't a chance of loose ears lingering around.

Uncle Tate pinched the bridge of his nose. "Well, the SMC knows, and I'm almost certain they will be going above me to call your father." He sighed. "They are far beyond believing my excuses for you. I can't be your alibi any longer."

I swallowed roughly, a roll of anger flying down each and every vertebra in my spine.

My eyes locked with his, and we stayed like that until I broke the dense silence. "So, what are you saying? They're expelling me? And then Dad will come up here to personally throw me into the Covens to control me even more? He won't let that happen. He needs me here."

There was once a time where I would have done anything to make my father proud. Now, though, it was the complete opposite.

My uncle's face dropped for a moment, guilt covering each and every woven line on his forehead. "I—I don't know. Just"—he took a moment before he glanced up at me—"get your shit together. I'll call your father in a few and figure out what's going on and see if he knows anything. I'll deal with the committee and do everything I can to keep you here. You need to make better choices, though." The lines of his face sharpened. "I'm being completely serious, Isaiah. You're going to need to get your grades up. Stop fucking around. For the love of God, get an alibi—someone who can collaborate your excuses—and stop getting caught doing shit. I want you to have your freedom here, because God knows you've never had it before, but there's only so much I can do for you."

A heavy feeling weighed on my chest because I could sense the urgency in his voice. I could feel the trickle of fear in the back of my head when I thought of my father and how he'd react if I was expelled. If I didn't stop rebelling, if I told him that I wouldn't be following in his footsteps, that I'd be taking the high road like Jacobi did...*fuck*. I wasn't afraid for myself. I was afraid for Jack.

"Okay," I finally said, and my uncle's head snapped up, shocked.

I was shocked too, but when it came to Jack, things hit a little differently. There was a miniscule part of me that felt something when it came to him. A slight opening in my numbness.

"I have it under control," I said, climbing to my feet.

His head tilted, and the shadows from the dim light on the edge of his desk clearly showed his skepticism.

"I don't even want to know. Just..." He glanced away. "Figure out what path you're going down, and stick to it. Yeah?"

I nodded, going toward the door, feeling all sorts of fucked up. Not only from the conversation with Uncle Tate but also from wondering how the hell the SMC could have known about me seducing—definitely using that word lightly here—Ms. Glenburg.

The only two people who knew, other than me and Ms. Glenburg herself, were the janitor and my uncle. And I knew that Mr. Clark hadn't told anyone. He and my uncle went way back. Mr. Clark knew more about my family than anyone else at this school. In fact, he had turned his head many times at my questionable behavior. Hell, he'd even helped me sneak back into the school after I'd left to be my father's errand boy in the middle of the night.

Then, it clicked.

There was one other person who could have known.

It didn't hit me until I walked into the dining hall for breakfast, after Brantley and Cade continued to prod me about the gossip on the stupid fucking blog that couldn't seem to talk about anything else other than me and the rest of the Rebels. Honestly, whoever filled their time with writing for the thing was desperate for my dick. Let's just put it that way. But that was when I saw her.

She was a little ray of sunshine sitting there at the table with Sloane. She stood out contrastingly compared to everyone else. Fucking gorgeous, *pure*, all things good—but there was something dark about her too. I wasn't sure if it was her features, where her skin was smooth and porcelain-like, completely flawless and angelic, but her eyes were sharp and vivid. They struck you when they latched on. Then, there was yesterday when she bit out a response to me but also blushed and clammed up afterwards. She was split down the middle. Soft but hard, light but dark. Looking at Gemma was like breathing in fresh air...but with black, murky lungs.

It was her, though.

The good girl. Gemma.

She was the only other person who could have known.

Mrs. Fitzpatrick's voice, in all its shrill glory, snapped me back to reality. Brantley and Cade were both staring at

Gemma with a devious look in their eye as she sat, completely unaware of anything going on around her.

"Okay, class. I want you to pick one object in the room—I don't care what it is—and start drawing." Mrs. Fitzpatrick's hands clapped, the sound reverberating around the room. "I just want to see where your potential is! There is no right or wrong way to do art, friends! Let's get creative!"

My lip curled as I took my eyes off Gemma and brought them back to my boys. "I need to talk to her alone." I flicked my head to her as she swiped a lock of brown hair out of her face. She began drawing on the paper in front of her, appearing even more angelic than before. She was completely focused, heedless of anything else—even me—as I stared at her, plotting something in the back of my head.

"We're on it," Cade said.

I grabbed my pencil and grinned, watching my boys divide and conquer.

Alright, Gemma. It's payback time.

CHAPTER SIX

GEMMA

I LEARNED LONG AGO that you had to find good in the littlest of things. The minute of silence in a house full of people you hated. The smell of coffee in the morning, even if you knew you weren't going to get a cup. The sun on your face, even for a fleeting moment, before a tsunami-like storm hit the grass below your feet.

This right here. This moment was good.

The pencil felt light in my hand, the metallic shine of the lead on the thick paper in front of me was like a little sliver of hope on this awful day. I couldn't shake the unease that had laid deep in my belly after breakfast this morning. My skin prickled underneath my brand-new uniform during my first two periods. I wasn't necessarily anxious about being at St. Mary's, because it really was better than home, but I did feel apprehensive when it came to people staring at me—and trust me when I say *everyone* was staring at me.

So, this moment here? Art class? Are you kidding me? This forty-five-minute class made up for the lingering gazes that kept following me around the expansive hallway this morning.

Art was my happy place. Art was the one thing he couldn't take from me. I always found a way back to it, even when I felt like my creative streak had vanished along with all rational thinking. Somehow, drawing was what grounded me. I got lost in it.

It felt like home, and that was a comforting thing to feel when you were a hostage inside the place you'd lived all your life. Not to mention, art had saved my mental state so many times I'd lost count.

My hand continued to flick over the thick, high-quality paper as my pencil moved languidly, sketching the small clay figurines on the top of a nearby shelf. I chose to sketch the first thing my eyes landed on, because as soon as Mrs. Fitzpatrick said, "Sketch", I jumped at the opportunity.

"Hey, that's really good."

The deep voice was close, and my head popped up quickly, a rushed breath leaving my mouth as my fingers wrapped around the pencil in my hand. I landed on a set of deep, honey-colored, almond-shaped eyes that sent a rush of warmth through me.

"Oh," I croaked. "Thank you." I smiled shyly and then put my attention back to my paper.

My heart started to skip in my chest when his presence grew heavier. He was still standing beside me, a little too close for comfort. But maybe he was just admiring my art work.

"I'm Cade," he offered as he plopped himself down in the next chair.

The art room wasn't set up like a traditional classroom, although I couldn't really be certain what a traditional classroom was since I'd only ever gone to one high school, and it was for a brief time, but it didn't look like my first two periods' rooms at all. Instead of desks sitting in an organized manner, there were several rectangular tables set up in different directions all over the room. There didn't seem to be any rhyme or reason to why they were placed where they were placed, but I kind of liked it like this. It wasn't so direct. It was a little messy and completely out of order.

It was strange that things out of order felt right to me when I'd been taught all my life that there was no middle ground. It was black or white, straight or crooked, right or wrong. There couldn't be an in between. Ever.

"I'm Gemma," I said, going back to my paper while trying to ignore the heat I felt from his skin radiating onto mine. A sense of urgency whipped through me, telling me to move away from him, but I didn't. I didn't move because I knew in the back of my head I wasn't feeling that urgent need to flinch because of him as a person. It was because of something else entirely.

Tobias' voice tickled the back of my brain: *Survive, but don't believe a single thing he says. He has plans for you, just like he did for Mom.*

Not everyone was bad, and I had to start trusting my gut more than trusting what I'd been told over the years. I knew that now.

Cade and I worked in silence for the next several minutes, and soon, I felt myself getting lost in my sketch again. My eyes moved back and forth from the little figurines and their ornate details every few seconds, making sure I got every last thing correct when he muttered, "Shit."

Glancing over briefly, I saw that he was staring at me.

"Can you do me a favor, Gemma?" His voice was sweet, genuine. Maybe even a little desperate.

I paused, my heart slowing. Placing my pencil down on the desk, I gulped a big lungful of air before looking over at him. Strangely enough, another wave of warmth went through my body. It was like I had taken a steaming cup of tea and gulped it down quickly, feeling the hot liquid coat my throat all the way to my stomach.

"Um, sure." I hated how my voice came out like a whisper. I'd always been a quiet person. Richard used to ask if I was afraid of my own voice, and honestly, around him, I was.

Cade tilted his head across the room, his jawline sharp as he angled it away from me. "Can you go over to that door right there." I followed his line of sight. "Yeah, that one," he confirmed. "Can you go and move that curtain out of the way? The end of it blew onto the statue that I'm drawing. Probably from the air vent."

"Oh, yeah. Sure."

"Thanks. I just don't want to lose my line of sight by walking over there. Drawing doesn't come easy to me." His eyes shot down to my sketch. "Unlike you." His smile was soft, and two dimples formed on his cheeks. He seemed nice, but when I glanced back at his eyes, they said something different. I couldn't pinpoint it exactly, but where his smile said he was innocent, his eyes did not. Either way, I chose to ignore it because there was no sense in being outlandish. I was nice, and it was okay to help someone, even if I was always taught to keep to myself. I hopped off my stool and began walking over to the statue he was drawing, feeling proud that I wasn't letting old habits decide my every move at St. Mary's, despite how out of my element I was.

The art room was the one place in this entire school, at least so far, that wasn't dimly lit. There were recessed lights above my head and a million other standing lamps placed all over the room. It was bright in here, so bright it took my eyes a moment to adjust when I'd first crossed the threshold.

Just as I was passing by a dark, half-opened wooden door on my left, likely a supply closet, a hand wrapped around my upper arm, yanking me into a dark area that smelled of acrylic paint and old, musty art supplies.

I yelped, immediately looking down to the hand on my arm, which was pointless because the room I was pulled into was dark. The only light source was the door outlined from the other side.

A gritty voice simmered in the darkness. "Who did you tell?"

My heart slammed against my ribcage as the hand on my arm tightened. My stomach bottomed out as I was dragged even farther into the closet only to be pushed forcefully up against a shelf with my next breath.

My eyes immediately began scanning the area, straining against the bleak darkness for a way out. *Always look for an escape first.* There was only one door, the one I was pulled into, and the person in front of me was blocking it, so that was out. *Look for a way to protect yourself second.*

Wait. I shook my head, clearing my thoughts and bringing myself back to the present. *You're not in that place, Gemma. You're at school.*

A short burst of air left my mouth. "Get your hand off my arm," I very calmly demanded, keeping my voice steady and my feet firmly on the floor. The rising anxiety was there in the back of my head, scratching the walls of my brain with panic, but I pushed it away, knowing I had been in much more compromising situations in the past. Being shoved into an art closet in the middle of art class was like child's play.

The firm grasp on my arm dropped, the scent of something enticing gone, and then I heard a shuffling noise before the click of a light which then shined down on my head. I glanced up to the single light bulb swaying above me before coming down and almost choking on air.

Isaiah's head tilted as our eyes collided. His gaze was like an icy stake being thrust into my chest, cooling me and burning me at the exact same time. The feeling was new and perplexing, and I felt my head tilting too. What was it with him? Why did it feel like he shocked me to life when he was near?

"Who did you tell?" Isaiah snapped again, this time while running a hand through his dark hair. His jaw clenched on the sides as his plump lips turned into a disapproving scowl. My body grew hot. The sip of tea I metaphorically had earlier when Cade looked at me, warming me on the inside, was *nothing* compared to latching onto Isaiah. It was similar to walking under a steaming shower after rolling around in the snow, the hot water washing over every inch of my flesh, burning the coolness instantly.

"Wh—what?" I stuttered, unable to catch my breath.

Isaiah's eyebrow hitched as he crossed his arms over his school uniform. "I knew you were eavesdropping yesterday when I talked to my uncle—in the privacy of his office, might I add—but I didn't peg you to be like the rest of the girls here. I didn't think you'd run your gossiping little mouth, especially after only being here for what? Twelve hours?"

My cheeks caught fire.

I *was* eavesdropping. I'll admit that. But I didn't tell anyone a single thing. Who would I have told?

My lips parted, and his eyes instantly flew down to my mouth. I felt a tugging on my stomach that was beyond unfamiliar, so I brushed it away before saying, "I don't know what you're talking about."

A rough chuckle rolled out of his mouth as he threw his head back, the muscles along his neck growing more prominent with each echoing laugh. "Here's the deal," Isaiah whispered, taking a step closer to me after abruptly ending his laughter. My eyes widened as his chest brushed against mine. My back was firmly pressed into the shelf behind me, causing a lone paintbrush to fall down to the ground with a slight thud. My breathing had quickened, and my pulse was speeding, but it wasn't out of fear. Isaiah was strong and commanding. He was definitely confident, and after seeing him this morning in the dining hall, and how everyone else seemed to gravitate around him, I understood why. But he didn't scare me—not in the way I was used to, at least.

Isaiah's chest was still pressed against mine as he gingerly reached up and brushed a stray hair out of my face. My cheek tingled where his fingers touched. "Oh, *Good Girl.*" He laughed under his breath in a condescending tone. "You kind of owe me now."

That stupid nickname he had obviously given me after meeting yesterday stirred up a bunch of shit that I'd pushed away from the moment I got into that town car to attend St. Mary's. It sent me straight to the red, and although I had a really good hold on my emotions, anger especially—a survival tactic, no doubt—I found it hard to keep myself in line when he said that. My hand reached up, of its own accord, and I smacked his away from my face. I peered up into his smug expression and seethed, "*Do not* call me that."

Whoa. Did I really just do that?

His lip twitched at my tone, and I could feel the weak girl inside of me, the one that was shattered long ago, pulling me back. But I stood my ground, tilting my chin upward as my brown locks fell behind my shoulders. "And I don't owe you anything, *Rebel.*" He wanted to give me a nickname? I'd give him one right back.

Surprise flashed across his face—and probably mine too. *Why was I acting like this?* I knew right then that Isaiah was dangerous to be around. He did something to me. Breathing his air gave me confidence and a feeling of power that I had never felt before. I found myself relishing in the feelings he was planting inside of me.

I went to push my way around him, eager to get out of the

tiny, dark room that apparently had me morphing into someone I wasn't, when his hands clasped onto my wrists.

I paused, my heart thudding to a complete stop. "Did you or did you not tell someone about me and Ms. Glenburg? Because I have to say, you just stirred up a bunch of shit for me." His voice lowered as he brought his head down to my ear. My entire body went haywire as his warm breath graced the sensitive skin. "I know you heard the conversation, Gemma."

I gulped, tilting my head over so he had better access to my neck. *What the hell was I doing?* I couldn't stop. I didn't want him to leave my personal space. I wanted him to keep breathing down on my neck like he was, because...I *liked* it. I liked it a lot. "I was eavesdropping." My voice was low and breathy. "But I didn't tell anyone."

There it was again, his hot, minty breath mingling over my skin, causing goosebumps to rise. "Are you sure about that? Because if you did tell someone, I will find out."

This time, I pulled my wrists out of his grasp, and I basically ran to the door. I peeked over my shoulder, my chest rising and falling like I was in PE instead of art. Isaiah was staring at me intently, looking completely unbothered in his school uniform. He was effortlessly attractive, and he knew it. "I'm sure, so again, I don't owe you anything."

And with that, I threw the door open and stepped back into the art room, breathing in the fresh air that wasn't nearly as intoxicating as Isaiah's.

But as soon as I took a deep breath and felt my shoulders relax, they shot up to my ears again because every single set of eyes, the teacher's included, were staring directly at me. And when Isaiah stepped out of the closet, I could see the wheels already spinning inside my classmates' heads.

A deep, throaty chuckle sounded as he walked past me. I stared after him, feeling my body go numb at the rumors that were likely about to be floating around this desolate boarding school.

Isaiah turned around on the heel of his shoes and began walking backwards, smiling from ear to ear at me like the devious bad boy that he *obviously* was. Once he slid back onto his stool, the classroom as still as if it were empty, he slyly said, "I guess I know who will be featured on the gossip blog tomorrow...with a new story." My eyes drove into his with a burning intensity. He winked. "Consider us *almost* even, *Good Girl*."

I was on fire from embarrassment as he spun around in his stool, putting his back to me. Cade and another guy stood beside him, snickering as they, too, winked at me.

Isaiah had no idea what he just started.

CHAPTER SEVEN

GEMMA

MY STOMACH GROWLED LOUDLY as I sat on my bed with my knees pulled up to my chin. The junky phone that Richard gave me months ago laid untouched beside me on the fluffy cobalt-blue comforter that had somehow appeared on my bed along with a few girly pillows thrown on top for good measure.

When Sloane had walked in earlier, after all of our classes were finished, she paused while taking off her maroon blazer that fit her like a glove and laughed.

"See?" She grinned, nodding to my bed. "He loves you."

"Who loves me?"

A deep voice from the past tried to weasel into my head with insults about no one loving me, but I pushed it away as I focused on my roommate.

She gave me a pointed look, kicking the shoes off her feet, which went flying across the room. "Headmaster Ellison. He obviously got those"—she nodded to my blanket and pillows —"for you—unless someone sent them from home?"

I couldn't stop the sarcastic laugh from tumbling out of my mouth. "Definitely not."

Sloane smiled, but it didn't quite reach her eyes.

We'd both fallen into easy silence while doing our homework after she'd asked about my day and complained for a solid ten minutes about the fact that we didn't have any classes together. I peeked up at her a few times from my desk, watching her type something on her computer, unbeknownst to her that I was literally sweating while trying to focus on my own homework, which took me no more than an hour to complete. Auntie was very thorough with my studies over the years, and a lot of the time, the only thing I had to occupy myself with was reading the textbooks she and Richard supplied me with. As sad and boring as it was, learning was the only thing I had to look forward to in my childhood.

But as each second passed with Sloane buried in her computer, my stress levels rose. Sloane didn't say a single thing about Isaiah and the whole art-supply-closet ordeal, so I assumed the news hadn't reached her yet. I had a big feeling that Sloane was definitely the type of friend who wouldn't let something like that slide under the rug. But what did I know about having a friend?

After another hour, she asked if I was ready to go to dinner, but I told her I wasn't hungry. Her lips pursed, but she didn't push me on it. She only nodded after asking me one last time before slipping out of the door, and I hadn't seen her since.

That was when I turned my cell phone on and laid it beside me. I knew Richard would hear about the rumor of Isaiah and me—whatever the "rumor" was. For all I knew, it would get back to Headmaster Ellison, and he would call Richard, letting him know what his *niece* was up to. I didn't know much, but I knew enough to know that if a girl was shoved inside a closet with a boy, especially one as popular as Isaiah, the rumors would be juicy.

I remembered every last thing down to the smallest of details from when I'd attended Wellington Prep for those few short months before coming here. *Sex. Parties. Drugs. Drinking.* I drank it all up in huge gulps as I stayed behind in the shadows, hoping no one would pay attention to the judge's *strange* niece as I eavesdropped on classmates and their gossip. Rebecca, the only other person in the senior class that talked to me, usually filled in the gaps for me. She didn't know it, but she taught me a lot. She brought me up to speed. And one thing I knew with absolute certainty, from attending Wellington Prep and Rebecca's short, one-sided friendship, was that high schoolers were vicious with their gossip, and scandal was the one thing that fed it.

I was lucky to have made it out of Wellington Prep without ever being the center of anyone's gossip. I knew how to blend in, and not many people paid me any attention, except when Ms. Weltings started *really* looking into my drawings, which was what landed me in St. Mary's in the first place. Although, now that I was here, I was wondering if Richard knew all there was to know about this school. He certainly acted like he did, but I also knew that one of his personality traits was acting arrogantly confident in every situation he was ever in. Even if he flew blindly, he still acted as if he knew every last detail. He made it seem like St. Mary's was a prison. A punishment. A way to keep me under lock and key while also getting the social worker off his back. It was his subtle way of reminding me that I was his and that I needed to follow the rules. As soon as I turned eighteen, the social worker would no longer look into Judge Stallard's hidden niece. There would be no need to pretend that he followed the laws that he so righteously protected. I was his, and his to do with whatever he pleased. Or so he thought.

Several shaky breaths shuddered from my chest as I glanced back down to my phone, seeing nothing but a blank, black screen. And then the door flew open. Sloane quickly darted inside our room, wearing tight jeans and an off-the-shoulder shirt that was knotted in the front, showing off her flat belly. The chains on the other side of the door jingled, and my stomach twisted at the sound before she slammed it shut and placed her hands on her hips.

"Holy hell, Gemma!" Her mouth gaped, and my face flamed almost instantly. *Here we go.* "You're here for less than twenty-four hours, and you score a closet date with Isaiah Underwood?"

The realization hit me head on, like the final snip of a thread. *A closet date.*

I flew up from my bed. "No! That is not what happened!" I let out a tiny growl and started pacing the room in my short sleep shorts and plain t-shirt. "He set me up. He thinks I'm the one who told that blog thing about him and the teacher!" I flung toward her, probably looking no less than a frantic mess. "But I didn't, and I told him that!" Anxiety from Richard finding out that I was caught in the closet with Isaiah was causing me to act erratically, and I would be lucky if Sloane still wanted to be my friend after I just rushed toward her like a rabid animal.

Her features were pulled together tightly, a little wrinkle in the center of her eyebrows from the confusion. "How did you end up in a closet with him?" She shook her head, her raven hair swaying as she walked toward me and pulled me back to my bed to sit me down by pushing on my shoulders. "Take a deep breath, and start from the beginning."

So, I did. I told her everything that Isaiah said to me in the closet. My mouth was like a speed boat, zipping through choppy waves, plowing down every single red light that my brain was throwing out.

When I was finished spilling everything, Sloane let out a loud, breathy sigh and popped up from my bed. She began pacing the floor back and forth, nibbling on her thumb, just as I was seconds before. "Okay, listen." She glanced at me, and I scooted up to the top of my bed, eyeing my phone that was still beside me. "It's not a huge deal. I mean, you totally have a crush on Isaiah—that much is obvious from the red on your cheeks when you talk about him—and it's odd that you can't see that yourself, but whatever. Everyone has had a crush on Isaiah, and by crush, I mean every girl would strip themselves bare and spread their legs wide for him. But this will all blow over soon. The blog will post about Isaiah's latest closet date, and then something juicier will happen, and it'll be over."

My heart sunk even deeper in my chest. Sloane had it all wrong. I didn't care what anyone thought about me at this school. That wasn't my issue. The issue was this rumor making its way back home. If Richard learned that I was in a closet with a boy, he would be here faster than I could even pack my getaway bag.

There would be no escaping him.

There would be no grand plan to elude him and his sick future for me.

And there would be no finding Tobias.

"Hey, hey." Sloane's hand landed on mine, and I flinched before recovering and glancing up to her soft features. "It's not a big deal. I swear. Everyone has been featured on that stupid blog, Gemma. Don't sweat it."

A weak smile graced my lips as I snuggled down onto my bed, dropping my head onto the comfiest pillows I'd ever felt. Sloane left the room for a few minutes, doing something in the bathroom before coming back into our room and sitting back on my bed. I scooted over to the very edge, pressing myself against the wall as she lay down and pulled her computer to her lap.

"What are you doing?" I asked, rolling to my side, clutching the cell phone in my hand with an empty feeling carving out my stomach. I was dreading the moment it would ring.

Nerves began eating away at my hot skin when a heavy bout of anxiety fell on my shoulders. *What if he just comes here and drags me back home? Like, gives no warning and just shows up?* I silently shuddered.

"High school is hard. Especially this one since we can't even escape all the bullshit." She laughed under her breath. "So, I'm being a good friend and lying here with you as we watch some cheesy movie on Netflix."

A little bit of warmth seeped in when she said the word friend, but I didn't let myself show anything on the outside. Instead, I asked, "What's Netflix?"

Sloane's head whipped toward me, the side of her face illuminated by her laptop screen. "Girl, where have you been?"

Hell. Hell is where I've been.

CHAPTER EIGHT

ISAIAH

I COULD ALWAYS FEEL when someone was watching me. The skin along my neck would prickle, the beating of my heart would thud a little harder against my ribcage, my eyes would snap to each and every last corner of the room I was in, waiting to see that overbearing shadow of what my future held. The SMC had nothing to do with my father's line of business, but their watchful eyes were just a mere glimpse of what it would be like when I took over his position. If I hated the SMC watching me, waiting for me to slip up so they had grounds for expulsion, how would I feel with the law circling every so often, ready to catch me in the middle of a massive gun exchange? Not to mention the enemies. Their presence was heavy and, at times, imperceptible. Some of them could be lethal and blend in better than a fucking chameleon. I knew better than anyone just how lethal human beings could be.

My phone vibrated for the fifth time since yesterday, with my father's name flashing along the screen. If I didn't answer soon, I knew he'd throw a goddamn hissy fit, so I finally snatched it from my pocket while swiping the apple out of Cade's hand.

"*Fucker,*" he mumbled under his breath.

"Hello, Father," I answered into the phone, taking a bite of the red flesh. The sweet juice hit my tongue, but it wasn't nearly enough to take the bitterness out of my tone when it came to talking to Carlisle Underwood.

He growled on the other end, hardly noticeable, but I could detect his piss-poor mood even being locked away at St. Mary's. "I hear you've been wreaking havoc on your uncle's boarding school. Is that true?"

I took another bite of my apple, shifting my eyes down that long wooden table lined with numerous plates of food until I landed on Gemma. "What are you talking about?" I asked, wiping my mouth off with the back of my hand.

Damn. Cade was right. Gemma *was* hot. Really fucking hot. Hot in the way that she didn't know she was hot. It was a pity that she was like the rest of the girls here: hungry for gossip and as shallow as the fucking kiddie pool.

My father's voice got louder on the other end. "Did you fuck a teacher?"

There was no hesitation on my part when I answered, "No."

Cade nudged my elbow, and I shot him a look. He mouthed, "Party?" Then he swirled his index finger around in the air. I knew what he was asking, so I gave him a curt nod and watched as the hushed whispers broke out along the table.

"Did you only call to ask about my sex life, or did you call for a less exciting reason?"

Now there was no hesitation on his end. "Both. I've heard rumors of Callum's son dabbling in the business. Is it true? Have you found out anything useful?"

Oh, right. The whole reason I was at St. Mary's.

I huffed out a sarcastic laugh, annoyed at how my blood pressure was spiking. My hand squeezed around the apple so hard juice began to seep out of the sides. "Can't just let me be until I graduate, eh?"

"I can't have you acting like a fucking immature fool, especially with Bain there."

My gaze shifted from Gemma, who was smiling shyly at something Sloane had said with her head barely even visible from the shelter of her hair, over to Bain.

Bain was the bane of my existence—no pun intended. Our fathers were rivals in the gun-trafficking business. They were both competitive, always trying to beat each other out of sales. They were shady as fuck. Both domineering. Both living up to the legacy that their fathers, and their fathers before them, and so on, left to carry out—thus Bain and I being forced to fall into line to carry the legacy out once the time came.

But the difference between Bain and me was that I wanted no fucking part in what my father did for a living, and Bain was the exact opposite. He was already a miniature clone of Callum.

And Callum was a shitty human being. I had my eye on Bain—and not only because that was what my father not so subtly demanded when he thrust me into this godforsaken boarding school.

"You have a choice to make, Isaiah." *He couldn't be serious.* I'd never had a fucking choice. "You can join the business as a snake. Or you can join as a lion." My jaw clenched tightly as I suddenly became very focused on the conversation with my father. "Stay unknown to Bain, fly under the radar, and knock him on his ass when you two meet again in the future. *Or* I can rip you out of that school and throw you into the Covens where you'll come out more lethal than I am."

A deep chuckle left my chest as I rose from the table and began striding through the dining hall with my phone pressed to my ear. Once I was away from wandering eyes, I gritted through my teeth. "You won't rip me out of this school because you want me here to spy on Bain." I was too valuable.

My father laughed in the most narcissistic of ways. "You might not give me a choice. Your uncle says the committee is ready to throw you on your ass." He paused, and a hot sensation of dread crept over my shoulder. I glanced behind me, only to see the long, dark hallway with shiny white and black tiles along the floor and nothing else. "I want you to listen very closely to me," he snarled. I swallowed, clenching my fist tightly with my ears perked. "Get your head out of your fucking ass, boy. This is real life. This is a real business. You're right. The last thing I want to do is send you to the Covens. Not because I necessarily care where you are until it's time for you take over—because, frankly, you probably need the discipline that comes with the Covens—but more so because you need to do your fucking job."

I was shaking with anger. My limbs vibrated as I held tightly onto the phone, wanting to smash it into tiny little pieces.

My father's voice sunk into my bones as the words came through the line, "Clean your act up and figure out how to dazzle the committee so they don't expel you. Fuck, just do your goddamn job. If not, you won't be the only one going to the Covens."

I stilled. "What does that mean?"

"Jack could use some discipline too, I guess. Think of this as a bargaining chip. Fuck up, and you both will be shipped off until the time comes that I need you. Do you understand that?"

Fucking piece of shit. My throat clogged, and I clenched my eyes. "Yes."

"Yes what?" I noted the uptick in his voice.

I swallowed my pride because I was quickly brought back down to reality when he brought up my little brother. "Yes, *sir.*"

Then, the line went dead, and I quickly shoved my phone into the side pocket of my blazer. My fist reared back quickly, and I pounded into the wall, feeling pain rip up from my fingers all the way to my neck.

Fucking Jacobi. It wasn't fair to blame my older brother for wanting out and leaving me behind, but I did. I fucking did.

———

MY SWOLLEN KNUCKLES still ached a little as I tore off my white button down and flung it back into my bag. Lockers were being shut all around me, and for a moment, it felt like I was back in my old high school, surrounded by precious trust-fund babies with their biggest worry being what kind of car their mommy and daddy were going to give them for their birthday, only to wreck it hours later.

A low growl came from me as I scanned the locker room. It was the only modern part of St. Mary's. Everything else was dark and dreary. Old and primeval. Even the weather was uncanny as rain seemed to constantly fall from the clouds.

"What did you do to your hand?" Shiner stood beside me as he whipped on his lacrosse shirt, nodding to my hand.

"Nothing," I snapped as he shot me a wary look, but with his usual easygoing personality, he brushed me off quickly.

Shiner's real name was Nash, but he refused to be called that, so he went by Shiner. Actually, mostly everyone called him One-Liner-Shiner. He gained that nickname his freshman year when it only took him one line to get the entire female senior class in his bed. The legacy had stuck, too. Shiner was a bit of a manwhore, but most of us were. After all, what were we supposed to do while attending a boarding school that didn't even allow us to have cell phones during class hours?

As soon as we were all geared up for lacrosse practice, Cade rushed out in between our warm-up laps. "Where're we getting the booze for tomorrow?" he asked, bending down to touch his toes in a stretch. I held my lacrosse stick tightly in my hand, glancing at the dark clouds above our heads, wondering when it was going to start raining—because it *always* did. "Some of the girls have some shit stashed." I cracked my neck, looking out along the field and over the grassy hills that laid behind the bleachers. St. Mary's stood in the distance, appearing like a castle—a broken castle for broken princes and princesses was more like it.

"Nice," Cade muttered before sticking a foot out and tripping Shiner as he ran another lap.

Cade cackled as Shiner fell to the ground, his brown hair flopping on his head. "What the fuck, Cade."

"Payback's a bitch, Shiner."

"Payback for what?" I asked, staring at my two friends. Cade was towering over Shiner, who had made himself comfortable on the grassy land beneath his back. He even went as far as bringing his hands up behind his head and crossing his ankles. "Fucker claimed the new girl for the party before I could."

My head snapped down to Shiner who was grinning deviously like the smug fuck he thought he was. "Not happening."

"You already had her!" Shiner's mouth fell. "It was the headline on the stupid blog."

Cade snickered, glancing at Coach who was about to

round us up. "You're on that damn thing more than anyone, Shiner. You love it. So, are you calling yourself stupid, too?"

I rolled my eyes at their banter. "For one, I don't share. You know this. And two"—I walked over and stood directly above him, peering down into his face—"I'm not finished with her."

I felt Cade's stare driving into my temple. "You're not?"

Pointing my lacrosse stick at Cade, I answered with, "Nope," and then stalked off to the huddle that was beginning to form.

I wasn't finished with Gemma.

She just didn't know that yet.

CHAPTER NINE

GEMMA

THE NEXT FEW days at St. Mary's were better than I'd imagined, but that wasn't necessarily saying much because I had expected it to be pretty shitty. I kept waiting around for the blog post to show, the same one that Isaiah taunted me with, and by day three, I was feeling relieved that I hadn't heard or seen anything about me being in the closet with him.

Sloane and I got into a good routine, and I met a few other girls too. My stress levels began to fall with each passing day of no calls from Richard, but when Friday rolled around, there it was. Just like Isaiah had said.

I snatched Sloane's phone out of her hand during breakfast, and the blood drained from my face. There was a picture of me, walking through the hallway with my head tugged low, my worn and tattered books clutched to my chest. My chestnut hair was draped around my cheeks like a veil, shielding me from everyone.

The headline was all that I thought about during class. I

didn't even look back at Isaiah and his friends during art. I didn't look at anyone.

"People have already moved on," Sloane said, tugging me by the fabric of my blazer toward an arched doorway that looked as if it belonged in a Catholic church. A thin stream of light fluttered through the colorful stained glass, making the green a little more vibrant than before.

Once she pushed the door open, I felt the warm heat from the sun land right on my face. I breathed out a sigh, feeling lighter than before when we were stuck inside the school with people no doubt murmuring about me behind my back, despite Sloane lying to make me feel better.

"They have not," I said, trying to find it in me to laugh. I came up short, and after a few minutes of walking in silence with Sloane by my side, she came to a sudden halt.

We were both standing up on a grassy hill overlooking St. Mary's on one side and some sort of sports field on the other. I could see a huddled circle of guys in the middle, all holding large sticks.

"What are we doing?" I asked, bending down and pulling up my socks a little higher. It wasn't cold out, but there was a tiny bite to the air which likely meant rain was soon approaching.

Sloane eyed me skeptically as I stood straight again, ignoring my question. "Why are you so worried about this? About being on the blog? Why does it bother you so much?"

I darted my attention away from hers, looking back down to my shoes. I'd only known Sloane for a few days, and I already wanted to tell her everything. That was how it was with Sloane, though. There was something special about her. Something welcoming. I wanted to be her friend in a way that I probably never could.

I shrugged, lying through my teeth. "I just don't want people thinking I'm like that right off the bat."

Sloane shuffled on her feet, the grass crunching underneath her weight. "Gemma." Her voice was low as a few girls walked past us, smiling. Sloane smiled back sweetly, whereas I glanced away. As soon as the girls were out of earshot, she shot me a look that had me wavering. "I like you..."—she glanced down to the field—"but I can tell you're lying to me."

"I'm not," I blurted, feeling the anxiety of losing the first friend I'd ever had.

God. How totally pathetic did that sound?

I sighed, bringing my arms up to cross over my chest. My lip teetered in between my teeth as a whistle sounded from the sports field. "I have..." *Shit. Should I be saying this?* I peeked up at Sloane, and she was waiting patiently, her delicate features loose and unbearing. "My uncle is really strict." The words rushed out like water breaking through a dam. There they were. Out there in the open. The first of many secrets I'd buried underneath this nice and tidy boarding school uniform.

Sloane's dark, delicately arched eyebrows crowded together. Her thick lashes fanned over her cheeks as she thought for a moment. "What does this have to do with your uncle?"

My legs were shaky as my chest constricted. "He'll find out, and I'm not really allowed to have..." *Anyone.*

Sloane's bright-pink lips formed an *O* as recognition dawned on her. "A boyfriend? Don't worry about that, Gem." Her smile reached her eyes as she grasped my arm, intertwining ours together. "There's no way your uncle will find out."

My stomach seemed to swallow itself. "He knows the headmaster."

Sloane threw her head back and laughed freely as we continued walking down the grassy hill toward a set of bleachers that were pretty empty except for a few lingering girls huddled together, watching whatever sport the guys were playing down below.

"Gemma, the headmaster isn't going to tell your uncle anything. Trust me."

I wanted to trust her; I really did. But I didn't trust anyone.

Shaking my head, I sighed and took my arm out of hers as she turned and leaned over a chain fence separating the field from the metal bleachers. "Trust *me*, Sloane. My uncle will find out." My gaze shifted from her to the field, and just like that, a buzz went through me. A jolt of something hot started from the very bottom of my stomach, zipping all the way to my burning ears. I gulped when my eyes collided with Isaiah. He was several yards away, glancing up to where Sloane and I were standing as he took the bottom of his shirt and brought it up to his forehead, wiping away the sweat. My eyes instantly dropped to his torso, and my lips fell open.

Sloane giggled. "Oh my God, your face is blood red, Gemma."

I sucked in a breath and quickly whipped around, putting my back to the field. "What? No, it isn't!"

Sloane laughed even harder. "Don't worry, it happens to us all. Those Rebels are *hot*. I'll be the first to admit it."

"Damn straight they are!" a few girls who were sitting on the bleachers called out from behind us, fake fanning themselves. "Tell us!" One girl grinned down at me. It was Callie. The same girl that I saw the first night I was here. She was still sporting her school uniform—we all were since school had just ended a little while ago—but her white blouse was untucked and tied in a knot right under her bra that was peeking from below. Her long, blonde hair was braided but not in a childish way. It was cute and preppy, and I was a little envious.

"What?" I asked, suddenly feeling *extremely* self-conscious.

Callie's group of friends laughed as she deadpanned, "How was he in the sack? Hopefully still as good as when I had him a week ago!"

In the sack?

Sloane must have sensed my confusion, because she stepped forward, placing her hand on my arm. "Oh, shut up, Callie! We all know Isaiah turned you down at the last party."

My lips parted as I tried to make sense of what they were talking about. It took me a while to catch on to what they were referring to, and it made me hate Richard even more. I was good at blending in and acting like I wasn't the strangest, most naive seventeen-year-old on the planet, but I was. I was so out of my element it wasn't even funny, and I couldn't just ask Sloane to fill me in because that would raise too many questions, just like it did with Rebecca at my last school. The thing was, I wasn't a normal teenager. I hadn't experienced the things most kids my age had. I knew that. It was just really hard to accept.

As I further listened to Sloane and Callie argue back and forth about the Rebels, I eventually caught on and interrupted Sloane when she growled—yes, actually growled.

"I didn't do anything with Isaiah."

"That's not what he said," another girl piped up, giving me a once-over. I ignored the urge to hide myself.

"Well, he was lying." Blood rushed to my skin, and I wanted to turn around, stalk down the grassy field, and yell at Isaiah for making everyone think something of me that wasn't true—which, to be honest, was completely out of character for me. But still, I could feel a smothered scream trying to climb out of my chest. I was angry. Really angry.

Another girl leaned forward. "Why are you denying it? It'll only make you more desirable if you admit being with him. He's the most popular Rebel there is. I bet all the other boys will want a taste of you now. Shit, maybe even I want a taste of you."

Callie rolled her eyes as her friend giggled. I knew right then what type of girls these were. I noticed girls like them at Wellington Prep. I'd overheard their conversations many times during class and even in the bathroom. I didn't quite understand their power play, but I envied them all the same. They didn't bow down to anyone. It seemed as if nothing scared them. They were fearless, and they definitely knew their way around a boy's heart...and body.

Sloane huffed as she pulled me around, putting our backs to the group of girls once again. "Ignore them. They're just bored."

My mouth spoke before my brain could tell me to stop. "I don't really understand. Do they not like me now? Or do they like me even more? Did she seriously say she wanted a taste of me?" That was weird. Right?

Sloane gave me a side-eye, and *shit, I messed up.* "Gemma?"

My teeth scraped along one another as I gulped. "Yeah?"

"Just how strict is your uncle?"

Strict was an understatement.

"Uh, why?" I gulped again. My fingers began playing with the cotton hem of my skirt nervously.

"You just seem..." *Weird.* "Different. Like you're...sheltered in a way?"

Silence passed between us as I debated my next words. There was a sudden halt to the conversation. A fork in the road. *Surely telling her I was homeschooled most of my life wasn't a huge deal, right?* It was the stuff I was taught and punished for that would raise suspicions. It wasn't even that I wanted to protect Richard. I wasn't *not* telling her certain things for his benefit, but it was purely for mine. I had to act smart, form my plan, and crush him like a Mac truck when the time came. If he knew I was spouting off things that he wanted to stay private because he *knew* they were wrong, he'd rip me away despite the suspicions from the social worker. He'd find a way to keep me stowed until the time came where he could use me for his own sick desires. It would be difficult, but he would find a way if he truly had to.

My head fell back down to the field until I landed on Isaiah again as I debated what to say to Sloane. This time, he wasn't looking at me. "I guess I am kind of sheltered. I was homeschooled for a really long time."

I felt the breeze from her head snapping in my direction. "Is St. Mary's your first school? Like...ever?"

"No." I followed Isaiah's tall, lean frame as he jogged down the field, holding a stick. I wasn't sure what sport they were all playing, but it actually looked kind of fun, even if this small, angry part of me wished that he would trip.

Turning to look at Sloane again, I found her watching me intently with her hazel eyes, obviously hungry for more information. "What sport is that?" My head tilted toward the field.

Her face blanched. "Um. It's lacrosse."

I nodded, tucking my hair behind my ear to watch them again. One guy flung his stick hard toward another one who was standing in front of a net. A ball went flying through the air. The girls behind me cheered loudly before erupting in gleeful laughter. I jumped at their shrill outburst, and then my shoulders slowly dropped. A feeling of despair snuck up behind me, like a ghost coming up and brushing its translucent fingers over my flesh. My heart sank as I let myself feel the envy burning my blood.

I'd missed out on so much, and in the past, I'd never really let myself dwell on that because when you're in an internal battle with yourself, filtering through what was the truth and what was a lie, resentment over not going to a real high school and having normal experiences seemed so trivial in the grand scheme of things.

But standing here, without Richard looking over my shoulder and no threats being whispered into my ear, I felt it. I felt that unbending amount of loss and anger, all wrapped up in one atomic bomb, ready to unleash at the first taste of freedom.

"Gemma?" Sloane saying my name kicked me out of my troubled thoughts. My eyes refocused as I landed on her soft expression. "One, I have so much to teach you." My cheek twitched as the bitterness slowly disappeared. "And two"— her eyes sparkled as she glanced back down to the field —"Isaiah is totally walking up here right now."

I gasped, a breath getting stuck in my chest. My head whipped to the right, and there he was, shirtless, striding up the field with a wicked grin sitting right between his high-arched cheeks.

"And he has his eyes on you."

CHAPTER TEN

ISAIAH

MY ATTENTION never once left hers. From the moment I saw her standing up above the lacrosse field, my plan seemed to get brighter and brighter in my head. Like a neon sign, blazing its iridescent colors in my direction.

She was beautiful, even more so as I got closer to her, and I didn't use that word often. I stopped walking for a second. I didn't think that I'd *ever* used that word to describe a girl.

But fuck, Gemma's face was beautiful. Even the air around her was beautiful. It was as if the sun was shining directly on Gemma and no one else.

I noticed Sloane standing beside her, turning her attention to me and then back to Gemma a few more times before nodding. A leaf crumbled beneath my shoe, and just like that, Sloane was glaring at me.

Wonder what I did to piss her off?

I quickly thought back to the last party, but *nope,* definitely didn't get caught up in her at any point that night.

"Sloane." I dipped my head as I brought my hands up

around my neck, pulling my bundled-up shirt tighter as it draped around my shoulders. I was shirtless and sweaty, but neither Sloane nor Gemma seemed to be affected by that. *Weird.*

Flicking my eyes to Gemma, I noticed that she wasn't looking at me. It was as if I didn't exist at all to her. If only she knew that that made her much more alluring to me.

"Don't you *Sloane* me!" Sloane snapped, placing her hands on her hips.

I heard a snicker behind my back, telling me that Cade and Shiner had finally caught up to me.

I clicked my tongue against the roof of my mouth and leaned my forearms on the metal fence, falling in between the two girls. "Why the cold shoulder, Sloane?"

She huffed as I looked toward Gemma again. The sun caught a few strands of her hair, making the chestnut color even richer. "Because!" she snapped, clearly irritated. "Poor Gemma over here is *stressing* because of your little show earlier this week! The whole school thinks she's a slut."

Cade wandered up beside me, running his hand through his sweaty hair. "Oh, now, come on. Isn't that every little girl's dream? I heard that being a slut in high school nowadays is like being prom queen. It means you're popular."

"Not every girl wants to be popular." Gemma finally turned herself toward us and leveled me with a stare that touched every single cell in my body. My stomach dipped, and my tongue darted out of my mouth as I licked my lips. *Oh, I like her.*

"Hmm," Cade murmured beside me, leaning back on the fence as he looked out toward the field. The girls were on one side, us on the other, but I suddenly had the urge to jump over the metal rod so I could be on the same side as Gemma.

"Make it go away." Her voice was soft and hesitant, but I could sense the fierceness lurking behind with urgency.

Silence fell over the group of us. We were all staring directly at Gemma who had dropped both of her arms down to her sides. She was on the taller side, at least taller than Sloane, with lean, long legs. The skirt she wore fell to about mid-thigh, much like all the rest of the girls at St. Mary's, but Gemma seemed to wear it best. Her skin was creamy and smooth, her cheeks flushing with the tiniest bit of pink.

I slowly swung my attention to Sloane, who had her lips pursed together in my direction, waiting for my answer. Her eyebrow suddenly cocked upward, and I appreciated how she didn't bat her eyelashes at me. Sloane had been attending St. Mary's since the time I had, so I knew her pretty well, but we'd never been alone in a closet together. She had never thrown herself at me like the rest of the female population, and I'd never pursued her because I didn't need to pursue anyone, really.

I kept my gaze trained on Sloane even though I wanted to look at Gemma in the most agonizing way. "Sloane, did Gemma tell you about Ms. Glenburg?"

Everything around me ceased to exist as I kept staring down into Sloane's hazel eyes. This was something that my father had instilled in me long, long ago: how to read people. Their mannerisms, their breathing, their eyes. I'd watch and then decipher the next words that came out of their mouth very closely. It was a quality that my father needed in his line of business, I supposed—and fuck him, but he taught me well. I could see through someone as if they were water in a glass cup.

The skin around Sloane's eyes wrinkled as she threw her hands up. "What? What about Ms. Glenburg?"

She looked to Gemma, who had kept her face expression-less, and then back to me. "Stop trying to change the subject, Isaiah. You may be considered the top dog at this school, but you need to fix this for Gemma until—"

"Until what?" I inquired, suddenly even more interested.

"Nothing," Gemma snapped at me. Her soft and hesitant expression morphed to anger as she locked onto me, and I felt a flame blaze within. "Let's just go, Sloane."

I didn't want her to go, but just like that, Gemma had turned her back on all of us and began walking down the grassy hill toward St. Mary's. My eyes trailed after her, following the smoke from the fire brewing inside of her.

Sloane narrowed her gaze on me. "Seriously, Isaiah. Not everyone likes attention. I know that's hard for you Rebels to understand, but figure out a way to get her out of the spotlight before she gets in trouble." Then, she growled at me like a rabid dog before ruffling her black hair in her hands with frustration. "Oh. And Gemma didn't tell anyone about you and that teacher, whoever it was. She had only talked to me that night, and she didn't say a word."

I assumed as much, since there wasn't even a flicker of recognition on Sloane's face when I mentioned Ms. Glenburg a few seconds ago. Thankfully, the blog didn't release any names, likely because they didn't even know who it was. Teachers came and went at our school often—probably because of students like me who liked to cause trouble. *Oops.*

Before Sloane followed Gemma, who was already down to the side door of St. Mary's, I asked, "Why would she get in trouble?"

"Just never mind. Get it taken care of. I'm done with letting my friends get walked all over by Rebels." Sloane shifted her attention to Cade briefly before whipping around and running after Gemma.

I turned to see Cade's face fall.

"Did she know...?" I asked, not wanting to dive too much further into choppy waters with his situation.

He pushed off the fence, sighing. "Probably. She and Journey were close. They were roommates." Then, he shook his sweaty blond hair out. "But Sloane is right. Not everyone likes attention, even if we thought she deserved some payback."

I heard Shiner in the distance as he walked beside Cade. "I like the attention."

Cade grunted, "Shut up."

Finally pushing myself off the fence and taking my eyes away from the door that Gemma had disappeared into, I realized the validity in Sloane's statement. Not everyone liked attention, and even glancing at Gemma brought attention.

CHAPTER ELEVEN

GEMMA

"THERE'S A PARTY TONIGHT, and we're going."

Well, with a statement like that... I warily looked over at Sloane who was shoving an Italian sub into her mouth. The dining hall was open pretty much all day on the weekends and didn't close until curfew, which was 9:00 on Friday and Saturday. On Sunday, it went back to normal hours: curfew at 7:00 and no later.

Still gripping my cell phone in my hand, waiting for Richard to grace me with his nightmare of a voice, I began picking at the fruit salad on my plate and glanced down to a few other girls that Sloane had introduced me to last night before lights out.

"I can't," I whispered, feeling uncomfortable.

"Why?" one of the girls asked. Peeking up through a few strands of my hair, I saw that it was Mercedes, one of the girls I met last night. She lived just across the hall.

I shifted in my seat, unsure of how to answer the question. I'd never been in this situation before, sitting with other girls my age, having small talk about a party that was going on later in the evening. It was nice, don't get me wrong. I'd thought of this exact moment and played it out in my head every night when I'd get home from Wellington Prep. I'd watch the girls during lunch, listen to their easy conversations, and wonder if I'd ever get that. And now that I was kind of living that dream and enjoying it, I knew it wouldn't last forever. None of this would. *But I still wanted it.*

"Um..." I started.

Sloane placed her sub back down on her tray before wiping her fingers on a napkin. She swiped at a few stray crumbs stuck to her black shirt before taking her hands and placing them on my forearms, squeezing lightly. "Listen, I know you said your uncle is strict, but there is no way he will find out that you went to a party. I mean, we're locked away in a boarding school, Gem."

I lowered my head, not wanting anyone else to hear me. "But my uncle knows Headmaster Ellison. What if he catches us and then tells him?"

Mercedes giggled. "Trust us when we say the headmaster won't tell your uncle. He knows so much stuff about me"—she glanced around the dining hall as if she were looking for someone in particular—"and he has yet to tell my parents, who, by the way, are on the committee."

"The committee?" I questioned, even more leery than before. *What freaking committee?*

I looked between the two girls and watched as Sloane grabbed her fork. She started shoving a bite of salad into her mouth seconds later. Not only did she have a greasy Italian sub on one end of her tray, she had a colorful, healthy salad on the other. She said something about *balance* when Mercedes commented on her two choices of food but quickly moved on and muttered through her chews. "Yeah. So the way it works is that Headmaster Ellison basically has the final decision on everything, but there is a committee—the SMC—that votes on grants, educational shit...discipline...and"—she shrugged —"whatever else it is they have meetings about. I don't know and don't really care. I just know that the headmaster has covered for us both on numerous occasions."

My face must have shown my confusion when Sloane added, "The only people the committee has beef with are the Rebels, and that's because they think they rule the school and are always doing stupid shit to get a rise out of them."

Mercedes laughed. "Especially Isaiah. They hate him."

That garnered my full attention. I was still totally infuriated with Isaiah over the closet thing, and not only was I appalled at how one look from him could make my chest tight but also elicit angry little fires throughout my bloodstream at the same time, I was also confused. And intrigued. I wanted to know more about him, and I didn't understand why. "Why do they hate him?"

Sloane rolled her eyes. "Because he's the baddest one of the bunch. He's always sneaking out and doing shit he shouldn't...like having sex with a teacher."

He didn't actually have sex with her. I knew that from listening in on his conversation, but I kept that to myself.

I looked back and forth from Sloane to Mercedes as they took the conversation in their hands, talking in between bites. "What teacher was it anyway? The blog, as usual, was vague as shit."

Sloane looked perplexed. "I'm not sure. I haven't seen Ms. Hayes around, but also...I haven't seen Mrs. Lanning either... or Ms. Glenburg."

Mercedes' mouth dropped. "Mrs. Lanning is married. It can't be her."

Sloane dipped her eyes down, casting her a look. "Isaiah is hot as sin and looks way older than he actually is. Not to mention he can basically convince anyone to do anything. I'm certain that even married women have fantasized about having his head between their legs." She paused as a grin graced her face. "And I mean *both* heads, if you catch my drift."

Mercedes and a few other girls laughed as they all began talking about Isaiah and the rumors that followed his legacy.

My cheek tinged with pain as I bit the side of it while listening to their conversation. My heart flopped as I silently agreed that Isaiah was very attractive. Quite possibly the hottest guy I'd ever seen in real life. Granted, all I had to compare him to were the guys at Wellington Prep and the imaginary ones in my head that I'd conjure up from the books I'd sneak from the girls at the group home, but he had all the perfect attributes. The ones that were used to describe the perfect specimen of a male.

Dark hair that somehow made the sharp lines of his face stand out even more. Icy eyes surrounded by a mass of thick, dark lashes. Tall and strong. And there was just a little something extra to him that made your heart zing with one look. But despite thinking all those things, it didn't take away the fact that I was still angry with him. In fact, it felt like a betrayal to myself that I felt something when his eyes were on me. It was far beyond what my little innocent brain could decipher, but my body felt alive when he was near. *I* felt alive. Maybe that was why I had no issue snapping at him the last few times we had spoken. It was like my subconscious was aggravated that he had some affect over me.

"No," Mercedes' voice brought me back into the conversation. She shook her wild, curly hair out. "I think he's hot because of his behavior. Did you see him kissing Breanna last weekend? The way he gripped her?" Mercedes fanned herself. "It was so...possessive, and for some reason, he made it hot."

Sloane snickered into her sub, eventually throwing her head back and laughing loudly.

I kept my mouth shut as envy filled up the gaps inside my chest that had been opening since I was young enough to know what jealousy was.

I didn't feel it often, but once I got to Wellington Prep, and I was able to breathe life for the first time in *ever*, I didn't realize how much more there was beyond the walls of my bedroom. Even the girls at the group home that Richard's mother ran wouldn't throw me a bone to let me know that my life was completely and utterly fucked up. I even thought that the books I'd sneaked from them were purely fiction. I had no idea there was any truth to them.

It was good that I was feeling that envy, though. That meant that I'd broken through yet another wall Richard had built in front of my eyes, demolishing it swiftly with the sudden curiosity of what else was out there.

"He's picky about his girls, though. Have you noticed that?" Mercedes took a sip of her drink. "That's why I've never tried to get his attention. I'm not sure my ego could take the hit if he turned me down."

"Isaiah would be an idiot to turn you down," I said before I could stop myself. "You're pretty perfect, if you ask me."

Mercedes' cheeks flushed as she smiled at me, but then her smile quickly fell, and I wanted to suck the words back in. *Should I have kept that to myself?* But it was true. She was the most welcoming of the girls I'd met so far, except for Sloane.

"I'd be an idiot, huh?"

My eyes widened at the voice coming from behind me. *Oh my God.* I understood now why her smile had vanished. Was she trying to warn me?

Isaiah's scent, something clean but enticing, wafted around me as he took a seat to my left. I kept my eyes on Mercedes, who was blushing even more than before. *Shit, now what?* Taking a quick pause to think, I then pushed my tray out in front of me. I tilted my body toward him, glancing at his hot, somewhat arrogant smirk. *Show no fear.*

"Yeah. You would be," I calmly stated, backing my opinion with confidence. "Mercedes is great."

Our eyes caught, and I swore everything else around me melted away. Just like that. I was certain the sounds from the dining room were still there: the silverware scraping against the bowls and plates, the low chatter of other students, even the distant whirring of the air conditioner, but I couldn't hear a single thing except the thumping of my heart in my ears. I was brought to life in those few seconds staring at him. Air whooshed into my lungs. My blood rushed through my veins. Everything sparked as our gazes caught.

What was it with him? Why couldn't I seem to function correctly when he looked at me?

Isaiah's head tilted just slightly, a small twitch of his perfect lips. His inky hair was laying untouched on his head, longer on the top than on the sides. "Gemma," he whispered, snapping our moment in half like a twig breaking in the middle of the forest.

My brows crinkled, my eyes slanting. One tip of his chin and the flicking of his eyes to someone standing beside me caused me to finally shake myself free.

"Gemma?" the headmaster's voice sounded from behind me. I glanced up at him quickly in horror, seeing him staring at Isaiah disapprovingly, like the other day when I'd first arrived at St. Mary's. I slowly glanced around the dining table, wondering how much time had passed. Sloane's lips were smashed together as she stared at me. Her short black hair was tucked behind both diamond-studded ears. Mercedes' eyebrows were shot straight up, her fork frozen in mid-air with a piece of lettuce dangling off the side.

There was a hush that came over the table as the headmaster bent down to my level. "I need to see you in my office, please."

A blinding white light flashed before my eyes. The floor underneath my feet felt like slippery mud. My limbs were trembling as I shot straight up from the table, banging my knees off the bottom ledge.

I couldn't even bring myself to look at Sloane, and definitely not Isaiah, as my shoulders caved in on themselves. My feet shuffled along the shiny floor as I felt every ounce of freedom I'd managed to grasp slip through my fingers.

This was it.

It was over.

My one chance was gone.

CHAPTER TWELVE

GEMMA

I COUNTED each and every square on the checkered floor as I followed the headmaster. Nothing but our breathing—his leveled and mine erratic—sounded in the long hallway, and before I knew it, we were walking into his office.

Ping-ponging my attention back and forth from one end of his office to the next, noting almost instantly that we were alone, I found myself relaxing a fraction.

Richard wasn't here. Yet.

"Gemma." The headmaster bowed his head to the chair at the foot of his heavy desk.

Shuffling farther into his office, I lowered myself down onto the leather seat, grasping onto the arms for dear life. Fear like no other crept over my shoulder, whispering dreadful things in my ear. Every time I shut my eyes, I could see nothing but a dark, wet concrete floor and chains swaying from the ceiling.

"He's coming to get me, isn't he?" I whispered, feeling

myself tighten. *Shit. Shit. Shit. I knew he'd find out about the rumor.*

The headmaster didn't sit behind his desk. Instead, he perched himself at the end, his shoes peeking into my line of sight.

"No."

"No?" I repeated, thinking over the little word carefully. The word no typically stood for something negative, at least in my life, but right now? It was full of sunshine and rainbows.

A light chuckle came from him, and I finally glanced upward, leery of what I'd find. "I just wanted to see how you were doing. I saw you made friends with Sloane, and..." The headmaster looked up at the ceiling as if contemplating something before bringing his green eyes back down and smiling. "Mercedes?"

Pushing my back onto the hard chair, I swallowed nervously. "Oh, um. Yes, sir. They're nice."

His heavy brow line deepened. "You don't need to call me sir, Gemma."

I let out a breath, bringing my hands to my lap. "My uncle told me—"

"I'm pretty positive your uncle told you a lot of things. Please do not call me sir. I want you to be comfortable here, and I can tell you're pretty uncomfortable right now."

Not necessarily uncomfortable, just extremely cautious.

"And..." He sprung up off the edge of his desk and walked around to sit in his chair. I eyed him the entire way. He was even more relaxed today than when I had met him at the beginning of the week. He wasn't wearing a tie but instead was wearing dark jeans and a button-down shirt, his hair a little messy on top. I had to admit, he was perplexing. "Gemma, did you hear me?"

Shit. No. I was too busy trying to figure him out. "Oh. I'm sorry. What did you say?"

"I said I can tell you don't trust me."

"I don't trust anyone except my brother." I was quick to answer him, and almost instantly, I wanted to slap myself. There was a definite dent in my heart as I spoke aloud about Tobias for the first time in a very long time. *Why did I say that?!*

I saw the shock on his face before he had a chance to recover. "You have a brother?"

My chest was wound so tightly that I could hardly breathe. "Yes. A twin." *Should I have been telling him this?*

The headmaster reached out and grabbed a green folder, opening it and placing it in front of him. Every muscle inside my body begged me to move forward just a bit, to see what was inside, but I didn't want him to think I was digging, so I stayed still in my seat. A few pages were flipped, the headmaster licking his finger once or twice, before he set it back down and brought his gaze back to mine. "So, where is your brother, then?"

If only I knew.

A few seconds passed as I had an internal war with what I was supposed to be sharing with the headmaster. I didn't trust him, but there was a very strong part of me that wanted to. I didn't know why. For some bizarre and unexplainable reason, he felt familiar to me, and not in the way that I'd seen him passing by on the street. It was something more. Something that made me feel safe, which, in the same breath, made me feel unsafe.

A knot made itself known in my throat. My chest grew even tighter, and the girl inside of me that longed for her brother, and longed for a way out, banged her fists against the contents of my brain, but at the exact same time, there was a door being slammed and a lock being clicked. *Don't trust.*

"You know what?" I switched my eyes back to him as he smiled. "Never mind that, okay? I called you in here for a few reasons, actually, and none of those were discussing your trust with me."

The headmaster, again, stood up from his desk and came around and plopped himself on the edge in front of me. One of his legs was touching the ground, the other was hiked up over his knee. "Your uncle wants you to check in every Monday with him, and he wants you to use the phone directly from the school instead of your cell phone. I told him you could come down here each Monday evening before curfew."

Can't wait. "Okay, thank you."

He nodded and glanced away for a moment. "I need you to know something, though."

I wavered before reluctantly saying, "Okay?" which came out more like a question than anything.

"As headmaster of this school, I take my students very seriously. I like to give them freedom and a chance to make their own decisions." Heavy silence filled the office before he continued. "You don't trust me, and that's okay because you don't know me. But you can come to me with any problems you may have..." His sentence trailed at the end as we had some weird, muted conversation with one another. I couldn't be sure, but I felt like he was skirting around what he truly wanted to say, and before I could nod my head in understanding, he leaned forward and lowered his voice. "And I mean *any* problem. It doesn't have to pertain to school... Do you understand what I'm trying to say?"

Don't trust. Don't trust. Don't trust.

My pulse quickened at his words, and the fear and loneliness I'd felt almost all my life—even more when Tobias left—came crashing down at the exact same time thunder rolled above the school. I jumped in my seat, taking that as a sign to keep my mouth shut. *If he only knew just how badly I wanted to trust him*. But I wouldn't. The only person I could truly trust was myself, and sometimes, I even questioned that.

"Also," the headmaster moved right along after I didn't answer him, and I was thankful. I was thankful because I wasn't sure what to say. "Mrs. Fitzpatrick was impressed with your artistic ability." He laughed, moving around to his desk again, acting as if we didn't just have a heavily deep conversation about trusting one another. "Actually, that's putting it mildly. She said you were brilliant. That you had the skill of Picasso himself."

That brought an instant smile to my face. A real, down-to-my-soul smile. "Really?" I asked with true surprise. I surely thought Mrs. Fitzpatrick would think poorly of me after seeing me pop out of a closet with Isaiah on my heels. *Jerk. A hot jerk, but still a jerk.*

"Yes, really." He grinned before pulling the green file open again. After flipping through a few papers, he read aloud, "Gemma has the potential for a full-ride scholarship to almost any prestigious art school in the nation, with a portfolio. Each and every piece she created for me in her few months of attending Wellington Prep blew me away, and I have been an art teacher for almost twenty years. Please give her a safe place to let her creative streak shine, because if you give her a chance, she will flourish."

My lips parted, and my cheeks were on fire as I sat there dumbfounded.

"I took it upon myself to contact your old school for transcripts since your uncle has yet to get them to me."

There was a reason for that, I was sure.

"Oh," I whispered, wondering what else he got from Wellington Prep. Did they tell him about my journal? About what was inside? About what Richard, my not-so-real uncle, had told them? The tips of my fingers prickled with the need to snatch that green folder from his hands.

"So, after talking with Mrs. Fitzpatrick, we've decided to let you use the art room at any hour of the day, except for after curfew or, of course, during your other classes."

Hope blossomed in my chest, warming me up from the inside out. "Are you serious?"

He nodded, this time grinning so big I could see his white teeth. A flash of something whipped through my head at the familiarity of his smile, but after a fleeting second, it fell, just as the feeling of warmth had vanished. "Just..."—he glanced away—"your uncle has made it very clear that you are to focus on your studies and *not* art."

That wasn't surprising in the least, especially considering what had happened at Wellington Prep.

"But...you're allowing me to use the art room? Why?" I couldn't help the words tumbling out. I was beyond confused. There were too many mixed emotions floating around my head, jumbling up my thoughts. From the second I stepped my wet shoe into St. Mary's expansive entryway on Monday, I'd been in complete disarray. Isaiah, the headmaster, Sloane... all together, mixed with the thick walls of this place, tucked away in the middle of the forest on the very brim of Washington...made me feel something that was almost taunting in a way: *safe*. I felt safe.

But I wasn't. I wasn't safe until I was far, far away from Richard. He had ties with this school in some way, and even if Headmaster Ellison had been all but forthcoming about his rocky skepticism regarding Judge Stallard himself, I wasn't totally sold on the idea that I was untouchable here.

If Richard knew of even one tiny misstep from me, I'd never ever get a way out. For all I knew, he was putting together a plan right this second to fend off the social worker and any unanswered questions and take me back. But still, I wanted to know why the headmaster was allowing me to do something *my uncle* forbade. I needed to make sense of it all.

"Because," the headmaster whispered, finally answering me, "you remind me of someone."

CHAPTER THIRTEEN

ISAIAH

"Because you remind me of someone."

Hearing my uncle and Gemma get to their feet and walk over to the door of his office, I scooted back slightly from the hinges and rested my back along the stone wall behind me.

Gemma was the first to walk out, stopping dead in her tracks at the sight of me sitting in the same spot she had sat a few days ago, when *she'd* eavesdropped on *my* conversation. There was a slight dip in her brows, her pale lips pursing. She recovered quickly, darting further away when I shot her a wicked grin. I cocked an eyebrow as if I were saying, *"See? I can eavesdrop too."*

"Isaiah?" My uncle cleared his throat, breaking Gemma and me away from our silent spar. She quickly shot me a withering stare before turning around and walking down the hall in her tight skinny jeans, which I may have preferred over her uniform. The uniform showed smooth legs, but her jeans fit her like a glove, showcasing her tight ass and curved hips.

My uncle cleared his throat again, and I finally tore my longing stare away from Gemma. "What do you need?"

I really only came down here to ask why my uncle needed to talk with Gemma, but after I'd heard their voices filtering through from the other side of his office door, I couldn't help but listen.

I needed—*okay, fine...*I wanted to know more about Gemma because there was absolutely more to her than met the eye. At first, she looked innocent, and there was no doubt in my mind that she was. She was shy, blushed a fuck-ton, which was actually kind of cute in a way, and fell into herself anytime there was attention on her. But she had a fire inside of her too. Gemma was fueled by something. Something dark and unforgiving. I was beginning to learn that she was hard to read, but all in all, she appeared good and respectful. For fuck's sake, she called my uncle *sir,* and each and every teacher adored her. I'd heard them discussing her in the teacher's lounge the other day when I bluntly walked in to use the vending machine that was off limits to students. Gemma was a good girl, even if she hated when I used that little pet name, and I wanted to know more.

After striding into my uncle's office and plopping myself down onto the leather seat at his desk, noting it was still warm from Gemma, I hiked a foot onto his desk. "What did the SMC say?" I had been acting nonchalant since we'd talked last, but after speaking with my father, I was on edge. I hardly slept. Instead, I stayed up until three, playing video games with Cade, and I *never* did that. Video games were like a suspension from reality, and although my reality sucked, I still liked to be in control of it.

He grunted. "You're on probation."

I paused. "What the fuck does that mean?"

My uncle ran a hand through his hair, looking more tired than usual. He put his back to me and angled his head up to the ancient map framed on the wall behind his desk. I followed his line of sight, roaming my gaze over each and every valley of earth, reminding me that there was so much more out there than this dreary place I called home.

"It means you have one more chance. You and Ms. Glenburg put them over the edge."

My nostrils flared as my boots thudded to the floor. "I talked to Dad."

He cocked his head over his shoulder. "I did too."

Silence fell upon us as it often did when my father was brought up. I ground my teeth, gripping onto the arms of the chair tightly. "He threatened Jack."

That had my uncle turning around with a disapproving scowl etched on his features. His hands graced his hips angrily. "Of course he did." Shaking his head, he sat down into his seat.

"So, I basically can't get kicked out of St. Mary's and also have to keep tabs on Bain, who loves trouble as much as any of us."

The scratching of my uncle's hand against his pebbled five o'clock shadow caused my eyes to drop down. He huffed out a sarcastic laugh, but I stayed silent. Thinking. Pondering.

"Why exactly can't *you* give my father updates about Bain?"

I'd never really thought of it before because when my father forced his little scheming plan of sending me to boarding school to keep watch on his enemy's son, Bain, I didn't really care. I was happy to be away from him and his bullshit, albeit a little worried about Jack, but with our nanny and Mom's nurses as a buffer, I was sure Jack was *mostly* fine. But now I was wondering. And I mean, did I have a choice? No. But why did I have to be his little spy when my uncle was the headmaster, for fuck's sake?

His answer came swiftly. "That's easy, Isaiah. Your father doesn't trust me."

I squinted. "That makes no sense. You're his brother."

My uncle darted his eyes away from me. "And you're Jacobi's brother. Do you trust him?"

I grunted. *Touché.* It wasn't that I didn't trust my older brother—he'd never blatantly lied to me—but I had been betrayed by him, and that was similar enough.

"The real question is"—his hands came and rested along the desk—"how are we going to keep you out of trouble but allow you to keep an eye on Bain? I know that when you sneak out, it's because of him, and the SMC will not allow me to make excuses any longer. I cannot be your cover. The SMC no longer believes my lies."

His admission didn't phase me. I knew he was aware that I snuck out, because he was always the one that had the final say in punishments, even if he wasn't the one who had caught me sneaking back in. It infuriated me beyond belief that Bain always snuck back in undetected, though. He was a sneaky little fuck.

My fingers came up and drummed against my chin for a second. "So, I need to quit getting caught or at least have a better cover for when I do get caught..."

"And you need to get your grades up. You're smart, Isaiah. So why on earth are you flunking?"

I chuckled under my breath before shrugging.

"You're so defiant. You're failing your classes on purpose, aren't you? Another one of your attempts to gain control like Ms. Glenburg had pointed out."

Whatever. I wanted to stew in silence, annoyed that they'd somehow made sense of my behavior that even I hadn't realized, but I didn't have time for all of that. They could take their Freud bullshit and do with it as they pleased.

I sighed, rubbing the back of my neck to ease the tension.

"I think I have just the plan that can knock out each of those things."

He raised an eyebrow, wafting his hand out for me to continue.

"What do you know about the new girl?" I asked as my cheek lifted.

His face faltered. "No." The word was like a bullet being fired.

"You haven't even heard my plan."

He snickered. "I'm certain that whatever it is, the answer is still no."

I propped my leg back onto his desk, ignoring the way it made him scowl. "Hear me out. Good Girl can be my tutor. You said I was on probation, right?" I didn't give him a chance to confirm. "I'm assuming they're going to be paying close attention to my grades along with my behavior. I'll get my grades up with my *'tutor',"*—I used air quotes around the simple term—"and she can also be a damn good cover. An alibi." My leg fell to the ground as I sat up taller, feeling the smallest amount of desperation kick in. "You can write a note that she and I have permission to use the library after lacrosse practice, which gives me a pretty good excuse to be out of my room and roaming the halls after curfew, and on the nights that the SMC is suspicious of or doesn't believe my bullshit, Gemma can lie and tell them that I was with her, studying. They would *never* suspect a girl like her to cover for a guy like me. She's too...*good*."

He gave me an incredulous look, but he didn't say no. "And you just expect her to lie for you? You are right. She is a good kid. She's timid, and sweet, and I'm assuming she's honest as well. What if she doesn't lie for you, Isaiah? What if she tells them straight up that you were not with her?"

My desperation, along with the anger that my father had instilled after our conversation, was beginning to rise to high levels. "Then I'll fucking convince her! Do you have a better idea, Uncle Tate?" I took a deep breath before cursing under my breath. "I didn't care much about what Dad had to say when he sent me here. Fuck him. But he threatened to send Jack to the Covens. Jack!" My voice grew louder. "He's fucking nine years old."

Another round of silence fell upon us, hushing my loud outburst. My chest was heaving, and for the first time in a while, I lost my control in front of another person. I felt a little unhinged.

My uncle didn't say anything. Instead, he brought his finger and thumb up to his nose and punched the bridge of it. Then, he moved to his temples and began massaging them. I needed to do the same because my head began to pound the moment I brought up my little brother.

After a few more seconds of silence, I leaned my elbows down on my black jeans. "Do you have a better idea?" My chest ached, the muscles along my neck tensing. "I know it's my fault the committee isn't happy with me—that's on me. But you're right. Half the time, the reason I get caught doing shit I shouldn't is because of Bain. He somehow twists shit, and he never gets caught sneaking back in after going in fucking circles. He always manages to sneak away without getting into any trouble at all."

"That's because Bain has been taught all his life to evade authority. His father has been grooming him from a young age."

I often forgot that my uncle was once in the same position I was in. That he was once a part of the family business, and he likely knew more than me.

"So was I," I answered, flicking my eyes to him.

He gave me a grin. "You're right, but there's a difference between you and Bain, Isaiah. You don't want to please your father like he does. And also, you're not the bad kid that everyone thinks you are."

I joked. "The committee says otherwise."

Another stretch of silence passed as he thought for a moment. His eyes wandered all over his office as he had an internal battle with himself. Then, he shook his head. "I suppose you can carry on with your plan...but don't break that poor girl's heart. She's...fragile. She can be your tutor." He glanced away as he mumbled under his breath, "It would probably do her good to make some more friends around here." After a moment, he locked back onto me. "She can lie for you on occasion, if she's up for that, but do not force her into anything she doesn't want. Every girl at this school seems to be wrapped around your finger. Don't mess with Gemma."

My lips ached to give him a cocky grin, but instead, I stood up from the chair and began walking toward his office door. "Don't worry, Uncle Tate. I won't corrupt the good girl."

I was certain he mumbled, *"Yeah fucking right,"* under his breath, but I couldn't be sure.

CHAPTER FOURTEEN

GEMMA

"AND THIS IS where we usually hang out on the weekends before curfew..." Sloane's voice trailed as she plopped herself down onto a couch with a ridiculous number of frilly pillows scattered on top. Her small frame was nearly invisible as the cushions swallowed her up.

Glancing around the dimly lit room, I found a few standing lamps and some candles resting along a high bookshelf, their flame flickering back and forth. The room was dark but comforting. I could totally see myself getting lost while sketching in here.

"Come sit with us," Mercedes said as she pulled a book from the shelf across the room. "What did the headmaster want?"

Slowly sitting down on the floor over a multicolored woven rug, I crossed my legs and rested my back against the couch Sloane was lying lazily on. There were a few other groups of students in the...lounge?...but they all went back into their own conversations after scanning me from head to toe.

"Oh, um." I teetered my lip back and forth. "He wanted to talk about my past transcripts and let me know that I could use the art room whenever I wanted."

"The art room?" Mercedes sat at the end of the couch, wiggling underneath Sloane's legs.

"Yeah." I smiled shyly, pulling my long sleeves farther onto my hands to hide my wrists.

"Oh, yes, didn't you know?" I quickly straightened at the sound of Cade's voice. He strode into the room, looking just as dreamy as he did in art, except I knew those honey-brown eyes could be deceiving. Sliding down beside me, resting his shoulder against mine, he peered over at me. "Gemma is quite the artist. You should have seen her sketch in art the other day."

I hastily moved my arm away from his, annoyed that he was touching me. "It would have been nice if I could have finished my sketch. But someone took advantage of my generosity." *Shit, why did I just say that?* What was it with these guys that fired me up?

A girl from a few seats down snorted under her breath. Mercedes smashed her lips together as Sloane mused, "Okay, I officially love my new roomie."

I wasn't sure why she said that, but I assumed it was because I had talked back to Cade. It wasn't on purpose, but I was still a little bitter that he had tricked me and worked alongside his friend to corner me in the closet. I was amazed at the confidence I had when allowed to speak my mind for once.

"Uh-oh. Someone's bitter." My eyes moved swiftly over to a pair of black combat boots that were so close to touching my own shoes I could have moved a centimeter and they'd have been joined together. I refused to travel the length of his legs to meet his face.

"Of course she's bitter," Sloane mumbled. The couch cushions moved behind my back, so I knew she'd sat up. "The school thinks she had an infamous closet date with you after one day of being here."

Brantley, one of the other Rebels that Sloane had pointed out during breakfast, made an appearance. "Did you hear that? Your closet dates are infamous, Isaiah."

Cade made a high-pitched whistling sound. "I don't know about you, but I think I hear some jealousy in Sloane's tone."

"Absolutely not," she was quick to rebuttal. "I don't screw around with Rebels."

Brantley stepped closer to us. "Who do you screw around with then?"

I finally turned around and glanced up at Sloane. She and I hadn't talked much about *her* since I'd arrived here. We'd talked about the school, a little about my life, but not so much hers. That probably meant I was a bad friend. I needed to ask more questions, get to know her a little better.

Sloane's face stayed even, but I saw the smallest amount of pink spread over her cheeks. Before she could answer, Isaiah cleared his throat, and the tip of his boot hit the edge of mine.

Finally, I brought my attention to him, craning my neck back to peer up at his tall stance. I tried to brace myself for the impact, but my stomach flopped anyway.

The angle of his jaw was even sharper from where I was sitting, the edges of it looking like a sharp blade. His blue eyes were icier than ever, too, but somehow soft as he peered down at me. "Can we talk?"

My mouth opened, but nothing came out. Butterflies were definitely swarming my stomach. I gulped when I pressed my lips together again, suddenly feeling dizzy. *Say no.*

I needed to say no. He made the entire school think I had done something with him in the art supply closet. He was the whole reason my cell phone was burning a freaking hole in the back of my jeans, just waiting for Richard's cold voice on the other end telling me he'd seen the blog post on Mary's Murmurs. I wasn't sure how to access the site, but Richard was a smart man. He'd figure it out.

"I think you've rendered her speechless, bro."

Another voice came from beside Cade. I think it was Brantley. "I think you've rendered everyone speechless."

Isaiah and I both took a quick scan of the room, realizing everyone was staring at our little moment. Not a single person was speaking. Their attention was solely on us.

It didn't take long for my body to grow hot. Gasoline was poured over my head, and their scorching eyes were the match. If there was a mirror in front of me, I wouldn't even have to look to know my entire body was flushed.

Once I peeked back at Isaiah, his head moved slightly. My breathing had quickened, the couch cushions behind my back shifting again, telling me that Sloane was about to swoop in and save me.

"Fine," I whispered, slowly climbing to my feet. Isaiah dipped his head down to my legs and then back up again. The single movement of him scanning me from head to toe made the room spin. I was in a time warp. Time had passed, I was sure of it—maybe only a few seconds—but to me, I felt it had paused all together. I was rooted to the floor, my feet becoming heavy in my shoes, but eventually, the moment was gone, and I trudged after him.

See? I could do this. I could get past the way he made me feel when he looked at me. *It was fine*. Isaiah Underwood would not become a distraction. And plus, I was pretty sure the only reason I was feeling so erratic around him was because I'd been so starved of human interaction my whole life. It had nothing to do with the way his blue eyes seemed to burn a little brighter when he locked onto me.

The very second Isaiah and I stepped out of the lounge, we were met with the quietness of the long, empty hall. A trickle of a faucet dripped in the distance as I tiptoed after him, my shoes barely making a noise on the floor. The water dribbling and the pounding of my pulse were like an orchestra playing in my head, but it quickly came to an end when Isaiah halted in front of me. I made sure to keep a good distance behind him so I didn't fall into the hard planes of his body again like the first night we'd met. I slowly looked at his attire from behind, seeing that he was wearing black jeans and a red-and-black flannel shirt that was rolled to the middle of his forearms, and I hated that my stomach dipped.

"Come on." Isaiah's hand wrapped around my wrist, and my eyes shot down to where he was touching. I was suddenly thankful I had pulled my sleeves over my hands before taking a stroll with him. *Why was he touching me?*

The art room was dark, uninhabited by Mrs. Fitzpatrick, but Isaiah didn't bother turning on any of the standing lamps as the outside light shined through the far windows, basking the room in a faint outdoorsy glow.

The shuffling of his cool, casual stride gained my attention as he strolled over and flicked my earlier sketch that hung from a piece of string over Mrs. Fitz's desk.

"You're talented, Gemma."

I said nothing as I shifted on my feet. Isaiah's cheek lifted in a coy grin, and although every submissive, rule-following bone in my body broke with my intense stare on him, I didn't dare look away. That was the girl Richard molded me into from the time I could walk, and I didn't want to be her anymore. I would look at Isaiah all I wanted, and I'd talk to him like I wanted, too. Maybe I'd even take it a step further just to spite my dearest Uncle Richard all together.

"What do you want?" I asked, surprised at how leveled my words came out.

Being alone with Isaiah somehow gave me even more confidence than earlier when I'd talked back to Cade. And that was extremely enticing. Nerves still littered my belly, but a small part of me craved to feel that electric current of anticipation he gave me. Standing here, staring at him all alone in a dark room had the realization coming into view. The very second Isaiah came into my line of sight that first day at St. Mary's, he opened up something that was buried deep within my soul, and I'd been chasing the high ever since. I hadn't even realized it until this single moment. *Did I like the way my stomach dipped when he looked at me? Did I enjoy talking back to him?* I think I did. I think I liked seeing his reaction.

Isaiah laughed under his breath, the sound making my lips ache to do the same. Then, he hopped up on the edge of the teacher's desk, his long, black-jean-clad legs dangling an inch above the floor. "Alright, Good Girl. I have a proposition for you."

I snorted, and surprise flashed on both of our faces. "A proposition?" I rolled my eyes before backtracking as anxiety whipped through my body from the shadows of my past. I cleared my throat as I moved to take a seat on the stool in front of my usual desk. *Did I just roll my eyes at him?* The last time I'd rolled my eyes, I'd been punished. Badly.

"Hmm," he mused, hiding a smile. "I really like that you don't put up with my shit. You are quite possibly the only girl I've ever met who isn't affected by my charm."

Cocky, much? I thought his statement over for a moment, placing my arms on the art table in front of me. I pulled my sleeves down even farther onto my hands, clasping my fingers over on the cotton to stay glued to my palm. It wasn't that I wasn't affected by his charm, because I was, it was just that I didn't know what to do with it. I didn't know how to flirt.

Wait. I shouldn't be flirting with him. I was *not* affected by his charm.

"Who said you were charming?"

Isaiah's face split in two, the smallest dimple appeared on his cheek, and I locked onto it. Okay, fine. Maybe he was charming—at least the dimple was. "You are"—he scanned my face once more, the dimple still there—"very interesting, Gemma."

I ignored his statement because I didn't even know how to respond. "Did you take care of the blog? Did you get it taken down like I asked?"

Isaiah's legs stopped swinging for a moment as his smile fell. "You're afraid of your uncle finding out?"

My head whipped up, a piece of my hair getting stuck to my lip. I hurriedly swiped it away, watching as Isaiah focused on my mouth before he said, "Oh, yes. I can eavesdrop too, Good Girl."

I recoiled instantly. "Stop calling me that."

His large hands shot up in mock innocence, another smirk gracing his chiseled face. Even from across the room, I could see the mischievous glint in his eye. "Okay, okay. I'll stop calling you that"—he paused—"if..."

I made a throaty noise, dropping my head. "I should have known there'd be an if." *There always was.*

His voice cut through the air. "I'll stop calling you Good Girl if you do me a favor."

I treaded slowly. "What favor?"

He shrugged. "For starters, I need you to...uh, tutor me."

My face scrunched. "Tutor you?"

He nodded before glancing away. "And on occasion...I might need you to cover for me. A white lie here or there. No biggie."

I jerked back, my fingers clenching down over my sleeves. "You want me to lie for you? What kind of favor is that?"

I was confused, and for a split second, I thought he was teasing me again. Maybe he wanted to see if I'd fall for his good looks and arrogance like every other girl did. Maybe he wanted to see if I'd be willing to do whatever he wanted. But one look from the near ground-breaking level of hope in his eyes told me he was being serious.

He wanted me to lie for him?

Why?

CHAPTER FIFTEEN

ISAIAH

"You're serious?" she asked, completely and utterly dumb-founded. Gemma glanced around the room, her hair swaying from one side to the other, before landing back on me. "Why would I lie for you? And to whom?"

She rolled her pretty green eyes, the same eyes that somehow sparkled even without any lights on. It was like they were the light themselves. "This is a joke. Isn't it? You're trying to see if you have any sway over me because you're hot and *charming*." The word dripped from her mouth with pure distaste, then she flew to her feet and shot me a dirty look. She mumbled something under her breath about this being a test then said, "Leave me alone, Isaiah. I do not have time for this."

I hopped down too, my boots thudding to the floor as I ran after her. Gemma was small, so her feet didn't carry her nearly as fast as mine did me. "Wait," I called out, wrapping my hand around her waist from behind. She gasped as I pushed the heavy door shut with my other hand. "I'm being completely serious with you," I whispered into her ear, leaning so close to her I could feel her warm heat cover me like a blanket.

She ripped herself out of my grasp and darted underneath my arm, panic set deep into her features. My eyes narrowed. It was damn hard to read her. One second, she was acting timid and innocent, the next she was rolling her eyes and spouting off insults.

"I can't figure you out." My sentence came out as a whisper, and to be honest, I didn't even mean to say it out loud.

Gemma put enough distance between us that the entire line of lacrosse players could stand comfortably.

She wrapped her arms around her slender waist. "Why would I lie for you? And to whom?" Her left eyebrow was raised, and her lips were pursed. "And tutor you in what class?"

I stayed put, giving her the space she desperately sought after I had leaned into her warmth. "All of them. After lacrosse each night, I'll need you to tutor me in the library after curfew." She opened her mouth to protest, but I held up my hand. "The headmaster already said he would write us a note, excusing us if anyone asked what we were doing out past 7:00."

Gemma seemed to think that over carefully as her fingers clenched even tighter over the sleeves of her shirt. "We don't even have any classes together."

My head slanted as I took a step toward her. "We have art together."

She huffed. "How could I forget that? You shoved me into a closet the first day here."

There she was. That fiery girl who excited me more than I'd like to admit came back just as quickly as she'd left. I took another step toward her as she sighed loudly. "I can't tutor you, and I definitely can't lie for you." She took a step back.

Hope crashed and burned around me. "Why not?"

She shifted, her feet shuffling on the floor. "Because I'm... supposed to be focusing on my own studies." She hesitated for a quick second. "And my uncle doesn't allow me to be alone with boys."

With *boys*, she said. As if I were a boy. The things I'd seen and done made me lose my boyish vibe years ago. But I already knew this would be an issue with her, given the conversation I'd overheard earlier. I didn't hear the entire conversation between her and my uncle, but I heard enough. Her uncle was strict. I got it.

"Your uncle doesn't have to know. He won't find out."

Skepticism washed off of her in waves as she shook her head and glanced to her feet.

I took a step closer to her. "I can promise you that he won't." Was it an empty promise? Maybe. But who was going to run to Gemma's uncle and tell him that she was tutoring someone? Who even cared? It seemed so trivial.

Gemma began biting her pale lip, and there was a strong urge that begged me to swipe at it. It began at my neck and traveled down to my fingertips, causing them to twitch. Her lips looked soft, and her mouth was kissable as fuck—especially when she insulted me.

Gemma began shaking her head again as she took another step back. I could feel my grasp on her loosening. The war she had brewing on whether to consider my proposition was slowly becoming nothing but useless words floating around an empty room. My tone was eager and almost pleading. "He hasn't found out about the blog, right?"

She paused, looking right past me, as if looking me in the eye was going to do something. "No thanks to you."

I fought a smile. "That's because no one knows about it but the students. It's for school gossip. Most of the parents and guardians that send their children here want rid of them.

What makes you think they're checking some random blog on the Internet? Everyone outside of these walls is under an illusion that St. Mary's is a strict boarding school without the normal shit that comes with teenagers, like drama and gossip." *Among other things.*

"The two things teenagers thrive on."

My eyes slanted as I tried to read her again. There was a hitch of melancholy in the way she'd said that. "But not you?"

Gemma finally brought her emerald eyes back to mine, the shine in them a little dimmer now. "No. Not me. I prefer to stay away from the spotlight."

I clenched my teeth because, unfortunately, even just tutoring a guy like me would bring nothing *but* the spotlight. Rumors would spread like wildfire. They already were just from me asking her to "talk" in the lounge moments ago.

"I really need this," I whispered, showing her a side of myself that I'd never in my entire life showed anyone before. *Desperation.* But shit. I was. I was desperate. Jack wouldn't survive at the Covens. He was a good kid. And if I got expelled, that was exactly where he'd go. My father did not bluff. I was in a shit position.

Gemma paused, her tightened features dropping for a fraction as she scanned over my face. Her lips softened into a sad smile, though the moment was fleeting because, after a second, she seemed to clam up as she shook out her long brown hair and breezed past me. Her clean and girly scent clogged up my senses for a second, making me forget my purpose.

But when I heard the door open, I quickly spun around. "I'll give you whatever you want," I said with her back to me. She peered over her shoulder, giving me a glimpse of her smooth cheek. "It doesn't have to be a favor. Let's make a deal. You give me what I need, and I'll give you something in return. What do you need? Money? I have plenty." Shit. Now

I truly was sounding desperate. Money? Did I just offer her money? *What the fuck was I doing?* I was quick to change my pace. "You name whatever you want, Gemma. I'll give it to you."

A loud swallow came from her throat, and I felt the hope lingering in the air right in front of me. But then *poof,* it was gone within a flash. Gemma clenched her eyes, and instead of saying anything, she stepped out the door, leaving the echoing slam the only thing I could hear.

Fuck. That did not go as planned.

CHAPTER SIXTEEN

GEMMA

GLANCING DOWN TO MY OUTFIT, I cringed. "I..." My voice was as wobbly as my feet in the heels Sloane had lent me. "I feel weird."

Sloane popped her head out of the bathroom with one eye full of dark makeup and the other bare. "Don't! You look fucking hot, Gem." *Gem.* A slice of the past rushed toward me. The only person to ever call me Gem was Tobias. *Cue the ache in my chest.*

"It's true. You do!" Mercedes was flinging clothes out of Sloane's dresser. The scattered articles of clothing covered our floor like a new rug.

Looking back into the mirror, I trailed my eyes down to my smooth bare legs and back up to the tight leather skirt that hit my upper thighs. The mesh, black, long-sleeve shirt hugged my body tightly, showing off my slender waist and medium-sized chest. The only compromise that Sloane and I had was letting me wear a long sleeve shirt. She had questioned my request but didn't push me on the matter, thank God.

"Here." Mercedes came up from behind me, wearing nothing but her pink bra and matching underwear with a full face of makeup, handing me tall boots. "I can tell you're uncomfortable, so this will help. It'll cover up some skin." She smiled at me through the mirror. "You look killer, though. You have this good-girl vibe to you, but"—her eyes trailed all over my face—"your features are...so striking. Intense. But like, in a good way."

There was that phrase again: *good girl*. The small muscles along my belly clenched as I bent down and pulled off the strappy heels, placing them nicely at the bottom of Sloane's bed. Mercedes threw me a pair of socks, and after sliding the boots on, I did feel a little better.

Turning around and glancing at the knee-high leather boots, I felt less revealed and more myself. I was used to covering up, so showing this much skin was a rarity, except for those dark nights I pushed clear into the back of my head. *Nope. Not now.* I would not think of those things on the night of my first party with my two new friends.

"Are you going to tell us what Isaiah wanted today? Or are you still going with your story that he wanted to apologize for shoving you into a closet under false pretenses?" Sloane walked out of the bathroom, looking like a totally different person from the girl I'd met a few days ago with the fairy lights hanging around her bed. Red lipstick covered her lips so eloquently that she reminded me of a doll. Her hazel eyes were shadowed with dark-gray, shimmery eye shadow, and for a moment, I wished I was like that. I wished I'd had the opportunity as a young girl to play around with the makeup that lined the shelves I'd seen at the store with Richard's mother on our monthly outing. She'd scold me each and every time she saw me looking and would tell me that makeup was a sinner's poison. That if I touched it, I'd turn unworthy and end up like my mother.

The smallest amount of fear had seeped in at the memory, my heart thumping hard. Now that I was older and away from the looming threats and uncertainty that surrounded my mother when she'd *disappeared,* I knew Auntie's words were empty at best, but it still sent me into shock.

"Want some?"

Want what? I looked down to the red lipstick Sloane was holding and quickly shook my head. Clothes were still being thrown behind her head as Mercedes huffed and stomped around.

"Not tonight. Maybe next time, though."

Sloane smiled, the softness of the gesture not matching the intensity of her makeup. She looked dark and mysterious, and I felt a little envious of how confident she was.

I'd watched in silent awe as Sloane went over and grabbed a few pieces of clothing and flung them out to Mercedes. She snatched them quickly and started to shimmy her way into them.

"I love you," Mercedes sighed, running her hands down the front of her short purple dress. "I wish I was roommates with you two instead of Shayna." She rolled her eyes. "She kicked me out for four hours today while she messed around with one of the Rebels."

Sloane laughed as she sat on her bed to put those same strappy heels on her feet that I'd removed from mine. "If I were into the Rebels, I'd probably do the same."

Mercedes paused, silence encasing us all. Then, she began to giggle. "You're right. Me too."

My face was hot as they began talking about some of the other guys they'd like to spend four hours with. As they talked and I listened, my inexperience seemed to drive me away from their conversation, and my mind began drifting to

Isaiah and then to the rest of the Rebels. They were the only guys I'd really come into contact with since arriving here on Monday, and I couldn't deny their popularity with not just the girls, but with everyone. They were just *it*.   Prestigious. Protective. Strong. Superior. Their ability to command a room was irresistible. I'd learned that much just from watching them in the dining hall and earlier, in the lounge, after I'd left Isaiah high and dry in the art room. I didn't last long when returning to Sloane and Mercedes after our talk, because my mind was reeling, and the nerves never left, especially with what seemed like a million pairs of eyes on me. *Everyone* was staring at me, wondering what Isaiah wanted to talk about. So, as soon he had walked back in, his intense gaze landing right on me, I excused myself and came back to my room, opened up my brand-new journal from the headmaster, and mindlessly sketched until Sloane got back with Mercedes in tow. That was hours ago, and I was still feeling antsy.

"Seriously," Sloane chided. "Tell us. There is no way Isaiah called you away from everyone to apologize. That boy doesn't say sorry."

A nervous tremor went through my body, zipping and whirling, telling me that Isaiah's little chat was not far off in my brain, even though I kept pushing it away. I, unfortunately, didn't have my pencil in hand at the moment, so I couldn't just...turn off my thoughts.

The thing was, I didn't *not* want to tell them about our conversation, but I still needed to process it, and I would be lying if I said I was totally put off by the idea. It wasn't until he declared, *"I'll give you anything you want,"* that made me pause. I'd been secretly weighing my options, and every time I'd tossed up the two choices, my body would fizzle out. *Life or death. Servitude or freedom. Stay or flee.*

And not only was I conflicted with him *asking* me for a favor instead of demanding it, but he could actually give me something in return that could propel my plan to get out of the trap that my life was in. So far, I didn't have this grand plan like I'd hoped to form the second I was away from home, but with Isaiah's tempting words in the back of my mind, things began to spin. It was a plan that could likely kill me later if I were caught. It was something that could probably kill him too, if it came down to it.

Sweat began to break out along my forehead at the thoughts and my ears began to ring. I was suddenly very angry that I was even put in the position where I had to think of these things in the first place. I was angry at my life, and my *uncle,* and sometimes—even though it made me feel irrevocably guilty afterward—I was angry at my mother. Angry that she somehow landed in Judge Stallard's lap and chose to stay even after she could have left. I knew that she wouldn't have stayed as long as she did if she knew everything that I knew now, but didn't she sense he wasn't a good person? Didn't she feel the same dark and unforgiving feeling in his touch that I felt? I knew Tobias did.

I cleared my throat, springing up suddenly from my bed and walking over to the mirror to glance at the fragile, clear-faced girl in front of me that desperately wanted to be strong and courageous. "I think I do want some makeup, Sloane." I peered over my shoulder, and I could see the confusion on her face but also the excited sparkle glimmering in her dark-framed eyes.

She bit her lip, her white teeth straining brightly against the red stain. "What changed your mind?"

I shrugged, running my eyes down my outfit. "Let's just call it...spite."

She looked at Mercedes, and they both got the evilest yet amused smile on their faces. Then, they rushed at me and got to work.

———

THE HALLWAY WAS EERILY quiet as Sloane and Mercedes pulled me along. I was stuck in the middle of them, my hands clasped in each of theirs. Mercedes gave me a tight squeeze, her palm colliding with mine.

"We should probably tell her about the types of parties the Rebels throw."

My heart caught at the mere mention of their name. Sloane whispered back to Mercedes, her warm breath hitting the side of my face. "She's never been to a party. She won't know the difference."

Mercedes' hand clenched on mine. "You've never been to a party?"

"Don't make her feel bad, Mer." Sloane didn't give Mercedes a chance to apologize—not that she needed to. I knew I was the odd one out in this trio. "But just a heads up—"

"What if we get caught?" I interrupted her, my heart slowly sliding down my body like a sticky sludge as the resentment from an hour ago turned into blinding anxiety.

We had to wait until the clock hit a certain time for us to sneak out and travel down the windy stairs to the main level of St. Mary's, and that was when I really began thinking about what I was doing. If we got caught and Richard got word that I was sneaking around at night after curfew, he'd likely come to St. Mary's himself to punish me, if not just take me all together.

Chills ran down my spine as we continued walking down the long hall. The only guidance we had were the flickering sconces on the walls, which seemed to get dimmer with each step we took, until we landed in front of a door at the very end of the long corridor. The tall, arched wood creaked as it opened, and once it shut, we were enveloped in pure black. I couldn't see a single thing in front of me, and without knowing it, I gripped onto both Mercedes' and Sloane's hands again.

They didn't let go, though, or laugh. They intertwined our fingers together, and my breathing calmed. After a few seconds of standing in the dark, a deep voice startled me. "Names?"

Sloane answered for us, and we heard, "I trust you to inform the new girl on our rules?"

She answered, "She'll be fine. She'll sit this one out." Then, she began pulling me forward. *Sit what out?*

My boot splashed in something wet, and for a split second, I was taken back to a different place at a different time. A coldness set in my bones, and I shivered, which definitely didn't go well with the already high anxiety swarming my body. "Are you okay?" Sloane asked, stopping her stride for a second.

My voice croaked, and I hated that. I hated it so much. "Yeah. I just don't like dark, damp places." My eyes still hadn't really adjusted. "Where are we? And you didn't answer about getting caught. What if we get caught?"

My nerves were getting increasingly worse, and I was certain it had everything to do with being in this place surrounded by familiar smells and sounds.

"We're underground," Mercedes answered.

I whipped my head over to her even though I couldn't see her. "Underground? Like a basement?" The fear in my voice was like getting hit by a bus. I hoped they didn't detect it too much.

Water sloshed as Sloane stepped forward, pulling us again. "Yeah. It's basically soundproof. And we won't get caught. The headmaster is usually asleep by now, and even if we did get caught, he'd tell us to go back to our rooms, and that'd be it. He's cool, Gemma. He lets us be *us*."

I breathed heavily through my nose, trying not to let the musty smell of the basement get into my head. *This is St. Mary's. Not home.*

"Okay," I answered, feeling irritated all over again at the mere glimpse of the past. I shook out my shoulders and nodded. "I guess it's time I learn what a real high school party is like, right?" *Screw you, Richard.*

Sloane and Mercedes both laughed, the sound echoing throughout the emptiness of the hall. "Oh, Gemma. This is *nothing* like a real high school party."

"No?" I asked as we continued walking forward. The closer we got, the more I could hear a slight thumping of music.

"No." I could hear the smile in Sloane's tone before she grew serious. We stopped in front of something. The air grew dense, the gap of emptiness closing. "And no judging. Okay? This is where we get to pretend we're not trapped in a creepy boarding school away from our families, acting like we're normal teens, because we aren't."

I swallowed back the fear and felt confidence slide back in. "I know all about not being normal, Sloane." *Trust me.*

She breathed out a light laugh and then opened the door.

CHAPTER SEVENTEEN

GEMMA

IT WAS JARRING. The lights, the music, the smells, everything. It took a few moments for my eyes to adjust, the mascara on my lashes feeling heavy as I blinked several times, trying to figure out what was in front of me.

Sloane and Mercedes didn't let go of my hands as they pulled me farther into the room. Multicolored lights danced along their features, making their hair look blue. The music vibrated off my bare skin, and it felt intoxicating. I stifled a gasp as I drank in the scene as if I hadn't had water in years.

"What—" I muttered, still being dragged by Sloane and Mercedes.

Sloane pulled me from the front, tipping her head back to see my reaction. "Hope you're ready to dance." Her voice was hardly audible from the loud music coming from the speakers, and I couldn't believe that I'd hardly heard it at all from outside the entrance.

The warm breath from Mercedes graced my ear as she

shouted, "The only good part of St. Mary's, besides the hot boys, are the parties. It almost makes it worth it."

"Almost?" I shouted back, glancing over several of my new peers that I had barely even imprinted into my brain since getting to St. Mary's. They looked like they were having fun. *Was this what I had been missing out on during all those years in the basement?*

She huffed a laugh over my shoulder but didn't say anything else to me.

It was obvious that Sloane and Mercedes—and probably almost everyone else that attended St. Mary's—felt that it was kind of like a prison. There were curfews set in place, no one was allowed to have a vehicle, and we couldn't leave the school grounds. But to me, it was freedom in the form of castle-like walls with chains hanging from iron-clad doors. St. Mary's was better than home. Home was *my* rendition of prison.

This boarding school was so much better than feeling like your very flesh was being eaten away as someone stared at you from across the dinner table, taking their longing eyes and dragging them down your arms and back up to your face again. Every bone in my body would break, and my stomach would recoil when the word *Daddy* flew effortlessly from my lips, as if it didn't fucking kill me to call him that.

Survive, Gemma. Just survive.

I tasted the bile in the back of my throat but clamped my teeth together and calmed my pulse as I was brought back to the present, still gripping both Sloane's and Mercedes' hands. I'd realized my palms were squeezing theirs when they both glanced over to me with suspicion.

My fingers flew open, releasing theirs. "Sorry," I mumbled, hiding my embarrassment.

Mercedes tucked a wavy piece of hair back. "It's okay. It's a lot to take in." She paused, glancing out to the open area in front of us that was packed with everyone moving and shaking their hips.

I'd never been to a school dance, or party, for that matter. The only social gatherings I'd ever been to were the ones that Richard would take me to with his closest and most trusted colleagues to save face. *Here is my niece that I took in when her mother went off the deep end. She's a good girl. She's polite and smart. Isn't that right, my dear Gemma?*

The *only* indication that this entire scene was normal for people my age was from some conversations I'd eavesdropped on at Wellington Prep or during the rare occasion that Auntie would let me into the group home for an hour or so, where I gulped up as much information as I possibly could without seeming too interested.

I was *technically* supposed to be a member of the group home that Richard's mother ran after my mother had left, but Tobias and I stayed in the main house with him because the group home was for girls only, and Tobias and I threw a fit when they had tried to separate us as young children. Who could blame us? Our mother had been ripped away at such a young age—so young that I could hardly remember what her laugh sounded like. If it weren't for the old photograph of her, I don't even think I'd be able to visualize her face. Or maybe I didn't want to. The only thing I could remember for certain was that I'd never felt safe again after she left. Ever. Not even when Tobias and I would sneak into each other's beds late at night because we were both sad and scared. Seeking comfort with each other didn't last long, though. Richard grew more furious each and every time he found us together.

He hated Tobias. He hated him so much.

Richard's mother didn't mind Tobias much. In fact, I think she may have favored him over me, along with most of the girls she took care of, but after her stroke a few months ago, leaving her basically brain dead, the group home diminished in its entirety.

That was when things began to get interesting.

Judge Stallard suddenly had to explain why there was a random girl living in his house that wasn't on record and had no ties to the group home—none that anyone was aware of anyway. From what I'd gathered over the years, it seemed that my mother had been one of the girls at the group home. Maybe even one of the first. I'm not sure how or why my mother ended up living in Richard's house, but that didn't really seem to matter in the grand scheme of things.

What did matter were the rumors of me and Tobias that started from the girls who attended the group home before Auntie had her stroke. Social workers flooded the home, having to place each and every girl into a foster home or a different group home. I'd even heard talk of sending some of the girls to jail, which never made sense to me, but that was where they learned that there was a teenaged girl—*me*—living in the main house.

Judge Stallard was favored in the court, obviously, and had many—*too many*—ties with police, lawyers, and even social workers, but you couldn't buy everyone. (His words, not mine.) There was one social worker in particular that continued to poke around, thus landing me in Wellington Prep and now St. Mary's.

It seemed things just got messier after he sent me to school to save face. Richard could no longer trust me, and I could no longer trust him.

"Have you taken it all in yet?" Sloane asked thoughtfully.

Swinging my eyes away from hers and back around to the ocean of bodies swaying, I really let myself look. Mercedes was right; we were definitely in the basement of St. Mary's. There wasn't a single window that I could spot, which made me a bit itchy to think about, the floor beneath my boots was hard and dirty, and there was a smidge of dampness lingering in the air. Huge pillars were standing upright around us with glowing lights winding around the durable stone almost as if the stone pillars were holding up the entire school above our heads. There was a long table beside the curved door that we'd walked through that had various sizes of glass bottles on the top that I recognized as alcohol from Richard's bourbon addiction.

But my attention was strictly on the bodies jiving and thrusting along one another as an upbeat song came through the speakers. They were sweaty. Girls' hair stuck to their foreheads, their dresses and skirts pushed up high, showing off their legs. Most of the guys were off to the side, watching the floor with likely the same amount of awe that I currently had in my expression.

A door opening across from the dancing bodies snagged my attention away for a split second before I went back to watching what was happening in front of me. It was like a drug, watching people dance and just *be*. My stomach hollowed out, jealousy surging through my limbs, causing them to twitch. I stepped a foot forward, wanting to let loose just like they were. Everyone looked so free and happy, and I craved that. I could almost taste it on my lips.

I wanted that. I wanted to feel that euphoria that I'd only ever felt when I was sketching, too lost in my own world to realize that I was actually living in my own version of hell.

"Now the real party can start," Sloane said, a sultry tick in her tone.

"What?" I muttered, still unable to look away. One of the guys came up behind a girl. It was Callie, the girl that had taunted me on the lacrosse field the other day.

"The Rebels are here."

My attention was whipped away when the words left her mouth, and almost instantly, I locked eyes with Isaiah. He was taller than mostly everyone in the room, easily able to look over the dancing bodies and pin me to my spot.

A rush of heat swept through me, causing my breathing to quicken. I watched with bated breath as his thumb came up and swept over his bottom lip, never once looking away from me. His friends had moved away, but he didn't step a toe in either direction.

He was staring at me, and I was staring at him.

Blue lights illuminated his cut cheekbones, his jawline sharper than usual from the dancing shadows, and then he flicked an eyebrow up, questioning me.

It was almost as if he knew I was considering his deal.

I gulped back the unyielding amount of anxiety and fear trying to claw its way up my throat at the thought of Richard sniffing out what I was up to. But if I wanted to avoid my future and disappear into thin air so he could never *ever* have me, I needed a plan.

I ran from him once out of fear, and it was a stupid, hasty decision on my part.

I wouldn't be that stupid again. I needed a plan, and Isaiah was going to help me with it. He just wouldn't technically know it.

CHAPTER EIGHTEEN

ISAIAH

WHAT'LL IT BE, Good Girl?

The party was in full swing tonight, everyone already buzzing on the hard liquor we'd snagged from some of the girls—not a hard task when you fucked their brains out for a few hours, making them come more times than they even thought possible—at least according to Shiner. And knowing him, he likely wasn't bluffing on that front.

Cade, Brantley, Shiner, and I were late, but that was only because I had to devise a plan with them regarding Bain. I knew he and his fuck boys, who were nowhere near as trustworthy as the Rebels, would be here, and I had a feeling he'd be a pain in my ass tonight. He was a sneaky shit. He often liked to slip out during these parties, and I usually had to tail him so I could keep an eye on his movements for Dear ol' Daddy and stupid fucking vengeance, but I knew I needed extra eyes tonight. I had a pretty big feeling someone would steal my attention, and I was right. I'd been here for three seconds, and I'd already found her.

"You comin'?" Brantley shouted over to me as the door clamored shut behind us. My heavy boots were stuck as if they were cemented into the floor as I kept a hold of Gemma's watchful expression. She was all the way across the party, a lengthy amount of distance between us, but still, every nerve ending in my body was aware of her being. We'd locked eyes almost the second I stepped foot into the room.

She looked different tonight, wearing clothes that weren't hers and makeup that didn't quite belong on her soft face. She looked hot, don't get me wrong, but she didn't look as angelic as she did in her schoolgirl uniform. More like an angel that was scorched by a sinner's touch.

A little sexy, a little dirty, but still shining as bright as the goddamn stars.

"Yeah," I muttered, my eyes still fastened tightly to hers. There was a definite unspoken conversation happening between Gemma and me at the moment, even with pounding music and moving bodies in between us. The only problem was that I couldn't read her like I could most people.

With that frustrating thought, I moved my attention away, feeling the dip deep in my core as I followed the rest of the Rebels toward the makeshift bar. I snagged one of the neon-colored plastic shot glasses and tipped it back, letting the burn of Fireball coat my throat. Wiping my mouth with the back of my hand, I quickly searched the room, waiting to find Bain. After all, he was the main reason I'd come tonight.

No.

That wasn't true.

I came to see Gemma. I was prepared to corner her and break down that very shaky wall she'd hastily thrown up earlier when I'd brought up my little plan. She'd hesitated when I offered her money. She'd glanced over her shoulder, just briefly, seconds before opening the art room door and running away, but I could see the minor crack in her strong-girl facade. Gemma needed something, and I hoped I could be the one to give it to her, at least for Jack's sake.

The Covens. My chest grew tight at the mere thought of my father sending him there.

Part of me wanted to call up Jacobi and flip my shit on him—*again*—for leaving us in the dust, but I refused to grace him with a phone call. He didn't deserve to hear my voice or know how Jack was doing. Because fuck him.

The sound of my knuckles cracking caused Cade to grimace. "What's eating at you, bro?" His lips flattened as he leaned in. "You're usually much more chipper on Saturday evenings."

Shiner elbowed me and waggled his brows. "Yeah, I mean...it's Claiming Night, bro. What the fuck is the sour mood for?"

Claiming Night was a century-old tradition founded by the original Rebels themselves—at least according to the history Shiner had found. It'd evolved over the years with each group of Rebels, but the same rules applied. If you wanted to get fucked, prepare to get claimed, and the girls at St. Mary's? They *loved* the idea of being claimed, especially by one of us. They all had daddy issues—no judgment here, I get it—and they craved the thrill that came with these parties. They desperately wanted our hands gripping their willing bodies tucked away in a dark corner.

"It's the new girl, yeah?" Brantley sighed from behind me, tipping another shot back and gasping at the end. "Fuck, that burns." He chuckled, running his hand over his short hair as he threw the hot-pink cup behind him. "But it burns so *damn* good."

"The new girl doesn't want our boy," Shiner sang loudly over the music. "That's what's wrong with him."

I grunted, crossing my arms over my chest as I watched Sloane and Mercedes drag Gemma in her fuck-me leather boots across the floor. The lights of the party played peek-aboo over her slight curves, and the bare skin on her upper thigh made blood rush right to my dick. "That's not what's wrong with me," I snapped, suddenly irritated as fuck that every other guy was watching her cross the party with her two new friends.

Being jealous wasn't my usual M.O., and I wasn't even sure why I was jealous. Was it because I needed something from her and she wasn't willing to give it to me? Maybe. Or maybe not.

I didn't really have time to decipher it all.

What I needed was for Gemma to let me claim her for the night so I could get her alone long enough to rehash my earlier advance. *Fuck, that sounded dirty.* I cracked my neck, evening my breath. I just needed to get her alone so I could work out some type of deal with her. There was something she needed, and I'd give it to her in exchange for what I needed. All she and I had to do was convince the SMC that my grades were improving due to her excellent tutoring skills, and she had to tell a tiny lie for me on occasion. It wasn't that hard. I just needed the SMC off my back and to take me off probation so I didn't have to worry about being expelled.

Easy day.

"Are you sure about that?" Brantley raised his eyebrows at me. "Looks like they're headed over this way." A wicked grin spread along his face, and my fist begged to wipe it off. "Shall we see which Rebel Gemma likes better?"

I scowled and drove my eyes into his. "Don't, Brantley." Something potent hit my blood, and I hoped he caught my slight warning. Brantley, along with Cade, knew all about the real reason I was at St. Mary's, because their fathers were in the *family* business. My father was their fathers' boss, for lack of a better word. We'd all seen shit that we wished we hadn't. Our lives weren't normal, and our upbringings would probably make grown men recoil, but that wasn't saying much for the students that attended St. Mary's. We were all a little fucked up in one way or another. It just depended on the cards each was dealt that determined whose life was worse.

"Has anyone spotted Bain yet?" This question came from Cade as Brantley and I continued staring at one another.

"I have," Shiner commented from the other side of me.

Shiner wasn't aware of what my father did for a living or that Brantley, Cade and I knew of each other before we all began attending St. Mary's. I knew my father had told their fathers to send their sons here at the same time I'd shown up, as a sort of intro to what our futures held, but Shiner somehow made his way into our friendship, and I liked him. He had our backs even if he was unaware of some things. He also knew the ins and outs of this school since he'd been attending here longer than any of us, and that came in handy.

Shiner's face remained relaxed as he stared out into the party. "Bain has eyes on your girl, Isaiah."

My blood ran cold as I sharpened my gaze on the room and landed on his beefy stance. Bain was surrounded by a group of guys, who'd all wanted to be a Rebel but didn't quite make the cut, in the far corner of the basement. Each and every last one of them stood back with their arms crossed over their chests like they were gangsters, gazing out onto the floor with their tongues half hanging out of their mouths as they watched Gemma, Sloane, and Mercedes on the dance floor. Bain's mouth twitched as he kept watching Gemma, my attention bouncing back and forth between him and her.

Nope.

Before I could even stop myself, knowing damn well that when he saw me with her, he'd want her *that* much more, I made my way onto the floor, leaving the rest of the Rebels behind. Gemma was in between Sloane and Mercedes, her dark hair tumbling down her back and framing her heart-shaped face as she stood with her back ramrod straight, watching everyone around her dance like their lives depended on it.

Sloane ruffled Gemma's hair as laughter rushed out of her. "Come on, Gemma. Dance like nobody's watching!" she shouted.

Gemma nibbled on her lip, slowly looking up at everyone around the room who was undoubtedly staring at her, until she saw me. Her eyes widened, the dark makeup surrounding the vivid green color showing me just how out of her element she was.

"What is it?" Mercedes asked, pausing her moving hips for a brief moment.

"It's me," I answered, coming around and lazily putting my arm around Gemma's tense shoulders. She sucked in another breath as our bodies touched, and Sloane gave me a warning look. Her hands graced her hips, but just before she could spit out whatever came to mind, the lights went out, and a voice sounded out from the speakers. *"It's claiming time."*

CHAPTER NINETEEN

GEMMA

I GASPED, my body frozen with pure, blinding anxiety. "Claiming time?" I asked, wincing at the unease evident in my tone.

"Isaiah," Sloane's voice warned from somewhere close by. "She is not ready to be claimed. Pull her off to the side —*now*."

Isaiah's arm that was draped over my shoulders didn't even move a fraction. "Relax, Sloane," he whispered. "Don't you trust me?"

She scoffed quietly. "No. Not even a little bit. Quit fucking around."

My heartbeat sped up to an inhuman speed. Short puffs of air escaped my chest as I willed my eyes to adjust to the darkness. The room was quiet...so quiet I could hear everyone's breathing. Confusion filled my senses, making them stall out altogether. I was frantically trying to get my mouth to open to ask what the hell was going on, but my tongue was twisted in a perfect knot with confusion.

Music suddenly cut on again, playing so loudly that I flinched. I snapped my head over to the nearest speaker, wishing I could see into the bleak darkness. "Breathe, Good Gi—" Before Isaiah could say anything else in my ear, a cold hand firmly grabbed my elbow opposite of him, and I was whooshed away, just like that.

Panic coursed through me, and I jerked my arm back so hard I stumbled over my own feet. I knew it wasn't Isaiah as his arm fell from my shoulders quickly, and his voice and body heat were long forgotten. A cold fear washed over me in thunderous waves, and I had to silently scream at myself to remember that I was far, far away from home at the moment.

"Let me go," I seethed, pulling my elbow back again. Whoever it was that had me let out a dark, rich chuckle. The music was still blaring, but he was so close to me I felt the rumble of his chest along my arm.

"Now, now, new girl." His alcohol-ridden breath tickled my ear, and my nose turned upward just before I tripped over something. The grip he had on my elbow grew tighter as he kept me upright. "I just wanted to claim you for the night. You want claimed, don't you?"

"What does that even mean?" I asked, my voice muffled by the upbeat song. My head was spinning with the mix of darkness and loud music. Everything was in overdrive from the second Sloane and Mercedes had pulled me down the dark hallway after curfew. I should have just stayed in my room and scoured through endless articles revolving around Judge Richard Stallard himself to see if I could uncover anything about what he may have done with my brother.

But *no,* I just had to come to this party with Sloane and Mercedes, for some godawful reason.

I knew the reason, but at the moment, I wasn't going to admit it. Not now.

A finger trailed over the side of my face as the guy's voice penetrated my ear again. I wasn't sure where we were in regard to where I was standing a few seconds ago, because whoever it was that had me in his grip dragged me several feet away, and I didn't even know in what direction. "They didn't tell you the rules of tonight? They didn't explain what Claiming Night was?" He huffed, his hand on my elbow tightening again as he pushed his body into my backside. Swallowing back the bile and the familiar feeling of disgust, I pushed my fear away and tried to level my breathing. *Survive, Gemma. Just survive.*

I shook my head, no longer resisting. My eyes shut as my shoulders loosened. I'd been in this position too many times before to let myself get all riled up. I knew how to calm myself down and just *deal*. Richard wasn't behind me, demanding that I call him *daddy*. I wasn't in a pit of emptiness where no one would hear me scream. I was at St. Mary's, and I was fine.

But was I?

"Let me go," I demanded through my silent protests of wanting anger to outweigh fear. Something thick and hard graced my back from the guy who ripped me away, and I bit down on my lip as I recognized what it was. My eyes closed. An empty black abyss was all I could see, yet somehow, it grew even darker. *No. You're fine, Gemma.*

Flashbacks began assaulting me, hidden memories creeping out of their vaults and taunting me in the back of my brain. I felt the tremor in my limbs, my body quaking with my rising stress levels.

His voice was muffled, morphing into something from the darkest parts of my soul. "They say you're a good girl, Gemma. But are you?"

And just like that, I was snapped back to a place I never wanted to be again.

. . .

THE FLOOR WAS hard and cold. Blood seeped from my bare, wet knees. Misery seemed to be the only thing to keep me afloat. It was the only thing I could feel. I was numb, except for that tiny amount of sadness that was allowing the tears to fall ever so gracefully over my dirty cheeks for the last...however long it had been. Time seemed to pause but move quickly at the same time down here.

A faint glow of light swept underneath the covered window, and that was how I'd been keeping track of the days, but when I was in and out of consciousness, it was hard to know if an hour had passed or an entire day. The only indication that I knew actual days had passed was because Richard's tie was a different color from the last time he'd come down here.

My eyes drooped again, my wrists aching from the metal digging into them. They were sore and weak as I hung below. Sometimes they'd be lowered, and I could rest my face on the cold dirty ground, but other times, I'd been extended. See? Time kept passing.

I snapped to attention, the metal chains ricocheting off one another, as the door opened and shut again. My brain told me to flinch from fear, but my body must have been too weak, because it didn't seem to move again after the initial startle from drowsy to alert.

My head hung as my arms were extended high, and the ends of my hair were a dark-gray color from the wet dirt coating them. The strands were thick bands of mud, hardly moving at all. His shoes were the first thing I could focus on, the shiny black of them gleaming and making my eyes hurt.

He shuffled past me, going behind to hopefully unchain me. This had to have been the longest he'd ever left me down here. With Auntie basically dead, no one came to check on me. Not that she did much, but it was comforting to know I wasn't truly alone when he'd get in these foul moods.

My arms fell with a thud, the chain screeching as it finally let up. My elbows cut as they hit the gritty concrete I'd been resting my knees on, and I cried out as much as I could with the dryness of my throat.

"Was that punishment enough, Gemma? Are you ready to be a

good girl?" he asked, a chummy tone in his voice like he was doing me a favor.

I wanted to spit at him, but that would require me to have strength to raise my head, and it would also require me to have actual saliva in my mouth, and I had neither of those things at the moment. Not to mention, he'd broken me. He broke that blazing, fiery spirit I'd had when I'd decided to stand up to him like Tobias had. It was a mistake. I knew that now. But I was hopeful. I was hopeful he'd send me to the same place he sent Tobias—wherever that was—but how wrong was I?

My head was jerked backward as his hand wrapped around my hair. "I asked you a question. Don't make me repeat it." He cursed under his breath as a dry yelp escaped me. "I will be damned if you act like your mother. I wasn't able to break her from that defiant streak she had, but I'll be sure to break you. You will be what I want and nothing more."

A strangled cry left my lips as my chest caved. "Y-yes." The word croaked out of me like a dying frog, and it damn near killed me.

"Yes, what, baby girl?" he whispered into my ear, pressing his core into my back. Something girthy rammed into my spine, and I silently belittled myself for learning what it was—which, ironically, was the start of what had landed me in this stupid predicament in the first place. Nothing got past Judge Stallard. With my Auntie gone, I thought I could be sly and figure out everything Tobias whispered to me in the mere minutes before he disappeared, but I was wrong. Richard checked on what I'd been up to. He knew every last Internet search I'd ever made.

Swallowing back nausea, I whispered through labored breaths, "Yes, Daddy."

A lone finger traced my bare spine, a shiver of chills coating my skin. He hummed in agreement as his fist tightened around my hair again. My head hurt when he'd pulled on my strands a little tighter. "If you're curious, just ask me." His warm sigh brushed over my shoulders. "You're almost eighteen. The perfect age. I can teach you all there *is to know about the human body. Just wait, little one." And just like that, he dropped me back to the ground, my knees all but shattering with the impact.*

"WHAT THE FUCK."

I gasped, my eyes springing open quickly as lights blinded me from above. My palms immediately went to cover them as I moaned, and that was when I realized my cheeks were wet. *Why are my cheeks wet?*

"Isaiah, back off," a voice said, sounding seriously concerned. "Calm down."

A growl sounded. "Calm down?" Then a loud gruff. "What the fuck did you do to her, Bain?"

Who is Bain?

"Gemma?" Sloane whispered. "Are you okay?" Soft hands wrapped around my wrists, and I let out a shaky sigh, and then I quickly snatched my arms away at the thought of my sleeves being pulled up too high. *Shit.* I flung my eyes back open, clenching my fists so tightly my nails dug into my skin. Despite Sloane's dark and edgy eyeshadow, I could see that she was truly worried about me.

"I'm..." I began to sit up. "I'm—fine." *Oh my God.* Did I say anything while I was out? Did I do something?

She took her plump red lip into her mouth, and she eyed me cautiously. Her hand gingerly went up to my forehead, and she raised her eyebrows, as if asking my permission. I gave her a slight nod, and she rested the back of her hand on my sticky skin. "You're in a cold sweat. Did you pass out?"

"Or did you knock her out?"

I turned my head to see Isaiah—in all his righteous glory, might I add—glaring directly at a guy I'd never seen before.

Isaiah's scowl was deep and furrowed; angry lines sliced over every angle of his face. He looked...intense. Two of his friends—one of them being Cade—stood in front of him, almost like they were a barrier between him and the other guy, who was looking pretty damn smug.

"I didn't knock her out, Rebel. Calm the fuck down." His laugh was a haughty one. It reminded me of Richard's. "She passed out or something. One second, she was standing in front of me, and the next, she was down. She slumped in my arms." He shrugged like it was nothing.

"And so you fucking dropped her?" Mercedes was standing off to the side of a room that I didn't recognize with her hands on her hips. *How did I even get in here?* Sloane was still checking me out, feeling my forehead again and frowning. Then, her hand went behind my head, and she gasped.

"You're bleeding."

Isaiah flung his attention to me so fast I jumped, causing my knees to buckle together as I sat on the floor. The glacial color of his eyes grew even colder as he zeroed in on me and then to Sloane's bloody fingers.

"Think first, act second," Cade said to Isaiah under his breath, not loud enough for everyone to hear, but I definitely picked it up, thanks to my well-honed listening skills. The other friend of Isaiah—who I now recognized as Brantley—had stepped toward Bain. Bain looked completely bored with the entire situation and not at all intimidated by Isaiah's murderous glare.

I knew right then that I didn't trust Bain. Just looking at him from down below made my stomach twist in knots, and that wasn't just because he'd been the one to send me into a full-on panic blackout. I just didn't get a good feeling from him. His dark eyes were hungry for something as he flicked his attention down to me, and after being around evil my entire life, I could tell, without a doubt, that he was corrupted in some way or another.

A light touch on my chin startled me as I continued

staring at Bain. My head pounded violently as I flinched, but then my attention was gently snagged away with the turn of my face. Isaiah was crouched down to me, his brows lowered, his icy eyes filled with worry. "Did he do something to you, Gemma?"

Gemma.

He called me Gemma instead of Good Girl.

Why did that bother me?

"Not intentionally." *But was he planning to?* I was suddenly aware that I was the center of attention in a very small room with way too many eyes. I cast my gaze downward, but Isaiah was quick to raise my chin again, his thumb brushing ever so lightly over my skin. "I blacked out," I admitted, blinking rapidly as he ping-ponged his attention between my eyes. I knew there were other people in the room. Too many people. But something about breathing the same air as Isaiah made me feel safe yet vulnerable at the same exact time. It was like I *wanted* to tell him all my secrets—even the scary ones that I preferred to hide from. "It's not the first time. I'm fine."

My lips parted as his hand came up and cupped the side of my face, weaving his fingers into my hair. My body was instantly awake, my head no longer pounding with pain but swimming with something else. It felt like I was floating. My body flushed; my skin prickled. His lips fell open slightly, and I glanced down to his mouth at the sound.

"For fuck's sake. You think I'm bad? You're about to make the new girl orgasm on the spot with that lustful look you're giving her, and she's fucking bleeding. You're a kinky fuck, Underwood. All I did was whisper in her ear, and yet I'm the one to blame?"

Isaiah's jaw hardened at the same time his nostrils flared. His hand dropped from my face, taking away the small escape of the situation with him. Then, he popped back up to a standing position.

He barked an order out to Sloane. "Take Gemma back to her room, and make sure to clean up her gash. Keep an eye out for a concussion."

"And you'll deal with Bain?" she asked with disgust as her hand wrapped around my arm. Mercedes came over and helped me up, too. The room spun a little, but I wasn't sure if that was from falling or from the up-close-and-personal encounter I'd just had with Isaiah.

Isaiah said nothing as I glanced back at Bain. He was staring at me intently, his eyes narrowing and his head slanting ever so slightly. Something flashed across his face, but before I could focus on it too much, I was pulled out of the room and enveloped in the dark hallway yet again.

CHAPTER TWENTY

GEMMA

SLOANE AND MERCEDES were both sound asleep on Sloane's bed, both of them snuggled underneath the lush lavender comforter. I nibbled on my lip as I reached back behind my head, my fingers diving underneath my thick hair, to make sure it was still okay. After we'd made it back up to our room from the party, Sloane went to work on cleaning the cut, inspecting it thoroughly with the flashlight on her phone, all while cursing out Bain—the guy who had tried to *claim* me— under her breath.

I stayed silent as she and Mercedes listed all of Bain's bad qualities, the two of them rambling on for what felt like hours. Apparently, he was the black sheep of St. Mary's, and he wasn't someone you wanted to be claimed by. Sloane could attest to that firsthand, although she didn't go into details.

After finally gaining the courage to speak again and agreeing that I would stay away from Bain, I very reluctantly asked what "claiming" was. Mercedes shot Sloane a worrisome look, as if they didn't want to tell me. I think they thought I was going to judge them, but I was the last person who ever would.

"Being at a boarding school doesn't give us a lot of free time to date or anything. We have curfews and can't really leave the premises, except for special occasions, and even then, it has to get approved by the SMC. But the rumor states that the Rebels, long ago, started something called Claiming Night. It's where the boys claim a girl for the night, and they fuck or do whatever, and come morning, everyone goes back to their normal boarding-school life filled with nothing but academics and shitty memories of their families who shipped them away in the first place."

I stayed silent as she and Mercedes gauged my response. A dreadful feeling of disgust and embarrassment slithered through me over the fact that this Bain guy thought I wanted him to claim me, and even hours later, it was still sitting nice and heavy in the pit of my belly like a bucket full of stones.

If I hadn't passed out in my fit of panic, what would have happened? And what about Isaiah? Didn't he say he was claiming me before Bain snatched me away?

A rush of heat swept over me. I clenched my legs tighter, ignoring how I kind of liked the idea of Isaiah wanting to claim me, and stared down at the laptop the headmaster had gifted me a few days ago.

I was already high on anxiety, with a pounding headache from the night's events, so opening up the laptop was just putting a cherry on top, but sleep was out of the question. And so was sketching. Taking pencil to paper was usually therapeutic for me, but sometimes, when I got too into it, I would have the same blackout spell that I'd had earlier, where I'd travel back to the not-so-distant past, and that was the last thing I needed at the moment. *No, thank you.* One traumatic visit from the past was enough for me.

Dropping my knees to sit cross-legged, I pulled the laptop closer, glancing at Sloane and Mercedes to make sure they weren't about to catch me searching stuff on the web that I *"shouldn't under any circumstances"* be searching, per Richard's threats. But if I wanted to get on with my plan, I needed to learn all there was to know about Judge Stallard and his many, many connections. I hoped it would lead me right to Tobias.

The keys of the laptop were cool under my touch, my fingers shaking slightly as they rested along flexible rubber. The ache in my head wasn't nearly as bad as before, but the brightness of the screen in the dark room caused my eyes to burn.

I'd just opened the search engine, my heart pounding wildly, the echo of it almost deafening in the near silent room, and that was when I heard a slight *ping*. A soft gasp escaped, as if it had sprung right out of my nervous stomach. My gaze widened at the little box in the far-left corner that said I had a new message. I had no idea what it was. I had hardly used my laptop since getting here, but the more it blinked, the more I panicked. Sweat started to form on my hairline, my head thumping in sync with my rapid heart rate. *Breathe, Gemma. Just breathe.* I shut my eyes, removing my hands from the laptop, and counted to ten before I went into a full-on spiral like earlier.

When I opened my eyes again, I glanced at the girls asleep on Sloane's bed. Mercedes had shifted a little, likely from hearing my little outburst, but her chest was moving softly like before.

After bringing my attention back to the glow of my screen, I took a steady breath and clicked the flashing icon. I hadn't even realized I was holding my breath until I began to see stars dance in front of my vision. A heavy burst of air left me, staring at the words in the message.

GOOD GIRL, *meet me in the hall in five.*

. . .

As EACH SECOND PASSED, my heart thumped harder. Blood rushed to my ears as my skin grew slicker with sweat. I reread the message a few more times before another one came in.

STOP SECOND-GUESSING YOURSELF. *I won't bite.*

MY FINGERS HOVERED over the keyboard as I tried to convince myself that it wasn't a trap. There was no way Richard knew I was sitting upright in bed in the middle of the night on a laptop he didn't even know I had, messaging me as if he were Isaiah. That was...irrational.

ISAIAH? I typed, still needing the confirmation.

HE MESSAGED BACK WITHIN A SECOND.

WHO ELSE CALLS *you Good Girl? Of course it's Isaiah.*

A SARCASTIC LAUGH threatened to escape my lips. If he only knew that he wasn't the only one who called me Good Girl.

Feeling brave, I typed out another response.

HOW DID *you know I was on the computer and that I'd get your message?*

. . .

ANOTHER PING SOUNDED as I bit my thumbnail.

I DIDN'T.

I SWALLOWED as I ran my hands down my face. Then I typed, ***How do I know it's really you?***

I WAS STILL RIDDLED with anxiety as I chewed on my nail, rereading the messages, when it showed he had sent another. A spark started in the center of my chest as the next message had a picture attached. It was of him grinning at me. His inky hair was messy on the top, his chin tipped upward showing off the harsh angles. His icy eyes, surrounded by a thick band of black eyelashes, looked playful and not at all like the dangerous, smug boy I'd met just a few days ago outside of his uncle's office.

Another message came through as another rush of heat swept through me.

I'LL BE outside your door in two minutes. We need to talk.

I SAT on my bed for another thirty seconds, staring at the empty search engine box as I contemplated ignoring Isaiah. I could slip underneath my blankets and push my laptop away, pretending like everything was fine and that this entire night never even existed, but he was right. We did need to talk.

Butterflies fluttered in my belly as I pictured him outside my room, waiting for me. A small smile tugged on my lips, which I quickly wiped away as I swung my legs over the bed, placing my feet on the soft rug.

Tiptoeing over to the door, I glanced back at my two new friends, making sure they were still asleep, as I gently placed my hand on the iron knob and slowly turned it.

Oxygen filled my lungs with my deep breath as I silently reminded myself there was no other option for me. Isaiah said he'd give me anything if I tutored him, and I knew, deep down, I wouldn't get another chance like this. I was going to think of this as a transaction. A deal. I would do what I needed to do in order to get what I needed in return.

So what if I found him slightly attractive? So what if my body sizzled like I was on fire when he was near? So what if he made me feel alive for the first time in my entire life? He was also arrogant, smug, and had a niche for breaking rules. *Obviously.* Isaiah needed me to tutor him and lie to...someone, for whatever reason, and there was no question about it—I'd do it because I had to. I was surviving, just like Tobias told me to. I desperately needed money and probably even a fake ID, and those were two things I knew for certain Isaiah could get for me after hearing his conversation with his uncle.

He and I would strike a deal, and then, when the time was right, I'd be soon forgotten by everyone.

Even him.

CHAPTER TWENTY-ONE

ISAIAH

THE WALL WAS solid against my back, and my feet were steady on the firm ground, but my heart rate was anything but. I stood in the girls' hallway with nothing but small flashes of light from the lanterns flickering with the obvious rising tension.

Even though it had been hours since I found Bain hovering over Gemma's lifeless body in one of the rooms in the basement, I still felt keyed up. Not only did Bain get me completely riled by just simply being himself, but when he pulled his fucked-up shit with Gemma, I pictured myself strangling him. From the moment she was pulled out from under my arm during claiming time, I felt unnervingly frantic.

The most frustrating thing about it all was that Cade was right: I couldn't do anything to Bain. My father would go ballistic if I outed myself or our family, and not to mention, I was under probation with the board. I couldn't do shit—not when Jack dangled in the crossfire. My father knew exactly what he was doing when he had threatened him, and I hated him for it.

It seemed Bain knew that I couldn't do anything, too. His smug, shit-eating grin nearly caused me to slice my hands open with my nails as my fists clenched together. When he walked past me, after having words about the *rules* of claiming, I saw the coy glint in his eye, that all-superior, pompous attitude that had him holding his head up high like he was untouchable.

He wasn't untouchable. Maybe at present, but not in the future. If only he fucking *knew* who I was.

The door slowly swung open, and all thoughts of Bain vanished right in front of me.

One long, bare leg stepped out into the hallway first, and the orangey glow of a candle flickered at the perfect time to show Gemma's quiet figure slipping into the hallway. The heavy door shut quietly behind her as she continued gripping onto the iron chain before it bucked against the wood.

Her soft footsteps were silent as she padded over to me. My lips twitched as she got closer. The oversized shirt she was wearing reminded me just how fragile she actually was.

"Hey," I breathed out, still leaning back onto the wall. I remained casual, but there was definitely something urgent tugging on the inside.

"Hi," she squeaked, glancing up at me with her doe-like eyes. Her attention shifted down both ends of the hall, and that was when I pushed off and clasped my hand in hers.

Her breath hitched, staring directly at our connected palms. A hot flare of desire punched me right in the chest with the sound of her lips opening, and that was when I began pulling her down the long corridor. Her bare feet shuffled over the dark-red carpet, and I quickly darted my eyes away from the dark polish on the ends of her toes. *Even her fucking feet were attractive.*

We stopped abruptly, and Gemma damn near ran into my back. "Sorry," she whispered, a bundle of nerves backing the word as it flew out into the silent hall.

"Shh," I hushed, gripping her hand a little harder, making our palms connect yet again. There was really no need to grab her hand, but there was a strong part of me that needed to touch her. It was very unsettling.

I opened the door to the closet lined with extra linens and pulled her through, shutting it as quietly as possible behind her.

"Where are we?" Gemma's hand tightened on mine when the bleak darkness surrounded us.

I pulled her a little farther into the deep closet, all the way until we got to the back. "We're in the linen closet. It's almost time for the duty teacher to walk the girls' hall, but we should be safe here."

"*Should* be safe?" She put a clearly implied emphasis on the word "should", and I couldn't help but chuckle.

Her voice grew stern, and I was instantly pissed that I couldn't see her angry expression. "Why are you laughing? I think I've used almost all my luck in the not-getting-in-trouble department lately. I'm bound to get caught for something soon. I am not a lucky person, Isaiah. And I don't break rules."

Her dark silhouette shifted in front of me, and I was pretty certain she had her hands propped on her hips. "Then why'd you come?" I asked.

She huffed, her warm breath hitting me directly in the chest. She didn't answer, though, and a heavy silence filled the small space.

I took a step toward her, finally able to make out her body as my eyes began to adjust in the room, and I wrapped my hand around the back of her head gently. I didn't know what I was doing or why I couldn't seem to take my hand away, but when the soft waves of her hair fell gracefully over my skin, I whispered down into her space. "Is your head okay?" My fingers continued to move around tenderly, feeling for a bump that I was certain was there.

The entire Bain situation didn't make sense to me, and when we'd questioned him further, he seemed to talk himself into circles, laughing casually every so often. Shiner came in during the tail end of the conversation, after shutting down the party as I demanded when Gemma was ripped out of my arms, and he was ready to throw down with Bain.

Shiner couldn't really understand why we wouldn't just throw fists for him fucking up Claiming Night by breaking the rules, but in order for him to understand, I'd have to tell him who my father really was, why I was at St. Mary's in the first place, and yeah, that really wasn't on my to-do list. Brantley had calmed him down in the end, and eventually, Shiner let it go. But he wasn't wrong. Bain absolutely needed to be knocked down a few notches. Body-snatching the new girl out of someone else's arms definitely crossed over quite a few claiming rules, and he fucking knew it. The question was, why did he do it?

"My head is fine," Gemma's voice cracked. My fingers were still woven in her hair as I rubbed the back of her head, relishing being so close to her.

Shit, what the fuck was I doing?

Not only was my body humming with something new and exciting with her so close, but my dick was beginning to twitch. There was just something about a good girl being shoved into a dark closet with me that turned me on.

Just as Gemma let out a wistful sigh, something echoed out in the hall, and she screamed. I flung my hand over her mouth and pulled her into my chest, shushing her. "Fuck," I muttered under my breath.

My uncle's words echoed throughout my head: *Stop getting*

caught. There are no more second chances. And this was exactly why I needed her to get on board with the tutoring thing. If that were already established, being out of our rooms after curfew wouldn't be that big of a deal right now, and I wouldn't have had to shove her into a fucking closet to talk.

If this were a week prior and I was in a closet with someone, mere seconds from getting caught, I'd probably make my chosen girl moan loudly just for the fun of it, but that was before my father had threatened Jack and I was put on probation with the SMC. Now, I was on thin fucking ice, and I wasn't stupid enough to jump on it.

Her head shook back and forth along my chest as my hand fell from her mouth. She whispered quietly, "Sorry. This is why I don't like breaking the rules. I'm not a thrill seeker. I can't get into trouble."

I stayed silent for the next few minutes, listening for movement. Gemma was still a warm cocoon of all things *her* pressed against me until my arms began to relax. Then, she slowly took a step away, taking her warmth with her, and I watched as she reached up and ran her hands down her face. *I wished I could see her expression.* Not that I'd be able to read her. She was guarded better than the fucking El Chapo.

I cleared my throat lightly. "So, what is it that you need from me so that you'll agree to tutoring?" I asked, cutting straight to the point. I wasn't sure how much longer I could stand in a dark, stuffy closet with her standing so fucking close to me.

"And lie..." she half-whispered. "Isn't that what you said the favor was? To tutor you and lie for you?"

I chuckled. "Yes, and I'm not at all surprised that you didn't forget that little piece."

She shifted, just barely, but I noticed. It was surreal how hyper-aware I was of her slightest movements. "Who will I be lying to?" she asked, as if she were still contemplating her decision.

"The SMC."

She was quick to reply. "The committee?"

"You know about the SMC?"

"Yes. Sloane and Mercedes were talking about how the SMC hates you. They said that they hate you the most out of everyone..."

Her voice trailed at the end as if she felt bad for what she was saying. I snickered, unable to help myself. "Yes, and I'm just absolutely wounded that they hate me." My lips split as I held back a laugh. "I'm trying to get in their good graces. That's why I need a tutor. I gotta get my grades up."

She paused for a few seconds. "I don't think you're telling me the truth. You're the type of guy who couldn't care less if someone didn't like him or the choices he made."

"Not true," I hummed, thoroughly enjoying the conversation with her. "I care if you don't like me."

She paused. The closet grew quiet. My lips were pressed together as I tried reminding myself that Gemma and I were about to strike a deal and that I needed to take it seriously. But instead, I was toying with her.

"I'm just messing with you," I said in a low voice, trying to remember the whole point of this conversation. "I mean, it would be nice if we could be friends." *Why did that word sound so fucking bothersome?* "But we don't have to be anything more than tutor and student, if you want to get technical. You tutor me, and the nights when I have to dip out early, you lie and say I was with you the whole time. That's all."

Time had passed. I wasn't sure how much, but it had to have been a while because I was becoming very observant of the smallest movements from her. I could hear her soft breathing. I could feel her body heat, smell the scent of her shampoo.

"Why?" she finally asked, her voice no louder than her quiet breaths. "Why do I need to lie? Why do I need to cover for you? Where will you be going?"

"Sometimes I need to leave the school at night, and since I'm on probation, I'm kind of out of second chances for redemption." That was all she was going to get from me. I couldn't dive any further into why I leave on occasion. I just couldn't.

She shifted on her feet and crossed her arms over her chest. I wished it wasn't so dark in the closet so I could see how her legs looked in that oversized shirt again. Did she even have any shorts underneath? Or just her panties? *Fuck. Pay attention.*

"You're on probation because..." She hesitated, and my head tilted, waiting for her to finish. "Because of you and... and...the teacher having..."

"Sex?" I hardly concealed my amusement. "You can say the word, Good Girl. It's not dirty unless you make it that way." I paused. "And we didn't have sex."

The air whooshed as she quickly stepped forward, placing her hands on her hips. "I know I can say the word!" she whisper-snapped.

I smashed my lips together to hide my laughter, but her arms dropped, and her hair fell forward like a shield. "I'm sorry," she started. "I don't know why you make me so...angry. There's just something about you that—"

"Gets you all fired up?" I smiled. "I noticed...and I like it."

Her head moved a fraction. "You like when I'm rude to you?"

My lips curved. "I kind of like that I have an effect on you."

"No one said you had an effect on me."

I laughed, knowing very well that I *did* have an effect on her.

Gemma took a step away from me, as if she could hear my thoughts. Then, she straightened her shoulders again. "So...you need me to tutor you to help you get your grades up and lie for you on the nights that you have to leave the school to do..."

Fuck. I held my breath, hoping to God she didn't ask what I did when I left the school. I wouldn't tell her. I'd have to lie, and for some reason, lying to a girl like her just felt wrong.

She sighed. "Whatever. That doesn't matter. So, I need to tutor you and lie sometimes...if anyone asks?"

It sounded like she was beginning to accept my proposition, and I felt instant relief at her words. "Yep." I pushed myself back a little farther and propped my leg up behind me onto the linen-lined shelves. "So, you're in, then?"

Her whisper cut through the air like a knife. "No one said I was in."

I suppressed a frustrated growl. *Goddamn. Was she toying with me now?* "But you're considering it. I saw the way you paused earlier when I said I'd give you anything you wanted."

Another heavy bout of silence filled the sultry closet that was no longer smelling like linens but more so Gemma. Something soft and girly. I liked it so much I wished I could taste it. I bet she tasted sweet.

"My uncle cannot find out." Her words were laced with venom but dripping in fear. "He wouldn't be happy if he knew I was tutoring you."

"You mean Judge Stallard?"

I *felt* the uptick in her stress level. The change in the tiny room was nearly suffocating with her tension. "You...you know my uncle? By name?" She stumbled over her words, and part of me wanted to reach out to steady her.

"I don't personally know him," I answered swiftly. "But

after going through the trouble of removing the blog post from Mary's Murmurs, I wanted to know just who your uncle was and why you were afraid of him."

"I'm not afraid of him." Gemma shot forward, as if her getting closer to me was going to convince me of the bald-faced lie coming out of her mouth. She was afraid. No amount of shoulder straightening, chin lifting, or confident stance was going to fool me. Her small frame nearly quaked with fear at the sound of his name coming from my lips.

Giving in, I sighed. "Whatever you say." And then I took a step toward her. "Then let's talk about payment because the sooner we do this, the better."

A slight nod in the dark was all I got.

CHAPTER TWENTY-TWO

GEMMA

"YOU WANT WHAT?" he asked as he stood over me in the dark closet.

A slight dip in my stomach filled with disappointment at the leeriness in his voice. If he wasn't able to pull through, I'd be devastated. *I needed this.* "I want fifty thousand dollars and a fake ID."

I watched as his arms came up behind his neck for a slight moment. "The money I can do, no problem. But a fake ID is going to take some time." Then, he paused as hope consumed me. "Why do you need a fake ID, Good Girl?"

"And that's another thing..." I prefaced my next request with as much confidence as I could muster up. Being shoved in a tiny closet with him—*again*—was making me feel all sorts of bold. "No questions."

I could hear the grinding of his teeth before he reluctantly agreed. "Fine. Same goes for you, then. No questions."

My brows furrowed. It was a fair trade-off, but I already

had questions nibbling away at my tongue, which annoyed me to no end. Why did I care?

"Who said I cared enough to ask questions?" *I totally did.* "You can do whatever you want as long as you can get me what I need."

He let out a light chuckle, and for some reason, I liked the sound of it. "I can get you the money and a fake ID, but you need to stay quiet about me leaving early or not showing up at all. No one can know I'm sneaking out of St. Mary's. Not even your friends."

"You mean Mercedes and Sloane?" I thought for a moment. *Were they actually my friends?* Yes. I guessed they were.

"Yes. Mercedes' parents are on the SMC."

I nodded, even though he couldn't see me. After thinking for a moment, I snuck a glance at his dark figure. "Okay, so..." My voice was shaky, and I was so frustrated by it. He probably thought I was a nervous wreck twenty-four-seven. "You need me to tutor you and cover for you, and I need money and a fake ID."

"Do we have a deal?" he asked in a voice so low I felt my stomach dip.

"Yes," I rushed out, feeling as if I'd just taken a leap off a cliff. Isaiah took a step toward me as I was finishing my thoughts. "But no one can know what I've asked of you. No one." If Richard knew I was asking for money and a fake ID, he'd know I was planning on running again. I mean, he already knew I wanted to run—I'd already tried—but I also knew he thought that my last punishment broke me. It nearly did. But even with broken pieces, I'd still run. And this time, I was going to be smarter. I would succeed no matter how good I was at playing the dutiful good girl he thought he had a future with. I wasn't his little doll to do with what he wanted, no matter how I portrayed myself to him. That was all part of the game.

Survive, Gemma. Just survive.

Isaiah's hand gently grasped onto my wrist, pulling me out of my thoughts. I flinched the second he touched the bumpy skin before remembering that we were in the dark, and he couldn't see the marks. "Shh." The word floated out of his mouth and tickled my skin like a feather. He pulled me closer to him and slowly turned me around, putting my back to his front, before pointing at the light seeping underneath the door.

Panic wrecked me in waves, havoc causing several stress-inducing scenarios to play out in my head. It was like I was watching a series of movie trailers, but I was the guest star being thrown back into a pit of hell.

"Someone is out there, so be very, *very* quiet, Good Girl." Isaiah's whisper did nothing to alleviate my stress. In fact, it might have made it worse.

I nodded with the pounding of my heart drumming in my ears. Isaiah gently pulled me back farther into the closet and behind a standing shelf of what I saw to be more linens. Laundry detergent and his body wash filled my senses, calming me for a fraction, before the door swung open, and a golden stream of light filtered through the tiny area.

Isaiah's hand instantly covered my mouth, and his other arm snaked around my waist, pinning me to his front side. His chest was sturdy along my back, his breathing calm and not at all frantic with fear like mine. I was damn-near hyper-ventilating, and my vision was growing fuzzy. *Shit. Shit. Shit.*

Isaiah shifted behind me silently, and his arm around my waist loosened. I was so full of fear and stress that we were going to be caught I almost grabbed onto his forearm, but then something switched.

My chest was still heaving, but instead of being consumed

by dreadful nerves, I was focusing on something else happening. Isaiah's hand was wrapped over my mouth with his breath tickling the side of my neck, but his other hand, the one previously wrapped around my torso, slipped up past my long t-shirt and landed on my bare stomach.

I sucked in a quick breath, wondering what he was doing, when my skin broke out in millions of tiny goosebumps. He traced small, soft circles lazily over my flat belly, and I leaned back into his embrace. Something tugged in my core, and a needy spark jolted between my legs at the constant feel of his skin along mine. *Okay...whoa.*

My eyes jolted open when his lips touched the side of my neck. For a few moments, I just stood there, frozen, mesmerized by his warm mouth on my body, but as soon as he let up, he whispered ever so quietly in my ear, "Calm your pulse, Good Girl. They're just restocking the linens."

And as soon as he said those words, the door slammed shut, and the light was out.

Another moment passed, and when the coast was clear, Isaiah took a hefty step away from me, taking a little slice of my dignity with him. What was that? How...how did he manage to keep me from spiraling? When fear came in huge waves like that, it usually took me under. That was the thing with fear, though. Right? If you let it simmer for too long, you could get lost in it. Fear wasn't a bad thing. In fact, it made you aware and kept you sharp, but if you let too much of it in, well...that was when it took you down. *Did he touch me on purpose? Did he just...distract me? And did I like it?*

A harsh swallow came from beside me before he mumbled under his breath, "Things are going to get awfully interesting between us."

My brows furrowed, but then he said, "We better get back soon before housekeeping comes back with more linens. Mrs. Dunes should be done with her watch by now, anyway."

My voice was breathy. "Okay, yeah. Good idea."

I shuddered at my awkwardness, but I was so flustered by what had just happened that I couldn't delve in that too much.

We were silent as we walked side by side down the hall. I put enough distance between the two of us that there was no way he hadn't noticed, but the space didn't allow the tension in the air to dissipate even in the slightest. We were both a little on edge. I wasn't really sure why he was, but as soon as we popped back out into the quiet hallway, I noticed the tense way he held himself. Wide shoulders tight, fists clenched, corded jaw muscles moving back and forth.

My hand hit the iron knob of my door, but before I could turn it, he cleared his throat quietly. "We start Monday. I'll let my uncle know you've agreed to tutor me."

I nodded briefly, unable to look at him. "Will I be lying to him too? If he asks me about our tutoring sessions?"

"No."

So, his uncle knows. Interesting.

Isaiah took a step toward me, wafting his clean-scented body wash into my personal space again. "The SMC might not even question you. You're more of a cover for me. They usually catch me in the act of sneaking out or back into the school. If they see me in the hallway, I'll just say I was tutoring with you. I highly doubt they will even ask you anything."

I kept my eyes trained to the red carpet on the floor beneath our feet. "And if they catch you in a lie? Or me? Then what?"

"You won't get into trouble. Trust me."

My head finally snapped up as I locked onto his eyes. It was too dark in the hall to see the light-blue color surrounded by dark lashes, but I didn't need to see them to know they were full of conviction. "I don't trust anyone, Isaiah."

His tongue darted out to lick his lips, and that familiar pull from earlier made itself known in my lower belly. "Well, you're gonna need to trust me." A slight tug on one of my long pieces of hair was as good as him saying goodnight as he turned around swiftly and strode down to the opposite end of the hall and made a turn into the darkness.

CHAPTER TWENTY-THREE

Isaiah

"You're failing 90% of your classes." I brought my eyes up
to the laptop screen, seeing that the face on the other side
was Mercedes' father.

The SMC consisted of ten members. Five teachers, my
uncle—the headmaster—three parents, and one of the
school's biggest benefactors. We all sat at a long, rectangular
table in the library before the sun even made daybreak. They
were all on one side, sitting across from me, each holding an
angry, disapproving glint within their expression that was
clear even on the parents' faces through the computer
screen.

Even my uncle appeared disappointed.

He was still pissed about the Bain ordeal on Saturday
night. He'd somehow figured out what had happened with
Gemma. He knew we threw parties occasionally, but he'd
never caught us in the act or even knew where we held them.
For all he knew, we crammed into one dorm room. But

regardless, I think he trusted me and the Rebels to handle things if they ever got out of hand—which was precisely why Saturday was cut short. I may have been a rebellious menace most of the time, but I wasn't okay with what Bain had done.

My uncle leaned forward onto the shiny table and angled the laptop that had the three parents on videos, "Isaiah is aware of his grades. We have come up with a solution."

"You have?" That came from Mercedes' father again. He didn't like me. He'd never met me, but I'd seen enough of his face over the last year for disciplinary reasons. "Please do tell, Tate. I would love to know how you are covering for your nephew again."

A strike of annoyance cut through me. Maybe even a little guilt, too.

"He isn't covering for me. It was my idea. My uncle threatened to kick me out of St. Mary's himself, actually." I leaned back onto my hard-backed chair, briefly smelling the dust that lined the bookshelves behind me, and raised my chin. "I found a tutor, and she has agreed to help me with my school work in the evenings after lacrosse until I get my grades up."

Mrs. Dunes' head slanted, her plump rosy cheeks lifting in amusement. "You found a tutor? Who, may I ask?"

I knew what they were thinking. I could read it all over their faces. They weren't taking me seriously and likely thought I'd seduced someone into tutoring me. Again, it drove a stake of annoyance through me, but also, I couldn't really blame them. "Gemma Richardson."

Silence raced through the group of teachers. They shared quick looks with one another, which were hardly noticeable to the naked eye.

"Who is Gemma Richardson?" one of the parents asked through their muffled microphone. I was pretty certain it was

Abby Clinton's mother by the similarity in features, but I couldn't be certain.

"She's our new student. Very smart and driven." My uncle's voice held a hint of authority, one that he didn't often use.

Another parent snickered. "What is this? A joke? I'm sure the school's bad boy has already had her under the bleachers."

I laughed. "As if I've ever taken a girl under the bleachers." There were far better places to fuck someone than under the bleachers. I may have been an arrogant asshole, but I did have some dignity. I wasn't a goddamn animal.

My uncle shot me a death stare, his green eyes widening and his mouth set in a deep scowl.

I rolled my eyes and wiped off my smile. "Honestly..." I leaned forward, eyeing the parent who had said such a comment. "The new girl isn't really my type. Plus, she's one of the only girls at this school who isn't trying to get me to fu—" I stopped myself before the word came out. "...date them," I was quick to add. "Your daughters don't count. They stay clear away from me, and I stay clear away from them."

That wasn't true, but I was trying to get into their good graces, after all, so I felt the need to add that in.

"Faculty?" Mercedes' father asked, drawing all of our attention to him. "Can you back up what Isaiah is saying? Mercedes has told me a little about their new student. It is on par with what the headmaster has said. She also said that Gemma was very quiet and, overall, a nice girl. I would like to hear your comments, though."

I glanced down to the benefactor, to see what his opinion on the matter was, but he was out cold. Mouth open and everything. I suppressed a laugh.

Each of the teachers shared looks again and nodded amongst one another. Mrs. Fitz was the first to speak.

"Gemma is a wonderful addition to our school. She is

sweet and smart, from what I gather, and an amazing artist. I don't see her becoming swayed by Mr. Underwood at all. She is too focused on her studies—on art, to be exact."

Mrs. Dunes spoke next. "She is very mature. Well beyond her years. Attentive in class."

Mercedes' father garnered our attention again, his brows lowered. "Okay, so she has agreed to tutor you. But why?"

I sighed. "It's simple, really. She's just...nice." I was totally fucking lying out of my ass. I mean, I was certain Gemma was nice. She seemed to have a caring, nurturing side about her, but that wasn't at all how the conversation went down when I'd asked her to tutor me in the first place. Granted, I had asked her to lie for me and to cover my ass too, but that was beside the point.

"You mean to tell me...you asked her to take time away from her own studies and free time, and she just...agreed. Just like that?"

"Yes," I deadpanned. "They'll tell you." I nodded my head to the teachers. "Gemma is nice. There's no other way to say it. I told her I needed help getting my grades up and asked for her help, and she said okay. As simple as that."

Mr. Cunningham nodded. "She is a sweet girl. She helped me pick up the books I'd dropped the other day when every other student laughed—your children included. And then, she called me sir afterwards, as if I had done her the favor."

The other teachers were all commenting on how nice and sweet Gemma was when the benefactor let out a loud snore. I laughed under my breath, and then it seemed the conversation began to shift.

"Okay, fine. That's settled, then. We will give you a month to get your grades up."

Thank fuck.

"Hold on now," Mercedes' father interrupted Abby's mother who was very much ready to get out of the meeting.

"What about your behavior? That is more of a concern of mine than your grades. Mercedes tells me all that goes on in the school, and you are always the star of the story."

I highly doubted Mercedes told him much of anything. Or maybe she told him about the things that didn't involve her. Mercedes wasn't necessarily a rule-breaker, but she wasn't a saint either.

Sighing internally, I put on a fake face and acted apologetic for the first time in my entire life. "Listen, I know I've been nothing but a nuisance to you and the rest of the SMC since attending St. Mary's, and I understand I have burned most of my bridges with you all." I glanced down to the table and then back up to the faces staring at me. "But—"

"But he understands that this is his last chance at redemption. Most of his time will be accounted for. School during the day, lacrosse afterwards, tutoring in the evenings. Isaiah and I had a long talk, and he is aware that this is the last straw, and he didn't like the alternative."

My uncle was right. I didn't like the alternative, but neither one of us could come out and say what that alternative was to the SMC. None of them knew what the Covens was or who my father truly was—at least I hoped not.

There was a long pause on the computer as the SMC took in what my uncle was saying. Most of their eyes swung toward me, and for once, I didn't wear a mask. I didn't try to hide my desperation or cover it up with a smug grin. I showed them that I was serious, because truthfully, I was.

Ms. Glenburg said I didn't have a choice in anything except my behavior, but she was wrong. I didn't even have that choice. My father's threat was as clear as the water in the Maldives. I either did my job or Jack would suffer the repercussions. That wasn't much of a choice, was it?

"One month for an improvement in grades," my uncle stated, pulling the computer to face him. "And no more excuses for behavior. No more fighting. No more sneaking out of the school or into the girls' hallway. No more ditching class."

Someone from the computer said, "And no more seducing teachers."

The benefactor had woken up at some point, and the old, gray-haired man snorted in amusement, which truly didn't help matters.

"Yes, and no more seducing teachers." My uncle caught my eye over the computer and gave me a look.

I threw my hands up with mock innocence. "No more seducing teachers. Got it." My eyes briefly caught Mrs. Dunes, and her round cheeks were a bit redder than before. I bit the inside of my cheek to hold in a laugh so I didn't blow my last chance with the SMC.

"We will have another meeting in one month, Isaiah. Prove to us that we didn't just make a mistake by not expelling you due to your uncle's convincing—*again*."

"Yes, sir," I replied coolly, standing up and pushing my chair out from the table. "If we are done here"—I began adjusting my tie—"I need to get to breakfast if I want to be on time for class—something Mrs. Dunes will probably appreciate."

"Yes, yes." My uncle waved his hand out. "Go."

And with that, I turned around and walked out of the library, feeling the smallest amount of relief settle in.

———

LEANING BACK onto my stool during art class, I continued to gaze at Gemma. We'd missed each other this morning during breakfast, so I wasn't able to let her know that everything was a go for tutoring this evening. She, Sloane, and Mercedes had skipped out for some reason, and I couldn't help but think that reason was me. After all, Gemma would barely even look at me from across the room now.

That really didn't sit well with me. How the hell was she going to spend the evenings *tutoring* me if she couldn't even look at me from across the room? She needed to loosen up some. She was always so...serious. Cautious, too.

"Better fix that hard-on before the bell rings," Brantley laughed from beside me.

I snapped my attention down to my pants before rolling my eyes, knowing damn well I just fucking fell for his stupid joke. His chest shook as he busted up with laughter, and Cade joined in with him.

"Fuck off and quit thinking about my dick," I snapped, bringing my attention back to Gemma. She was sitting on her stool, looking like a poised schoolgirl with her spine straight and shoulders pulled back. Her hair was in one long braid that I imagined wrapping around my fist as I fucked her. *Fuck. Wait. That took an abrupt turn.*

I shifted on the stool again, taking my eyes off the soft skin of her legs peeking out from below her plaid skirt. I was already imagining myself kissing her breathless, which I absolutely could not do. It would be a huge mistake. I'd end up fucking her one way or another, because there was no way you could kiss a girl like that without wanting more, and then things would get messy between us. She was definitely the type of girl to let her feelings get involved, and that just couldn't happen—not with someone like me, at least. Plus, I couldn't have my cover-slash-tutor hating me and backing out on our deal now, could I? I was much smarter than that. Mixing business with pleasure was never a good idea. *But damn, I hadn't screwed around with anyone since Ms. Glenburg, and I didn't even get to finish.*

Cade began pulling on his backpack, even though the bell hadn't rung yet, while Brantley slipped his backwards baseball hat onto the top of his head, knowing very well Mrs. Fitz would scold him to take it off until he was out of her class. "Have we seen Bain anywhere today? How's he lookin'?"

My gaze snapped to Cade as my blood pulsed. "What do you mean, 'how's he looking?'"

Cade's eyes widened as he shot a panicked look to Brantley. "Apparently, you haven't seen the latest blog post."

That stupid fucking blog.

Clenching my jaw, I placed my feet from the stool back onto the ground, glancing to Gemma once before looking sternly into Cade's *oh-shit* expression. "Explain."

Cade looked about as uncomfortable as Mrs. Dunes today when the SMC had brought up me seducing Ms. Glenburg. Brantley rubbed his forehead roughly with his free hand. The bell rang, and I slapped my hand down onto the table. "Get on with it!"

"Shiner didn't listen to you. You know how pissed he was that the party got shut down..." *That could only mean one thing.*

"And you're just now telling me this?" My voice shook with unshed anger, and it killed me to keep it low. Gemma was seconds from rushing out the door, still keeping her attention away from me, which I found to be irritating, but thankfully, at the last second, Mrs. Fitz placed a hand on her arm and began talking to her with a glitter of awe in her eye.

I shot up out of my seat and gripped my backpack forcefully. I glared at Cade and Brantley before turning back to get my eyes on Gemma. "Tell Shiner he is on my fucking shitlist. I specifically told him to drop it." I was silently cursing myself for not taking a closer look at Bain this morning, too.

Cade mumbled under his breath as I began walking past. "Maybe it's time we clued him in, bro. He wouldn't have done it if he knew..."

I cut him another glare, and he threw his hands up innocently. "It was just a suggestion." Then, he nodded to the door where Gemma was standing. "Just FYI, the article said a Rebel—unnamed, of course—attacked Bain, fighting on Gemma's behalf because of what he'd pulled with her on Saturday. Probably why she's avoiding you."

Great. "I want that shit taken down *now*."

"We'll get it taken care of," Brantley urged. "We thought you already knew and had talked with Shiner."

I grimaced. "Well, I didn't, and now things are about to get messy."

CHAPTER TWENTY-FOUR

GEMMA

Watchful eyes followed my every move. They trailed me as I walked down the hallway, as I washed my hands in the girls' restroom, even as I sat in the back of World History, listening to a lecture on the Seven Seas. Everyone was mumbling under their breath and whispering about the blog post that I was featured on—*again*—so by the time I rounded the corner to art, I was ready to crumble.

My stomach was already filled with nerves, and the thought of being in class with Isaiah, who I hadn't seen since our linen-closet meeting Saturday evening, truly made me want to vomit all over the place. *Did he attack Bain? Was it all a rumor?* I wasn't sure, and neither was Sloane or Mercedes. The three of us huddled over Sloane's phone this morning while eating granola bars for breakfast as we read the blog post, mortification swallowing me up whole, not even bothering to spit out my bones afterwards.

On shaky legs, I gripped my sketchbook tightly to my

chest, relying on the fact that I was about to be in my favorite class of all to get me through the rest of the day. I purposely left my crappy cell phone in my room, already too keyed up over everything to be bothered with the fact that I still had Richard's threats echoing in the back of my mind.

I shuddered at the thought of *Uncle Richard* flashing across the screen with an incoming call but then froze when a hand reached out from a hidden corner at the end of the hall. I was pulled through as a light shriek clamored out of my mouth. My first thought was that it was Isaiah, because it'd been twice now that he'd shoved me into a small space to *talk,* but when my eyes adjusted to the dark crook blanketed in cobwebs, I froze.

Bain. It was the first time I'd been up close and personal with him—well...besides Saturday night.

"What are you doing?" I asked, keeping my voice steady, even though my heart currently had wings and was flying right out of my chest. "Coming to claim me against my will again?" I mentally smacked myself for not keeping my mouth shut. *What was going on with me?*

Bain's left eye was pretty swollen, and if the lighting were better, I was certain I would be able to make out the ashy-colored bruises. His dark eyes were stern, and for a second, I swore I saw his pupils dilate. "I have a little message for you, Good Girl."

I snarled, my lip rising with disgust. Then, I paused for a millisecond, realizing that the last few times Isaiah had called me Good Girl, I didn't recoil like normal. *Weird.*

My tongue stayed tied as I pulled my arm free from his touch. I eyed the light from the hallway from behind his wide stance. If I just slipped past him quickly and kept my back to the other side of the wall, I'd make it out and into the open area. But running wasn't a specialty of mine, and without having a solid plan of escape, I needed to stay put. I knew that from experience.

"A message for whom?" My voice didn't shake with my question, and pride filled me.

But just because I didn't seem afraid on the outside, didn't mean I wasn't on the inside. Bain gave me the creeps. He had given me the creeps on Saturday, especially when we were in a pitch-black room, and he gave me the creeps now. There was something cold in his touch. Something that felt too familiar to me. "Your little boyfriend, that's who," he snarled, squinting his other, uninjured eye at me. "Tell him that I know who he is..." He huffed out a laugh, and I pulled back even farther from his space, annoyed that his breath was touching me. He pushed his unbuttoned white cuffs up to his elbows before grinning at me wickedly, pausing for dramatic effect. His square jaw dropped as he reached a finger out and stroked the side of my face, despite me pulling away. "And it won't be long before I know who you are too. I recognize you. I just don't know where from yet."

I felt the blood drain from my face as he trailed his nail over my cheek, like he was summoning the blood to leave my body by the request of his finger. Then, he spun around and left me standing in the dark, spider-infested corner alone as the late bell rang throughout the hall.

I hurriedly rushed into art, and I'd been a frazzled mess since.

Mrs. Fitzpatrick was still talking with me about the painting I'd done early yesterday morning before breakfast as all my peers were still asleep in their beds when I felt the looming danger from behind. I knew Isaiah was staring at me; I could feel his eyes the entire class. The skin on the back of my neck was prickly, and Bain's words played on repeat as each second passed.

I recognize you. Did that mean Bain knew Richard? Did he know me? Better yet, did he know what went on behind closed doors? Richard was very private when it came to me, except for when he'd drag me to his elite dinner parties that consisted of other shady businessmen and politicians. I didn't realize it at the time, but the way they'd talk to me and run their hot gazes over my body told me all I needed to know now: Richard's closest allies were not good people. Not at all.

I wouldn't have been surprised if they knew the details of *my uncle's* plans for when I turned eighteen. He didn't think I knew, but I did.

"Gemma." Isaiah's hand wrapped around my small bicep just as I began walking out of the art room like I had a fire trailing me. "Wait up."

Blinking through thick moisture, which infuriated me to no freaking end that my thoughts had caused such a thing, I glanced up to his face.

The blue color of his eyes caught my attention first, and for a single, fleeting moment, I felt at peace. Calm. But then everything came tumbling back into view, and my lips turned downward.

"We need to talk," I rushed out, feeling the words waiting to explode out of my mouth.

"Come on," he said in a low voice as some students passed by but not without looking at us with their greedily receptive eyes. Drama: it was what made high schoolers thrive.

I shifted my attention to Cade and Brantley as they tipped their heads to us and walked away with furrowed brows and phones in their tight grasps. They definitely looked like they were up to something.

"They're taking the blog post down. I didn't know about it until right now. I know you feel uncertain that it won't get back to your uncle, which it won't, but I'll get it taken care of." Isaiah pulled me into the classroom beside the art room that must not have been used in quite some time, because it smelled of dust and had white sheets draped over every last piece of furniture. He shut the door behind me quickly, pulled me away from the dirty glass window, and let go of my hand.

He stood back and watched me with a careful eye, and I did the same to him. A small, barely noticeable flutter of butterflies swarmed my stomach, and it seemed all my thoughts disappeared. He wore his maroon school blazer today, which fit his wide shoulders perfectly. His tie was still a little loose around his neck, his tanned skin peeking out from the top of his unbuttoned white shirt. His coal-colored hair fell over to the side in a deliciously messy way, and before I knew it, my mouth was gaping, and heat was blasting to my cheeks.

Words died on my tongue as I went to say something, because not only was I checking Isaiah out, but I think he was doing the same to me. His eyes were locked and loaded on my bare thighs as I squeezed them together, and I swore there was a strong magnetic pull that was almost forcing me over to him. *Wait...why did we need to talk again?*

"Um," I finally managed to breathe out. The short word seemed to bring us both back to reality as his head snapped up, and his icy eyes left my legs.

"Fuck. Right." Isaiah shook his head and leaned back onto the sheet-covered desk.

I stayed exactly where I was to begin with, too afraid to get any closer. "Did you attack Bain? Did you do that to his face?"

His jaw was tense. "No." Then, he shrugged. "That's not to say I didn't want to, though. But I'm on probation with the SMC, remember? I can't afford to get in trouble."

I sighed in relief but shifted nervously in my new shoes that had magically appeared on my bed yesterday morning when Sloane and I got back from breakfast. She laughed and rolled her eyes playfully, mumbling something under her breath about the headmaster. "Bain talked to me before class," I said, pulling my blazer sleeves down over my wrists.

Isaiah's eyes hardened before he shrugged off his jacket and crossed his arms. "He talked? Or did he do something else?" The hardness in his gaze made me gulp.

Just how dangerous was Bain? And how dangerous was Isaiah? My inner voice whispered the answer to that question before I answered him. "He said to tell you he knows who you are."

Isaiah's chest heaved, and I watched as veins popped out over his hands. "Was that it?"

My gaze shot down to my new shoes. They shined with the little bit of light coming through the window as rain slashed at the glass. "No."

"Good Girl..." Isaiah was closer now, and I quickly brought my head up to see where he was. His strides were slow and casual as he approached me, stirring up the dust in his wake. "I know you don't trust me, but if it has to do with Bain, I need you to tell me."

My tongue swiped over my lips as my heart thumped against the walls of my chest. A really big part of me wanted to trust him, but I had a really hard time trusting myself to do so. My judgment was skewed. After all, I'd trusted Richard for seventeen years before I'd learned that all he was, was a devious man hiding behind the gavel in his hand.

But in the end, my heart won against my mind. "He said he recognized me...and that he'd soon know where from."

The only reaction I got from Isaiah was a slight twitch in his eye.

I wrapped my hands around my torso as a sort of

strength-inducing embrace. "If he knows me, then he likely knows my uncle, and—"

"He's just fucking with you to get to me," he interrupted me.

"I don't know." My mind was spiraling as I thought over Bain's words. It was the way he looked at me that had me thinking otherwise. *What if he did know me?* Could he have seen me at one of the gatherings Richard made me attend in the past? I didn't look many people in the eye at those frivolous, high-society parties because I knew I'd be punished later. "I don't trust him."

Isaiah's lips moved, showing off a grin. "I thought you didn't trust anyone." His slight smile grew wider, and I stared at his perfect white teeth. "We haven't even established a friendship yet, and you already trust me?"

I pulled back. "No one said that I trusted you." I paused, crossing my arms over my chest. "And no one said we would become friends."

He shrugged. "But you wanna trust me."

My brow furrowed as my arms flexed across my body. "I do not." And it didn't matter if I was lying. I wouldn't trust him. I wouldn't.

His smile caught my eye, and I swore the breath left my body like a soul ascending to heaven. "And you want to be friends with me." He reached over with his long arm and flicked my braid off my shoulder. "And that's a start, Good Girl."

A flicker of warmth basically caught me on fire at the mere sight of his dimpled cheek. *I couldn't be friends with him.*

Isaiah erased the open space between us until we were a foot away from one another. I tipped my head back to look at him and saw that his light expression had morphed into something darker. "Are you rethinking things now? With Bain making threats?"

I clenched my teeth together to suppress anything that wanted to run out of my mouth. It was hard to keep my thoughts straight with Isaiah this close. Something danced over my skin as if he was touching me. But he wasn't. It was scary how exhilarated I got with him near. Almost scarier than Bain knowing who I was.

"No. But if he found out what I was really up to, what you were getting for me, and he told my uncle..." I trailed off, my brain almost screaming at me to shut the hell up. "Just never mind. I don't want him running back to my uncle and giving reports on me. That's all."

Isaiah pushed his hands into his pockets, and as I peered up at him, all I could see was the side-eye he was giving me. "Your uncle must be a force to reckon with if Bain can inflict that much fear into you at the mere thought of him making the connection." He glanced away, watching raindrops trail down the window. His sharp jaw was the only thing I could focus on. "If you want out, you need to tell me now so I can come up with a better plan to get my ass off probation."

"Out of what? Tutoring?"

His icy eyes found mine again. "Yes."

Panic pushed me toward him, my shaky hands grasping into his forearm. "No!" The word was a jolt of desperation flinging through the empty room. "I need what you promised me." I needed it so badly I could almost taste the freedom on my lips.

His arm flexed under my touch, and I immediately dropped my gaze to his mouth.

"Good. Because the SMC already agreed to allow you to tutor me. We start tonight." Our eyes locked, and something passed between us. A bond? An understanding? I wasn't sure what it was, but something seemed to click into place for me.

"I'll meet you in the library at seven, then." The panicked

tone of my voice had vanished with relief, and Isaiah's grim frown had morphed to his normal, sly grin.

"Make it eight. I have a lacrosse game tonight."

I nodded. "Okay. I'll see you at eight." I began to turn away before his hand reached out and snagged me back.

"You should come to the game."

My brow furrowed as his hand stayed on my arm. "Your lacrosse game? Why?"

His eyes darted away, and his sly grin was nowhere to be found. His dark brows were slanted over his eyes as he stared at the window again. There was an unfathomable pull in my chest that made me want to reach out and place my hand on his, letting him know that whatever he was conflicted about was fine—which confused me altogether. Why did I even care if he was conflicted about something? Where was this coming from? Boiling anger began to surface at my irrational notion to make someone like him feel better. Isaiah and I weren't friends, and last I checked, he had thrown me into a closet on the first day of school as *payback*. I didn't know a single thing about Isaiah, and my need to put his feelings over mine was going to need to make a swift turn right out of this room.

But then... My mouth opened, and the words that came out surprised us both. "I'll come to your game." *What?!*

He snapped his attention back to me, and he sighed out a breath. "Good." And just like that, he walked over to the door and held it open for me. I began walking out with my lips sealed because I was so appalled by my behavior.

Right before I stepped back into the hall, Isaiah leaned down and brushed his lips over my ear. Goosebumps broke out along every inch of my skin, and unlike before, when Bain and I were in close contact and I'd had fear slithering through my veins, Isaiah caused nothing but an exciting thrill of butterflies to flutter across my belly. That was, until he said, "Do me a favor. Stay away from Bain."

His hand left my arm, and his breath no longer tickled my ear. I swallowed roughly and nodded curtly before he left to walk down the hallway with his unknowingly pretentious stride.

CHAPTER TWENTY-FIVE

ISAIAH

I STALKED into the locker room, whipped the maroon tie off my neck, and threw it to the floor. Cade flicked his eyes over to me as he was pulling on his white lacrosse jersey. Just as soon as it was over his head, I barked out a demand. "I need everyone on the field but you, Shiner, and Brantley."

"Bro," Cade started. "The game's in thirty..." His sentence trailed off because the look I shot him caused him to close his mouth quickly. "Everyone out. Now!" he shouted, waving his hand in the air. The rest of our team paused, some with their jerseys on, some shirtless and mid-laugh. It didn't take them long to see that something was going on with us, and they knew better than to ask. Locker doors were slammed, lacrosse gear was snagged, and soon enough, they were all filing out of the locker room, and it was the four of us surrounded by metal lockers, empty showers, and the echo of my racing heart.

As soon as the last person piled out—Mason, that slow fuck—I shot a venomous look at Shiner before giving no indication that I was about to take my fist and plummet it into his pretty-boy face. I watched for a split second as his expression went from confused to *oh fuck* before my closed hand landed on his cheekbone with a loud thud.

"What the fuck, Isaiah!" Brantley stepped in between us the second I pulled back, and his brows clearly showed his anger. "What are you doing?"

My hands immediately went to my hips, creeping underneath my jersey. I ignored the pain in my hand from punching one of my best friends, but that was what happened when you deliberately disobeyed an order that I gave.

Granted, Cade was right earlier. Shiner was in the dark, and it was biting me in the ass, but I wanted to set this conversation off on the right foot, friend or not. I needed him to understand that there were bigger things at play here. Because what he didn't know was that innocent lives quite literally dangled in the crossfire when it came to me and Bain and this school. A little punch to Bain's face from Shiner was all in fun childish games to him, but to me? It wasn't. It wasn't a game at all.

"I looked you right in the face, and I told you to drop the Bain thing." My voice was calm as I leveled Shiner with a glare. His hard cheekbone was red and swelling, but it didn't deter from his narrowed eyes and clenched jaw.

"And I didn't listen," he bit out. "I don't think that fucking deserves a punch to my face, does it? This isn't the fucking mafia, Isaiah."

My voice echoed against the metal of our lockers. "If it were the mafia, I would have chopped your fucking hand off." Something my father would have no issue doing.

Brantley was still standing in between us as a buffer, but he didn't need to any longer. I wasn't going to do anything else. My intention was to get Shiner's attention, and I needed him to shut his bantering mouth for more than three fucking seconds so I could get out what needed to be said. "There are things you don't know, Shiner," I started, dropping the firmness in my voice for a split second. "Things you are better off not knowing."

He huffed, shaking his head with what seemed to be disbelief. "Yeah, no shit, Isaiah." His chin tipped to Brantley and Cade. "You three have something going on, a secret bromance or some shit. I'm not fucking blind. I've seen the way you three have silent conversations."

Cade scoffed. "It is not a bromance, you fuck."

I ignored Cade and crossed my arms over my jersey. "Well, congratu-fucking-lations, Shiner. Welcome to our fucked-up lives." I flashed a look to the clock hanging over the door, seeing we had fifteen minutes to get on the field before Coach came in here and chewed our asses for skipping out on warm-up. "Sit the fuck down and listen, because I'm only going to tell you this once."

Shiner glanced at Cade and Brantley as they slowly came over and stood behind me, backing me with my decision to tell Shiner that we weren't just a bunch of bad-boy shitheads trying to get through their senior year at a stuffy boarding school by pulling pranks and skipping classes. In fact, we were trying to drag this year out as long as possible because what awaited us afterwards was nothing but stripped-away freedom with danger on the horizon at all times.

"My father didn't send me to St. Mary's just to get rid of me, like most students here," I started before shooting Cade and Brantley a quick look over my shoulder. "I'm here on behalf of my father. We all are." It almost killed me to say his name out loud. Not the name he used to front his many contributions to orphanages and group homes. Not the name that was signed off on checks for donations and charitable goods. No, I meant the name that others had been known to shiver at the sound of. The name that I'd someday take as my own, even though it cut me in half to think about.

"Your father?" Shiner asked, cocking a brow.

"Yeah. My father...*The Huntsman*."

———

AFTER SHINER finally picked his jaw up off the locker room floor and wrapped his head around what I'd told him, the four of us rushed out onto the field with our crosses in hand.

The air was dense with fog, the sun completely forgotten by the coverage of thick clouds. Our cleats stuck in the wet ground as we kicked back clumps of mud to the opposing team every so often. We were already in the second quarter, and just when I was getting in the zone and giving myself that break from the everyday nagging of my father's voice in the back of my head and his threats laced with sin over sending Jack to the Covens, Shiner came up behind me with his crosse in hand, eyes set on a defender on the other side of the field. "I can't fucking believe that your father is *The Huntsman*. Like..." He gasped for a breath of air, ready to jog past me. "*The* fucking Huntsman. Shit, Isaiah." I caught the look of anguish on the tight creases of his eyes, and I shook my head.

"It's whatever," I muttered. "Get your head in the fucking game. We're down by two." I brushed off the pity he was unintentionally giving me and acted like my father being the Huntsman wasn't a big deal, but it was. God, it fucking was. My father was feared by most. When people said his name out loud, they shuddered. Death followed everywhere he went. He'd killed people. He'd killed people right in front of me. I'd felt someone else's blood splatter across my face as he held the cold gun in his hand. The same cold gun that he'd later sell in his multi-million-dollar illicit trade business.

People knew of the name, even if they were in no way affiliated. The elusive Huntsman was the center of the news most of the time, while my father kicked back and laughed. I was certain the authorities had given up trying to put a face to the name.

I blinked away the thoughts as Shiner nodded sharply before sprinting past and slyly cross-checking someone twice his size, causing their body to thud to the ground. Mud splattered over the side of Shiner's white jersey, and I grinned. *That's what I'm talking about. Fuck the future.* Seeing Shiner cross-checking a prestigious pretty boy from Washington High was what I needed to bring me back to the present. Washington High's biggest concern was fucking up a game of lacrosse in front of their girl. Mine? Mine was keeping my brother out of hell and keeping myself in check long enough to find a way out for both of us. But right now, I'd focus on this. The game.

After Shiner cross-checked the opposing player, causing the ball to fly through the air, Brantley snagged it and began working his way down the other side of the field, where I trailed him, body-checking a few guys of my own who stood too close. My gaze wandered momentarily, locking onto Gemma for the fifth time in the last half hour. She sat in the same spot on the metal bleachers, with Sloane on her right and Mercedes on her left. She stuck out like a sore thumb because she was in a completely enthralling trance of the game. Every other girl around her was chatting away or laughing with their heads thrown back, but not Gemma.

Her eyes followed me. Even with the disadvantage of distance, I could feel her lingering gaze. My lungs burned with the thought, which was something new for me, but it was a flame I'd gladly keep lighting.

Because for once, I felt something more than dreadful numbness and the smallest amount of trepidation. Gemma, the Good Girl, gave me a spark of hope that I could keep Jack safe, and that wasn't something I'd felt in a long fucking time. I think the last time I'd let myself feel anything other than blinding anger was before Jacobi up and left me high and dry with our fucked-up father.

A smack to my back brought reality down on my shoulders again. The sounds were back, the wetness of the light rain pelting the skin of my arms. "You're talking about me getting my head in the game?" Shiner tapped me against the back with his crosse, and if we weren't in the middle of a game, I'd take mine and slice it behind his knees to make him fall. "You get *your* head in the game. Don't worry. Gemma isn't going anywhere, and Bain is tucked away nicely on the top bleacher with his eyes on Callie. He isn't even paying attention to Gemma."

I sighed, wishing I believed what Shiner said, but I knew, deep down, that Bain had his eyes not only on Gemma, but on me too.

Fucker.

CHAPTER TWENTY-SIX

GEMMA

LACROSSE WAS PROBABLY the most entertaining thing I had ever watched. The way each player chased after a ball with unyielding determination on their faces, kicking up mud and grass with their heavy strides down from one end of the field to the other. The strength in their arms as they used their stick for protection and what seemed to be a sort of weapon, beckoning the ball to a certain side of the field.

It was fascinating. The whole experience. From sitting on the bleachers in my favorite black jeans and borrowed St. Mary's lacrosse shirt from Sloane, with two of my new friends on each side of me, to the sounds of other people clapping and cheering in the background and whistles being blown that the game was coming to an end. It was all so...*normal*. The smallest seed of happiness planted itself inside of me, and it was hard to fight its sprout as Sloane and Mercedes dragged me toward the chain-link fence separating the field from the bleachers.

"What are we doing?" I asked as their expressions were

set on the field toward the left side. I followed their gazes and watched as a bunch of guys whipped off their helmets and wiped away the sweat dotting their foreheads.

Mercedes sighed wistfully as she rested her chin under her hand. She leaned against the wet fence without looking at me. "Checking out Washington High players."

"Oh," I answered, looking at each and every one.

Sloane snorted out a laugh. "Pretty sure Gemma isn't interested in Washington's players, Mer."

I sucked in my bottom lip, shrugging. "They're okay, I guess." Then my gaze wandered over to St. Mary's side of the field, and I immediately started comparing the two teams.

Aside from both teams wearing jerseys, albeit different colors, and being damp from sweat and the short spurt of rain we'd gotten halfway through the game, they were nothing alike. It seemed our guys were taller, stronger, and broader. Wide shoulders, chins held high. Each and every last one of them—even the few that I didn't recognize—looked determined and resolute. Determined to do what? I wasn't sure, as they'd already won the game.

My heart flipped when I saw Isaiah standing toward the end of their bench, talking with Cade, Brantley, and Shiner. He ran a hand through the sweaty ends of his dark hair, shaking it out slowly. Then, I ceased to exist altogether when he snaked a hand up underneath his jersey, showing off a stomach lined with hard muscles. His head tipped backward as if he were massaging a shoulder muscle or something, and then he slowly twisted his neck, making his well-defined Adam's apple bob up and down.

My throat closed. My legs prickled with heat. He was... He was really, *really* attractive. I felt a slight crack in my chest as I continued to stare. Isaiah was so beautiful that it was scary to look at him. In the few months at Wellington Prep, I'd hardly noticed any of the guys because I was too busy taking in everything else that was so new to me. I was in overdrive. But here? Away from my home and that town? I noticed *everything,* and the tingling in my core did not go undetected.

"Gemma!" Sloane's tone was loud but playful as I snapped my attention to her. I shoved a thick piece of brown hair behind my ear, feeling the heat sear my skin. A gust of cool, moist air wafted around us, but it didn't cool me down in the slightest.

"What?" I asked.

She and Mercedes both laughed but quickly stopped as wet footprints began to approach. We all turned our attention to a group of guys who began to walk up the muddy field, still in their hunter-green uniforms with smirks gracing their faces.

"Hey." One of them nodded to us as he seemed to lead the pack. "Did you babes enjoy the game?"

"We sure did," someone said from behind us. "You boys played a good game."

The leader of the pack, with his damp blond hair, looked over our heads, and his eyes lit up.

"Thank you, *beautiful.*" The interest in his voice was totally obvious, even to me. Sloane, Mercedes, and I all turned around to see who he was talking to.

"*Figures,*" Sloane mumbled, turning her back to Callie. "She's already fucked everyone at this school, so she has to start scouting newcomers."

I whispered back to Sloane, even though she had no issues verbally insulting Callie. "What's the point if they just up and leave after the game, though?"

Mercedes answered for her. "She's just looking for a quickie, probably. Callie has no self-worth. She uses guys and sex to make herself feel better." She paused before pulling herself out of my space. "I'm not judging...that's just what it seems like, anyway."

And before we knew it, the fair-skinned, blue-eyed Washington High player was jumping over the fence, and he and Callie were sneaking off behind the bleachers. The unwanted feeling of curiosity tickled the back of my brain as I turned back around. I wondered for a fleeting moment what it would be like to be her. To be a girl who wasn't afraid of what it felt like to be with a guy like that. I wasn't even sure what it felt like to kiss someone...well, not really. Not a guy I wanted to kiss, at least. Not a guy who made my skin tingle with something enticing...like Isaiah.

Sloane and Mercedes moved down to the group of guys that were still standing near the fence, and I followed reluctantly, curious to see them in action. My mouth was glued shut as Sloane took a piece of her hair and wrapped it around her finger, laughing at something one of the players whispered in her ear, and Mercedes blushed as a shy smile found her lips. I felt the jealous snake curl around my neck. I wanted to do what they were doing: garnering the attention of guys, flirting, all of it. I wanted that. I wanted to be comfortable enough with myself to do what they were doing. Would I? *Could I?*

My heart raced as I watched as one of the boys who had dark-brown hair and a scruffy jaw began to approach me. I started to panic, looking at Sloane and Mercedes for assistance, but then someone cleared their throat. *Isaiah.* I bristled at the excitement that came with seeing him so close. *When did he walk up here?*

"What are you doing, Graves?" He cocked an eyebrow as the sentence effortlessly flew from his mouth but dropped it when he moved his attention over to me. "Hey, Gemma. Did you enjoy the game?"

Mercedes and Sloane stopped talking mid-flirt and stared

a hole in the side of my head. Cade looked at Isaiah suspiciously, and I was suddenly aware of everyone's eyes on me. Again.

Isaiah's eyes were soft and inviting, but I saw the same look in them as I had earlier when he'd asked me to come to the game. It was as if he was conflicted about something. The blue color was warm, like an ocean in the middle of summer, but cold too. Glacial. The words were unspoken, but they were lingering in the air with our silent exchange. *Trust me.* My feet shuffled along the sidewalk, and I inched closer to the fence separating us. He was still sporting his jersey, although the white fabric was dotted with specks of grass stains and mud. His lip tipped upward, his eyes exuding the smallest flicker of approval before he glanced at the Washington High player. Then, he quickly whipped his attention to the bleachers behind my shoulder and narrowed his eyes.

Confusion filled me as something passed over Isaiah's face. Cade moved closer, and his gaze followed Isaiah's, eyes hardening at the last second. Just as I began to turn around to see what they were glaring at, Isaiah rested his elbows on the metal rod between us. His mouth twitched as he leaned his head beside mine, pushing my thick hair, which was now wavy from the moisture in the air, off my shoulder. I squeaked out a surprised sound as my heart thudded to the ground when Isaiah's hand crept into the back pocket of my black skinnies. My entire body hummed as a jolt ran down my leg and back up to my heart. *I liked it when he touched me.*

Isaiah smelled like the outdoors, and for some reason, that was comforting to me. "I know you're confused, but just trust me." He paused, and I swore I could feel his lips brush my skin. "Please."

Uncertainty swept me off my feet, and just as my thoughts unmuddled, Isaiah whispered along my ear again. "I'm going to kiss your cheek." My breath caught, and before I could react, he quickly moved his mouth from my ear, and he placed his soft lips on my high cheekbone in front of everyone.

My teeth clamped down over my plump bottom lip before I could allow myself to smile. It wasn't a fake smile either. It was a real, ripped-from-the-deepest-parts-of-my-soul smile, which was exactly why irritation soon followed.

I wanted to ask what the hell he was doing and why he thought it was okay to touch me like I was his, but God, there was a secret part of me that liked it. I liked it too much, and liking it took away the fear of Richard somehow finding out that someone had touched me, *kissed* me—even if it was just my cheek.

But before I had the chance to clear my head and say anything, Isaiah quickly pulled back, whipping his hand out of my pocket and putting a safe distance between us. "Meet me outside of the locker room in twenty. We can walk to the library together for tutoring. Sound good?"

I blinked a few times, trying to steady the earth below my feet. "Ye—yeah," I said, finally letting my lip plop from my teeth. *What the hell was happening?* I knew I was naive and completely uncertain in this situation, but everything about this encounter was confusing to me, and I was pretty sure it had nothing to do with my lack of social skills.

Isaiah shot me a nod just as someone began to walk behind me. Glancing over my shoulder, I saw that it was Mrs. Dunes. A tender smile graced her face as we locked onto one another, and I saw that she was wearing the same St. Mary's lacrosse shirt that I had on but with dangling silver earrings that looked to be lacrosse sticks hanging from her ears. Her gaze briefly moved to Isaiah, and she gave him the strangest look before sighing and walking down to the side door of the school.

Then, someone shouted in the distance, taking all of our

attention. The guys from the opposing school seemed to recognize the catcall, and they began saying their goodbyes to Sloane and Mercedes and a few other girls from Callie's tight-knit group of friends—not before giving up their numbers—and they turned to leave. The one that had spoken to me before Isaiah swooped in and sliced the moment in half raised his angled chin to Isaiah and chuckled. A moment passed between them, and then they all turned around and stalked down the wet grass to their teams.

My brows crowded with even more confusion as Sloane tipped her head over the fence to look down at me. "Did Isaiah just say you were tutoring him?"

I opened my mouth but was interrupted by MaryAnn, one of Callie's closest friends, as she popped in between us. "Um. Did Isaiah Underwood just kiss your cheek? In front of everyone? Does that mean it's true what the blog said? Are you two…a thing?"

"What? No! I'm…I'm just tutoring him. That's all." That didn't explain the whole kissing-my-cheek thing, but I'd figure that out later when we were alone and I could ask what he was thinking.

Blonde ringlets bounced off MaryAnn's shoulders as they fell with relief when she flipped around to lean her back on the fence. "That makes sense. You're definitely not his type."

A sting of annoyance pelted me just as Sloane scoffed. "What makes you think that Gemma isn't good enough to be his type, MaryAnn?"

She shook her head. "No, no. That's not wha—"

Mercedes leaned forward into my line of sight. "Yeah. Gemma is gorgeous, and she's—"

"Late." Headmaster Ellison appeared out of thin air, and I jumped in my spot, whipping around so hard I hit my back on the chainlink fence. The second our gazes collided, I was smacked face first with reality.

It was Monday.

It was Monday at 7 o'clock.

I was supposed to call home every Monday at the same exact time, and Richard did not like to be kept waiting. Shit. How could I have forgotten?

Dread slithered into my veins, making all the happiness I'd felt in the last few minutes turn to stone.

"Let's go." The headmaster's voice wasn't disciplinary or even angry, but it did hold a certain amount of caution to it, which told me that he'd likely already been graced with a phone call, demanding to know why I was late.

Richard was probably waiting by his phone, and the second it hit 7:01, he dialed up the headmaster and threatened something.

Probably his life.

CHAPTER TWENTY-SEVEN

ISAIAH

STEAM from the locker room surrounded me so thickly that I hoped I could duck away from the guys and snag my clothes before meeting up with Gemma outside in order to evade more questions. After dropping the "my father is the psycho they call the Huntsman" bomb on Shiner earlier, there wasn't time left for me to fill them all in about the deal I'd made with Gemma. So, when I treated her like she was something more than what any girl here had ever been before, Cade nearly combusted with questions. It was the sight of Grayson from Washington High that threw me off course. There was a flame of jealousy that flickered through me when I saw the way he was looking at her, but a wave of protectiveness quickly dimmed that light, and I took control of the situation. Grayson had no business talking to anyone at this school, and he knew it. His father was just as much a rival as Bain's was to my family, which meant that he and I were a conflict of interest. What was mine was mine, and he was not coming near anyone or anything at St. Mary's. I already had

Bain to deal with. I didn't need Grayson fucking poking around too.

I fended Cade off long enough to shower the sweat and mud off my body before he was able to corner me again, and I reluctantly filled him in. Curfew was soon, and I didn't have time to be chatting like little old bats at the hair salon on a brisk Saturday morning regarding my little show with Gemma.

Just as I slipped my black Vans on and stood up to leave the locker room, thankful that there were no more questions being thrown at me, Brantley's palm came down on my shoulder, and he squeezed my sore trap muscle. I yelled out in agony and slapped my hand over his, peeling his firm fingers off my muscle. I bent it backward until he screamed out and flung forward, cradling his hand that I nearly snapped in half. "Don't fucking touch me, Brantley. I'm sore as fuck."

He stood up, red-faced, but then quickly recovered. "You gonna fill us in on you and Gemma? What was that about?"

I shot a look at Cade, and he threw his hands up in protest. "I didn't say anything." How the fuck did word get around so quickly in this school? Brantley hadn't even been nearby when I'd bent down and kissed her cheek. *That soft, rosy fucking cheek.*

Shiner chimed in after Cade. "And *now* you're staking a claim on the new girl in front of everyone? First your father, and now this?" He scoffed out a sarcastic laugh, whipping off his towel with no regard to anyone else in the locker room.

I cringed, looking away. "Shiner, no one wants to see your dick."

He made a sarcastic noise. "Psh, they don't call me One-Liner-Shiner for nothin', Isaiah. Everyone wants to see my dick."

We all paused, and then Brantley shook his head. "I thought about it, and nope, still don't want to see your dick."

Cade laughed under his breath as he pulled a shirt over his head. We all ignored Shiner as he got dressed.

"Seriously, though. What's going on? Why did you make a scene like that? Are you trying to get Bain to fuck with her again? Because we all know the only reason he pulled that shit on Saturday was because he had watched you with her earlier that day."

A few of our other players walked into the room, also drying off from the shower. I eyed them briefly before shooting the rest of the Rebels a look.

"She's tutoring me because I'm on probation with the SMC." I shrugged. "As for the other stuff..." I trailed off, nodding to our midfielders briefly. I told them, "Good game," in a gruff voice and then began leaving the locker room. "I'll explain later."

I wasn't going to lie; I'd had the sudden urge to jump the fence and wrap my arm around Gemma's waist over the fact that Bain and Grayson were looking at her like they wanted a piece, but the main reason I'd put on the show was because they needed to know their place. At least, that was what I was telling myself.

Things with Grayson would slowly die off. He wasn't near Gemma enough to be much of a threat. But Bain? There were only two choices: I could try to keep my distance and hope he'd move past his little game of using her to get to me, or I could get even closer to her and make sure he stayed the fuck away.

I knew Bain. I knew his games. I knew most of his moves before he did. I saw the way he was looking at her and then at me. There was the smallest glint of excitement in his eye. Leverage. He wanted to hold something over me. It was becoming clearer and clearer that Bain didn't dislike me because of who I was in this school but more so because of who I was outside of it.

He'd told Gemma that he knew who I was, and I was beginning to believe it. It was possible that he wasn't bluffing.

I couldn't seriously consider Gemma and myself to be more than what we were now, even if my blood ran hot with her near. She couldn't be my girlfriend or anything even remotely close to that. I wasn't staking a claim on her like Shiner had said.

I didn't stake claims on anyone, not only because no one held my attention for long, but because I'd never in a million years give myself the chance to feel something like that for someone.

Having a girlfriend, or even just a relationship with someone that went further than the surface, wasn't in the cards for me. It was a no-go. It would be nothing more than a trap. Could people fall in love? Sure. Would I? No. I wouldn't allow myself the luxury because if I did that, then that would mean there was one more person that could get caught in the web of some very dangerous and illegal shit.

My own mother was a casualty in my father's little game, and even at age nine, when I was still so goddamn naive and impressionable, I knew I wouldn't do that to another woman. I wouldn't fall in love and bring an innocent being into a world full of lies and pain—almost always emotional but sometimes physical too. A rough swallow worked itself down my throat as broken and fragmented memories came rushing in at the sound of my mother's bones snapping. That same cry for help I'd shouted years ago almost worked its way to my lips, but I clenched my fists until my knuckles went white, and I exhaled a deep breath.

I'd make damn sure that Gemma and I went our separate ways after I was taken off probation with the SMC, so that way, there wasn't even an inkling of suspicion that she truly meant something to me after it was all said and done.

Because she didn't. She was just a means to an end. A

glimmer of hope that Jack would be fine—for now. *But then, why was I trying to protect her so fiercely?*

After letting the locker room door shut, rather aggressively, behind me, I scanned the hallway for Gemma but came up empty-handed. This addition to the school was built only a few years ago when my uncle had taken over the position of headmaster. Sports weren't always a necessity at St. Mary's, but my uncle fought with the SMC, arguing that sports were a great way to get aggression out that most of the students here were burdened with. That was why our lacrosse season was all year long. We had practice games during the off season with the schools that were close by to *'give the students something to look forward to.'*

After stalking down the hall, I pushed open the swinging door and was met with fat, thunderous clouds and a light mist of rain. I jogged along the sidewalk, past the bleachers, and made my way to the back entrance of the school, pulling open the brass-handled door, and slipping inside with even wetter hair. I flung the damp ends back and forth and let my eyes adjust to the dark entrance until I spotted Sloane and Mercedes a few yards away.

But no Gemma?

Mercedes was pulling her wild, spiral curls up into a bun when I approached them, and her cheeks instantly ripened with color. "Where's Gemma?" I asked, ignoring the way she blushed.

Sloane looked suspicious, her eyes crinkling on the sides. "She had to go with the headmaster." She darted her attention away as if she were hiding her concern. "She looked..."

"Scared," Mercedes answered quickly, actually looking me in the eye for once.

A weird notch of concern hollowed out in my chest, and I casually pushed it aside. A cool breeze wafted around our ankles as the door opened, allowing Cade and Brantley to walk through. I had no idea where Shiner was, but I could only guess it had to do with a set of warm lips.

My attention went directly to Sloane as she lightly growled under her breath at the sight of Cade. Then, she turned toward me. "I'm going to go look for Gemma."

"No."

She raised her dark eyebrows, her short hair swaying over her shoulders with the jerky movement of her head. "Excuse me?"

Tipping my head to the rusty clock above the archway, I said, "It's almost 7:30, which is curfew on game nights. By the time you grab something from the dining hall, it'll be time for you to go back to your rooms. I'll go find her. We have tutoring soon."

Sloane flicked an arched eyebrow up. "Right...*tutoring*."

Mercedes' voice was small when she spoke up beside Sloane. "But won't you two get in trouble if you're out past curfew, like the rest of us?"

"The SMC has allowed for Gemma and me to tutor after lacrosse in the evenings—after curfew."

Sloane rolled her eyes. "Has Isaiah ever cared if he got in trouble, Mer?"

Cade spoke up as soon as I turned my back and began striding down the hall. "Want me to grab you girls something from the dining hall? He's right. It's almost curfew."

Sloane didn't miss a beat. "No one wants anything from you Cade. We all know how you don't show up when needed anyway."

I wanted to laugh at the insult because neither I nor the rest of the Rebels usually got turned down for anything. Cade being insulted by someone would have been fucking hilarious had there not been a reason why Sloane hated Cade so much. I knew, without even looking back, that Cade's face was an ashen gray. He knew why Sloane hated him too, and it fucked with his head.

Rounding the corner of the long entryway, I found myself alone. Everyone would soon be tucked away in their rightful halls: boys on the left, girls on the right. I hadn't heard from my father since Friday, but I yearned to hear from Jack. Just for confirmation that he was doing okay, more than anything.

I didn't trust my father, and my mother was too far gone to take her word on much of anything these days.

Pulling my cell phone out of my pocket, I quickly typed a text to Jack and then slid my phone back into my jeans. My uncle's office door was shut, so I leaned my head against the thick wood to have a listen.

A loud, stern voice played on the other side, the end of a sentence filling the office. *"Were you studying? Or were you doing something you know I wouldn't approve of?"*

My brow furrowed as I tried to decipher the reasoning for that question. Then, my frown deepened when Gemma's tender voice came next instead of my uncle's. "Yes, sir. I was studying."

The man's voice, who I assumed to be Judge Stallard, didn't let up. "Are you alone? Where is the headmaster?"

A pause on Gemma's end. "He's in here with me."

"And how often do you go into his office alone, young lady?" There was an icy-cold bitterness to his tone that had my shoulders squaring and teeth clenching. It was obvious that Gemma was fearful of her uncle, no matter how many times she defied such a notion, and I could see why. He didn't scare me, but I understood why he scared her, if his tone was anything to go by. My breath hitched with anger at the thought of someone scaring her, and I had a primal urge to barge into the office and rip the phone off my uncle's desk.

Gemma didn't hesitate when she answered her uncle. "Only to call you."

"I don't know if I believe you," he sneered, and just as I was about to turn the knob to make it known that Gemma was *not* alone with the headmaster like her uncle was insinuating, the door flew open, and my uncle stepped out, red-faced and aggravated beyond belief.

He quickly shut the door, eyeing me briefly, as if he knew I had been standing there, and rested his ear against it just like I was. *Well, shit, I now knew where I got it from.*

My uncle rolled his eyes at me, loosening his tie from around his neck as we both listened to Gemma and her uncle, who was still on speakerphone.

"The headmaster just left the room. I'm alone now. There is nothing going on. I'm following the rules. I'm in my room by curfew each night, and I'm doing everything you've asked of me."

Gemma said her uncle was strict, and she wasn't lying. He sounded like a real son-of-a-bitch, to be honest. I didn't like him.

"Good." His voice was gruff, and there was a clunking on the end of the phone, like ice sliding against a glass cup—likely surrounded by amber liquid. I knew that sound by heart. "And your art? You've stopped sketching, yes? If I hear that you've been sketching up those—"

"I'm not. You asked me to stop, so I did."

Something loud banged on his end of the phone, and my brow furrowed again, trying to piece together what was going on. "Did you just interrupt me?"

"I—I..." Gemma's voice grew leery, and I found myself praying to God that she would dish out that same fiery spirit to him that she did to me. *Who did he think he was, talking to her like that?* I almost laughed at the thought. I knew men like him. I knew men like him so well it made me see red. He sounded just like my father—high on power and hungry for violence.

"I'm sorry," she finally managed to say, and that notch in my chest seemed to hollow out.

"I'm sorry?" he asked. "I'm sorry..." The way the words floated out of the speaker made it seem like he was insinuating something only he and Gemma were aware of. I cleared my head, shaking it slightly against the wood, trying to get a better read on him, when Gemma's fear-laced voice turned cold and empty.

"I'm sorry...*Daddy*."

My eyes flung to my uncle's, and I jerked back slightly. *Did she just call him...Daddy?*

A very loud and muffled sound of breathing made its way past the wood door, and it sounded an awful lot like a moan. My head was spinning in different directions, all of which resulted in barging inside my uncle's office and snapping the fucking phone in my hand, but I fought to keep myself present and grounded. Calculated behavior was better than impulsive behavior. I'd take this little moment and stash it away for a later date and use it to my benefit if it ever came to that.

"That's right. I am your Daddy," her uncle finally said after more heavy breathing. "And soon enough, you'll be home, back where you belong."

My heart began thumping a little harder at his words, and I didn't know why. What I did know was that I didn't particularly enjoy the thought of her leaving and not coming back.

"I will talk with you next Monday. And this time? Don't be fucking late." There was a strange sense of awareness as the words trailed from his mouth. Like there was a threat to be delivered. Maybe a silent one.

"I won't be late," Gemma answered. "Would you like to speak with Headmaster Ellison before I head up to my room? It's almost past curfew."

"No," her uncle answered sharply. "Go back to your room.

You know I don't like when you break rules. Remember what we say?"

"Good girls don't break rules." Then the line went dead.

Just as my uncle and I pulled back from the door, both of us looking equally as perturbed, the loud bang of the phone slamming into the receiver told us all we needed to know.

Gemma's uncle thought he had her wrapped around his finger, but he didn't. Because Gemma was angry.

CHAPTER TWENTY-EIGHT

GEMMA

MY ENTIRE BODY twitched as I stood above the headmaster's mahogany desk with my hand still on the phone. I slammed it so hard onto its receiver that my arm went numb. His voice was like a million little spiders crawling into my ear and filling my head with unjust lies and bigoted thoughts that only stemmed from years of looming threats and punishments. I hated him. I hated him so much I felt a scream threatening to tear through the empty room. But instead of screaming or taking the globe off the end of the headmaster's desk and throwing it against the wall, I peeled my fingers away and counted backward from ten until my breathing grew less erratic.

My stomach churned as I continued to replay his words: *you'll be home soon, back where you belong.* I couldn't. I couldn't go back there. I wouldn't survive. If this thing with Isaiah didn't work out, I wasn't sure what I would do.

The money I could probably do without. I would make ends meet one way or another. There would be no other choice, but it was the new identity that was my true ticket. I needed a fake ID with a new name. A way to blend in without raising flags to the officials—the officials that Richard had spent years forming relationships with so they could stay nestled in his deep pocket.

Being a judge came with many perks, and having everyone on your side—police chiefs, fire officials, attorneys, judges, you name it—meant that if I were spotted, I'd be tucked away nicely in a police car and taken right back to Richard himself.

I should know. It happened before.

This was no speculation. It was a very real possibility.

I pushed the heels of my palms into my eyes to force away the frustrated tears before the headmaster walked back into his office. It was already awkward enough that he had heard my *uncle* insinuating that something was going on with the two of us while on speakerphone. Crying in front of him would only make things worse.

The look on the headmaster's face flashed across my mind, and he was no less than mortified. But knowing Richard, that was his plan in the first place: embarrass the headmaster and conjure up some power play to show that *he* was in charge here, not the other way around.

A long, drawn-out breath left my chest just as the door swung open again and in walked Headmaster Ellison. My hands lifted from my eyes immediately, and I tried to force out a smile, which only turned to shock when I watched Isaiah walk in after his uncle.

"Isaiah," I blurted, startled that he was now standing in the office too.

His lips curved at the sight of me. "Already ditchin' me for tutoring?"

Shit. I was supposed to meet him outside of the locker room. I darted my eyes around the room, searching for a clock to see what time it was. I was never sure how much time had passed when Richard was involved. Anger and fear seemed to contort my senses, and everything was skewed.

"It's almost curfew," Isaiah said, coming a little closer to me. My heart skipped inside my chest at his nearness, and it surprised me. It surprised me that I could feel something other than that lingering fear and resentment that I was always left with after playing the dutiful niece. "Good thing we have the okay to tutor after curfew, yeah?"

The headmaster was standing behind his desk, opposite of Isaiah and me. He eyed us both cautiously before clearing his throat. The red tie around his neck was looser now than it had been when he grabbed me from outside a little while ago. "If anyone gives you trouble for being in the library after curfew, send them to me." His dark brow rose at Isaiah, like he was silently threatening him, but when he turned toward me, his expression softened. "Same time next week, yes?"

I stared at the headmaster from across his desk for a few moments, eyeing him subtly as the same familiarity that I'd felt on that first day tinged my senses. *Maybe I could trust him.*

I stilled. *No. Don't trust.*

"Yes, sir." I nodded and quickly turned to look at Isaiah because I was ready to get out of his office with Richard's voice lingering in the open air. Everything felt tarnished after he spoke. Once I locked onto Isaiah and got over that dip in my stomach that kept happening when he was near, I hesitated.

Trailing past the sharp curve of his cheek and straight jaw, I moved down his tight black tee and found his hands in fists. His posture told me that something was wrong. It was as if he was angry, which was confusing to me—much like earlier when he had leaned in and kissed my cheek before disappearing back down to the field. The more I was with Isaiah, the more I learned just how complex he was. Or maybe it was just that he threw off my senses. I felt so jumbled near him.

After glancing back at Isaiah's face to decipher what was going on, I saw his laser-like stare locked onto something on the headmaster's desk. But no sooner than I snapped my head down to the messy contents on top, Isaiah grabbed a hold of my hand, stealing my attention away and completely blinding me.

"Let's go, Teach." Isaiah pulled me behind him, his calloused hands—likely from holding that stick in his tight grip during lacrosse—brushed over my soft palm. I let him lead me like a blind fool because his hand in mine muted something that screamed *urgent* in the back of my head.

I glanced back once at the headmaster and watched in a daze as he picked up a file and shoved it in the top drawer of his desk before slumping down in his chair.

He was definitely upset about something, and I had a very strong feeling that it had to do with me. *Great.*

———

As soon as Isaiah and I were out of his uncle's office, I felt like I could breathe again. The hallway was a little brighter, and the long, narrowed corridor leading to the dining hall was bathed in a warm glow from the overhead chandeliers. The air was fresher, and soon, my senses were filled with the scent of delicious warm food that made my stomach roll from hunger. *My weekly phone call was done. I survived.*

Isaiah's hand was still in mine, but I didn't pull away or comment on it. I was silent as we walked, too captivated by everything else around me that seemed to mute the dark voice lingering in the background. "Is that why you don't like when I call you Good Girl?"

I paused, my feet stuck to the black-and-white floor

beneath my shoes like cement. My eyelashes fluttered with shock as I tore my hand from his. My head flung up, and all I saw were two icy eyes peering down at me. "Wh—what?" My heart drummed against my chest.

Panic set in when his lips set into a firm line. "Just answer the question."

"Were you listening to my phone call?" Embarrassment flooded my cheeks, and a small amount of horror seeped in. How dare he listen.

There was a small twitch of Isaiah's mouth that I zeroed in on, which sent a new batch of fire to my blood. "Just like you listened to me and my uncle the first day we met?"

My eyes shifted to the floor, suddenly feeling stupid, because he was right. I had eavesdropped on him first, so I guessed I kind of deserved that. But I was still annoyed, and just as I was trying to rationalize why it was okay for me to eavesdrop and not him, he interrupted me.

"I was listening in, yes, but regardless, your uncle wasn't exactly quiet on the other end of the phone. And surprisingly enough, you can hear very well through that thick door." I stayed silent, mulling over what I should say next. I was upset with myself that I didn't even think about the fact that the headmaster could hear the conversation on the other side of the door after he'd very abruptly stepped out. And I had no idea that Isaiah was even out there. I grasped at the conversation that I was trying my hardest to push away, replaying it in my head to figure out what I had said.

"Answer me," Isaiah pleaded. His voice had a sternness to it, and there was a tiny divot in between his brows.

"I thought we said *no questions asked*." I shifted in my shoes, crossing my arms over my chest. A few students staggered out of the dining hall, holding cans of soda, passing us by as slowly as possible. They looked at Isaiah and then to me, and I wasn't sure what we looked like to everyone else, but I assumed it looked as if we were sparring. Isaiah was staring down at me sternly, and I was peering up at him with one eyebrow raised, waiting for his response.

I heard a loud sigh escape him and maybe even the light sound of a growl as he spun around on his heel and stormed through the dining hall doors. Another group of students had quickly shot out of his way as he stalked into the large room with as much authority as Richard had in the courtroom, and then their attention went to me, likely wondering what I'd done to make the top Rebel of the school so angry.

I was wondering the same thing. Shouldn't I have been the angry one in this situation?

And why was there a small part of me that was feeling out of sorts, knowing that Isaiah was angry at the moment? Was he angry at me? Why was I even concerned that he was angry in the first place?

Stepping farther into the nearly empty dining hall, I watched as Isaiah moved like some sort of predator as he casually swiped food from the line, even as the workers were putting it away. He didn't even bother paying as he turned back around with his eyes dead set on me standing in the same position that he left me—arms crossed, one eyebrow raised.

His dark hair fell onto his forehead as he came closer, then he thrust a bag of chips into my hand and stormed past me, knowing I'd follow. Even if I didn't follow him, I'd see him in a few minutes anyway as we both headed to the library for tutoring, and not to mention, I was through being intimidated by people or letting their behavior affect mine. That wasn't the new Gemma. That was the old one that Richard had formed between his slimy fingers.

The halls were empty and dark as we walked down them, side by side, eating our separate bags of chips. The only sounds were the bags crinkling and our very subtle chewing.

My tongue was burning to yell at him or spew something angry, mainly because he had stormed off, acting as if I was the one who had just eavesdropped on his conversation and not the other way around, but as soon as we were in the desolate library and the door slammed shut behind us, something else entirely came out of my mouth, stunning me right there in the entryway.

"Yes." *Wait. What are you doing, Gemma?!*

Isaiah was a few steps ahead of me, his tall stance nothing but a dark shadow in the enormous room with tattered books lining the shelves. His back went still.

I belittled myself silently, irritated that I had answered his question that we both should have forgotten about, but it was like an invisible power had coaxed me into it. There was something heavy weighing on me from the very second he brought it up. Like he pushed away one of my many masks and saw beneath my stony glare that I was certain didn't intimidate him at all.

My voice broke in all the wrong spots before I cleared my throat and tried again. "Yes, that's why I didn't like it when you called me Good Girl. That's why it made me angry."

I saw a tremor rip up Isaiah's spine, and I swore he grew another three inches as I stared at his back. It only took him seconds to recover, but I knew that what I'd said had jolted him. He turned around quickly, the bag of chips still in his hand. "Then I won't call you that anymore."

"No!" I blurted, pushing myself farther into the library with desperation hot on my heels.

It wasn't hard to see his muscles tighten with the moonlight filtering through the far windows. "No?"

I swallowed, keeping a hold on him. Why couldn't I just stop talking? Why was I spilling the dirty truth all over the library floor as if I hadn't spent years hiding from it? "Don't stop calling me that."

The faintest of smiles touched his lips as the bag crinkled in his hand. "Okay..." He dragged the word out before rubbing his thumb over his bottom lip and then licking the salt off. "But why? It's apparent you don't like your uncle."

Understatement of the year. "I don't." I wrapped my hand tighter around my bag of chips, feeling incredibly vulnerable for saying that out loud. If Richard heard that confirmation come out of my mouth, I'd be chained up for weeks until I proved to him that it wasn't true. "But..." I looked away, almost suffocated with the words that wanted to come out.

A throat cleared from behind me, and I jumped so far I bumped into Isaiah. His free hand wrapped around my waist to steady me as I searched the dark library for whoever had made themselves known.

"What are you two doing in here?" The librarian, who I recognized from the other day, pushed her glasses up so she could see us better. "It's after curfew. The library is closed, hence the lights being off."

The older woman skittered her gaze past me and locked onto Isaiah. "Out after curfew again, Mr. Underwood. I wish I could say I was surprised." The cool disappointment was clear in her tone, and for some reason, that set a fine line of protection through me.

Stepping forward out of Isaiah's grasp, I plastered a soft smile onto my face. "Actually, I'm here to tutor Isaiah. Didn't the headmaster tell you?"

She eyed me cautiously. The whites of her eyes moved quickly as she scanned my face. "He did no such thing."

I peered back at Isaiah. I could tell she didn't believe me; there was a certain hitch to her voice along with a knowing glint in her eye. Knowing what? I wasn't exactly sure. She probably assumed I was one of the willing girls that Isaiah shoved into closets to mess around with. My face heated at the thought—more so because curiosity tickled the back of my brain again.

I slowly turned back around. "Well, the headmaster said that if anyone gave us trouble, to direct them to him. Isaiah is failing his classes, and I was asked by the SMC to tutor him in here after lacrosse to bring his grades up." I smiled sweetly, and it felt like I was falling into my past self whenever I was questioned by Richard when he thought I was lying about something. I could play this part well—so well that it felt like slipping into my own skin. "We can walk down to his office together, if you'd like. I don't mind at all. It'll give Isaiah a chance to gather his study materials anyway."

The woman looked at Isaiah and then back to me. The library keys dangled in her hands as she jostled the books in her arms. I could see the leeriness fade as she bounced her attention back and forth between us again. "That's okay, dear. I can check with him on my way out. Just make sure you two lock up when you're done."

I smiled once more. "Of course."

Before she turned around, she leveled Isaiah with another withering stare that only older ladies seemed to possess. I silently laughed, remembering Auntie giving that look a time or two. "Don't get crumbs in my library, Mr. Underwood. Or else you'll be doing Mr. Clark's job. Got it?"

Without even looking back, I could hear the cunningness in his voice. "Yes, ma'am. I'll lick them up if I need to."

The older woman's face flickered with shock before she let out an exasperated sigh and spun around. Her long dress swayed as she hurried to the door, and then she slammed it shut.

My free hand found my hip as I spun around. "Really?"

Isaiah's cheek lifted as he casually shrugged. "What?"

"You'll *lick them up* if you need to? Who even says that?"

Isaiah's smile grew wider, and my eyes went right to the

dimple in his cheek. I felt my own lips tingle with the need to smile but gritted my teeth together so I wouldn't. If there was one thing I'd already learned from Isaiah, it was that he didn't need any more encouragement.

"Her reaction was entertaining. Could you imagine what she'd do if I actually bent down and licked the floor?" He paused, looking thoughtful. "Do you think she'd be mad?"

I sighed. "I think I can see why the SMC is tired of you. And it has nothing to do with your grades."

His hand fell to his chest as if he were gripping his heart. "Ouch. Bring back the nice Gemma who just batted her eyelashes at the meanest old bat in this school and somehow got a smile in return." He chuckled. "I didn't even know Mrs. Groves could smile."

I rolled my eyes as I breezed past him, heading straight to one of the long tables. "It's called having respect." I knew everything there was about that tiny word. Richard made me memorize it, and I was pretty sure I could recite the Merriam-Webster definition in my sleep.

Isaiah's bag crinkled again, and I peered over my shoulder, watching as he tipped his head back and put it up to his mouth to eat the leftover chip crumbs. A wistful thought flew through me as I recalled seeing Tobias do that on the rare occasion that we were given an unhealthy snack as a child. A small bag of chips to us was a once-a-year treat.

Pushing the thought away, I shouted over my shoulder to Isaiah. "Better not get those on the floor."

The now-empty bag had vanished from his face as a devilish smirk appeared. The silvery moonlight hit the side of his chiseled jaw as he flashed me his white teeth. Then, he lifted his finger and popped it into his mouth, sucking it to remove the salt from the tip. My small, teasing smile instantly vanished as something forbiddingly hot fell to the bottom of my stomach. I jerked my head away and pulled out my chair, slinking into it as sweat coated my hairline.

I heard his shuffling feet before he appeared at the other side of the table. The chair creaked as he sat down, his empty bag of chips lying beside my half-full one. "You think I don't have respect for authority?" he asked as he leaned back onto the chair, tipping it back far enough that I just *had* to look at his face. "I told her I would clean up after myself."

A breath left my lips. "You made her uncomfortable."

He smirked. "I can't control others' reactions."

My brow creased as Isaiah pushed my bag of chips to me, nodding to them. I gingerly stuck my hand in the bag and pulled a chip out, not bothering to put it up to my lips. "But you can control your actions," I reiterated, pushing the chip back into the bag. "Actually, now that we're on the subject of *actions*...care to tell me what was up with earlier? Why did you kiss my cheek in front of everyone?"

And why did I like it?

Isaiah stilled, his chair balancing on only two legs. I glanced up at the small lamp that sat on the table between us, and my fingers itched to turn it on so I could see his face better. "I'll answer yours, if you answer mine."

I knew very well what he was referring to, and the last thing I wanted to do was talk about the phone call he'd overheard, so I deflected the topic as if it were my main reason on this earth. "I think we better get to studying. What do you need help with first?"

Isaiah's arms came down and rested on the glossy wood that separated us. I kept my eyes trained to the dancing shadows along his forearms that seemed to move every other second as his fingers drummed over the hard surface. "I thought you trusted me, Good Girl."

My eyes moved to his, and it drove me mad that I couldn't see the blue color. I suddenly found myself reaching over to the light in between us and clicking it on. "I already told you I don't trust anyone."

His head tilted, his thick black eyelashes falling once, then twice. "You trusted me earlier when I leaned in and kissed your cheek. Didn't you?"

I did. The muscles along my mouth tightened, and I was left speechless.

"So, tell me, Gemma. Why do you still want me to call you Good Girl? Now, after knowing that your uncle calls you that—which I am one hundred fucking percent certain isn't in an endearing way—I'm going to need an explanation."

The beating of my heart grew in speed as I stared up into his cool eyes mixed with uncertainty and something else I couldn't quite decipher. Every single part of me was screaming to abort this conversation and put him and his pleading face in his place, but there was a teeny-tiny stab in my chest that had me pausing. I didn't owe him an explanation. I knew that. So why was I considering it?

Could I trust him? Would it be so bad to trust someone here? The hollow part of me grew deeper as my heart continued to climb in speed. The thumping was hard—I could feel the beat in every corner of my body—until I just let go. I blurted out my answer, and it was like thunder cracking in the background. "Because every time you call me that, it cancels out each time he has called me that." I licked my dry lips as I shrugged. "Maybe if you say it enough, it'll erase them all."

Silence filled the library, and it was just as heavy as my vulnerability. There was no change in Isaiah's facial expression, no hitch of breath, nothing. Isaiah only stared at me. He stared at me so long that I began to grow uneasy, and I wanted to slash at the air to make the words disappear. But that was the thing with words. Once they were out, they were out. There were no take-backs.

Anger began to seep in at Isaiah's lack of response. I wasn't even sure what I wanted him to say, but I needed him to say *something*. Anything. Another few seconds passed, and I finally straightened my spine. "Was that enough trust for you?" I snapped, leveling my chin and glancing away. Shame settled in my bones, weighing me down to the chair as if I were permanently one with it now.

"I kissed your cheek earlier to protect you." His words cut through my anger for a second.

"What?" I asked, completely confused.

Isaiah repeated himself. "I kissed your cheek earlier to protect you."

"I heard what you said. I just don't...understand." My brows puckered for a second before I recovered. "Protect me from who?"

Isaiah pushed my chips toward me again. "Eat, Gemma. The dining hall is closed, and I've heard your stomach growl three times now."

I brushed the chips away, too eager to know his answer. "I answered you. Now you have to answer me."

The biggest, megawatt smile appeared on Isaiah's face, and the warm glow of lamplight shone on that stupid dimple again. "Oh, is that how this is gonna go, Good Girl? An answer for an answer?" His brow hitched. "That can lead to some very dangerous places."

I ignored his grin, sitting up taller in my seat, feeling slightly exasperated. "How is placing a kiss on my cheek going to protect me?"

"Why are you so afraid of your uncle?"

I placed my hands down on the table. "Why are you so dead set on not getting expelled?"

He leaned forward, our eyes leveling. "Why are you always scribbling in your journal?"

Anger brewed. "Why did you tell me to stay away from Bain?"

"Have you ever been kissed?"

A soft breath left my mouth as my eyes jolted down to Isaiah's lips. The traitorous pair that they were betrayed me right there on the spot. I thought for a hopeful moment that Isaiah didn't notice, but by the twitch of his upper lip, I knew that I'd been caught. *Isaiah: 1, Gemma: 0.*

"You haven't, have you?" His smile fell, and when I met his eyes, my cheeks flooded with heat. *And shame.* There was a whole lotta shame that came after the initial feeling of embarrassment. His jaw tightened at the edges as his chest filled with air. Once he let his breath out, I did the same. I hadn't even realized I was holding mine until I watched his chest expand. "Bain will try to use you to get to me. I kissed your cheek to show people that you were mine. I was making a point."

Why did his words sting so much? What? Did I want Isaiah to kiss my cheek for any other reason? No. That couldn't even be a possibility. I had enough to worry about. Isaiah was already close enough to becoming a casualty in Richard's games if he caught on to our agreement. If Isaiah and I somehow became more than what we were now, it would only seal his fate. No one was allowed to touch me, and I knew it killed Richard to know that there were people here who could see me—and possibly touch me. Even if they weren't looking at me in the way that he did.

You are mine. I held back a shudder as his voice filtered in, but it was quickly replaced with resentment and anger. I wasn't his. And I wasn't Isaiah's either.

My face felt tight. "I'm not yours." The words were like a slap in the face with how much anger stewed behind my lips. "And you think something as simple as kissing my cheek will keep people away?" I laughed bitterly. "People take what they want, Isaiah."

Isaiah cracked his knuckles before placing them back down onto the table. "It'll take much more than a simple brush of my lips to keep Bain away from you. But at least it's a start." Isaiah leaned back, clearly unphased by my temper-tantrum, and pulled his phone out of his pocket. "People will start talking, Gemma. And soon, there will be a lot of specu-lation about us. More eyes on you means Bain will have even less of a chance to mess with you."

I shifted my gaze away, slightly embarrassed that I had just lost my cool and a little annoyed that he wasn't even looking at me. My eyes squinted as I glanced at the library doors, swearing that I'd seen a shadow pass by, but that was likely my head messing with me because I suddenly felt exposed. "So..." I started as silence encased us. "You kissed my cheek so people would talk? And watch me?" My hands fell to my lap. "I'm not really a big fan of having eyes on me." *This was already off to a bad start.*

"I know." Isaiah finally glanced up at me from his phone. His expression was soft, but his voice held an undeniable amount of sternness to it. "But there are things you don't know, Gemma. There is a lot more riding on me staying at this school than I'd ever care to admit."

Silence pressed on us, as if we were stuck in that tiny linen closet again. "And there's a lot more riding on me getting my hands on a new ID than I'd ever care to admit."

Our eyes clashed together again, and I swore time had stopped. Everything had stopped existing except for the two of us. There was something heated about our conversation, like hot coals seconds from bursting back into flames. I felt the walls caving in, the room growing smaller.

But then, Isaiah's phone buzzed, and the moment was gone. The air conditioner kicked back on, and the papers on

Mrs. Groves' desk fluttered to life. I watched as Isaiah ran his hand through his dark hair, pushing it off his forehead to reveal two slashes of brows.

My chin jerked when he raised his phone in his hand. "Duty calls."

"What?" My voice was all breathy, and I quickly shook my head. "Wait. We're done for tonight? We didn't even study."

His lips curved. "I don't need a tutor, Gem."

Gem. "I thought you were failing your classes?"

Isaiah stood up, hovering over me. "I am. But it's not because I'm incapable of learning. I just don't do the assignments."

My mouth opened as I peered up at his tall stance. "Oh." I began to stand up, feeling somewhat bothered by the fact that Isaiah was pretty much just using me as a cover and that he didn't actually need my help studying. But then again, I was using him too, so I had no right.

Isaiah grabbed the chips off the table, and I stood back and watched as he swiped the crumbs back into the bags. His gaze shot to mine at the last second, and his brow hitched. "Should I lick it to be sure, or..."

My lips begged to curve upward, but I didn't allow myself to smile. I only sighed and shook my head, acting as if I were just as exasperated as Mrs. Groves was earlier, but I wasn't.

As soon as Isaiah flipped the lamp off, he came up behind me and opened the door, allowing me to step into the hallway. His arm brushed mine as he reached over and turned the lock, and even though I was wearing long sleeves, tingles still flew to my skin. My blood was humming as he walked in stride with me. The hallways were empty, the lights dimmed to a minimum. I peeked up once, only to see him staring straight ahead with his face completely free of anything going on inside his head.

Leveling my gaze with the hallway, I took even breaths,

willing my body to behave in the way that it always had before, but the truth was, I'd never been alone with a boy as much as I'd been alone with Isaiah since coming to St. Mary's. It seemed the more we were pushed together, the more silent exchanges we shared, and that only led to my body reacting in ways that scared me. It scared me because I had the strongest urge to step in front of him and beg him to *see* me. To put his eyes on me and learn of everything that lurked inside.

That was the total opposite of who I was. I didn't want anyone to look at me. I didn't want anyone to see what was on the inside, because it was dark there. It was really, really dark. But still, Isaiah Underwood and his hot and sultry looks and random dimpled grins were becoming more and more alluring to me. It was the way that he could somehow coax me into speaking my mind, instead of hiding behind shy smiles and hidden thoughts, that was enticing. In a way, Isaiah *was* seeing me, and that was because I wasn't holding much back when it came to him, and I had no idea why.

Once we'd rounded the girls' hallway, he stopped, stepping in front of me. His dark hair swayed down on his forehead again, and I wanted to push it away just so I could see him better. "I need your phone number."

I stumbled over my words even though I'd just spent the last several seconds practicing leveled breathing. "Wh —what?"

His lips moved slowly. "I want your phone number, Gemma."

"Why?" I asked, still very aware that he was only a few inches in front of me. If I breathed too deeply, I bet our chests would brush.

His brow furrowed, another stray piece of dark hair tumbling down. "Because I'm not done with you, but I have to go do something." He slowly raised his hand and brushed his hair back, showing off his clear skin.

I rocked back on the heels of my shoes, feeling the pressure intensify in my chest. "I can't give you my number."

His head slanted. "What do you mean you can't?"

I blew out a breath, placing my hands into the back pockets of my black jeans. "My uncle will likely pull my phone records. He gave me the phone before I got here, and I haven't touched it." I felt stupid for asking my next question, but I did it anyway. "Can you see who people call? Or text? He can look that up, right?"

Isaiah looked to the tall ceiling above our heads and sighed. "Yes." I heard the grinding of his teeth before he shook his head. "Okay, don't worry. I'll figure something out." His phone vibrated again. He didn't even bother looking at it. "Don't come back out of your room tonight. Okay?"

My brow furrowed as I glanced around the dark hall. "Okay..." I wasn't sure why he said that, but either way, I wouldn't be leaving my room.

Isaiah's brows crinkled for a fleeting second before he recovered. "And if anyone asks, we were tutoring together until ten, okay?"

"Until ten?"

He nodded sternly, his jaw hardened to stone. "I have to go. Go back to your room."

On top of Isaiah's pushy words, I detected a very small amount of pleading, like there was caution lingering there. I was curious, but not curious enough to ask. Instead, I nodded and then began walking past him before his arm caught me around the waist, and he pulled me backward. His breath moved over my ear, and my entire body heated with excitement. "If I'm ever not around and something happens, you can trust Cade, Brantley, and Shiner. Okay? Find them if you need something."

I swallowed past the hot knot in my throat. "Isaiah, I already told you I don't trust anyone."

His chuckle hit me in all the right spots. "You trust me, Good Girl. Even if you want to pretend that you don't." His arm slowly dropped from my waist, and I almost pulled it back over before I realized that would have been completely insane. "I'll see you tomorrow."

He began walking in the opposite direction, leaving me standing there with my skin warm and my heart moving in triple speed.

My blood didn't stop rushing until I got to my room and slammed the door shut behind me, not even remembering that Sloane would be on the other side. But that was what Isaiah did to me. Being around him made me see nothing *but* him. He had some crazy, uncontrollable power over me that shunned everything away except his icy eyes, which sent me into overdrive. It was terrifying.

Sloane gasped as I stepped inside our room, pausing right in the middle of it with her black hair in a messy topknot and huge pink, fuzzy slippers that looked like bunnies below her legs.

"What on earth are on your feet?" I asked, halting as I locked onto the two fuzzy creatures.

"Where have you been?!" She rushed over to me, the bunnies' heads bobbing back and forth. "Isaiah said he was going to look for you, and I know you had tutoring, but I've been worried. The headmaster ripped you away, and I'm not going to lie, you looked spooked." Sloane placed her hands on my shoulders. She looked over my body quickly, her eyes running over my face and clothes. "I do not trust those Rebels for even a second. I don't know what Isaiah is playing at, but are you really tutoring him? He isn't stupid. I've seen his SAT scores. Is something else going on, because I have never in my life seen him kiss a girl's cheek like that. It was innocent and tender, and those are two adjectives that I would never use to describe Isaiah Underwood. When he has his eyes on someone for claiming, he ravishes their face greedily before the lights even go out." She glanced away, like she was reminiscing about something. "Not that anyone complains. It's just...he doesn't do the whole *sweet* thing."

"Um," I started, glancing at her big, round eyes. "Yeah, we are just tutoring." I knew I couldn't tell Sloane about our secret conversations in the bleakness of night, tucked away in dark closets or dusty classrooms. Especially because those conversations seemed to circle my past and hidden secrets.

Sloane dragged me over to my bed and pushed me to sit. "Then why did he kiss your cheek?" She then ran the four feet to her bed and hopped up on top, scooting all the way to the wall. "This is so unlike him. Usually, he's a *wham-bam-thank-you-ma'am* type of guy. Not the type that would randomly kiss someone's cheek and bat those eyes, tutor or not." She thought for a moment, looking distrusting. "What is he playing at?"

Unlacing my shoes, I asked, "What does that mean? Wham-bam-thank-you-ma'am?"

Sloane placed her hand to her lips, muffling her next sentence. "You are more innocent than I thought." Her hand dropped. "I have so much to teach you."

Just as Sloane was about to continue on with her rambling, there was a faint knock on the door. Both of our heads swung in that direction. Sloane mused, "Expecting someone?"

I shook my head, the teeniest amount of anxiety creeping over my shoulder. Would I ever not be afraid that he was coming for me? "Who would I be expecting?"

Sloane slowly climbed off her bed and walked over to the door. A weird sense of urgency flew through me and seemed to push me off my bed. What if it wasn't Richard, but it was Bain? Isaiah's words echoed through my head, remembering that he was silently begging for me to stay in my room for the rest of my night. He'd said that duty called, which ended our "tutoring session" much quicker than I had anticipated. Did Bain know Isaiah had gone somewhere and he was coming to mess with me?

"Wait," I called out as I followed Sloane. "Let me get it."

Sloane's face dropped, her pink lip jutting out, but she didn't protest. Instead, she stepped out of the way, the fuzzy bunnies flopping on her feet. My heart thudded against my ribcage as I slowly opened the door and peeked down the hall. It was hard to see with the flicking sconces, but a familiar, broad-shouldered lean body was walking down the hallway slowly, as if he didn't have a care in the world.

Isaiah?

Sloane bent down and grabbed something before pulling me back and quietly shutting the door, hardly making the chain on the front rattle at all. A note was crumpled in her hand along with a familiar bag of chips. "I think this is for you." She smiled as she handed the note to me.

With a less-than-stable hand, I opened the piece of paper that had my name written on the top in huge lettering.

Don't think I forgot about you not eating, Good Girl. Eat your chips. I need my tutor well-fed.

A surge of something warm rolled through me, like the sun finally gracing the skies again after weeks of thunderous storms. I fought to keep my heart relaxed and smile at bay, but I failed miserably at both—something Sloane most definitely managed to point out.

CHAPTER TWENTY-NINE

ISAIAH

I EYED Cade's sleeping form on his bed through the darkness of our room, stepped over the PlayStation controller that had fallen from his hand sometime in the night, and headed for the door. I snagged my tie off the back of my chair, whipped it on over my damp hair, and exited my room as quietly as possible.

I'd never cared in the past if I had woken Cade up—or the rest of the hall, for that matter—but it was way before the moon disappeared and gave way to the sun, and also, I didn't want anyone to know what I was up to.

My Vans shuffled along the red-carpeted floor as I pulled out my phone and reread the texts between me and my little brother. He was fine but had mentioned spending a lot of his time with Mary, our lifelong nanny who could take someone down with a frying pan if need be. She was a stocky woman with olive-colored skin and eyes like the sea. Her crazy, curly hair had begun to gray the last time I saw her, and wrinkles now lined her round cheeks, but she was still the same woman who had stepped in after Mom's *accident,* and she'd been there for me and Jack ever since.

I trusted Jack with our nanny, but I didn't trust him with our parents. *Such a healthy, happy family we had.*

Once I stepped onto the landing, I eyed the girls' hallway briefly before Gemma's face had flashed behind my eyes. Not that it was the first time I'd thought of her this morning. I thought of her from the moment my alarm sounded, drifting me out of my sleepy fog. I'd wondered briefly if I had dreamt of her too, because her vivid jade eyes and pouty mouth were the first two things in my head this morning.

Or it could have had something to do with the fact that I was about to go snooping in my uncle's office for that file titled "Gemma Richardson" that he not so subtly shoved into the top drawer of his desk yesterday.

If my uncle were smart, he'd guard that file with his life. Because one way or another, I was getting back into his office, and I was reading all there was to know about Gemma and her secretive life, along with her extremely suspicious uncle. *She called him Daddy.* What the fuck was up with that?

A growl sat deep in my throat as a strangely possessive feeling came over me, causing my shoulders to tense and my jaw to clench. I wasn't sure why I felt so agitated over Gemma and her life that she obviously wanted to keep private. I hardly knew her, although it didn't feel that way when we were alone. I was eager to touch her and be close to her, but I had no right to feel protective. Maybe it was because her uncle reminded me so much of my father. I wanted to destroy all the Carlisle Underwoods in the world— not just my own flesh and blood. That was another reason why I despised Bain so much and the way he looked at her. She was a toy to him. A toy he wanted to break just because I'd touched it first.

Stepping down off the last step, my phone vibrated in my

pocket. I reached in my black pants and read the latest blog post from Mary's Murmurs. After Gemma seemed so put off by the whole blog post and being featured on it, I'd set up alerts for new posts. Her uncle would likely never learn of Mary's Murmurs, but after last week's scandal, I'd made a decision to become informed of all things in this school—even the insignificant gossip that filled the halls.

The top headline was bolded, like always, and my name was the first to be seen.

BAD-BOY REBEL, ISAIAH UNDERWOOD, TO BE SNAGGED BY OUR NEWEST STUDENT, GEMMA RICHARDSON.

RUMOR HAS it that Gemma is tutoring Isaiah in the late evenings, but is that all that's going on? Is Gemma Richardson the beauty to our beast? Beautiful, quiet, shy, and seemingly naive to all the bad in the world. Is she Isaiah's ticket to a clean slate? Can she help him with his grades...and more? Or is he her ticket to life on the wild side? Only time will tell.

I CHUCKLED UNDER MY BREATH, putting my phone back in my pocket. They had one thing right: Gemma was beautiful. Everything about her was beautiful. Her eyes, her skin, the curve of her cheek, the soft flesh of her waist as my arm snagged around her last night. Gemma was the full package, guarded or not. Was she my type? No. But that didn't seem to deter me from thinking about her twenty-four-seven, now did it?

When I reached my uncle's office, I placed my ear to the

door and listened. Oftentimes, my uncle would fall asleep at his desk and wake the next day, looking disheveled and confused until he was able to get his hands on some of the coffee in the dining hall, so I needed to be certain he wasn't trapped behind his desk from the night before.

Silence filled the other side, but the uncertainty was still there as I turned the knob slowly, noting that it was unlocked. I pulled the door open, glancing inside with hesitation.

My uncle *was* in his office. But he wasn't asleep. Instead, he was staring directly at me.

"What are you doing?" he asked, raising a wary eyebrow in my direction. He was standing beside his desk, holding a paper in his hand with a cup of coffee in the other. *Fuck, he's already up and has had his coffee.*

I only paused for a second. "Oh, hello, Uncle." There was a light and airy notch to my tone, completely bypassing the fact that I had just walked into the room, looking suspect as fuck.

His eyebrow didn't lower as he continued to stare at me.

I walked in a little farther, my tie still loose around my neck. A fire was burning in his wood-burning fireplace on the other side of the room, the flames licking with intensity as I shut the door behind me.

"Trying to break into my office?" My uncle's eyebrow finally fell, but the wary expression only worsened.

I shrugged. "No. Just wanted to catch up. How ya been?"

"Isaiah, what do you want?" He took a sip of his coffee before sighing.

I sat down in the seat at the foot of his desk, the one that I was sure Gemma had sat in the night before. "I came to check out that file you stashed away last night."

My uncle's eyes flicked up over the brim of his coffee mug.

The cup hid his mouth, but I heard the words plain as day. "I knew you'd be back."

I leaned back in the leather chair, propping my feet up onto his desk. "You did, did you?"

Placing the mug down, he walked over to the fireplace and put his back to me. His hands were clasped behind him, and a dense silence filled the room. The popping of embers was the only sound to break the quiet every few seconds.

I was the first to speak as I lowered my feet to the ground and walked to stand beside him. "What do you know about her?"

His chest inhaled and stayed like that for so long I turned my head and focused on the fire. Whatever it was that he knew, he was struggling with it. That part was clear. What was also clear was that I was eager to know everything. If it were anyone else, I wouldn't care. I wouldn't have come back here early this morning to see what the file had said. It would have left my head the second my uncle had shoved the file into his desk.

Gemma was quite literally digging herself underneath my skin, and she didn't even know it. I had no reason to want to know more about her, but I did. I desperately did, and I couldn't blame that on wanting to protect her from Bain. This had nothing to do with him at the moment.

Finally, my uncle exhaled, the fire fanning underneath his heavy breath. "I do not trust her uncle. The things he has told me don't match up to her file. She'd apparently been homeschooled until two months ago, then sent to a nearby prep school, and then he abruptly ripped her away from it and called me to send her here."

"And what did he say when he called you?" I waited a beat. "*Why* did he call you?"

I slowly turned and fixed my attention on the side of my uncle's profile. He stared into the fire as if it were challenging him to look away, which he wouldn't because, deep down, he was an Underwood, even if he didn't claim the name, and Underwoods never backed down from a fight. "He's, uh... I owed him a favor. He asked me to take in his niece because she was a troublemaker."

I laughed without hesitation. "A troublemaker?"

He scoffed. "Yeah. And it's obvious that it's not true."

We stood in silence for a few more minutes before he turned his head to mine, and I did the same to him. We locked eyes, held each other there for too long before he said, "He's hiding something."

I nodded once. "So is she."

"She's fragile and scared."

"Scared? Yes. Fragile? Debatable." I thought back to her snarky little attitude the first couple of times we'd talked. She may have been shy at times, and she blushed so much it was actually cute, and she was definitely afraid of her uncle, but she had a fighting streak in her. She wasn't as breakable as my uncle thought.

My uncle sighed again before walking back over to his desk and slumping down behind it. "She reminds me of someone I used to know." He looked back at the fire instead of at me, and it was like he wasn't fully there. Like he was revisiting the past as the orange and red flames coursed with life. "She was a fighter by nature, but she was sweet, too. Kind."

More silence passed between us, and I finally went back and sat in the seat I was in before. I was sure the sun was beginning to rise, and I was eager to get to the dining hall to not only see Gemma, but to catch sight of Bain too. He'd disappeared last night when he'd snuck out during my tutoring session with Gemma. That was why things had been cut short, and it infuriated me that I'd lost track of him. I never did that. The only good thing was that I'd made it back to my room without being caught by the duty teacher.

"Have you talked to your father?"

I shifted uncomfortably at the change in the conversation. "No. I did talk to Jack, though. Mom must be feeling down lately. He said he's been spending a lot of time with Mary."

"That's probably a good thing."

My mouth stayed closed, but it was the truth. Mary was a sense of normal, and normal was what Jack needed.

"Gemma needs a phone."

My uncle's head fell to the side as his mouth slanted. "I can't give her a phone. How would I explain that if anyone found out?"

I shrugged. "How do you explain giving her a laptop, blankets, and those extra uniforms?"

His eyes narrowed. "How did you know I did that?"

"Uncle Tate"—I crossed my arms over my chest—"you know I have my ways."

He rolled his eyes and rubbed his hand over the scruff on his chin. Then, he pulled his bottom drawer out and scooped up something before dropping it on his desk. Several phones clinked together from his arms. "Take your pick. It'll only work on the Wi-Fi, so pick one that is adaptable to your phone for messaging."

"Thanks," I muttered, picking up a phone that was identical to mine. I assumed they were confiscated in the past when phones were banned, or maybe students had accidentally left them behind and didn't want to come back here for even a second to grab it. I didn't really care. All I cared about was Gemma having a phone. Not only so I could talk to her when I felt like it, instead of waiting for her to get on her computer to chat, but also because Bain was a troublesome thought in the back of my head when it came to her.

Gemma needed a way to call me quickly if he decided to corner her again, which I knew he would. Bain was a lot of things, but stupid wasn't one of them. He would wait until I wasn't near to do so.

"Keep her close, Isaiah." I shook myself from the thoughts and regained focus on my uncle as determination covered his features like a steel mask. "I have an inkling that something much bigger than what we think is going on with Judge Stallard."

"What do you mean?" I asked, eyeing the clock. Breakfast started in five minutes.

He shook out his unkempt hair. "He doesn't have any siblings."

"Who doesn't?"

"Her uncle, Judge Stallard. He said Gemma is his niece, but he doesn't have a sister or brother. Nor does he have a wife—or anyone in the family with the Richardson surname." He looked around his office at nothing in particular. "I've looked into it. I don't think Gemma is related to him—which makes me wonder where she came from."

I let out a breath as I stood and placed Gemma's new phone in my pocket. "Well, that's... interesting...and, quite frankly, not comforting in the fucking least."

The things going through my head were dark and twisted, which I knew were a direct result of how I grew up. I wasn't a stranger to gruesome upbringings and traumatic pasts, but it didn't sit well with me to think those things about Gemma.

"I suspect abuse."

My heart stopped, and my back went rigid.

"So, keep her close, Isaiah. We do not want a repeat of Journey." My uncle was remembering exactly what I was. I looked down at my hands hanging down by my sides, the veins pumping some seriously hot blood throughout. I still felt Journey's limp body in my arms as I handed her off to Cade.

"I've got it under control," I said before stalking out of his office and shutting the door behind me. My eyes clenched tightly as I ran a hand through my hair, tugging on the ends slightly to get myself to clear my head. A few heavy breaths left my tight chest, and just like that, I was fine.

For once, I was thankful for all the fucked-up shit I'd seen as a child. At least now I had the capability and threshold to deal with traumatic shit and push it away until it disappeared altogether.

Did that make me fucked up?

Probably.

But hey, we were all a little fucked up at St. Mary's.

CHAPTER THIRTY

GEMMA

MY FINGERS ACHED the next morning, and up until just a few moments ago, charcoal had covered every inch of my hands. Now they were red and raw from scrubbing them in the sink so no one would suspect that I was in here instead of in my room, tucked away underneath the comfy blankets that were given to me by the headmaster.

After Isaiah and I had parted ways last night, and Sloane had finally drifted to sleep after drilling me about Isaiah and our tutoring session, I couldn't sleep. Not a single freaking wink. Which wasn't at all unusual, but since arriving at St. Mary's over two weeks ago, I had slept better than I had in months. Ever since Tobias was sent away, my dreams had been more potent than normal, and they occurred more and more as I aged. They felt more real than reality, at times. It was terrifying, and every time I closed my eyes last night, all I could hear was Richard's voice lingering in the back of my head. His familiar sickening breath of pleasure that floated through the phone after I'd given in and called him his favorite little pet name caused my stomach to twist with unease, and I knew the only way to untwist it was to get it out.

I needed to spill everything onto the canvas—my outlet.

So, at around five in the morning, I climbed out of bed, tiptoed over to the bathroom, and hurriedly got ready for the day. A quick shower, moisturizer, a little bit of lip gloss (just to spite Auntie), my uniform, and I was out the door and creeping along the dark hallway with only the flickering sconces as my audience. Nerves pushed at my belly with each corner that I turned, wondering if it was okay to be out of bed that early in the morning, especially given Isaiah's warning. But the sun was going to peek over the tall, lush trees any minute, so I kept going. And I had to admit, breaking the rules—even by a few minutes—felt good. Dangerously good.

The very second I stepped in the empty art room, I breathed in a sigh of relief. It only took me minutes to gather my supplies and get ready. I pulled my damp hair into one long braid, freeing any stray pieces from my face, and slipped my blazer off my shoulders. I draped it over a stool, my lips twitching when I saw that I'd placed it on Isaiah's stool that he sat on during class. Next, I took my white blouse off in case I got charcoal on it, because I knew I would. I was only in my knee-high socks, maroon plaid skirt, and a tight, white tank top, which sent a chill over my skin.

But then, I got to work.

Time flew by, and before I knew it, the hallway lights were turned on, and the clock showed that I had been working for nearly two hours. Breakfast was soon, and I didn't want to make Sloane worry, so I rushed over and washed the charcoal off my skin before standing in front of the canvas with my raw hands. I scanned the creation that I had no recollection of even creating. Sketching had always been a release for me. A way to work through my secrets without revealing a single thing. My head was in a different space. *I* was in a different space.

I was there, reliving whatever horrendous memory that wanted to resurface, and in a way, it was therapeutic. It was a way for me to take control of the situation and then toss it right the hell out of my head.

But it never really left.

A shaky breath fell from my lips as I looked at the smudged charcoal. It was mostly the color of ash, but some parts were darker than others. It was a messy, rushed sketch, but that was exactly why I liked it. In the middle of the canvas, it was me—half of my face, at least. I trailed down the sharp black curve of my button-like nose and the shadows around my right eye. The arch of my high cheekbone was encased with long stray hairs, and my lips were split, like I was gasping for air. Then, on the other side of the canvas, where the rest of my face should have been, were the words *Good girls don't break rules,* over and over again, getting messier and even more smudged as they trailed down the entire length of the paper. The words blended with my face, and something in my chest cracked. Animosity and the slow burn of anguish tore through my soul as I quickly spun, taking my eyes off the shattered girl that I'd drawn.

The sudden urge to whip back around and tear it into pieces consumed me as a scream clawed at my throat. I was fighting like hell to make the torturous memory disappear. I even glanced down at my hand to see if the blisters were still there from the last time he made me write the phrase over and over again until my hand had bled, but no. The only thing I saw were the scars that circled the diameter of both wrists. The shiny skin that was lighter than the rest of my golden flesh.

Counting backward from ten, I stared at the ceiling, calming myself. Movement outside the classroom door was beginning to catch my eye, and I knew I needed to get a move on. Forcing the sickly feeling of the past from my mind, I hurriedly ran over to Isaiah's stool and grabbed my blouse and blazer. I pulled my shirt up and over my head, not once looking at the mirrored, charcoaled version of me. I knew I couldn't leave the canvas sitting out in the open like that, and Mrs. Fitz and I had never discussed what I should do with my projects if I were to use the art room like she and the headmaster had suggested, so I did what any sane person would do. I unclipped it from the easel and ran over to the supply closet—the one that Isaiah had pulled me into on that first day—and hung my work in the very back, near the broom that looked as if it hadn't been used in years. The ends of it were frayed, and cobwebs hung off the wooden stick as dust danced around me. *Perfect.*

It was vital for me to keep these sketches a secret, and I was too proud of the actual work to throw them away. I made the mistake of letting someone else see them once, and that bit me in the ass.

Just as I shut the supply closet door, a deep voice floated around me, causing me to freeze.

"I was wondering if I'd find you here." Isaiah's tone was light and airy, and it was a welcomed sound from the angry and panicked beating of my own heart.

"Isaiah," I started, then I felt stupid because I seemed to always address him by his name when he popped up out of nowhere. It was like my brain and mouth were no longer connected when he was within sight. Clearing my throat and hoping that my cheeks didn't give away my embarrassment, I asked, "What are you doing here?"

He leaned back onto the table that he usually sat at, his feet somehow still touching the floor as his butt rested along the edge. He was utterly beautiful sitting there, and my fingers twitched to sketch him instead of the nasty memories that kept resurfacing. There was a shadow under his jawline, and the maroon blazer he wore was snug around his biceps and cut off just below his waist, showing his slim hips and black pants that led to his shoes.

Yes, Isaiah was definitely the definition of dark and dangerous.

Until he smiled.

Which he was currently doing at the moment.

Wait. Did I miss something?

"Did you say something?" I asked, quickly darting my attention away.

He hummed out a laugh and stood up from the desk. His strides were slow and easy as he walked toward me, causing my heart to jump up to my throat. *What was he doing?* Just as the panicked thoughts began to consume me, his finger graced the bottom of my chin, and he tipped my head backward. My braid swung behind my shoulder, and I watched in awe as he brought his other hand to his mouth. A flush started to creep up my neck as his tongue darted out from behind his soft lips to lick his thumb. I felt the slick pad of his finger swipe over my cheekbone, just below my left eye, and I almost fainted.

I was hot. Burning up. I was completely captivated by whatever was forcing me to stay in his tight grasp. Something throbbed within, and desire annihilated any reminder of the inexperience I had. The entire room was festering with flames. I wanted to kiss him. *Did I really want that?* I did. I knew I did. I wanted to know what it felt like to be kissed by *him.*

"You had something black on your face," he said, still keeping his hand on my chin.

"Charcoal." The single word had cracked around the edges like a firework.

He nodded once, our breath mingling together as we stared at one another. His eyes held something wild and tempting, and I really, really wanted to chase after it.

"What are you doing to me?" His question was nothing more than a raspy whisper as his hand left my chin, and he finally stepped away, allowing me to breathe again. His fingers ran through his dark hair, ruffling it a bit, and I just stood there, completely and utterly dumbfounded. Did he mean to say that out loud?

My lips were still parted as Isaiah crossed his arms over his chest and lowered his gaze. "I thought I told you to stay in your room."

Blinking myself back to reality, I pulled down my blazer sleeves and leveled my chin, forcing out a lie. "I waited until curfew was over."

His angry slash of an eyebrow hitched. "You've been in here for hours, which means you left your room before the sun even came up."

I pulled back. "How—"

Isaiah shot up from the desk he was leaning against and crept toward me. "Your hair is messy," he said, reaching out and pushing a piece of brown hair away from my face. "You had charcoal on your cheek." His lip twitched, and I couldn't seem to tear my eyes away as he crowded me again. "And I went to your room to grab you this morning, and Sloane couldn't seem to find you." He sighed before flinging his blue eyes to mine. "Leave a note next time."

My heart hiccupped at what sounded like panic in his voice. "Why did you come to my room?"

There was a beat of silence that lasted a second longer than I wanted. Isaiah's thick lashes lowered as he glanced away. "You shouldn't be in the halls before curfew is up, Gemma. Not alone, anyway."

"But why?" Isaiah's jaw was bracketed with tension. "Does it have something to do with whatever you had to do last night? Does it have something to do with me covering for you?" I couldn't seem to stop the questions from spilling out.

His growl was low, but I heard it. "How long have you been in here? Please tell me it hasn't been all night."

A sarcastic noise left my mouth as I threw his words back at him from the night before. "I'll answer yours, if you answer mine."

My lips curved at the sight of his narrowed eyes and dimpled cheek. "My uncle does not give you enough credit." Then, my slight smile fell. I swore he was talking in riddles. What did that even mean? "Tell me, Good Girl. Are you this snarky with everyone? Or just me?"

The tiniest laugh left my lips. "Just you."

He grunted with a half-smile before grabbing onto my hand and pulling me toward the classroom door. Butterflies coated my belly that I hastily pushed aside, pretending they weren't there. The second we were in the hallway, he pulled his hand away but glanced down at me. "For some reason, I feel privileged."

"Privileged?" I asked, glancing back up at him.

He nodded, looking straight ahead as we walked side by side. "I kind of love that you dish it back out to me and no one else."

I fought a laugh. "Why would you love that?"

His dimple reappeared just before I saw Cade, Brantley, and Shiner walking toward us from the dining hall. The bell rang over our heads, and I cursed myself for getting so caught up in my sketch—and let's be honest here, I was caught up in Isaiah licking that freaking charcoal off my face too—that I had missed breakfast altogether. Sloane was probably busting at the seams to ask me where I had gone so early this morning.

Just before the rest of the Rebels appeared in front of us, Isaiah bent down and whispered into my ear. "I love it because it means you trust me enough to be yourself, and even though I'm probably unworthy of a girl like you trusting someone like me, I'll take it anyway."

He winked as he pulled back and then began walking in stride with the Rebels, who'd all dipped their chin at me like they were approving something, and I felt the pride swell. I liked the fact that Isaiah said he felt unworthy of me, and I liked that his friends seemed to approve of me, too. I was beginning to like a lot of things that I shouldn't, and as the hallway began flooding with students from breakfast, all trying to get to their first class, I was left standing there, feeling my inability to trust someone disappear right into thin air.

Deep down, I knew I needed to control the butterflies that had been dormant in my belly for so long. I knew that Isaiah's intentions were good, and he probably didn't even realize that the simplest of touches made me burn on the inside. He wasn't really flirting with me or insinuating that he wanted anything from me other than what I was already giving him. He said it yesterday: he had kissed my cheek in front of everyone to prove a point. But still. My thoughts were muddled when we were brought together. I wasn't living in fear, or hiding from the past, or even contemplating my next move. Instead, I was secretly watching out for his dimple to reappear or waiting for that scorching heat to wash over me when he'd glance down to my mouth, even as fleeting as the look was.

Somehow, the bad boy of St. Mary's, who I'd found to be egotistical right off the bat, put a pause on my dark and troubled thoughts, and I didn't realize it until now, but that was exactly what I was starved for. I was ravenous for Isaiah Underwood and for the way he silenced all the shit in my head, and I found myself looking forward to seeing him again later, even if I knew there would eventually come a time where I wouldn't see him ever again.

CHAPTER THIRTY-ONE

GEMMA

WALKING INTO THE LIBRARY EARLIER, I had felt a little pep in my step. I'd been like this all day. My cheeks were twitching to smile for no reason at all other than the fact that I was beginning to feel ease settle over me with the hint of freedom chasing after my heels.

I wasn't sure if it was because I'd sketched this morning, or maybe it was because I was able to sit down in the dining hall with people my age who really weren't all that different from me—even given my upbringing—and eat lunch with them. Or maybe I was feeling elated because I'd gotten the highest grade on my English 4 test—thank you, Auntie, for making me read *Jane Eyre* in one single sitting last year. Or maybe it was because I was truly feeling at ease without two dark and beady eyes staring at me from across the dinner table each night just hoping I'd mess up so he could fulfill his sick pleasures and punish me.

"What's all this?"

My body hummed at the smooth voice coming from

behind me. Spinning around with my uniformed skirt still on, I raised my brow at Isaiah, all fresh and clean from his shower after lacrosse. *He smelled so good.*

"This," I answered, flipping back around to hopefully hide my heated cheeks, "is called tutoring, Isaiah. How will you explain the pair of us just sitting here if someone walks in? We need study materials. We have to actually act like we're tutoring, right? Even if you say you don't need it."

I didn't give him a chance to answer as I sat down in the same seat I used last night, moving a piece of paper off my laptop.

Isaiah mumbled something under his breath as he pulled his seat out and slumped down, looking all relaxed. His long legs were sprawled out in front of him, his feet hitting the tips of my shoes, making my toes tingle.

"What was that?" I asked, opening my laptop to distract the tingling in my legs. The light of the screen was so bright in the dimly lit library that I had to close my eyes. The librarian had shut most of the lights off before leaving me alone in the expansive room with as much life and history that one person could hold lining the deep shelves.

"I said I guess I should do my homework since my grades really are shitty."

I smiled. "Killing two birds with one stone. Who knew you were smart under all that no-cares-given attitude?"

Isaiah chuckled, pulling something out of his pocket. "I may act like I don't have a care in the world, but that's not true."

I glanced up to his face, and we caught each other. Deep down, I knew there was much more to people than met the eye. More than anyone, I knew such a thing. Whatever was on the outside was most definitely more potent on the inside. It was obvious that Isaiah was troubled, as was I. Although, I tried to hide it as best as I could.

Isaiah's black lashes swooped down to whatever was in his hand, and I followed his line of sight. "If I didn't care about anything, then I wouldn't have gone through the trouble of getting you this." He pushed something black and rectangular in shape across the table, and my brows furrowed. I moved my laptop to the side with the search engine still open and tucked loose pieces of hair behind my ear.

"What's this?"

"A phone."

My eyes rolled of their own accord. "I know I'm a little backward, Isaiah, but I'm aware that this is a phone. I'm just wondering why you're handing it to me."

His hand fell to mine as he wrapped his fingers around my wrist. My eyes jolted to the skin-on-skin contact, and everything in my body seized. It wasn't because he was touching me, although that made me feel warm, but it was more so because of what part of me he was gripping onto. If he saw my wrists...

"Because you need a way to get a hold of me."

I swallowed back a tightness in my throat as I looked up at him once again. His hand was still wrapped around my wrist, and the longer it stayed there, the more my heart thudded. "And maybe I want a way to talk to you other than the lame student chat."

I said nothing as I stared at his face. I didn't know what to say. My body was frazzled for many reasons.

Isaiah's palm finally left my wrist, and I jerked it back, putting it in my lap. He didn't seem to notice the dip in my mood.

"The phone only works on Wi-Fi, but you can still text me and use the Internet. I put my number in there, along with the rest of the Rebels', and added a few apps I thought you might like."

My lashes fluttered against my cheek a few times before I

regained the ability to speak. "How did you even get this?" I turned the device in my hands a few times, inspecting it. This was nothing like the phone Richard had given me. It did look a lot like Sloane's and Mercedes', though.

He shrugged, leaning his arm on the chair beside him, looking nothing less than smug. "I have my ways. I just needed peace of mind that you had a way to call me if..."

"If what?"

"If Bain said something...or cornered you again." He glanced away. "He won't do it if I'm close by."

My pulse began to drum. "He's been pretty silent since the other day." With every breath I took, it seemed my heart pounded twice as fast. I hadn't forgotten about Bain or what he'd said to me. But he hadn't said anything since. In fact, I'd hardly seen him at all. It seemed our schedules didn't align, and I was thankful for that, but he was still a quiet thought lingering in the back of my head. He was nestled up right beside my dearest Uncle Richard.

Isaiah's gaze heated, his eyes appearing like shards of glass. "Never trust a snake that's silent, Gemma. Bain may be quiet, but I can assure you he is still just as deadly." The muscles along Isaiah's temple flickered. "Bain and I have history, even if he doesn't exactly know how deep that history runs yet. He has it out for me and would like nothing more than to have power over me. He sees you as a bargaining chip or a way to get back at me, because I've given you attention, and not to mention, you're one of the sole reasons I'm not being expelled—something Bain would fucking love."

There were too many questions floating around my head, and even though I'd always been told to keep my wandering tongue silent, I still wanted to ask him more. I wanted him to elaborate. What history did they have? Why did Bain want Isaiah to get expelled from St. Mary's? But I didn't say a word because just as soon as my mouth opened, the library doors flew open, and Cade's glare traveled over each and every table until he landed on us.

"Ever think about checking your phone?" Cade looked agitated as he walked over with his set jaw and slight scowl.

Isaiah slowly looked back to see Cade, who had his hands pressed to his hips. His chest was heaving. *Did he run here?*

I watched as Isaiah pulled his phone out of his pocket. His eyes scanned whatever it was that he was reading, and then a feral growl left his mouth. "You don't know where he went?"

"No. And the car hasn't moved."

"Who? Bain?" I asked before I could stop myself. I *almost* shrunk back into the chair from past experiences of speaking out when I shouldn't have, but that wasn't me anymore. I didn't have to stay quiet to stay safe. I wasn't going to get punished for asking an innocent question.

Cade's mouth flung open as he snapped his gaze back to Isaiah.

Isaiah shot him a look that I couldn't put my finger on, and then his features softened a little as he looked over to me. "Tutoring is coming to a sudden halt." Isaiah pushed himself from the table, his tall stance looming over me like some type of enticing nightmare. His inky hair fell onto his forehead, and the blue of his eyes that were warm seconds ago turned glacial. "If anyone asks..."

"I know. I know. We were here, tutoring together."

His lips twitched so subtly that I doubted he even knew he did it.

Before Isaiah left, I asked, "Should I go back to my room? What if someone comes in here and doesn't see us sitting here? Like someone on the committee?"

"I don't think anyone is actually going to come in here. All the teachers who are a part of the SMC dip out right after school unless they have hall duty."

A leery feeling of unease settled over me. "Are you sure?"

Isaiah sighed as he ran his hand down his face feebly. I could be his alibi like he wanted, but if someone actually came here and asked where he was, what would I say? It was one thing if they asked me the next day. It was another if they were standing here looking at an empty chair.

Cade mumbled under his breath as he looked away, too, clearly thinking of a new plan. Silence fell over our group as I sat in the chair with the new phone in my hand and my laptop pushed to the side as Isaiah and Cade both stood above me with a tenseness in their shoulders that even I could feel.

My fingers grasped the phone tightly. "I'll just text you if someone comes in here. I'll say you ran back to your room for a book or something." I paused. "Unless you are leaving school grounds?"

Cade spoke this time, looking at Isaiah. "The car hasn't moved. He didn't leave the school—yet."

Isaiah's brows knitted together as he gripped the back of the chair he was standing above so tightly his knuckles began to change color. His gaze pierced mine once more as he said, "Text me if anyone comes in here. And I don't just mean a teacher. If any other student pops in here, don't trust them."

A chill flung to my limbs as Cade let out a grunt. "Still think your plan of showing Bain that Gemma was yours the other day was a good idea? Because now he's really unpredictable."

"Did I have a choice?" If looks could kill, Isaiah would be a cold-blooded murderer right about now. But so could Cade. He had those dreamy, all-American-boy features, whereas Isaiah had dark and dangerous ones, but when he narrowed his eyes and clenched his jaw? Thunder rolled. Watching them stare at one another was like watching a hurricane brew over an ocean. "I saw the way he looked at her after our initial conversation when I'd asked her to tutor me in the first place, and then at the claiming?" He shook his head with rising anger. "Bain isn't stupid, Cade. You know that. It's either I keep my distance from her and act like she's nothing more than a piece of fucking dirt on the bottom of my shoe"— *Ouch.*—"which I fucking can't because she's my…"

"Tutor," I answered, inserting myself to the conversation so they'd both remember that I was sitting right here even though they were acting like I wasn't. *A piece of dirt on the bottom of his shoe?*

"Exactly." Isaiah's voice was tight around every single word, and my stomach flopped. "She and I are being thrown together no matter what, so it's either I keep a close eye on her, or…"

Cade sighed, crossing his arms over his chest.

"Or nothing. You're right. We know how Bain gets when he becomes…centered on something." I slowly raised my chin and looked at Cade. His sentence threw me off course because the anger that was just radiating off him was no longer there, but instead, there was anguish. His big brown eyes deepened as they found the ground. His shoulders dropped. His breath was unsettled.

"I've seen him looking at her too," Cade said. "But is it because of you? Or because…"

Isaiah huffed. "Probably both."

Silence encased us all again as they stared at each other, obviously sharing a silent conversation that made me feel pretty damn insignificant.

Pride washed over me as I opened my mouth. "Is anyone going to fill me in? Because it sounds like you two are talking in code, and I don't like to be left in the dark." A simmer of anger began to brew right after pride. I'd been in the dark my entire life. I'd been lied to, forced to keep my mouth shut, and physically thrown into a dark basement so I was "*protected*" from certain things. Being unaware of your surroundings or things that were going on around you was nothing less than dangerous. I deserved to know what was going on. I'd always deserved to know what was going on around me. It had just taken a while to realize that.

"There isn't time right now." Isaiah shook his head and began typing something on his phone. "Cade is going to walk you back to your room when I give the go-ahead." He glanced up at Cade briefly before beginning to walk away. "She shouldn't be alone if we can't find him. I don't trust him. If anyone comes in here asking why you're here, just say it's a group tutoring session or something."

The tiniest growl left my lips when Isaiah dismissed me. Both boys snapped their attention to me as my hands flung to my waist. "I've been lied to my entire fucking life." I paused for a split second at my choice of words before continuing. "I've only been told certain things because..." I trailed off, pushing away the past, gripping onto my rising anger. "It doesn't matter why. What matters is that something is going on that pertains to me, and I deserve to be brought up to speed. I am so tired of being dismissed because I'm a *good girl.*"

One second passed as my heart whacked against my chest. Blood rushed to my fingertips, and I wasn't sure what it was, but I was *mad.* Was I finally just at my threshold for all the bullshit in my life and taking it out on Cade and Isaiah? Maybe.

My fists tightened even more as Isaiah's mouth split wide, and he let out a laugh that only fed my rising temper. "How often do you curse, Gemma?" Cade chuckled under his breath, and I pursed my lips. "You're seriously adorable when you're angry. I might just start pissing you off to see your reaction." Then, he grinned at me and turned around, leaving me standing there with fumes coming out my ears.

I stomped my foot like a five-year-old would, but to be honest, I don't think I'd even done that as a child, let alone at seventeen. "Isaiah!" I barked. "You will tell me what's going on, or else I won't be your alibi if the SMC comes knocking." An evil grin slid onto my face, and I *loved* the fact that I had power. I loved it too much. "How easy would it be for me to tell them that you leave during our tutoring sessions to sneak out and go do God knows what."

Isaiah threw his head back and laughed without even looking at me over his shoulders. "You'll continue covering for me, Good Girl." I crossed my arms over my chest, feeling that surge of power dissipate. He continued walking to the door as he talked. "Or did you forget about our deal? Didn't you need something in return? A fake ID or something?"

The door shut seconds later, and my arms slowly fell in defeat. Isaiah was right. How could I forget that he was my ticket out of here? That he was the one carving my path to freedom? That he was paving a way for me to hopefully find my brother? It was scary that Isaiah could take my worries and turn them to dust within seconds, making me forget all that had weighed me down in the first place.

When I turned toward Cade, he was standing there with his arms still crossed and his gaze pointed to the ceiling like he was trying his hardest not to look at me.

"Will you tell me what's going on?" I asked.

He laughed sarcastically, bringing his gaze back down. "Not a chance in hell. Isaiah brought you into this; he can be the one to deal with the repercussions."

"Rude," I whispered under my breath, plopping myself back down into the chair. I pulled the laptop over and began typing furiously into the search engine, pretending that Cade wasn't standing just a few feet away and that Isaiah didn't just leave me in the library, totally empty-handed and restless. He wanted me to cover for him, but he wouldn't tell me why?

Whatever. Fine. It wasn't like I was willing to tell him my secrets either. But it seemed that both of our secrets affected the other in ways we didn't want to admit. He said he was protecting me, but how was I protecting him when it came to Richard and my secrets? After it was all said and done, if Richard somehow learned that Isaiah was the one who gave me the necessities to get away from him, would he go after him?

I sighed, easing the stress from my shoulders as I tried to be proactive with my time. I typed the words *Judge Stallard* rather aggressively into the search engine and hit enter, waiting to dig into every last thing that Richard was related to. Knowledge was power, and maybe something would pop up that would lead me to Tobias. Maybe the smallest of clues would appear, and I'd know where to start once I got out of this school with my wad of cash and new ID. Nothing like distracting myself with a little search that Richard would nearly kill me for. It was all part of his control: him knowing everything about me, and me knowing nothing about him.

"Judge Stallard?" Cade startled me, and I had no idea that he'd even moved from the other side of the table.

I slammed the laptop shut. "Stop snooping," I snapped.

Cade's brown eyes widened. "What? You can trust me. Maybe I can help with your little search there."

"I *do not* trust you," I said, even though there was a really small voice inside of me that told me I could.

Cade's lips twitched. "I'm bothered that you don't think I look trustworthy."

I raised my chin. "You *do* look trustworthy, and that's exactly why I don't trust you." I began pushing the laptop open again with my fingers. "Plus, you were the one who tricked me the first day in art when Isaiah pulled me into the closet."

Cade's shoulders slumped for a second, his light hair

falling into his eyes. "Well, shit. I did, didn't I?" He batted his thick eyelashes at me. "I'm sorry. Do you forgive me?"

A smile tickled my lips as I fought to keep them even. "Does batting your eyelashes like that really work on girls?" I knew for fact that it did. I'd seen him in action a couple of times this week. His target always seemed to fall into his lap like he was some type of female magnet.

A huge grin covered Cade's face. "Of course it does." He pulled out the chair beside me and rested his hands behind his head. "But for the record..." He glanced away. "I won't betray your trust. I promise. I won't look at your computer anymore."

I wanted to believe that. I really did. A warmth settled into my bones, and it seemed to spread over my skin. I pushed my laptop the rest of the way open, only peeking at Cade a few times before I typed enter on the search engine again and began reading all there was to know about Richard. For some reason, the bitter taste I'd always had didn't surface like usual when his round face appeared in front of my eyes. Instead of feeling that rising panic, I felt powerful. Like digging up all this information was giving me a sense of strength against him. The last time I'd started to dig, he caught me red-handed, and it did not end well. Even when I groveled at his feet and acted like the devoted and loyal girl that he wanted me to be, he still punished me.

Out of the corner of my eye, I saw Cade shift with his phone in his hand, but he didn't look at my computer screen again. I wasn't sure if he was making a point not to look because he said I could trust him, or maybe he just didn't really care. Either way, I was relieved. My chest untightened as each second passed with his head down, and my breaths eventually resumed to their lazy rhythm as I scrolled over articles and newspaper headlines.

That was, until I felt a vaguely familiar feeling creeping up behind me, causing my fingers to pause over the keyboard. I glanced at the little time icon in the corner and saw that it was well past curfew—something the rest of the Rebels didn't seem to care about.

I peered over my shoulder slowly, prepared to see something or someone standing there, but all I saw were sky-high bookshelves and an empty, dark aisle that led to the back of the library.

"What's wrong?" Cade asked, putting all four of his chair legs back onto the floor.

"I...don't know." I bristled at my rising anxiety. I was probably feeling uneasy because of all the searching I'd done. My subconscious was poking at me to tread lightly. "It's probably nothing. I just feel like we're not—" My sentence came up short when something thudded in the back of the library. There was a flash of movement, and within seconds, Cade was up out of his seat, and he was pulling me up and pushing me behind him. I stumbled onto the edge of the table with the phone Isaiah gave me clutched in my hand and my face pressed to Cade's back.

"Text Isaiah and tell him we're going back to your room right now." His grip on my arm tightened, and within seconds, we were heading for the door.

"Wait!" I shouted. "I need my sketchbook." I had no idea what was going on, but there was a feeling of urgency in my blood that was instinctual. If someone found my sketches, things would get bad—fast.

"What?" Cade's face was a mix of pressing caution.

"Please," I begged, trying to whip my arm out of his grasp.

The shadows over his face deepened, but he dragged me with him to the table, keeping his eyes trained to the back of the library. I hurriedly swiped the worn sketchbook off the table, and then we were out the door.

"Stay quiet since I'm technically not allowed to be out after curfew." His hand loosened a little. "So let's not get caught."

"I wasn't aware that you cared much about that."

Cade's chuckle was short and sweet, but he stayed silent the rest of the way to the girls' hall. We didn't run into anyone else. The hall was just as unmoving as it usually was during curfew hours. I pulled the phone up during our walk and began texting Isaiah, which Cade had to help me with because I had no idea which button to press. Just as we reached the girls' hall, Cade's phone began vibrating, and he answered it quietly.

"Check the library," he whispered, glancing behind us once. "There was a loud thud in the back, and instead of investigating, I decided to take Gemma back to her room." Then, the line went dead, and Cade pushed his phone back into his jeans.

"Was that Isaiah?" I asked, watching the darkened corners of the girls' hall. We were almost to my room now, and thankfully, the duty teacher hadn't made her rounds yet, but I still felt unease moving through my blood like sludge. I was on edge—likely with good reasoning.

"Yeah." He glanced down at me. "He said to tell you to stay in your room all night."

I rolled my eyes, but before I could say anything, Cade sighed. "And he said to put an emphasis on the words *all night*."

My lips twitched as I pulled the phone out and texted him again.

ME: Yes, your highness. I will stay in my room.

. . .

His response was instantaneous.

Isaiah: All night.

"Just listen to him."

I pulled the phone to my chest and glared up at Cade. "Again! With the snooping!" I whisper-yelled. He was worse than Tobias when I used to hide my sketches from him.

Cade's lips curved, but he said nothing as I quietly opened my door and slipped inside.

Sloane popped up off her bed, her hair falling back behind her shoulders. She sighed before plopping back down onto her pillow. "Finally! I've been waiting for you to watch our show. Tutoring with Isaiah should take, like, one hour, max."

A light laugh floated out of me as I tucked the new phone into my pocket, pushing away Isaiah's text from my mind, along with everything else. I was safe, and that was all that mattered at the moment. "Let me get changed for bed, and we can watch it. You didn't have to wait for me, though. You could have skipped ahead and filled me in later."

She sucked in breath. "Absolutely not." She peeked up at me just before I went into the bathroom. "And you better never watch without me. Our friendship depends on it."

I couldn't even hide my smile as I shut the door behind me.

CHAPTER THIRTY-TWO

ISAIAH

I'D WAITED until mostly everyone was in the common room to slip out early Saturday afternoon. Cade and Brantley were currently creating a diversion and getting everyone stirred up over our lacrosse game that ended with thrown punches to the other team.

The Wildcats didn't accept that we'd beat them in the last few seconds of the game, and a few of the guys had words, and before I knew it, Shiner was flying over our goaltender's back to defend him after a sucker punch to the jaw.

Coach brushed it under the rug, although I was sure my uncle had heard all about it.

I, for one, did not partake in such felonious acts. In fact, I was the one who had pulled Shiner off and held the peace. There was definitely a time for throwing punches, and being on probation with the SMC wasn't one of them.

Before leaving the common area, I found Shiner attempting to one-line one of the girls that Bain often frequented, which stole Bain's attention away instantly. Which meant my plan had worked like a charm.

Gemma was nowhere to be found in the common area, but that was because she was in the art room, and I was fine with that, knowing we had eyes on Bain at the moment. The last few nights of tutoring had been tense. Aside from a few bantering comments about how I needed to do my homework so the SMC felt that she was doing her job as my tutor, along with quick, heated glances from me that I was certain she didn't even notice, we'd mainly kept to ourselves. I had a feeling she was still angry about the fact that I hadn't given her any more information on Bain, but it was better that way.

Cade, Brantley, and Shiner had been on their A-game with keeping up with Bain after Tuesday's slip up, and he'd yet to leave the school grounds like he had in the past. Bain had fucked with us the other night, as if he knew there were eyes on him. I'd had a suspicion for a while now that he was getting antsy, and Tuesday confirmed as much. There was no one in the library after Cade had taken Gemma back to her room, and once we were done searching the darkened library aisles, finding not even a single page of a book out of place, Bain suddenly reappeared and slipped back into his room after we'd gotten back. It was a damn miracle that neither of us had gotten caught by the duty teachers scouring the halls that night.

Shaking the feeling of pressing anxiety from my shoulders, I crept up the stairs and walked down the hall slowly. It didn't take long to find myself in front of Bain's room, and I was inside the dorm even quicker since I had the master key—well, a copy of it, at least. Something I wasn't sure my uncle knew, considering I'd stolen his and made a replica the first week I'd arrived here.

I knew it would come in handy eventually. *Always think ahead, Isaiah. Cover your bases.* A swallow worked itself down my throat as one of my father's lessons came to mind. He'd always taught me to think ahead, and even though I hated him more than anything in the entire fucking world, I'd stayed true to that piece of advice. I had a backup plan for every aspect of my life—except for being the heir to my father's business. There was no backup plan for becoming the Huntsman, because that meant harming Jack, and I wouldn't do that. Jack was my limit.

As soon as the door clicked behind me, my gaze grew sharper and my ears more alert. I wasn't sure what my father wanted me to find. He'd been too cryptic over the phone yesterday, and I wasn't in a spot where I could question him further. I could only assume it was related to drop-offs and sales, though. I knew Bain's phone would likely hold the most information, but that would be much tougher to snag, so his room was my first stop.

I stepped over his bundled clothes on the floor and lifted up his mattress, searching for any makeshift holes inside for hiding spots. The pillows in my hands were just the same as any other pillow, soft and fluffy, lacking any weight that would indicate something shoved inside. His dresser was full of boxers and extra uniforms, along with a few pieces of street clothing for after classes and weekends.

Just as I stepped back from his desk, something caught my eye. *A Polaroid camera?* My brows pinched as I picked it up and inspected it. Then, I placed it back down quietly and searched the rest of his room for what I was absolutely certain would be here.

I stood in the middle of his floor, searching every corner of the room until I paused, staring at a book. It wasn't unusual to have a book on your desk at a boarding school, right? But what was unusual was that it was neatly pushed up against the back end of his desk. Each book was ramrod straight, almost looking like a decoration that would be on a shelf in a house versus an actual textbook that the school had given us.

My finger ran down the spine slowly, and instead of skin-like leather touching the pad of my pointer, it was plastic. Hard, unbending plastic. As I tipped one book back, the entire thing moved in one fluid motion, revealing the smallest cutout in the wall.

What a fucking idiot. I changed my opinion from earlier. Bain was stupid.

The hole wasn't any bigger than a few inches wide than it was tall. There were frayed pieces of drywall all around the edges, and as I reached inside, I easily grabbed the photos.

I flipped through them quickly, knowing that, at any given moment, Bain could head upstairs. The guys were instructed to text me the second he stepped out of the common area, but still, that wouldn't give me much time to exit his room without running into him. It was doable, though. Otherwise, I wouldn't be here.

The first few pictures were of Journey, which was no surprise to me. Everyone knew of his obsession with her, and although her accident was ruled just that—an accident—I still suspected he had something to do with it. I didn't buy his alibi when we'd cornered him, and without anyone suspecting that someone was at fault other than Journey herself, no one else had questioned him. I wasn't convinced, though—not with the things I knew. Which was another reason why I didn't want Gemma alone—not with a direct threat from Bain himself.

After pushing aside the few stalker-like photos of Journey, who had obviously been unaware that her photo was being taken, there was one of Ms. Glenburg that had me snarling. Not out of protection, because from the looks of the photo, it was quite obvious that she wasn't just lusting over me but over Bain as well. Her tits were on full display in a lacy bra with what I assumed to be Bain's thumb in her mouth. Her red lips were wrapped around his finger with hollowed out cheeks as she sucked. I didn't give a flying fuck that Bain seemed to be having some sort of an explicit relationship with her. I wasn't jealous in the slightest. But what I did care about was that the next photo was of me as I hovered over her with my hand up her skirt.

That fucker.

Bain was the one who told the SMC. It shouldn't have been much of a surprise that he'd been following me—my suspicions have been there for a while, especially with what he'd said to Gemma. But now that I was certain he was the one trying to get me kicked out of St. Mary's, that likely meant he knew I was following him and reporting back to my father on his whereabouts. Did he know my father was the Huntsman? Or did he just know my father was in the same line of business as his? Most of the time, you could put a face to someone's name, but what name did he know my father by? Carlisle Underwood? Or the Huntsman?

My teeth gritted together so hard my jaw throbbed. Finding this meant that Bain knew too much. I knew calling my father was inevitable. He needed to know that Bain was onto me, but what did that mean for me? For Jack?

I shoved the photo of Ms. Glenburg behind the next, careful not to crinkle the edges, but when I settled on the image in front of me, my fingers clamped down.

Golden brown hair fell down her back in those luscious waves that I found myself wanting to touch out of the simple notion that they looked soft. Her bottom lip was sucked into her mouth as she stared at the computer screen in front of her. Even through the bad quality of the photo, I could see the intense look in her gaze as the screen illuminated the perfect planes of her cheeks and—*was that Cade beside her?*

It was. My firm grip grew tighter, the edges of the photo

bending in my fingers. This photo was taken Tuesday, after I'd left Gemma in the library with Cade as I searched for Bain's sneaky ass.

Goddamnit. My heart began climbing in speed, the thumping so hard my chest rumbled. I cracked my neck as I shoved the photos back inside the hollowed part of the wall.

My phone vibrated, and I angrily pushed the fake book back in its place and read the text.

CADE: on the move.

I WAS out of Bain's room before I even put my phone in my pocket. My strides were slow and easy down the hall, and I knew I appeared as I usually did on the outside, but I was burning with a million little fires on the inside, all of which formed a blazing circle around Gemma.

A feeling of protection like no other had surfaced, and I wanted to find Bain, shove him up against a wall with my hand wrapped around his throat, and demand he never look in her direction again.

There were two reasons Bain would be taking photos of Gemma, and none of them settled well with me. He was either interested in her because of me, or he was interested in her because she reminded him of Journey. Both options added on another layer of anger that all stemmed from my fucking father.

Which only made me hate him more.

CHAPTER THIRTY-THREE

GEMMA

AFTER SPENDING MOST of my day in the art room, I was feeling better than before. The week had been interesting. I was finally getting in the groove of my classes and finding myself more relaxed than ever with Sloane and Mercedes, whereas before, I was a little nervous to be hanging out with them in fear that I'd act too suspicious or say the wrong thing, but things were becoming easier for me. Everything seemed to be looking up, except for my tutoring sessions with Isaiah, which were nothing more than a nerve-wracking ending to my day.

I wasn't afraid to be around him, but I found myself glancing up at him every few minutes as we'd work silently in a room that seemed to have an even eerier feel since Tuesday night. I was also a little perturbed with myself, because even though I was half-angry with him that he still hadn't given me any information on Bain and the vague threats or even answer my question about who was in the library that night with Cade, I still found my breath faltering when we'd lock eyes for the briefest of seconds. It lit me on fire each and every time, and then after I cooled down, I would berate myself for even looking up in the first place.

It was maddening.

He was maddening, and I didn't even think he meant to be. It was just my body's reaction to him. I kept blaming it on curiosity that came with never being alone with a boy, or feeling hands on me that belonged versus hands on me that were forced, but whatever it was, I couldn't seem to get it to stop. The thoughts that were put into my head like tiny little seeds were fed and watered by Isaiah's icy eyes and perfect, arrogant mouth. I couldn't avoid him—or the wicked thoughts that made my skin itch.

And tonight, there was another claiming party that Sloane and Mercedes were dragging me to—something that Isaiah was well aware of. It was made known at the breakfast table yesterday morning when Sloane had very loudly demanded that I go. Even despite the whole incident that happened last time, she wouldn't hear of me staying in our room. Once it was decided that I'd go, which I really only agreed to because she was making such a scene, Isaiah's gaze slid right to mine and then ripped right past me, as if he were looking at someone from afar.

"I can't believe Isaiah gave you a phone." Sloane was doing her makeup in the bathroom, but she'd kept the door open so Mercedes and I could still chat with her.

"That is really odd." Mercedes glanced up before looking back at her nails that she was painting red polish onto. "Why did he even get you a phone? Don't you have one already?"

Unease settled in. I really liked Mercedes and Sloane, and I truly did hate that I was keeping them in the dark, because what a contradiction that was. But in order to keep things in line, I had to evade the truth some. "Yeah, well..." I glanced away, unable to look either of them in the eye. "He wanted to be able to get a hold of me about our tutoring sessions. Sometimes he runs late because of lacrosse and..." The hole in my chest was getting bigger as I forced a little bit of the truth out. "My uncle is pretty strict, and he checks my phone records. He wouldn't be happy about me texting someone that he had never met—especially if it were someone like Isaiah." That was definitely putting it mildly.

Mercedes let out a loud laugh. "My dad would lose his shit if he knew I was even talking *about* Isaiah. My father doesn't even want me to look in his direction."

"Isn't your dad on the SMC?" I asked as she glanced back at her nails.

She blew out a breath, her blush-covered cheeks puffing. "Yep, so he *really* doesn't like Isaiah since he knows of everything that he's done." A light laugh left her. "Well...the things he's been caught for."

There was a question at the tip of my tongue that caused it to burn. "Why are you at St. Mary's, Mercedes?"

Sloane was sent here because her parents were in the military and deployed often, but I wasn't sure why Mercedes was. She was nice. Really nice. And if her parents were on the SMC, that meant that she actually had parents, and well... something didn't quite add up. Sloane said everyone at St. Mary's was a little messed up, but I didn't get that from Mercedes. I didn't really get that from Sloane, either. But then again, did people get that from me?

"Because Mercedes' parents want her to get into Harvard or some ritzy school like that."

I shifted on the bed. "And you can get into one of those schools by going here?"

Mercedes shrugged. "St. Mary's has an excellent reputation for getting students into the Ivy Leagues—or at least a well-credited college. It was the closest high-end school to my hometown, so they decided to send me here instead of allowing me to attend regular high school with fewer chances at getting a good education. Or so they say."

I began picking at the threads on my blanket. "So, St. Mary's is considered to be a high-end school?" I thought back to Wellington Prep. It was absolutely the type of school that could get you into an Ivy League college—or at least that was what mostly everyone had talked about when I attended for those brief two months. The curriculum there was on-par with what it was here, but of course, nothing like what Auntie used to make me do.

Sloane laughed. "I'd say so. It's expensive to go here if you're not on a scholarship. My parents had the same thought that Mercedes' did. It is one of the only boarding schools in the nation that produces Ivy-League-destined graduates, even despite some of our shitty upbringings. It's like the SMC thought we had nothing else to do but study, so they made the coursework hard as shit." She rolled her eyes at the last part of her sentence but quickly changed her tune as she gave me a pointed look.

"I have a question for you, Gemma."

My attention bounced to Mercedes and then back to Sloane, my fingers now basically tearing the blanket apart. "Okay?"

"Where do you keep sneaking off to in the middle of the night?"

My heart halted as my fingers stilled.

Mercedes' voice squeaked. "She's sneaking off? What? To where?"

"Is it to see Isaiah?"

I sucked in a breath, sitting up taller. "What? No!"

"Is that why he's always looking at her?" I snapped my attention back over to Mercedes. *Wait, what? When does he do that?*

Sloane pointed her straightener at Mercedes. "Exactly

why I'm asking! He kissed her cheek the other day, and ever since then, he has been watching her like a hawk." Her lips pursed as she glanced back at me. "What exactly are you two doing while tutoring? Is it him you're going to see in the middle of the night?" She sucked in another breath, her chin dropping. "Oh my God. Are you guys having sex?" She placed a hand to her heart. "I swear to God, if he takes your virginity and then breaks your heart, I will burn him alive with my flatiron! You are too sweet. God, he will ruin you! I knew this tutoring thing was such bullshit! It makes no sense!" At some point during her rant, she'd begun waving her straightener around the small bathroom like a maniac.

Mercedes hopped off the bed. "For the love of God, put the straightener down before you burn St. Mary's to the ground, Sloane!"

I couldn't help it. A loud laugh escaped from my mouth, and once it was out, I couldn't seem to stop. I couldn't remember a time in my life where I'd ever laughed so much, and I didn't even know why. Was it because I was elated that she didn't know I was sneaking off to the art room to draw the most horrific yet beautiful depictions of my most buried memories? Or was it because she threatened to burn Isaiah alive on my behalf? Whatever it was, I liked it. I was laughing hard. It only took a few seconds for Mercedes to start giggling and then for Sloane too.

We were all mid-laugh, trying to catch our breath, when a knock sounded on the door. I jumped to my feet quickly, but Mercedes brushed me off. "It's probably Callie. I told her to bring me my necklace when she was done getting ready."

Relief settled in, and I relaxed again. I wasn't even sure who I thought would be on the other side of the door, but with how things were going lately, I was skeptical that they would stay normal for me. "Isaiah and I are not having sex," I said to Sloane, finally addressing what she'd assumed I was doing when I left my room. Maybe I'd laughed so hard because the idea that I was sneaking off at four in the morning to go do the one act that was absolutely forbidden to me above all else was so absurd it was hilarious.

"Yet." Sloane pointed her straightener at me, and I laughed again.

"Put that down before you really burn St. Mary's to the ground." I pushed off the bathroom door frame. "And what do you mean by *yet*?"

"I mean... I see the way he looks at you, Gemma." She began straightening the last few strands of her black hair. "I know you say that you're just tutoring him, but he...I don't know. It's like he can't stop looking at you. Even when he's at lacrosse practice. His eyes find you every time he takes a break."

Just as Mercedes began opening the door, she rolled her eyes at Sloane. "It's true."

I let out a tight laugh, trying to figure out a way I could brush off her speculations of Isaiah. Even if he was looking at me as much as she said he was, I was certain it was because of the Bain thing. They didn't know that Bain had made that vague threat against me. They didn't know that Isaiah was concerned that Bain was going to try to use me as some type of pawn to get back at Isaiah for whatever it was that they were feuding over.

"Oh!" Mercedes' tone was like the squeak of a mouse. "Headmaster Ellison."

My thoughts faltered as I glanced at the door and caught the eye of the headmaster. He was staring directly at me, and my stomach somersaulted. *Oh no.*

"Umm..." Mercedes looked between us. "So sorry, Headmaster. I'll go back to my room."

His expression changed swiftly with the slight shake of his head. "Oh, there's no need for that, Mercedes."

She stepped back farther into the room, closer to me now. Her nail polish lid was still off, and the strong scent flew under my nose. "But...it's after curfew. I should be in my room."

"Oh?" The headmaster smiled deviously, and it shocked me because, for some reason, the way his lips tipped upward was so...familiar. A warmth settled over me. "I suppose that may be true." His statement was more of a surmised one at that. He winked innocently at Mercedes and then caught my eye again. "I just came to see if Gemma was adjusting well with everything. Especially with the new tutoring gig. We didn't really get a chance to talk much on Monday after you left my office. But it seems like you're doing just fine."

He was definitely surprised by this but also looked... happy? I had to admit that Headmaster Ellison was very confusing to me. I really wanted to trust him, and there was something about him that I connected to almost instantly, but there was also the smallest voice in the back of my head, reminding me not to trust a single person—least of all someone who owed Richard a favor. Their initial conversation was not far from my memory.

I nodded. "I'm doing okay." My lips smashed together as Sloane and Mercedes came to stand beside me. "We were just"—I glanced at both of them—"having a...girls' night. Is that okay?"

The headmaster was bewildered by my comment. Something flashed along his features before he smiled. "Of course." He looked at each of us. "Have a great night. Don't tell the other girls I let you three have a sleepover." He chuckled. "Although, I assume this is a common thing around here? I don't make a habit of coming to the girls' wing often." Then, he nodded once and muttered a goodnight awkwardly before shutting the door.

The three of us stood in the middle of the room for a solid minute before Sloane said, "That was weird as fuck."

Then, we all started laughing again.

———

THE SPLASHING of water beneath my feet sent a thrill of exhilaration up my spine. My stomach dipped with excitement, which was a vast improvement from the last time I'd walked in the tunnel underneath St. Mary's. After the headmaster had left the room, Sloane, Mercedes, and I commenced our "*slumber party*," which just involved getting ready for the party. Sloane had taken the straightener to my hair, even if I was a little hesitant at first because of how she had been aggressively waving it around all night. But in the end, my darkened mess of brown waves had fallen over my shoulders like a shiny sleek curtain.

It was amazing the transformation I'd had in the few short weeks I'd been at St. Mary's. I had been away from home for less than a month, and with each passing day, I felt Richard's slip on me lessen more and more. It was a troubling thought as I walked arm in arm with Sloane and Mercedes to attend a party that revolved heavily around something that had always been presented as *bad* to me. I was taught that breaking rules was bad and so was anything beyond that. In the past, the thought of breaking rules would have sent me into a spiral of panic, but now? After being away from Richard and that house? And everything that reminded me of what I'd missed out on and what I had lost? Like Tobias... I was welcoming the feeling of rebellion. It wouldn't last forever. I knew that. But the contrast between home and here was transformative in a way. Like the iron shackles were off my wrists. Metaphorically and literally. I was almost thirsty for what was to come of tonight—whatever that may be.

Suddenly, Isaiah's face flashed within my thoughts, and something achy came over my body. Then, I began sweating as Sloane's and Mercedes' arms, intertwined with mine, pulled me along the abyss.

We were getting closer to the door of the party, and I could feel the thumping of bass underneath my feet. I pulled down the sleeves of my shirt to cover my wrists when Sloane stopped walking.

I looked over at her, even though it was pitch black. "Sloane?" I asked as trepidation came rushing to the surface. "What's wrong?"

"Gemma." Her voice echoed against the empty walls surrounding us. "I need to ask you something else."

The excitement I had been feeling moments ago fell so hard I listened for the splash below my feet. "Okay…"

"What's going on, Sloane?" Mercedes whispered. "We're almost to the door."

"I know," Sloane whispered back. "But I don't want to ask this around anyone but you."

Now dread was really starting to set in. Sloane's arm unwrapped from mine, and the scratchy material of the long-sleeve sweater she lent me rubbed against my arm. Then, she grabbed a hold of my hands and gave them a quick squeeze before rushing up and pushing my sleeves past my wrists.

I jerked back from instinct, trying to unwind myself from both her and Mercedes.

"What are you doing, Sloane?" Mercedes' voice was still low enough that if anyone were to come up behind us, they wouldn't hear, but to Sloane and me, it was like a rubber band snapping in the wind.

I began shoving my sleeves back down, knowing that it

didn't really matter because it was so dark that no one would be able to see.

"Why do you do that?" Sloane asked, ignoring Mercedes. "Why do you hide your wrists?"

Mercedes gasped, and my brows furrowed with confusion.

"Gemma." Her voice was sweeter this time, and her hands found their way back to mine. "Are you...suicidal?"

I paused before Mercedes broke the heavy silence. "You can talk about it, okay? It's important to talk about it. We're here for you."

My mouth opened, then shut, and then it opened again. "I'm not suicidal."

That wasn't to say it hadn't crossed my mind once or twice in the past, but only in the darkest pits of my head did I ever have those thoughts, and as soon as I'd said them, the voice of Tobias would cut through with his steel armor and sword, slashing them away no sooner than they came in. *Survive, Gemma. Just survive.*

And I would. I'd spend every one of my breaths trying to survive, just so I could find him.

Neither Sloane nor Mercedes said anything, and it was probably because they didn't believe me. I couldn't blame them, though. I was quiet and kept to myself a lot. I disappeared for hours at a time, and I couldn't imagine what they'd think if they ever saw my sketchbook.

"Then why do you shove your sleeves down? Why do you never wear a t-shirt or undress in front of me?"

"It's not because I'm hurting myself," I answered with full honesty, and I wished I could tell them the actual reason I shoved my sleeves down. The words were on the very tip of my tongue, and for the briefest of seconds, I almost said them.

"Then why?" Sloane asked, completely dumbfounded. If I could see her face, I bet she'd look skeptical.

I sighed. "Because I broke the rules." I sucked in a sharp breath, intertwining my fingers with both Sloane's and Mercedes' through the sea of darkness. I began pulling them farther, and once we reached the door to the party, I squared my shoulders and raised my chin. "And good girls don't break rules."

CHAPTER THIRTY-FOUR

GEMMA

A GUST of air whipped my straight hair around as I pulled Sloane and Mercedes into the room. The party was in full swing. Everyone's faces were familiar to me now, and it seemed as if we were the last to arrive.

Sloane's hand clamped on mine as the door shut behind us. "What does that even mean?"

"What?" I shouted over the loud music, eyes catching on the dancing lights that fluttered around.

"What does breaking the rules have to do with your obsession with pulling your sleeves down?"

My mouth clamped shut, and after a few seconds, Sloane swung herself around and cut through my view of carefree classmates.

Her black-winged eyes dropped slightly, her pink lips frowning. "Are you sure you're not..." She looked to the left as someone walked by. As soon as they were out of sight, I took my hand from Mercedes, who was still holding on tight, and I placed my palms on Sloane's hardly covered shoulders.

"I *promise* you I'm not hurting myself. That's what you think, right? That I'm..." My voice trailed off as I tried to remember what I'd learned in psychology class during those brief months at Wellington Prep. "Cutting?" I said this as a sort of question because I couldn't remember if that was the correct terminology.

But I must have been right, because Sloane briefly nodded.

"I'm not." I smiled gently, seeing that there was the smallest flicker of sadness in her eyes. I wondered what that was all about. She looked sad for a moment...or affected. "There is a reason I cover my wrists, but that's not why."

Mercedes' hand touched my arm. "You don't have to tell us all your secrets, Gemma. But please come to us if something like that happens. Okay? If you...feel alone."

My brows crowded in, and even with the chaotic happenings around us, I felt a sort of bond form between our trio. "I promise," I answered, suddenly feeling very lucky to have them by my side even if I knew I wouldn't be able to reach back out to them after I left St. Mary's for good.

They shared a worrisome look but both ended up shooting me a little nod before my hands fell from Sloane's shoulders. We clasped hands again, catching the eye of a few other groups of students who all stared at me like I'd shown up naked instead of in what I actually wore.

My eyes glided over my outfit, and my stomach tumbled. There was a lot more leg showing tonight than at the last party. And even though I wore a skirt during the day for class, I'd always worn knee-high socks so there was only a thin sliver of thigh peeking most days. But tonight, Sloane had talked me into wearing her ankle boots—Doc Martens was what she'd called them, completely baffled that I didn't know the name. She'd lent me a black mini-skirt that hit mid-thigh but had a gold zipper down the back that seemed overly accessible to anyone who'd try to sneak up on me from behind—like Bain. A shiver danced over me when the brief memory of the last party crowded the edges of my mind.

As Sloane and Mercedes pulled me toward the back of the party, I scanned the open space for him. My feet stalled when I found him standing against a stone pillar with a few unfamiliar guys standing nearby. He was leaning his broad shoulder against the casing, looking just as dangerous as I suspected him to be. Cropped hair close to his skull. A thin scar over his cheekbone. Handsome smile, which was extremely deceiving.

I kept my gaze on his when he found me, as if he knew I was staring at him from afar. His eyes were a deep amber that looked like they'd burn me if I went near. One cheek lifted in a half-smile/half-snarl, and chills raced over my skin. *Shit, maybe Isaiah was right.* I needed to be more alert, especially when sneaking to the art room in the early morning.

"Damn, ladies," a deep voice said from up ahead, stealing my attention away from Bain. I could still feel him staring, though, like his eyes were leaving a trail of warnings over my body. "You three look downright edible."

Warm pools of honey greeted us as we stopped walking. Sloane pushed the guy's shoulder, letting her hand fall from mine. I briefly recognized him, and I was pretty sure he was in my Chem II class. His skin was dark and rich with a smile so bright I felt like I'd been touched by the sun. "How would you know? I wasn't aware you knew what a lady tasted like, Mica."

He tsked a couple of times before grinning at Sloane. "Sure, I do. How would I know that I didn't particularly enjoy the taste?"

I kept my face steady as I tried to comprehend what they were talking about. I had a very strong feeling they were using code. Sexual innuendos were not my thing.

"How could you not like the taste of pussy, though?" This came from behind Mica, and I swiveled around to see the Rebels coming to the group. My heart locked in my chest as I caught the eye of Isaiah who had already spotted me.

Heat kissed my cheeks, and the room seemed to shrink around us. He wore dark jeans and his usual Vans, but he looked more casual tonight. Instead of wearing a shirt like he'd worn last week, showing off his toned arms, this week he wore a zipped-up jacket and had the hood pulled over his head just far enough that it made me pause. My fingers nearly twitched with the need to shove it back from his face.

His famous grin made an appearance, and I swore his hand reached right into my chest, and he squeezed the life right out of it. *Shit.* He had an effect on me. A really big one. One that I wasn't very familiar with. It was like standing on shaky legs or like being pushed underneath icy water and not knowing how to swim.

"Enjoying your night off from tutoring?"

I shrugged just enough that my sweater fell off my shoulder, allowing musty air to dance over the bareness of it. Isaiah's eyes immediately shot down to it, and I watched as a swallow worked itself down his throat. "I guess." My voice was a tiny squeak, and I internally cringed.

Isaiah's head slanted. "You guess?" His eyes were filled with something that caused me to taste that tiniest bit of anticipation on my tongue, and for the life of me, I couldn't figure out what it was. Or what it meant. It was like the last few nights of us "tutoring" in the library with nothing but the sound of his tapping pencil against the thick wood and my racing pulse had led me to this moment right here, where one heated look from him had the small bundle of nerves in my belly exploding to full capacity. "We can always leave now and get back to..."—he took a step closer to me—"tutoring...if you want."

My eyes narrowed as Isaiah's grin grew wider. *Was he toying with me?* Was he making it seem like we weren't tutoring when we said we were? What was he playing at?

Mica, who had moved out of the way some, whistled loud enough that it cut through the music and my racing thoughts. "And suddenly, I wish I *was* into girls. I think I just got a boner watching you two talk."

Sloane threw her head back and laughed as Shiner blew out a breath. "Fuck, I think I got a boner too."

I knew my face was beet red, and I wasn't sure if I was more angry or embarrassed. Once again, I was in the dark with whatever the hell Isaiah was doing at the moment. It was like the lacrosse game all over again, when Isaiah leaned in to kiss my cheek and put on a show for people. Was that what he was doing? Putting on a show again? For Bain? Making people think that he and I were up to something so they'd watch us closely and keep Bain from interjecting himself? I knew the blog had been mentioning Isaiah's and my tutoring sessions, as if there was something else going on.

Isaiah shot Shiner a quick glare. "Shiner."

Shiner winked at me secretly, and I held back a smile. I actually liked the rest of the Rebels, even if they did walk the halls like they had crowns upon their heads. I mean, I did see Shiner throw a serious punch earlier today at the lacrosse game, so I guess I could see why some people stayed out of their way, but over the last few days, the Rebels had been exceptionally nice to me. Cade even introduced to me a game on my phone during lunch this week, and we'd been playing back and forth for the last two nights. I was beating him, and it felt really good to beat someone that seemed to be perfect.

Isaiah sighed agitatedly once more in Shiner's direction before he took another step toward me. The group had parted some, and his walk was more of a prowl than anything else. I swallowed back the need to glance away, knowing that it would only show how confused I truly felt in the moment. But as soon as Isaiah was close enough that his chest brushed against mine, everything else seemed to fade away. There was definitely a shift in the air. I could feel it. Eyes were on us. All of them. They tried to prick my skin, but as Isaiah's hands fell to my hips, a shield that was impenetrable locked down around us.

"What are you doing, Isaiah?" I whisper-seethed, realizing the music had grown softer at some point within the last ten seconds. "Is this another repeat of the lacrosse game? Everyone is going to start labeling me as—"

"Mine." The black hood on top of his head had fallen back, showing off those black-framed blue eyes that sent an icy burn whipping through my body. His fingers around my waist were splayed out, and I was almost certain he could pick me up in one single whoosh, and it would be nothing to him. His hands were large, and my waist was a perfect fit.

My breath caught as his head dipped to my ear, a dark lock of his hair brushing over a sensitive spot. I was suddenly in a frenzy, wanting to pull him in farther, but I was too rational to do so. I wasn't sure what was happening, but my body was feeling all sorts of things, and I was toeing the line of staying in the present and jumping back to the past. *You will remain untouched.*

Richard's voice was like whiplash, but I was quick to dodge the blow.

Stay present, Gemma. Just stay present.

This time, I didn't really care what Isaiah was playing at. I was going to let my instincts lead and push away the uncertainty of right or wrong. This one was all me. I wasn't listening to anyone but myself right here and right now. Not Richard. Not even Tobias, as his last words filtered through. *Survive, Gemma. Just survive.*

"I'm going to kiss you, Good Girl." My mouth opened,

and a rush of heavy-laden breath surrounded us. "Because right now, I need people to know you're mine. I found something today and..." My back curved as his soft lips swiped at my skin. "Just trust me, okay? I'm going to kiss you, and I'm going to act like I'm claiming you." His lips were moving over my ear like some type of synchronized song, and I was falling for it. Every last word. "There is no way I'm letting you out of my grip with Bain in the room." He paused, and I was pretty certain the entire room swayed. "Are you okay with that?"

My hands clamped down onto his wrists, my chest brushing over his. I leaned up on my tiptoes the second he pulled back and placed that dangerous gaze on me. My lips moved over his ear slowly. "I don't know how to do this," I whispered, briefly catching the eyes of our friends at his back. "But I am okay with it." *Was I okay with this?*

Slowly, I placed my boots back onto the ground and peered up at him with a realness that I hadn't shown a single person in this school. I was being completely and utterly transparent with him, even if it did make me feel inexperienced and frazzled. My blood hummed, my heart beating so hard I felt it in every crevice of my body.

He caught the eye of something or someone behind me, but it was fleeting. "You don't know how to do what?" There was the tiniest pinch in between his eyebrows, a small show of confusion on his features.

Another bout of warmth washed over my body as the room grew tighter. Was the music off now? I was pretty sure the music was off. "Kiss," I finally said, glancing to his lips as my chest caved in. "I don't know how to kiss."

His mouth opened almost instantly, those picture-perfect lips parting. His hands around my waist tightened, and his jaw locked. Then, his lips tipped, and his eyes grew hungry. "I thought so. I remember the look on your face when I asked the other night. But don't worry," he said as his hand came up and wrapped around the back of my head. "I'll teach you."

And then... And then he kissed me...and I was floating. I was floating just as high as the butterflies in my stomach, and I didn't care if my feet never touched the ground again.

Isaiah kissed me gently at first, his lips firm but soft at the same time. His hand gripped my hair, and a strange noise left my mouth, and that was when my feet seemed to touch back to the ground, but only for a quick second, because as soon as I caught up to what my heart was doing in my chest, his tongue jolted out, and he licked the seam of my lips, and mine opened without even realizing it. And then...I began kissing him back.

It was a bittersweet feeling. I knew it was fake and that Isaiah was just kissing me like he'd kissed other girls, but it replaced every other time my lips had been touched.

This wasn't my first kiss, but it was the first kiss I'd ever *wanted*. And that meant something to me.

Isaiah's growl vibrated my cheeks as his tongue swept against mine. His grip was death-like around my hip, and something new and hot pulled at my core. Before I could stop myself, my teeth nipped at his bottom lip, and if it weren't for the lights suddenly going dark, I would have pulled back and apologized.

A voice that I'd heard before—Brantley?—flew through the room over the speakers. "I guess we can let that moment right there declare the time for claiming. I think we're all ready now. Lights go back on in one hour. Remember the rules. Don't touch people who don't want claimed. And pick wisely."

"Fuck, Gemma," Isaiah murmured against my lips. "*Fuck.*" Then, his hand clasped with mine, our fingers intertwining instantly, and I was being pulled so fast I could hardly keep up. My eyes hadn't adjusted to the room. Everything was dark, especially with it being underground, but panic didn't creep in like usual.

In fact, the only thing I was thinking about was how my lips were tingling and how every inch of my body was on fire.

I wanted more. Something as forbidden as letting someone like Isaiah touch me and kiss me should have left me feeling tainted and fearful. After all, that was what had been pounded into my skull from a very, very young age. *You are to remain untouched and pristine. Otherwise, you'll end up just like your mother, with a corrupted mind and a twisted heart.*

But after one brush of Isaiah's lips over mine, he could have been the devil asking me to give up my soul, and I would have.

Isaiah just started something that I would make damn sure to finish. His lips made me feel unstoppable.

Richard said good girls didn't break rules, but he could watch me break each and every one.

CHAPTER THIRTY-FIVE

ISAIAH

THE LOCK on the door clicked, and everything intensified. The room was just as dark as the basement had been, but I knew my way around. My hands pushed Gemma's tiny frame up against the back of the cool, concrete wall, and my knee pushed in between her bare legs.

The skirt. The fucking leather skirt. My fingers twitched to unzip it from behind, but I knew I was getting ahead of myself. In fact, this was going against the entire fucking plan.

Kiss her, claim her, bring her in a side room, and ride out the rest of the party letting everyone think you fucked her. That was the plan. Make everyone talk and draw their attention to her, because the more eyes on Gemma meant that Bain would be forced to take a step back. The students at this school were far more loyal to me than they were to him. If he even dared to step too close to her after everyone thought she was mine, they'd rat him out within seconds. Some would even interfere. He'd have more eyes on him than ever. I wasn't confident that the plan would work to its fullest potential, but I had to do something. I had to deter him somehow, especially after finding the photos. This was a plan that was orchestrated by me and the rest of the Rebels. It was all we had at the moment because, unfortunately, Bain was untouchable, per my father's recent orders.

A soft whimper echoed against the stone walls, and I was suddenly brought back to the present. Gemma and I were both still heaving at a complete standstill with our sudden lack of oxygen. My hands touched her soft, warm skin, and my dick was as hard as a rock as it pushed up against her belly. So badly did I want to hitch her legs around my hips and grind myself onto her warmth.

I wondered if she was wet. I wondered what she'd do if I crept my hands up her thighs and pushed a finger into her tight pussy. Would she let me?

Just as I had the thought come through, Gemma jumped up, and her legs were around my waist as if she had read my mind. My head spun, and blood rushed. *Jesus.* Gemma said she didn't know how to kiss, but her tongue was back to being tied with mine, and sexy-ass noises were coming out of her mouth, and it was making me lose control.

I never lost control.

But fuck me, Good Girl was wrapping her tiny little hands around my body—and *Christ,* maybe even my soul—and making them her own.

The strangest pull in my stomach had me faltering for a second.

Fuck. I'd never felt like this. I didn't know what to do with it.

I pulled my mouth from hers, sucking in a chestful of air.

"What the fuck," I said through choppy breaths. Gemma's small frame wiggled in my arms, her warmth radiating to my jeans, and I threw my head back, letting out a ragged breath.

"What?" she asked, her voice heavy with about as much lust as I felt.

My fingers dug into the bare flesh on her legs, and she sucked in air.

Put her the fuck down.

"You!" I growled, fingers still biting her skin.

Lights. Where the fuck were the lights?

I moved us quickly, feeling for the door and then the light switch. A soft glow basked the room from the light above our heads, and I felt the dilation of my pupils as I stared down at her lustful green eyes and swollen lips. The apples of her cheeks were flushed, and when I trailed my eyes down to her split legs around my waist, her skirt was pushed up just far enough that I could see the color of her panties. I almost fell. My knees shook. The entire fucking school shook.

"I'm putting you down."

Hurt flashed behind the lush green, but just as quickly as she looked hurt, she looked...disappointed? Her plump bottom lip jutted out, and it was a swift punch to my dick.

She was pouting, and a twisted part of me wanted to bite that pouting lip. *Fuck yes.*

Was this the Gemma that she liked to hide? The one I caught a glimpse of every once in a while? The one that sat so quietly behind the good-girl act?

Physical pain soared through me as I put distance between us. Her fingers fumbled with the bottom of her skirt as she pulled it down, hiding the marks my fingers had put on her. "Why did you put me down?"

"Why did I put you down?" I asked, almost roaring. My back flung toward her as my hands gripped the back of my neck tightly. Then, I spun around and gave her a look that had her mouth shutting. "You said you didn't know how to kiss."

She nibbled at her lip as she pulled her chestnut-colored hair to the side. "I know."

"You lied!" I snapped. I didn't like to be lied to.

Her gaze flew to mine as she bit back a response. "I did not!"

"You honestly cannot stand there and tell me that I was your first kiss. If so, then you were a fucking stripper in your past life." *So hot. It was so fucking hot.*

Gemma's shoulders stiffened, and a flicker of something went across her face. "I never said that you were my first kiss."

A burning, fire-flaming zip of jealousy slashed up my spine. It was irrational and without logical reason, but that didn't make me any less aware that I wanted to rip any person before me who'd had the opportunity to kiss a girl like her to fucking shreds.

Her shaky voice seemed to ground me. "I said I didn't know how to kiss. Not that I hadn't been kissed."

I thought over her words carefully, repeating them in my head as my hands fell to my sides. "So, then you have been kissed. I wasn't your first?"

Conflict was evident on her face. Her beautiful, angelic traits, even with the rare bout of makeup on her features, pulled together with confusion. "No. But...yes?"

I pulled back, my hands shooting back up to my neck. I felt as tight as a string on a fucking crossbow. "That makes absolutely no sense."

"I know!" she snapped, obviously trying to work through something as she began pacing the small room. There was nothing in her way except for a dingy, tattered couch that had enough cum on it that I could smell the dried sperm before even stepping foot in here.

"I'm confused," I finally said after following her every move. Was that what I was feeling? Confusion? I was definitely feeling something, but it was so new I couldn't decipher it.

She stopped and spun on her black boots. I caught the smoothness of her leg and felt the rise of my dick again. *I wanted her.* I felt wild, staring at her from across the room. My chest started to heave again as blood pumped harder.

I licked my lips, and she placed her hands on her hips, just underneath the cream sweater that was now only half tucked into her skirt. "You're confused?!" she shrieked, and I took a step toward her. "*I'm* confused!"

My head slanted. "Why are you confused?"

Her eyes shot to every last corner of the room before she grabbed onto me. I was closer now, and I hadn't even remembered walking the rest of the way over to her. "Because this is all so new to me! And I like it! I like it a lot, and I'm not supposed to. It's something that I was taught was *so* bad for so long."

Bad? My hands reached out for her when she squeezed her eyes shut, bringing her shaky hand to the bridge of her nose. Her words were like rapid missiles shooting out of her mouth. "And it's not even real. You were kissing me because of Bain, right? I'm just another pawn in a game, and it's whatever... I know that you're trying to protect me or put more attention on me so he'll leave me alone or...whatever—"

"Who said it wasn't real?" I interrupted her before she could get any further.

Two big, beautiful green eyes flew open and snagged me. My hand came up and rested underneath her chin. My thumb rubbed her swollen bottom lip, and every nerve ending in my body stood erect. "This situation is...unorthodox. I know. I asked you to tutor me and to cover for me when I needed to leave the grounds so I could have a way to dodge being caught and expelled by the SMC and still do what I needed to do..." I glanced away, knowing very well I shouldn't have been bringing her further into this shit, but she deserved to know the truth—something that I had been contemplating since Tuesday. "I'm here at St. Mary's because of Bain." I couldn't even look her in the eye as disgust and anger filled me. "My father sent me here to report all there is to know about Bain and his father. You want to talk about a pawn? That's exactly what I am. Bain leaves the school, and I follow him. That's why I need you to cover for me and to have a reason to be in the halls after curfew. It's why I leave the school. My father and Bain's father are *bad fucking men.*"

Gemma jumped as my words grew angrier, but I continued to hold her chin in place.

My gaze left the couch, and I found hers again when her soft voice echoed in the room. "I know all about bad men, Isaiah. You don't have to explain anything else to me."

My jaw clenched as I fought to keep myself from kissing her again. Gemma was not a pawn. I wouldn't let her be. That was exactly what Bain was trying to do. He wanted to use her against me just like I suspected he was trying to use Journey against Cade, for whatever fucking reason that was still unknown to me.

"I kissed you in front of everyone to put on a show; that part is true. But kissing you wasn't fake. What just happened was anything but fake." I swallowed, licking my lips. Even with the impossibility of her and me ever being anything at the forefront of my head, I couldn't help myself. My body was aching to have her. My heart was beating fast with an intensity that made my blood sing. It was much more than attraction. I wasn't dense. There were things I was feeling that were buried deep below the surface, and that in itself should have pulled me away from her. But instead, I got closer.

I bent my head to hers, shoving any last thought of Bain, my father, the future that awaited me, and the secrets she was keeping away. It was just her and me, locked away in a room underneath the unmoving halls of St. Mary's Boarding School. Something shifted inside my chest, and I craved to know if she felt this way too. She was my little mystery girl. I was bending in half without knowing the things that went on behind those green eyes. Things were moving so quickly. The ability to deny the hole she was carving with just a single glance from across the dining hall was long gone. *Fuck, I needed to touch her.*

Gemma's back curved as she pressed herself to me, and her doe-like eyes nearly stole my breath away. My tongue darted out as I licked my lips again, my chest growing tight as it begged me to shut the fuck up. "We probably shouldn't go here, Gemma." Our eyes caught, and the room was caving in. "It won't last. It can't go anywhere." My mother's face was crowding the outskirts of my memory, and again, that right there should have been the push that I needed to step away, but I didn't.

"I know," she whispered, darting her eyes from my mouth and then back to my face. "I'm leaving this life behind one way or another."

I nodded sternly. "And I can't leave mine."

A short breath came from her sweet mouth, and my eyes shut as I inhaled. "That's the whole point, right? Keeping you here at St. Mary's. Keeping you from being expelled?"

I didn't answer her because I couldn't get my thoughts to stay in that straight, controlled line that they never veered from.

"Isaiah?" My eyes opened in an instant as I locked onto hers. The green pulled me in quickly. "Will you kiss me again?"

My hands around her waist grew firmer until it felt like she was the only thing I'd ever need to ground me. *Shit. This was so bad. So fucking bad.* "My uncle told me not to corrupt you, Good Girl." I knew, staring down at her soft expression and perfect parted lips that she was about as innocent as they came. She may have kissed me like she was made for me, but she had exuded innocence from the first moment I laid eyes on her. And I wasn't going to lie...it was fucking tempting. I wanted to grasp her purity in my devilish fingers and dirty her in every way. I wanted to make her body respond to mine and no one else's.

"And you're going to listen to your uncle?" The sincerity in her question made a deep, throaty chuckle float out of my mouth.

"I never listen to what my uncle says. I will kiss you over and over again until you tell me to stop." *And maybe not even then.*

The smallest lift of her lips made the room tilt. "Good."

CHAPTER THIRTY-SIX

GEMMA

Isaiah's eyes shut as I sucked in a shaky breath. His hand splayed out over my torso, resting along the bare skin of my stomach. The feel of his palms on my body was all-consuming. I was suddenly aware of everything he was doing and nothing else. The hardness of him that should have scared me but instead excited me. The way his breath was like a feather brushing against the crook of my neck. The feeling of his chest moving against mine. And at some point, his head had dropped, his hair tickling the side of my cheek as his warm breath coated my flesh, making goosebumps rise on the ends of my arms.

Before I could panic and rethink the last few moments, Isaiah's teeth scraped over my collarbone, and a jolt of something hot rushed through me, canceling out the hidden threats of Richard that laid ever so quietly in the back of my head. Isaiah's presence gave me a fraction of safety...of normalcy, and I was running with it.

"So, you've been kissed," he asked as his lips pressed

against the side of my throat, right over my pulse point. Everything inside of me came to life, and a need so hot was causing my back to bow and my breath to quicken.

What the hell was he doing to me? I'd always thought I'd be afraid or too nervous to actually enjoy myself if I ever got the chance to feel another's touch. But I wasn't afraid. Not at all. I was exhilarated. I wanted more.

"Ye-yes," I answered, tilting my head to the side to give him more access.

"But have you been touched?"

Such a difficult question, and one that I would rather not explain.

Isaiah pulled back just a fraction. The hard planes of his chest still moved against mine. He waited with patient eyes as his grip tightened. The cut arches of his cheekbones were flushed, and his eyes were nearly feral. He was dangerously attractive, standing in front of me like that. Like...like he wanted to consume me.

I swallowed as I let the bitter question leave my mouth. "Touched how?" I knew I was avoiding some of the truth, and he probably knew that too.

Isaiah's eyes had darkened, like a hooded veil covering the depths of his blue hues. "If you have to ask, then the answer is no." He paused, taking his palms from my waist and cupping my hands in just one of his. He pushed them up above my head, and I fought the urge to glance at them to make sure my sleeves were still covering my wrists. "Or..." He was looking at my lips now instead of my face. "Whoever touched you before...didn't know what they were doing. They didn't know just how unworthy they were to have you in their grasp."

His lips were a breath away from mine, and I tipped my head. "But...you do?"

"I know how to do a lot of things, Gemma, which probably makes me that much more unworthy of this moment right here."

He wasn't unworthy. He had no idea what unworthy was. He had no idea the vile things that had been whispered into my ear as my knees hit the cold, damp floor of a dirty basement tucked ever so nicely underneath a pristine house with my wrists in heavy chains. If I thought hard enough, I could still feel Richard's length pressed against my back as I cried from hunger. The desperation in my shaky voice as I apologized for something so completely innocent, like holding my brother's hand. I could sense the way he got off on punishing me. The man I'd never thought of as a fatherly figure *loved* to watch me beg for his help. He loved having me at his mercy, and when I turned eighteen and was back in his grasp, I was sickened with the thought that I'd be at his mercy, and he'd get on with his sick dreams of having me the way he had my mother.

Fury, fear, and rebellion wrapped around my body like a vise grip as Isaiah's lips hovered over mine. "Teach me," I pleaded. The words were jutted out like a sword thrusting forward into its opponent. My mouth brushed against his, and he let out a noise that made my stomach dip. "Teach me what feels good, Isaiah."

"We're going down a rocky path," he answered, pulling back just a second before his lips touched mine again. Sparks flew, and I felt my hips jerk toward him all on their own.

He pulled back and shot me a dark look. "Do that again and I'll end up destroying you." His free hand landed on my hips as some sort of warning. His fingers dug into my skin, branding me as excitement flared within. "I'll make you feel good, Gemma. But trust me when I say you are not ready for what your little hips are trying to do."

He was likely right, but he had no idea how desperate I was to rebel. My body and mind were in sync for what seemed like the first time in my life, and I was rioting on the inside. I wanted to live and breathe in the freedom that I had in this very second. I didn't want to think about the future, or the looming threats, or even finding Tobias. I just wanted to...feel. I wanted to feel like I did when Isaiah kissed me. I wanted that high. I was hungry for it. Things were coiled tightly in my lower stomach, and I wanted them to unravel. I wanted Isaiah to pull the string that was keeping me bundled so tightly.

Before I could plead with him, his palms went underneath my skirt, and he touched the curve of my butt just below the lining of my panties. His fingers gripped the soft skin as he hauled me up against the wall and kissed me feverishly. His wet tongue ravished mine, and I was pushing up against him, and he was pushing right back against me. There were no second thoughts between us. When one of us moved, the other did the same. We were like magnets, unable to pull apart, completely captured by one another like we were ensnared in a trap of hungry kisses and hot touches.

"Do you feel that?" he asked as he hauled himself back for a fleeting moment. My pulse had quickened, and my legs prickled. "Do you feel that burning need inside of you, Gemma?"

My answer came out as a rushed breath. "*Yes.*"

His chest rose as his fingers dug into my skin once more. His jaw ticked, and his voice was as raw as I felt on the inside. "That's how you should feel every time someone kisses you. If you don't feel this way down the road, when you grace some guy with what you're giving to me... You fucking leave and go find someone who elicits this feeling inside of you."

Wow.

At some point during our kiss, Isaiah had let my wrists fall free, and my fingers found their way to the back of his head and intertwined with his thick hair. "Is this how you're supposed to feel?" I asked, fighting the urge to look away as my inexperience and vulnerability came crashing down. "Is this how you feel when you kiss other girls?"

Did it always feel like this? If so, I now understood why everyone got so excited about Claiming Night.

Isaiah's wet lips glistened under the dim light. "No."

The answer shocked me. "No?"

He shook his head slowly as his sharp gaze landed on my lips. A swallow worked itself down his throat, and his next words were nothing more than a whisper. "And you've ruined all future girls for me now." He paused as we locked eyes. "*Shit.*" Then, his mouth was on mine again, and the room was spinning, and all my thoughts vanished. Everything was gone except for Isaiah and the feeling of something so enticing licking over my core.

A soft noise came out of my mouth as Isaiah continued kissing me, moving away from my mouth so we could catch our breath every so often and nipping my ear and my neck, and it was honestly too much to handle, until there was a sharp knock on the door. Both of our heads snapped to attention, and panic cut through me so deep I half expected to be bleeding.

"Isaiah," came a bark through the thick slab of wood. I was pretty sure it was Cade, but I couldn't be certain. My thoughts were so fuzzy that if Isaiah didn't also look at the door, I wouldn't have even trusted that the knock had happened. For all I knew, it could have been my heart thudding to the ground. "Did I finally get your fucking attention?"

Isaiah's tone was as sharp as a whip. "Cade. What do you want?"

Isaiah glanced back down to me, staring directly at my lips like he wanted to kiss me more. "We have a slight problem. He's on the move."

A curse left Isaiah, and his face looked pained as he

glanced at my mouth once more. Hope crashed and burned around me, and I felt the disappointment come between us. The second Isaiah let my legs down, cool air brushed over me, and I felt...damp.

"Fucking hell." A groan left Isaiah as he righted my skirt on my hips and then ran a hand through his hair rather aggressively. "You're..."

My attention flew to him. "I'm what?"

I stood on shaky legs and felt...different. Branded? Less pure? Tainted?

No. I wasn't tainted. I wasn't. Even if Isaiah and I had done more than kiss, I wasn't tainted.

Richard would definitely think that if he ever found out. His words were an echo in my head that seemed to climb out of the darkest areas of my mind. *You are to remain untouched. You belong to me. You are mine.*

But I wasn't his. I wouldn't be. Determination ran through my blood like I was born with the primal notion. The submissive little angel Richard had created was slowly self-destructing, and it gave me the tiniest bit of leverage.

There was a time in my life where I had believed everything that came out of his mouth. I obeyed his rules and thought true to his threats. He told me that if I didn't allow him to punish me, to take care of me, that I'd end up just like my mother. *Dead.*

But it wasn't true.

It was all a fucking lie.

Just like it was probably a lie that my mother had been mentally ill. An omission of the truth. Over the years, I thought long and hard about my mother and her behavior. I was so young when she left that it was hard to grasp onto what was real and what had been fed to me from such an early age, but if my mother had gone through what Richard had put me through (was *currently* putting me through) maybe he was the reason for her illness—if there ever was one to begin with. Maybe he broke her so deeply that she couldn't remember how to put herself back together.

Trepidation started to creep over my shoulder as the thoughts began pulling me under. My mind was trying to remember her laugh or the song she used to sing to me and Tobias, but I was quickly ripped away from the memory when a hand landed on my arm.

"You okay?" Isaiah's other hand found my chin, and I blinked rapidly, focusing on his thick eyelashes and stern gaze. "Where did you just go?"

"Um…" A shaky breath left my lips. "Nowhere. I'm here."

He shook his head once, and a dark tendril of hair fell over his forehead. His brows knitted. "I thought you said you trusted me." I said nothing, and I was pretty sure he was waiting for me to say something. Anything. But I didn't. I couldn't. "I know you're running from him, Gem. But why?"

Another rap on the door sounded, and I jumped. "Isaiah." Cade's voice was less playful and more urgent. "If you want to follow him, you better go now."

"Bain?" I asked as Isaiah's hand fell to mine, and he began pulling me beside him.

Just before he opened the door, he shot me a wicked grin. "Wanna go on a field trip?"

"As in leave the school grounds?"

"Mmhm." He swung the door open, and Cade locked eyes with him before he glanced over at me.

"And what if we get caught? Who's going to be your alibi when your alibi is right there beside you?"

He shrugged once, looking his usual cool, calm, and collected self before that dimple appeared on his cheek. "We better not get caught then, huh?"

CHAPTER THIRTY-SEVEN

ISAIAH

SILENCE STRETCHED all around us as Gemma placed her shaky hand in mine. My fingers collided with hers as she walked beside Cade and me through the darkness of the party.

I whispered into her ear, "Stay quiet. I don't want people to know we're dipping out early."

"Early from the party?" Her voice was hardly audible.

I straightened my back as Cade answered, "The Claiming."

Sounds of kissing and soft moans came into contact with the three of us as we swiftly made a beeline for the exit. I knew my way around this basement even with the blanket of darkness that surrounded us. My hand reached out as I touched one pillar, then another one, and then one more before I knew we were exactly three yards from the door.

Skin slapping against skin and a flirty giggle came from the left, and Gemma's light gasp filtered out into the heated air. It smelled of sex and alcohol, just like any other claiming, but it was new to her.

Everything was.

A throb settled deep inside my tight core as I let myself picture what was underneath her skirt. She was wet. I could feel her pressed up against me. I had the sudden urge to pull her back into that room and shut Cade out to spread her legs and taste her perfect little pussy.

What an obsessive, wildly hot thought.

Fuck, what was it with her? Gemma had awoken something inside of me, like an unbinding of my most secret desires. A sense of protectiveness and possession came over me the second my hands touched her, and it was a dangerous thing.

It was risky bringing her with me right now.

I knew that.

Cade knew that.

Mixing business with pleasure was likely going to fuck me over in the end, but here I was, shoving her through the door and pulling her along the musty, damp underground hallway made of wet stone and cobwebs.

"You're bringing her with you?" Cade asked, hinting at disappointment.

"She'll be fine," I answered, my hand clenching down on hers. "Who's trailing him?"

"Brantley," Cade answered as we walked briskly through the dark. "As soon as you and Gemma began that very, *very* convincing kiss, he snuck away."

"Goddamnit," I mumbled. "He does know I'm onto him."

I still hadn't informed my father that Bain was suspecting something, mainly because I didn't want to deal with the weight of his words right away. But I knew I had to let him know. I just wanted to be one hundred percent certain Bain knew I was watching him—or at least, that was what I was telling myself. Maybe I hadn't told him because I liked feeling as if I had some type of control, which I didn't. Not really, anyway.

Nonetheless, Bain waiting until I was preoccupied before dipping out was smart and calculating. I had a big feeling he would do it, though. Half the time when I'd follow him, he wouldn't do anything other than drive around in circles before parking his car down the street near the abandoned warehouse and walk back to St. Mary's. The students weren't allowed to have vehicles here, but Bain always had a backup parked down the street. Every once in a while, the type of car would be changed out and the tracker we'd place on it would go rogue, but we still managed to trail him. He was paranoid. Or maybe it was his father's paranoia. Either way, he was a deceitful little fuck.

"Have you told your father yet?"

"No." My answer was as short as it was abrupt, and a second later, I heard Cade sigh. Then, a second after that, we pushed through the doors, and the cool air of the hallway clung to my hot skin.

Gemma stood between Cade and me, staying as silent as a mouse. Her brown hair framed her stoic face, her eyes showing nothing at all.

I pulled my hoodie back onto my head and jerked a nod to Cade. "Let Gem wear your jacket."

I needed her to be in something dark. Her black skirt worked, but her light-colored sweater would catch an eye if we had to hide.

Cade sighed disapprovingly as he unzipped his dark-gray jacket and shrugged it off his shoulders. "You're seriously bringing her with you?"

Gemma shifted nervously and glanced to the floor.

Cade held out his jacket to her and ignored me while saying, "It's nothing against you, Gemma. It's just that Isaiah is being fucking *reckless*." He shot me a glare. "And you could end up as collateral damage."

A throaty laugh erupted from my chest as I tried to remind myself that I wasn't my father, and I'd never act like my father. Sure, I was the Huntsman's son, and I was viewed as the next boss, meaning not only would my two best friends work for me, but so would their fathers—if they managed to stay alive that long—but I didn't want to power trip them. I never would. "You know I wouldn't let that happen, Cade. You more than anyone should know that."

A tick of pain hit me with the quick reminder of my mother and what had happened when she was caught in the crossfire. Cade knew all about it. He and his father had shown up later that night.

Cade's jaw tightened as he helped Gemma zip up the jacket. She stayed silent, and it irritated me not knowing what she was thinking.

"You don't always have that choice, Isaiah." He ran a hand through his hair. "And she's right. What if you two do get caught?"

"We won't get caught. I was careless before. You know this."

Why was I even explaining this to him? Why was I justifying myself to him? I glanced away, knowing why he was so concerned. And I should listen. I really should.

"We need to go. You know what to do if anything arises while we're gone."

Cade shook his head at me before winking at Gemma, and then he slipped through the door to head back to the party.

I grabbed onto Gemma's hand once more, and we began the long walk down the empty hallway toward my uncle's stone cottage.

It was right behind St. Mary's, just through the far left

entrance of the school. Our feet shuffled over the cobble-stone walkway as the night air cooled our skin. Leaves rustled with rising tension as if they knew Gemma and I were sneaking away from the school in the middle of the night. Or maybe it was a warning to me that I should send her back with Cade. But fuck me, I liked having her near.

Stopping just behind the large trunk of a tree that smelled of pine, I peered at my uncle's far left window where I knew his bedroom was. This house was an old servant's house. Small and subtle, nothing more than a bed and a small bathroom inside. But his car was parked just a few yards away in the makeshift driveway. Gemma and I headed toward it.

My phone dinged, and with my free hand, I pulled it out and read Brantley's text.

BRANT: He's on foot. I see a new car up ahead. It's a Bentley. I think it's his. He must have found the tracker. Sending a pin.

I SIGHED and shoved my phone back into my hoodie and pulled my uncle's spare key from my jeans. Gemma stopped dead in her tracks, the loose pebbles shifting underneath her boots. "Isaiah. Are we really leaving?"

Placing a finger to my lips, I nodded once and then opened the door to my uncle's newly restored '75 Mustang. Gemma hesitated at first, and I felt the strangest little tug in my chest at the thought of her backing out, of having to follow Bain on my own—as usual—without her near. It was fucked up. Cade was right. I was being risky and reckless. A taunting voice in the back of my head whispered, "*Selfish.*"

A heavy breath left me as I came face to face with the realization that I *was* being selfish and impulsive, knowing very well that whatever it was I was feeling for her was never going to last. I wouldn't let it get that far. Nothing would change for me. I was still taking on the responsibility of my father's fucked-up empire, and I would never put someone like her in a position where she could end up as a suffering victim from the life I led.

I would never let it get to that, even if I could feel the pricking of deeper feelings underneath my skin. Gemma meant something to me—and in such a short time, too. It was fucking terrifying, and I didn't admit my fears easily.

The car came to life a second after I climbed behind the wheel. The engine was loud, but I wasn't worried about my uncle waking up and finding me. He knew I'd taken his car before and why. He likely wouldn't approve of Gemma being with me, but what he didn't know wouldn't hurt him.

"We could get into some serious trouble if someone catches us leaving the school," Gemma whispered, sitting stark still in the passenger seat. "Wouldn't that ruin everything?"

"Put your seatbelt on." I pushed the car into reverse and slowly began creeping away from St. Mary's. I flicked the lights on just as we made it through the entrance, the car dropping down as we rolled over the dip in the driveway.

Gemma's soft tone filled the dark interior after her seatbelt clicked. "Whose car is this? I didn't think students could have cars."

I chuckled, making a right turn to follow the pin that Brantley had sent me. "That's correct." I paused, scanning the street for any other moving vehicles. "It's my uncle's."

Her gasp made me smile.

"What?!"

I rested my hand on her bare knee for a quick second before putting it back on the wheel. *Bad idea.* "Will you relax? I thought you said you trusted me."

Her arms whipped across her chest. "You're totally taking that out of context."

"Ah," I murmured, still scanning the empty street. We were parked across from the address I had on my phone, wedged between a few other cars. "So you only trust me with my hands underneath your skirt. I see."

She gasped again, this time whizzing her entire body toward me. My lip jutted upward, and if it weren't so dark in here, I knew her face would be a *lovely* shade of red. "I...I..."

A laugh started to creep up my throat, and as soon as it was out in the open, bellowing from my mouth, she sighed. I was pretty sure she was trying to act annoyed with me, but instead, her cheek twitched, followed by her smashing her lips together.

My laughing eventually stopped when I watched a midnight-colored Bentley prowl through the entrance of a dilapidated warehouse and whip out onto the road, taking a right up at the stop sign. I crept my foot along the gas before speeding up just far enough that I could keep eyes on which direction he'd gone but not close enough that he'd see me.

Or maybe he had seen me.

Unlikely. But it was possible.

My phone dinged in the cup holder, and I caught Gemma's eye. "Read that to me, will you?"

She looked shocked for a split second before she uncrossed her arms and pulled the phone to her face. "It says it's from Brantley. He says he remained unseen."

I nodded once, and she placed the phone back down and re-crossed her arms. After a few more seconds of tense silence, her voice cut through the stuffy air. "Why am I with you right now?"

My eyebrow hitched as I kept my eyes on Bain. "Do you not want to be with me right now?"

"I didn't say that." She waited for a moment and then

shifted in her seat. "But what if you get caught? You're on probation. Isn't that the whole reason why you have me? To cover for you when you...follow Bain?"

I put my blinker on and turned left, slowing down a little as Bain's speed had decreased.

Gemma didn't give me a chance to answer her as another question popped out. "Do you make it a habit to sneak out of St. Mary's to follow Bain? Is this where you go when you leave tutoring early?"

"So many questions," I deadpanned.

"Isaiah!" she shouted, and I couldn't help but smile. *God, she was cute when she was feisty.* "If I'm going to get in trouble, I better know why!"

"You won't get in trouble, Gemma. I wouldn't let that happen."

She threw her hands out and pushed her lithe frame into the leather seat. "If we get caught, we will get in trouble!"

"We can just say we're studying the stars if they catch us walking back into the school later. Astronomy." I fought the smile wanting to crawl onto my face.

From the corner of my eye, I could see her shoulders slump. "So that's why you brought me? You're still using me as your cover?" She paused. "Do you even take astronomy?" I didn't, but that was besides the fact.

I caught her staring at me intently, and instead of answering her, I threw a question at her. "Aren't you using me too, though? You need fast cash and an ID, right?"

She quickly glanced away, unable to come up with anything to say because I was right, even though we both knew that it was total bullshit, especially now after crashing our lips together for the world's hottest fucking kiss to ever exist.

Bain made another left turn, and I was beginning to think we were going in circles again until he made another turn, and we started on a winding road. There were three cars in between us, making it difficult to keep my eyes on his blacked-out Bentley, so when I spoke next, I kept my attention on the road. "I'm not using you."

Her voice was soft, and I could hardly hear her over the sounds of the car. "You're not?"

"It's a shame that you even have to ask that question after what just happened. And I wouldn't have brought you if I thought we'd get caught." I swallowed back the regret I knew my next words would bring. "I brought you because I like having you near."

"Oh," she whispered, glancing down at her intertwined fingers. It took a moment for her to speak again, but when she did, there was a swift change in the air. "Why do you have to follow Bain for your father?"

Gemma's hands unclasped, and her arm brushed against mine as she placed it on the center console. Even through our clothed arms, I felt the heat. "That's a question I can't answer."

"Can't or won't?"

My response was quick. "Won't. Just like you won't answer any of the questions I want to ask you."

A moment passed before she nodded. "Fair enough." And then an easy silence came over us. It was as if she knew that we were crossing over into those dangerous depths of questions and answers that neither of us wanted to get into. It was so fucked of me to bring her tonight, and even more so if I were to start filling her in on everything that my life entailed. It was better if she were left in the dark on this one.

"So..." I glanced at her, and she caught my eye. Need pulled deep in my stomach as my arm brushed hers again. "Are you liking St. Mary's?"

An abrupt, choppy, squeal-like laugh left her lips, and I snapped my attention over toward her for a second before putting it back on Bain's Bentley. "What?" I asked. "Why are you laughing?" And why did I feel my lips turning upward at the sound?

Her light laugh filled the car again, and it was like an awakening. Why haven't I heard her laugh before? My chest was twisting, and I suddenly wanted to make her laugh again.

"Because..." She dropped her head so low that her hair fell forward, but I could still hear the amusement. "We go from talking about sneaking out of school to follow Bain on some secret mission, and now you're asking if I like St. Mary's?"

My fingers flexed on the wheel. "Don't forget the whole kissing and touching thing before all of this."

Out of the corner of my eye, I noticed how she brushed her hair away from her face, and without even looking, I knew her face was flushed. "Right. How could I forget that?" Then, she began again. "Let's see... My first few days here, I've been shoved inside a closet with the school's most popular bad boy, had a rumor started that I was the new slut of St. Mary's, then I was dragged underneath the school to my first-ever party, and someone attempted to *claim* me before I even knew what that meant, and I ended up with a concussion later that night. Oh, and then I was shoved in another closet after curfew. *And* I somehow started tutoring said bad boy from that first day of school...which really isn't tutoring at all, so..."

I finished for her. "So basically, you fucking love it."

Her laugh was loud, and I grinned. "Actually..." She leaned her head back onto the head rest. "I do."

"Let me guess." I sat up a little taller, squinting through the mist that fell onto the windshield to see where Bain had pulled into. My stomach knotted, but I didn't let Gemma see my concern. "Your favorite part was being shoved into a closet with me on the first day. Am I right?"

Her smile lit up the whole goddamn interior. There was a

glossy gleam to her eye, and at some point, she'd raised the hood of Cade's jacket, making her look adorably mischievous. Most of the time, she looked so focused and stoic, almost sad at times. But tonight? There was a glow around her. A care-free spirit that was just begging for a taste of life. Maybe it had something to do with what had happened earlier.

I wanted to kiss her again.

In fact, I wanted to do a lot of things to her.

Putting the car in park, Gemma glanced out the window. "Where are we?"

My fingers flexed around the wheel. I glanced through the windshield once more and held back a growl. "Somewhere I hope you never learn about."

The Covens.

Why the fuck was Bain at the Covens? Was his father supplying guns here now? This was my father's domain. The Huntsman's. This entire city was my father's, and when he learned that Bain had been over here, he would go on a rampage to find out why. This was grounds for a fucking war.

Gemma's voice brought me back down to the ground as my thoughts began jumping. "*The Covenant Psychiatric Hospital.*" Her head turned away from the window as the sign for the hospital glowed brightly against the wet glass. "Why is that so familiar to me?"

Ice coated my veins. A hand squeezed around the muscle inside my chest. *No.* "Maybe you've driven past it?" A million and one questions rushed to the tip of my tongue as I began fishing for information. It wasn't common for someone to know of this place. It was a psychiatric hospital, yes, and in the front, it looked like any normal facility for the ill. But on the backside? Underneath the floors of those who truly were sick, it was hell. Pure fucking hell. If Gemma knew what the Covens was, then there was a lot more to her than I thought.

"It's unlikely that I've ever driven past." Gemma seemed

to think this over before giving me a quick, fleeting glance. "Before St. Mary's, I didn't really get out much."

I wanted to continue digging and asking questions, but time was getting away from me, and I had a job to do. It was the whole reason I was at St. Mary's and the whole reason why Gemma and I were thrust together in the first place: to keep me here, to feed information to my father, and to keep Jack safe.

I left the car running as I pulled my hood up further onto my head and opened the door. A gust of wet rain rushed in, and I turned toward Gemma. "Climb over here, and keep the car running."

"Wait, what?" she asked, eyes wide and completely shocked.

"I'll be right back." I tapped the top of the car. "Honk if something goes wrong."

Then, I climbed the rest of the way out and watched as she began climbing into my seat. The door slammed as she started to protest, but I knew time was a fleeting thing, so I jogged through the slashing rain droplets and ducked behind a bush, just far enough that I could see through its wet branches.

The hairs on my arms stood erect as I stared at the side entrance of the hospital—the same one my father took me to when I was Jack's age. I knew the inside had lights so bright they could burn your irises if you stared too long and that the hallway reeked of body sweat, blood, and tears that was hardly covered up by antiseptic. My nostrils flared as my mind tried taking me down memory lane, the pinch of my neck still twinging like my father's hand was still there, gripping it, making me watch, breaking that last tiny bit of innocence that I still had in my youth.

Jack entered my head as I stared ahead through the drooping branches of the bush, rain drops clinging to the leaves for dear life. I watched as someone came out of the entrance of the hospital, letting the metal door shut loudly behind him. He was a stocky man, wearing a nicely pressed suit, so I knew right then that he wasn't one of the employees. He didn't have that distinct color of scrubs on: blue for the psychiatric part of the hospital and black for the Covens. I pulled my phone out and zoomed in on Bain backing his Bentley up to the door underneath the awning. There was a bright light that flickered above the man's head, allowing anyone to see clearly.

I snapped several photos of Bain climbing out of the driver's seat and rounding the Bentley with his trunk popped, then a few more as Bain pulled out a bag and rested it on top of the car. Then, out came a sleek, black pistol, and my stomach plummeted as a twist of anger clung to my bones. *Now he's doing his father's dirty work?* It wasn't hard for me to grasp the idea of Bain working alongside his father, because I knew just how dark and deceitful this life could be. And if Bain were anything like me, he'd feel as if he had no choice. But that was the thing with Bain. Even if given a choice, he'd still take his father's side. Bain loved power. The potency of it was clear on his face as he and the man talked back and forth, turning the gun in their hands like it was a gift straight from God.

They were corrupted men.

Both of them.

I wasn't a saint, and I'd witnessed things that I wished I'd never seen and regretted not stopping, but I, at least, had the humanity to feel guilt and torment. I, at least, had the ability to recognize humanity for what it was.

But men like Bain, my father, his father, even Brantley's and Cade's fathers...they looked down upon others and didn't care who got hurt.

A human life wasn't much to them. If it were, then the Covens would be burnt to the fucking ground.

They wouldn't allow torture and the breaking of a person's mind to fester like it had.

They all got off on it.

It made me want to walk over and snap their necks in half.

Maybe that made me as bad as them, but punishments were vital to the world when someone deserved them. And they all did.

After I clicked another photo of Bain handing off several guns to the mystery man, I pushed my phone into my pocket and began to stand up. The ground was slick against my shoes, mud sloshing as I turned my back to get back to Gemma.

That was my first mistake. *You never turn your back on someone with a gun, son.*

The sound whirled past my ear, and for a moment, I paused. *Was tha—?*

The next thing I knew, I was taken to the ground by my own subconscious ability to save myself from getting shot, and then I was ducking and rolling and climbing to my feet before running like hell to get back to Gemma.

That was my second mistake: bringing her here.

What the fuck was I thinking!

I wasn't sure if Bain had spotted me or if it was security. The Covens was highly protected on the inside, and it wouldn't surprise me if it were protected on the outside, especially with a goddamn gun exchange.

My heart lurched as I heard another pop of the gun, and it killed me to have to run right toward Gemma, but I had no other choice.

Cade's voice rung out in my head. *"You're being reckless."*

Reckless should have been my middle fucking name.

My breath was ragged, and my shoes were hardly keeping traction as I skidded to a stop right beside the car. I flung the passenger door open and flew inside.

Gemma was sitting in the driver's seat, and as soon as she saw me, I shouted, "DRIVE!"

CHAPTER THIRTY-EIGHT

GEMMA

I FROZE. My lungs had stolen my ability to breathe.

"Gemma!" Isaiah was completely wet from head to toe. His black hair was even darker than usual as it stuck to his forehead. Tiny raindrops clung to his lashes, and they stayed even as he opened his mouth and yelled, "Gemma, drive!"

A loud noise rang out through the air. *What the heck was that?*

"I can't drive!" I panicked, looking down at the wheel as if the leather would burn my hands. There was panic in his voice, and it only took one look from him to know we were in trouble.

"What the hell do you mean you can't drive?" Then, his hand gripped the shifter in between us. "Gas is on the right, brake is on the left!"

Blood rushed through my body so viciously I itched.

"It's life or death, Gemma! Go! Now!" Then, he popped the car into drive, and my foot moved off the brake, and I slammed onto the gas. The tires spun under wet asphalt, and then we whooshed forward, rushing down the street.

Something from behind sounded again, and Isaiah cursed. "Let off the gas for a second."

I did as he said, my foot completely coming off the pedal, and then he reached over and jerked the wheel to the left, and we went flying onto another street.

He wasn't paying much attention to the front of us but more so behind us. He kept his tight grip on the wheel from the passenger seat, but I was able to straighten it for us before pressing back down on the pedal.

"That's it, Gem. You're doing great. Keep your foot on the gas."

Isaiah was looking out of the side mirror, his jaw set into a tight, firm line. I didn't look for long, though, because the reality of the situation was weighing down on my shoulders, and I needed to keep us on the road.

I'd run before, on foot, but I knew what it felt like to be in a life-or-death situation, and there was no time for worry or second-guessing. What I was feeling was parallel to what I'd felt before, and I knew I'd do what was needed to get us far away from whatever it was he was running from. *Bain?*

"More gas," he urged, his large hand still on the wheel. He glanced out the front for a second before he went back to the mirror. Both of our bodies flew back onto the leather seats as I pushed us forward, trying my hardest to keep us straight on the road. The rearview mirror was too far up for me to see, and I was lucky I'd messed around with the seat while Isaiah was looking for Bain, otherwise my feet wouldn't have hit the pedals.

"Fuck," he muttered under his breath. It was so angry sounding that it sent a wave of caution to my ears. "I need to get you out of here."

"Us," I corrected, pushing even harder on the gas as my

gaze stayed steady on the road. There weren't any other cars in front of us, but up ahead, I saw the white lines curving, and my stomach revolted. *Gas? Or brake?*

"Isaiah, what do I do?"

He snagged a quick look to the road before he answered, "Let up on the gas. I'll turn for you."

My breaths were coming in hot, but I tried my hardest to focus on the task at hand, even with the nagging feeling of being chased scratching at my back. Although I'd been in a similar situation, where I'd been chased before, it didn't make matters better even in the slightest. My body was still just as panicky as it was then, and for a moment, I swore I could still feel the twigs slashing across my arms and legs, my skin burning with the cuts.

"Gemma," Isaiah's voice cut through my foggy brain, and I shook my head. "Breathe. I can feel your slip on the wheel."

I stuttered, shaking my head. "I'm—I'm sorry," I urged through clanking teeth. *Shit, I'm doing it again!* "I do this sometimes."

My fight-or-flight instincts were coming in like stinging slaps against my skin as I decided to fight. I'd fight against the panic. The fear was an exact mold of what I'd felt before. The dread of being caught and the pain that would come with it. It was maddening.

Isaiah turned the wheel for me as I focused on even breaths and letting up on the gas. My foot hovered over the brake and accelerator before he straightened the wheel. "Gas!"

My foot slammed down as my hands gripped the leather.

"You do what sometimes?" He turned the car for me again, although I was pretty sure I was getting the hang of it. Though, I had yet to come to a complete stop, so I knew I probably still needed his guidance.

"I sometimes space out. Black out. Remember with Bain

at the last party? When there is panic rising and it's too familiar to what I've felt before, I…"

He jutted through my confession. "You've run for your life before, Gemma?"

My answer came out before I could stop it. "Yes." Then, my hands squeezed again, righting the wheel so I was in between the lines of the road. "Is that what we're doing? Running for our lives?"

Isaiah's hand dropped from the wheel, and instead, he rested it on my knee. My leg jumped, and little sparks flew to the very tips of my toes. He didn't look at me, still leaving his stern gaze on the side mirror. "I shouldn't have brought you. I'm sorry."

It seemed the panic in his voice had lessened some. He was still glancing out the side mirror, but his jaw was no longer hard like stone. I focused back on the road, the dotted white line growing more blurred as my speed increased. "It's okay."

"It's not okay." I could feel his gaze on me like a million little spotlights. "And how the hell have you never driven before?"

I laughed—actually laughed. "Well…" I began to turn the wheel a little as the road had a slight curve. Isaiah's hand left my knee, and he helped guide me. "No one has taken the time to teach me." That wasn't the whole truth. Richard didn't want me to know how to drive. Just another way I needed to rely on him and ask for his help.

"There is no way I'm letting you leave St. Mary's without having the skill to drive. I'll teach you."

Something bloomed in my chest, and although I could feel the remnants of anxiety still brewing under the surface, a smile graced my lips. "There's no way you're *letting* me leave? I wasn't aware that I needed your permission."

He shrugged. "You don't need my permission, but you do need money and a new ID, so..."

I didn't respond because *yeah, he got me there*.

"We're almost back at St. Mary's," Isaiah said. "Keep up on the gas, though. We're not being followed anymore, but I don't want a run-in with anyone."

I nodded as my foot continued pressing onto the gas. So badly did I want to ask what exactly he was running from and why he was in a life-or-death situation from following Bain to a psychiatric hospital of all places, but I didn't. I knew how it felt to have secrets you couldn't reveal. Not to mention, I had my own answers that I needed to figure out. Like why that psychiatric hospital had felt so familiar to me.

"Make a left then roll into the school slowly. Switch the lights off."

I paused, letting up on the gas and slowly turning my wheel.

"Nice work, Good Girl. You're a fast learner." Just as the compliment came out, he chuckled because we both lurched forward from my foot landing heavily on the brake.

"Sorry," I said as I lifted my foot back off the pedal and inched it onto the accelerator again.

I saw the lazy half-grin appear out of the corner of my eye. "You have nothing to apologize for. In fact, I think you're pretty fucking amazing."

It felt like I'd swallowed my heart. Then, I stopped breathing as Isaiah reached over my body, his damp hoodie brushing over my cheek as he flipped a switch to turn the lights off. Once he was back in his seat, I managed to breathe again. "Amazing at driving? I think you're lying to make me feel better."

His large, warm hand rested back on my bare knee again, and he tapped the inside of it, making me see spots. "I'm not referring to your driving skills."

My mouth opened as a rush of something hot flung to my cheeks. I caught his eye as I glanced over at him, trying to read what exactly he'd meant by that, but then his eyes widened, and he shouted, "Brake!"

Brake?

Isaiah's hand left my leg, and he slammed it onto the middle shifter just as my foot slammed onto the pedal. We both jerked forward, but he was quick to push his arm out to my chest to keep me from colliding with the wheel.

My fingers covered my mouth. "Oh my God! Did I just wreck the headmaster's car?!"

It only took one second for Isaiah's loud laughter to fill the interior. His head was thrown back, his strong jaw catching devious shadows from the lack of light.

Oh my God. "Isaiah! This is all your fault!"

He laughed harder. His shoulders shook as he put his fist up to his mouth to stop himself. I stared out to the stone wall I had run into before slamming on the brake. I felt a shower of embarrassment and fear come down on me like a thousand bricks.

"You are truly fucking amazing," he said through more broken laughter.

"Amazing?!" I shouted. "Isaiah! Never mind the fact that we just snuck out of St. Mary's, but we also just wrecked the headmaster's car! And..." I took a shuddering breath in between my rant. "I don't even have a license! I've broken every rule possible tonight!"

Never in a million years did I think coming to St. Mary's would end up in me wrecking the headmaster's car, in the middle of the night, with someone like Isaiah beside me. Never in a million years did I think I'd be so...careless. Not to mention the fact that I was so blindly ignoring the conse- quences that could follow. But even with all of that, I could feel the amusement bubbling on the inside. It was totally the wrong time to be smiling or laughing, but my cheeks ached to do it.

"Relax." Isaiah was still chuckling with a smile on his face so large it could compel me to do anything if I looked too long. "It's only rule-breaking if we get caught, which we won't."

Then, he opened the door and climbed out effortlessly, taking my panic with him. Sloane had said that the Rebels were dangerous, and Isaiah was just that. He was so incredibly dangerous because he muddled my brain anytime we were alone. Rational thoughts evaporated, fear slowly dissolved, and dread no longer existed. The only thing that did exist was him and my wildly chaotic heart that seemed to soar higher than ever when he was beside me.

As soon as I climbed out of the headmaster's car, feeling the mist of cool rain dampening my hair, Isaiah's hand clasped mine, and we jogged through the wooded area until we got back to the school.

"You are insane, Isaiah," I whispered as he pulled me closer to his body, continuing our conversation. "It's still rule-breaking, even if you don't get caught."

"Says who?" he asked, glancing behind us at the tall trees. "And don't tell me you didn't enjoy breaking the rules."

I didn't answer him as he pulled me the rest of the way through St. Mary's door. He was right. I did enjoy it. I enjoyed it too much.

"You think I enjoyed being chased and then wrecking a car in the process?"

"I sure do," he whispered along my ear, making me jump a little. The farther we walked into St. Mary's, the louder the silence became. Our wet shoes squeaked as we walked along the shiny floors, but that didn't deter Isaiah from keeping silent. His hand still stayed in mine as he leaned in even closer to me, making me freeze. "Just like I think you enjoy it when I whisper in your ear."

He wasn't wrong. I did. My body flamed and ached in such a tortuous way that I was left speechless. It was so incredibly messy inside my head. Feelings and hormones were rioting so much that I stopped right there in the middle of the hallway.

I tipped my head up to his, both of us standing there with nothing but the flicker of sconces along the wall as our witnesses. Isaiah stared down at me, a devilish grin gracing his undaunting facial expression. Things were shifting. I could feel it.

"We shouldn't have kissed like we did earlier."

His sentence threw me off, and I felt my emotions slipping. His eyes didn't change, though. The swirls of blue still held a wealth of wickedness in them.

"Why?" I turned toward him even further.

His chest brushed against mine as he took a step closer, erasing any empty space that was hanging in limbo. His hand gripped my chin hard enough to gain my full attention but not hard enough to hurt. "Because now that I've had a taste of the good girl, all I want to do is corrupt her."

My stomach bottomed out, and my next words surprised me. "Then what are you waiting for?"

Isaiah's face darkened, his dark brows a cloak over his eyes, and then...and then I was spinning.

CHAPTER THIRTY-NINE

ISAIAH

I won't corrupt the good girl. I won't corrupt the good girl. I won't corrupt the good girl.

No matter how many times I said it, it wasn't getting through. My lips were on hers, and everything else was long gone. Her mouth was sweet and inviting and surprisingly needy. A growl tore up my throat as I pulled her small frame into my chest, and when she shuddered against my hard abdomen, I almost ripped her clothes to shreds.

Need like I'd never felt before drove through my body, mangling every part of me to distortion. I didn't care if she was fragile like my uncle had said. I didn't care if she was inexperienced or that she and I could never be anything more than what we were now. I didn't care that I was feeling something much stronger than desire whip through my blood.

Her kiss sucked me in. *She* sucked me in. A connection. We had something brewing. Something so big that it made everything else just...stop. Her tongue dragged over mine, and I pulled back to catch myself before I began inching underneath her shirt, as if we weren't in the middle of the fucking hallway, and that was when a thundering wave of awareness dragged over my shoulder. *Wait.* Faint footsteps pulled my attention, and I gripped her. We couldn't get caught. Not now. Not after realizing just how hungry I was for her. And possessive. And protective. And fuck, what was I saying?

"Let's go," I whispered, hurriedly pulling us through the nearby door. The second we were inside, I shut it quietly and spun around to check our surroundings. The dining hall was closed as it was the middle of the night, so the expansive area was quiet. The gleam of silvery moonlight shone through the arched windows, allowing me to see just enough to know that we were alone. I turned back to see Gemma nibbling on her lip, looking half scared and half excited. My mouth twisted a fraction, but it quickly disappeared as I saw a light shine underneath the door. *Shit.* Thinking fast, I snatched Gemma's hand, and a sweet puff of air left her mouth as I rushed us three tables down. My back was on the floor within a flash, and I pulled Gemma on top of me in a less-than-graceful way. She toppled and let out a little squeal, and before I knew what I was doing, I was silencing it with my mouth.

As my lips moved over hers, I was somehow able to pull myself from the impulsive behavior and began wiggling us both underneath the long bench and dining table. It was the same damn one I sat in all week, stealing glances at her as she sat with Sloane and Mercedes, looking damn near perfect while eating her oatmeal in the morning.

Gemma dragged her mouth from mine, and I placed my finger over her lips. "What the hell, Isaiah," she hissed over my fingers, her warm breath falling on my face. I inhaled and had to turn my head to stop myself from plunging my tongue down her throat again. "How did one kiss from you end up with me being under a table?"

"Because you're just as hungry as I am. You feel exactly

what I feel when we touch." My tone was hushed, but the validity to my sentence was in full force. Her body tensed on mine but quickly eased as I removed my fingers from her lips and pressed a quick kiss to the tip of her nose. "I like kissing you, and you like it too. There is no shame in that."

My heart strained, and I cursed the fact that her kiss was like a fucking truth serum. There *was* shame in that. I knew deep down that my words were truthful, but I also knew that we were destined to end in tragedy. It felt wrong to be feeding her my emotions, even if they were true, because she and I would never have something real. Even if she were a different girl who wasn't planning on dipping out of St. Mary's with a new identity and handful of money, I wouldn't go down this path with someone.

I needed to push back on the feelings that were there. I needed to stop kissing her, and touching her, and looking for her the second she stepped into the room. I needed to get off probation so I could stop using her as my way off the SMC's radar.

But need and want were two very different things.

Gemma opened her mouth to say something, probably to deny that she liked kissing me back, because I had a feeling she was going through the same emotions in her head, but the door to the dining hall creaked open, and she gasped. "Shh," I hushed over her lips that were still hovering over mine. "We're fine. Stay quiet."

Fuck, I wanted to kiss her again. And touch her.

A few moments passed before Gemma's mouth moved over my ear. "Why..." She spoke so low I could hardly hear her. "Why do I feel like laughing?"

My lips twitched as my hand slowly cupped the back of her head to keep her still. "Because deep down you like breaking rules with me. It's fun."

The softest, throaty noise left her, and she let out a soft

giggle. *Oh, shit.* "Gemma," I warned, also feeling a laugh bubble up in my chest. I saw the sway of light from a flashlight as the dining hall door shut loudly. Whoever was patrolling the halls tonight was suspicious, and I had a big feeling it was someone on the SMC, because why wouldn't it be with us shoved underneath a table in the middle of the night? Part of me wondered if I should have just let us get caught and tell the duty teacher that Gemma and I were walking back from tutoring, but it was late, we were far from the library, and I wasn't done with her yet. I didn't want the night to end.

Gemma's body started to shake on mine as she buried her head into my chest, holding back a laugh. I cursed the fact that we had to be quiet, because I wanted to hear her laugh again. It erased some of the darkness that rested inside me. Like a soothing balm. And I liked the fact that she wasn't panicking like earlier. Did she finally trust me and believe that I wouldn't let her get into trouble?

The light grew closer, and although Gemma's giggles were as quiet as a mouse, a small fraction of reality set in. We couldn't get caught. Even with my grades improving, mainly because I actually turned in my assignments now, I still needed to keep my nose clean. My grades would simply pacify the SMC, maybe sharpen their trust a little, but if I got caught sneaking out again, or alone with a girl shoved underneath a table in the dining hall at midnight—if I got caught breaking any rules, really—I would find my ticket out of here.

Gemma was still shaking on me, and her grip on my hoodie had tightened. *Fucking shit, Gemma.* I wanted to laugh just at the mere fact that she was laughing, but instead, I pushed my hips up and gained her attention. Then, I peeled her head from my chest and smacked my lips onto hers so hard it silenced every bit of laughter that was hanging on her tongue. It only took her a second to move past the shock and begin kissing me back, and although I kept my eyes open, watching the beam of light sway from one end of the dining hall to the next, the heat and intensity that her mouth caused on mine was electric. My hips moved, and Gemma's legs fell to the side slowly, letting my hardness touch her warm core, and *Christ,* I could feel the hot heat sourcing from the only piece of fabric that covered her. My hands gripped her hips to keep her steady so she wouldn't move over my jeans. The scratching noise would only bring more attention to us, and that was the last thing we needed.

Our lips moved in sync with each other, and Gemma must have caught the hint that we needed to be quiet, because there wasn't a single sound of smacked lips. Our kiss wasn't sloppy. Or rushed. It was slow, intense, and hot as hell.

As soon as the door slammed shut again and the beam of light was gone, Gemma pulled herself from my mouth. My hand left her waist, and I brought it up to my lips, telling her to be quiet. She nodded, and a piece of her hair fell forward, landing on my shoulder. The muscles in my neck stretched as I inclined my head and searched through the darkened floor to see if anyone was still standing there. I felt Gemma suck in more air. My hips had pressed up in the action, and she and I were like one. We were so close I could feel the burning throb all the way to my soul.

My eyes clung to hers, and for a second, we just stared at each other, eyes locked, bodies joined. Her chest had risen and stayed, her grip on my shirt never lessening. I gulped down a hot swallow, and then at the exact same time, our lips crashed together again, and our slow and steady kiss from earlier turned vicious and unforgiving. I didn't hold back this time. My hands were on her bare ass, the fabric of her panties bunching as I squeezed. Her hips moved over mine as if she knew exactly what she was doing. I suppressed a grunt and felt the need to growl as I nipped her lip with my teeth. We were moving so fucking fast I didn't have time to even ask if this was what she wanted. If we were going to go down this path, the one where we shared nothing but intense kisses and lustful touches, we were both going to go down afterwards. There was likely to be guilt, maybe even regret.

No. I would never regret kissing her. It was too hot and too pleasing.

I broke our kiss as I pushed us back out from under the dining table, allowing the open air to cool our heated bodies. As soon as we were on our feet, I picked her up underneath her skirt and placed her firm ass down on the slab of wood where we placed our trays for every meal, and then I shoved her legs apart.

"I told myself I wouldn't cross this line with you," I muttered through clenched teeth as her hands laid on my shoulders. "But then we kissed."

"And things changed," she finished, wiggling herself up to be closer to me. Our gazes met, and the air shifted. The truth was evident in her eyes. The same truth that I had. We both knew that this was something much more than a simple touch, and that it was something that would likely punish us in the end, but it didn't matter—at least not to me.

I wanted nothing more than her at that moment.

"Do you want to cross that line?" I asked, tipping her head back with the pad of my finger. Her long hair fell behind her shoulders, showcasing her rising chest.

She glanced at my lips. "I don't know what the line is...but I think I want to cross it with you." She swallowed quietly. "I told you earlier that I wanted you to teach me how to feel good, and that hasn't changed."

My one hand stayed on her delicate chin as she looked up at me with curious eyes. Her body language spoke volumes. The arousal radiated off her so strongly I could hardly focus on anything other than my own racing pulse. The innocent part of her was evident within her gaze, and I wanted nothing more than to take that innocent piece of her and distort it until she was fully fucked and unrecognizable. She was going to know what it felt like to be pleasured and treated like nothing less than a goddamn queen.

"The lesson is long," I started, gripping her knee that had somehow clenched around my hip. "But we'll start at the beginning." A rush of breath left her as my hand trailed up her leg and past the hem of her skirt. I watched as she squirmed under my touch and how her eyes darted away.

"Look at me," I pleaded, gripping her chin again. Once our gazes were joined again, my hand crept up a little higher. "It's okay to feel good, Gemma. If it doesn't feel good, then you deserve better."

A ragged, nervous breath left her mouth. "I was told that this was wrong...what you're doing to me...what I'm feeling."

My fingers stilled for a single second as I filed that little piece away for later. "They lied."

My other hand, the one on her chin, brushed over her slick, bottom lip, and I fought myself when I pictured devouring her mouth again. If I were kissing her, then I wouldn't see the wild hunger on her face as I dipped a finger into her. I wanted to watch her come undone. I wanted to be responsible for the flush on her cheeks.

Her eyes dipped as my hand reached the side of her panties. Her chest heaved. Her back bowed. Her hair flung out of her face, and the subtle moonlight shined directly onto her high cheekbones. Goddamn, she was fucking beautiful. Achingly so. It almost hurt to look at her.

As soon as I hooked a finger inside her panties, she shuddered. *So responsive.* "Isaiah," she whispered, peering up at me with wide eyes. She was already so fucking wet. My finger ran down her slick seam, and she whimpered. I couldn't believe no one had touched her before. Had they touched her before?

A raging dose of jealousy clawed at my back. I couldn't fathom anyone else watching this. I wanted her to be mine. The nerves were intensified in my stomach, and the overpowering protectiveness over her was coming alive in my very being as I stared down at her. "You're fucking beautiful, Gemma." I circled her clit gently, hardly keeping a hold on my steady pace. Rushing this wouldn't be smart. I wanted her to trust me with her body.

"It feels…" Ragged breaths left her as her cheeks darkened.

"*Good*," I whispered along her lips before I kissed her breathless. Her tongue caressed mine like it was pleading for something, and that was when I pushed the very tip of my finger into her tight, wet folds.

She moaned against my mouth, the echo of it sending a shock of pleasure down my spine. Her hips jutted forward, and it surprised her just as much as it surprised me. My finger inched in even farther, and her hands gripped down onto my shoulders, her tiny fingers digging so hard I could feel them through my hoodie. Our kiss broke, and she threw her head back, gasping as I began to move my finger slowly in her tight embrace. "Do what feels good, Gemma," I whispered along the exposed skin of her neck. I knew what would make her come undone, but she needed to explore this feeling of euphoria. I wanted her to be comfortable, and *Christ* if it wasn't the hottest thing I'd ever seen with her moving her hips to meet my knuckle. *God damn.*

My lips kissed her soft skin again, and I had the sudden urge to suck on her neck, but I knew that would leave a mark, and although I wanted nothing more than the whole fucking world to know that I had left my mark on her, I knew it wasn't in our best interest—at least, not with the SMC. I didn't want them to know I was corrupting the good girl of St. Mary's. My tutor. But that was exactly what I was fucking doing. I was corrupting her, and it was so selfish of me, yet I couldn't stop myself. It felt too good.

"Oh, my God."

My hand moved underneath her shirt, and I felt the tight bud of her nipple against my hand, even through the thin cotton of her bra. Her sweet little pussy began constricting, and that was when I lost my hold on everything. I pushed my finger in farther and curved it toward the spot I knew she was itching for, and my palm brushed over her swollen clit. My mouth was on hers as her legs widened, my hand squeezed her perky breast, and I mumbled, "Unworthy. I'm so unworthy of this." I pulled back just in time to watch her mouth open and her eyes fly shut. I felt her come undone on my finger, and I knew right then I was fucked.

I was royally fucked.

Gemma Richardson had my soul.

CHAPTER FORTY

GEMMA

As soon as I came down from my high and Isaiah pulled his hand out from under my skirt, I flushed so hard I began to sweat. Or maybe I was already sweating before. I wasn't sure. I was incapable of coherent thoughts or sentences, which was exactly why I peered up at him and said, "Th—thank you."

His face split into the biggest smile I'd ever seen, and I wanted to die right then. Actually, no. I didn't. Because if I were dead, then I'd never get to feel what I just felt from his hand again. It was... I was speechless.

Isaiah stood back, peering down at me as I slowly brought my legs together. I was wet and sticky and nearly blinded by another round of embarrassment.

"What are you thinking?" he asked as he pulled his hood back up onto his head. I couldn't see the exact shade of his blue eyes in the darkened room, but I had a feeling they were dancing with amusement.

I sighed, adjusting my skirt as I still sat on the dining

table. *Oh my God.* What if the table was wet from me? "I—I don't know what I'm thinking."

His cheeky grin caught my eye. "That's a lie. Tell me."

"What are you thinking?" I countered, feeling bold.

He chuckled. "You are not ready to hear what I'm thinking."

He was wrong. I was more than ready.

Isaiah had come closer to me, causing my pulse to race so fast I had a hard time focusing. "Tell me what you were thinking," he urged, and there was something in his voice that tricked me into spouting off from the mouth like I had no control over it.

"I'm thinking that I want to do that again...with you." I slapped my hand over my mouth. *Did I just say that out loud?*

Isaiah's eyes clenched for a single second before his hands gripped my thighs, and he pulled me to the very edge of the dining table. My hands fell to my lap. "We will. I promise." He ping-ponged his attention to my eyes and mouth before sighing. "But it's late. We need to get back before the kitchen staff starts prepping for breakfast." He paused, staring at my lips. "And it's almost time for you to sneak out of your room and go to the art room."

My eyes flicked to his, and I paused. "How did you know that?"

A slight dimple appeared. "How do I know you sneak out of bed every morning before school to work in private?"

I nodded.

"You think I'm going to let you sneak through these halls alone after finding out that Bain has some sort of infatuation with you?"

My brows puckered. "He has an infatuation with me? I thought you said he just wanted to use me against you."

He shrugged. "Those two things go hand and hand, which is all the more reason why you shouldn't be sneaking through the halls in the middle of the night." Isaiah's hands gripped my waist, and he plopped me down onto the floor. "But since I know you won't listen, just know you're covered." He winked at me, and I quickly looked away before my pink cheeks gave me away as I pulled my skirt down. I glanced at the table where I was sitting, and when I looked back up to Isaiah, he was smirking.

Why wasn't I more embarrassed? Why wasn't I more embarrassed that Isaiah's finger, the same one that was currently touching mine, was just inside of me moments ago? Why was the thought of him going back to his room without me so disappointing? Why wasn't I looking forward to the moment I was free from my obligation of tutoring him? Because after that, came freedom. That should have been the only thing on my mind. Not Isaiah and what he just did to my body.

"Stop overthinking," he said before slightly opening the door to the hallway. He looked both ways and then pulled me through.

I stayed quiet as we walked through the halls, hand and hand. I was going to break free from his grasp once we reached the girls' hall, but instead, he walked me all the way to my door, glancing back behind us several times.

Once we were in front of my door, I slowly turned to face him with my heart trying to race right out of my chest. Nerves sprouted from the very bottom of my belly as I thought about kissing him again. "Thank you for walking me to my room."

I was sure he had walked me so we didn't get caught by whatever teacher had night duty this evening, probably the same one that almost caught us in the dining hall moments ago, but a small part of me wanted to think it was because he wanted to spend as much time with me as I did him.

"I'm sorry I took you with me tonight. It was reckless of

me." He dropped my hand and took a step away from me. "It won't happen again."

We stared at each other for a scarily long time, and each time I tried to sort my emotions and figure out what exactly I was feeling, I came up short. Because the truth was, I'd never felt like this in my entire life.

I felt different. Isaiah made me feel something big, and even though I understood why he was apologizing to me and why he was telling me that it wouldn't happen again, I still felt the sting of disappointment. It was like he was closing off a part of himself to me, and that was silly because had he even really opened up in the first place?

He had. He told me why he was at St. Mary's. He told me a little bit about himself, and I was certain it wasn't without caution.

He opened his mouth to say something, but I interrupted him. "Remember earlier when you said your father was a bad man? That Bain's father was? That Bain was?"

Isaiah's brows lowered, and he dipped his head in a nod. I gulped back the fear that was crowding my throat and took a step toward him, placing my hand on his hard jaw, splaying my fingers out over his warm skin. "And how I told you that I knew all about bad men?" Isaiah's gaze darted to mine as I whispered something so raw and unforgiving. "My uncle is a bad man too, Isaiah. And you were right. I am running from him."

His hands were around my face so quickly I stumbled backward. Our lips joined together as he cupped my cheeks hard, crashing my body into his with a speed that made my pulse pause. His tongue dipped in my mouth, and that same coiled feeling of sparks that I seemed to feel every time he touched me erupted in flames. Was it the weight of my words that made this kiss even deeper than before? Or was it all in my head?

Isaiah pulled away quickly as he backed me all the way up to the door, pushing my back against it. "Why did you just tell me that? Where did that come from?"

I gulped a lungful of air before saying the same exact thing to him. "You told me some of your truth, and you deserve the same from me."

We stayed quiet for a few moments before Isaiah ran a hand down his face. "We're going to go up in flames, you and I. You know that, right? This..."—he pointed at me and then to him—"is...different."

"Different?" I asked before shaking my head to bypass my question because it didn't matter. "I don't care if I go up in flames." At least here, at St. Mary's, I had the choice.

A quick breath-stealing kiss landed on my lips before he let go of me, and I was met with a shadow of something dark on his features. Torment? Pain? Regret? It was like a knife being lodged into my chest with either option.

"It would be a shame for someone as innocent as you to go up in flames, Gemma."

Then, he turned around and walked down the hall as stealthily as he had crept into my life.

———

Sloane was sleeping when I snuck into our room, and I was grateful. I smiled at the sticky note taped to my pillow in her handwriting that read, *Details*. I knew she'd want me to spill everything that had happened with Isaiah, and I didn't want to lie to her. In fact, I wasn't sure what to say at all. Did I tell her about what he did to me? The kissing and the...other stuff? Did I tell her that we'd snuck out of St. Mary's and that I'd wrecked the headmaster's car?

No.

I would take that to my grave. I couldn't believe what the

night had held, and I especially couldn't believe that I didn't regret a single thing. Not even driving illegally with my heart lodged in my throat as someone chased us from behind. I was certain the adrenaline was still flowing throughout and that was why I was so calm at the moment. Tobias would be so proud of me if he knew of all the things I was doing. He'd always been the more daring twin. He used to tell me that I needed to live more and bend the rules. Figure out who I was. Which was probably why Richard hated him as much as he did.

As soon as I stripped out of my clothes and quietly washed up in the bathroom, paying extra attention to how swollen my lips were and how my cheeks held the faintest tint of red on them, I slipped into bed beneath my fluffy covers and replayed the night over and over again as I tried to fall asleep.

I should have been tired, and I was. It was almost three in the morning by the time I'd laid down, but there had been one thing nagging at me from the second I let myself breathe again: the conversation with Isaiah when we'd pulled up to the place that Bain had gone to. I knew there was more to that story than Isaiah had told me, but I wouldn't dig any further than I had. If Isaiah wanted me to know more, he'd tell me. He didn't expect me to tell him my life story, and I didn't expect him to either.

But what confused me the most about the entire situation was that the psychiatric hospital was vaguely familiar to me— like a photo in my head that was clear but tattered around the edges, leaving out the important stuff. And then there was the moment when I'd asked Isaiah where we were, and he said, *"Somewhere I hope you never learn about."*

But I had learned about it.

Or seen it.

Something.

Something had clicked when we pulled up to the dark, ivy-covered building. It was almost as creepy looking as St. Mary's.

I lay in bed for the next hour and a half, tossing and turning, in and out of sleep, willing the visual of the psychiatric hospital to rid from my brain. I'd even thought about Isaiah and his hungry kisses, but each time I'd let my mind wander, the nagging question popped into my head.

Why was it so familiar?

Then, it hit me.

I lifted the blanket off my body and peeled it away slowly, hoping the rustling wouldn't disturb Sloane. Though, she had hardly moved an inch since I'd gotten back into our room.

I pulled Cade's jacket around my shoulders, pushing my arms into the sleeves, smiling as I remembered how Isaiah had pulled the hood over my head as we dashed through the grounds of St. Mary's just hours prior. I tip-toed to my door in bare feet, slowly opened it, and slipped into the darkened hallway.

It was the same eerily silent corridor that greeted me each morning when I snuck out to head to the art room. Thankfully, I'd never run into anyone, but now that I knew someone was "covering" me, I'd made a quick mental note to make sure my back wasn't to the door when I sketched again. No one needed to see what was on my canvas.

It didn't take me long to roam down the stairs or to make it to the art room. I was usually already dressed for class on the weekdays when I'd come here, so the cool floor was jarring on my bare feet as I stepped through the threshold and headed straight for the supply closet.

The door thudded as I pulled it open, and it creaked so loudly I paused for a moment, looking over my shoulder. I half-expected Isaiah to be standing there, but instead, the only thing that moved in the distance were the dust particles as they danced through the air.

After walking a few steps into the supply closet, letting the smell of musty paintbrushes and mildew curve under my nose, I pulled on the tattered string and let the swinging lightbulb bathe the room in a faint glow.

The shake of my hand didn't stop me from pulling down my sketches from the past week, along with my art journal that I'd sketch in when I had any down time during the day. I now replaced most of my down time with the game that Cade had downloaded onto my phone, but that wasn't the point at the moment. With each piece of thick paper in my fingers, my stomach tightened at the things I found beautiful but also horrific.

The first was the sketch I'd done just two days ago, the charcoal still somewhat fresh on the paper. It was almost a blur if you were to look at it too quickly, but I knew by heart what it was even as I pushed it away. The spine of the girl, who I knew was me, was at the center of the sketch. Each vertebra was like a thick knot going down in a straight line with protruding ribs spreading to black smudges. Her head was bent down low with a messy bun of hair in fine detail on top, and the word *mine* was carved into the back of her neck as a thick hand laid on her bony shoulder.

I shuddered a breath as I pulled the next sketch out, which was the one that I'd drawn the first time I'd stepped foot in this art room as the sun still laid behind a blanket of night. It was half my face and the words *Good Girls Don't Break Rules* over and over again, line by line, floating down the other side of the paper.

I didn't even want to pull the last sketch out, so I didn't. Instead, I grabbed the leather binding of my notebook and flipped through sloppy pencil sketches until my throat tightened so quickly I lost my breath.

I knew it.

There, staring back at me, from just a few weeks ago when I'd first started at St. Mary's, was something I'd created in a lull of past trauma. I didn't remember precisely the moment that I'd drawn it, or why, because that was how it was when I took pencil to paper. My mind went to a dark place, and everything else disappeared except for the shunned-away memories that were hidden behind a thick wall in the present. My finger traced over the curved lines of the building, focusing solely on the smeared lead-written words that read *The Covenant Psychiatric Hospital.*

It seemed I was right to feel the sting of familiarity as Isaiah and I pulled up to the chilling ivy-covered stone building just hours ago...but why?

CHAPTER FORTY-ONE

ISAIAH

"WHO IS THIS?" I slammed my phone down onto my uncle's desk early Monday morning before anyone was up—well, anyone but Gemma. I already knew she was in the art room, drawing something with that adorable smudge of charcoal that was probably smeared across her soft skin by now.

My uncle sat at his desk and had no intention of moving as I stormed to the front and tossed my phone down.

"Did you wreck my car?" The crease in his brow was deep, but I knew it would lessen eventually.

"Not technically. Who is this man?" I asked again, nodding my head to the photo from Saturday night of Bain handing off a black duffel of guns at the Covens. "Do you recognize him?"

My uncle made no move to look at the phone. Instead, he continued staring up at me with distaste in his eyes. *Jesus Christ. Fine.* I pulled back, leaving my phone on the desk and sitting in the leather chair in front of him. "I didn't wreck your car. Gemma did."

His eyes grew wide. "What?!"

Shame filled me as I glanced at the books on the shelves, too guilty to even look him in the eye. I wasn't afraid of what he had to say about that. But I did feel shame and guilt rock through my body like an avalanche. Cade's, *"I told you so,"* echoed in the back of my skull like my own personal cadence after I'd filled the rest of the Rebels in on Sunday morning.

I glanced back at my uncle. "She recognized the Covens."

His eyes grew even wider. "Wait, you took her to the Covens?" His face was a shade of red that sent a mild line of concern through me.

"Let me explain before you start throwing shit."

His teeth clanked so hard I heard the clink from across his desk. *Impressive.* "Bain had left during a party. So...we followed him. I took your car." I gave him a pointed look. "And don't act surprised. You know I take it when he leaves randomly through the night. Anyway, we followed him."

My uncle's brows were still crowding his face, his jaw molded of marble as he continued to clench it. "And he went to the Covens?"

I pointed a finger at him. "Bingo. But why does Gemma know of the Covens?" An uncomfortable feeling split my chest open, and it shouldn't have surprised me that I was more concerned with how Gemma knew of the Covens versus Bain selling guns in my father's area, but the shock was still there. "If she knows about the Covens..."

"What did she say about it?" He paused, pulling my phone toward him. *And we were past the wrecked car...just like that.*

"She said that it looked familiar to her. But she didn't know why."

"What happened after that?" His eyes squinted as he zoomed in the photo on my phone.

"I got out to take some photos for Dad and told Gemma to slide into the driver's seat, just as a precaution. You never know what you're going to get with Bain involved. And then..."

"And then what?" he snapped, gripping my phone so hard I almost leaned forward to pry it out of his hand.

"And then someone started to chase me." I paused, not wanting to say the next words. "With a gun. So I made a run for it, and Gemma and I sped off. She wrecked because, apparently, she's never driven before." I held back a tight laugh even though it was more sad than anything. "Something I was not aware of until we were in a very compromising situation."

Silence encased the room as my uncle glared down at the screen. It had long since grown dim and eventually shut off. The second the screen was black, his eyes snapped to mine. "That was an incredibly dangerous and stupid thing you did by taking her with you."

"I know," I bit out, not even attempting to deny it.

His hand slapped down onto the desk, but I didn't flinch. I wasn't afraid of my uncle or his temper tantrums. He wasn't my father, by any means. "No. You don't understand." He pinched the bridge of his nose. "The man in that photo is Judge Stallard."

I stopped breathing. My heart seized for a moment, and then the anger came rushing in. "Wait." *Judge Stallard.* The room suddenly seemed colder.

My uncle's hoarse voice scratched at my confusion. "Tell me he didn't see her with you."

"No. There is no way. He was with Bain when I was spotted by someone. My guess is the Covens' security."

He seemed to relax a little before asking, "Did she see him?"

"No. She saw nothing. She did know we were following Bain, but I haven't given her much more than that. I don't want to drag her into this."

"But you have, Isaiah. By taking her with you. What were you thinking?" His expression showed a small amount of pity, and I looked away. "Have you learned nothing from what happened to your mother?"

Anger began to rise again, and I clenched my hands down onto the arms of the chair. "Of course I fucking have! I was there!"

"Then, why are you being so careless?" His voice boomed throughout the room as he stood up and rounded his desk. I didn't dare move in my seat. I didn't even look up at him. If I did, I was too afraid I'd lose the hold on my emotions and start breaking things like a child. I was feeling more and more lately, and I fucking hated it. The numbness I usually felt was gone. Instead, frustration, anger, and maybe even fear were working inside my stomach, and I fought to keep my breathing controlled.

"I thought you and her were just friends—well, that was until I saw the latest blog post. Something about you two and a party? Sneaking away? Was that when you left and followed Bain?" He shook his head. "Don't tell me..."

That stupid fucking blog. I ignored the alert I got this morning, too eager to get to my uncle's office.

I snapped my attention to him. "Don't tell you what?"

"Is that why she agreed to help you? To be your tutor? Are you making her think she's someone special to you? That you care for her?" He scoffed, pinching the bridge of his nose again. "Let me guess, you're fucking her...*goddamnit*. I told you not to mess with her, Isaiah!"

I inhaled a deep breath and glanced down at my shoes. Even if I wanted to explain things to him, I wouldn't know how. It wasn't why she agreed to help me, and I wouldn't tell him why she had, but there was a blinding light in front of my eyes that almost pushed me to tell him that I did care for her.

After a few more deep breaths from me, I took my eyes

off my shoes and placed my stoic expression back on my uncle, only to pause. "Why the fuck are you looking at me like that?" My brows pinched as he clasped both hands and leaned back onto his desk. "Unless..."

"Unless what?" I snapped, leaning forward.

"You do care for her." He hummed out a sound as my sharp glare caught the framed map behind him. *I do, but fuck, I shouldn't. I couldn't.* The admission was there in my mind, but I wouldn't say it out loud. If I said it out loud, then I couldn't take it back and act as if it never happened when our time came to an end. Because it would.

"Gemma is fragile, and there is a lot to her that we aren't aware of. You shouldn't be messing around with her, whether you care for her or not."

"She is not as fragile as you think, Uncle Tate." She wasn't. There was definitely a lot she was hiding underneath her shyness and rosy cheeks, but being fragile wasn't one of them. And she was smart. And courageous. Little did he know, Gemma had a plan. A plan that was full of strength and bravery. Some could say that running away was cowardly, but that was not what this was. Gemma was running away because she knew that going forward was better than going backward. And it wasn't like it was with Jacobi. He ran away and left me behind, along with Jack. There was nothing holding Gemma back, and I fucking envied that.

I moved past the discussion of Gemma, needing to get back to the real reason I came here versus the therapy session that my uncle thought this was. "What was Judge Stallard doing at the Covens in the first place?" Never mind the fact that Bain was selling him illegal firearms.

"My only guess is that he is connected to the Covens in some way, and that makes a lot of sense with what I've uncovered in the last week."

Now that got my attention. "What do you know?"

"What do I know?" He raised an eyebrow as he walked over to his desk and plopped down in his seat. He pulled out the same file that had Gemma's name stamped on it like before. "That he is a far worse man than I thought."

Something ticked inside of me right along with Gemma's confession Saturday night. The thought of her being with someone that she felt the need to run from set an ice-cold feeling straight through my veins. "You knew him before Gemma came here, correct?"

"Yes."

"How?"

My uncle sighed as he looked back down at the file. His muscles tensed, his eyes staring at something in particular, or maybe it was nothing at all. I couldn't tell. When he opened his mouth again, his tone wasn't as cold as before. It was on the brink of devastation, if I had to guess. "Judge Stallard's mother, Anne, used to run a group home for girls."

Silence stretched around us, and my patience began to run thin as he continued staring down at the file that was half closed. But then he began again. His gaze found mine, and his jaw was set like a thick line of steel. "You know how your father donates and makes his charitable dues as a front for what he truly does? How he sways people and misleads them into thinking he's a charitable man with a good heart?"

I scoffed before nodding.

"Well, your grandfather did the same. You know this, I'm sure." I said nothing, and he continued after leaning back in the chair that creaked against his weight. "One of the places he donated to was Anne's group home. They'd take in juveniles who were to serve time in a detention center for a crime they'd committed, but instead of going to prison, they'd go to the group home as a type of punishment. They'd work for free and ride out their sentences that way. Like therapy for young women going down the wrong path. The court would decide if it was the right place for these girls, or sometimes they'd just end up sending them to prison or jail if their age allowed."

"Okay..." I thought for a moment. "And this has to do with Gemma's uncle, how? How are *you* connected?"

He swallowed so roughly it sounded like the pencils that sat at the end of his desk were being forced down his throat. "I had a friend, a good friend. A young woman. We were your age at the time."

I cocked an eyebrow. "A *friend*?"

He ignored me. "She got into some trouble. Judge Stallard was the judge on her case." He thought for a moment. "It was one of his first cases. He was a young judge. I remember that much. He'd been given the job after his father had passed from a heart attack."

Now we were getting somewhere.

"Long story short, Judge Stallard sent my friend to his mother's group home as a favor to our family. With the ties your grandfather had with them, it wasn't hard to sway his decision. It was a well-known group home until recently, actually. Judge Stallard's mother, Anne, had a stroke, and the group home was shut down."

It didn't take long for things to click in my fucked-up brain. "So that's why he said you owed him. Because they took in your...friend? Saved her from what? A few months in jail?"

He grunted. "Try a few years in prison."

Okay, moving on. "So that's how you and Gemma's uncle are connected. What doesn't make sense to me is why he was at the Covens and why Gemma seemed to know what it was —or at least recognized it."

He licked his lips. "From what I've learned as of late, Judge Stallard is not a good man. He's hiding things about Gemma, has ties with the police force in the city, *and* there have been many rumors floating around about the group home that I'm pretty sure Gemma came from." He paused, opening the file again. "My theory is that Judge Stallard runs the Covens. He is definitely affiliated in one way or another." He looked up at me. "I'm thinking he sends criminals there instead of jail. He deems them insane during the trial, sends them to the psychiatric unit, and from there..."

"From there what? He's there making these criminals even more unworthy of living? Molding them into men like the ones my father has working underneath him? Filling the world with more murderers? What?"

"Yes, Isaiah. That's exactly what I think." His voice was too calm for my liking. "People like your father pay good money for the men created in that sinful place. If Judge Stallard is the one sending men there, he's likely to be a multimillionaire."

My anger was back, and my heart was slamming against my chest. I knew what went on underneath the floors of that psychiatric hospital. I knew the horrors and spine-stiffening pain that could be inflicted within those dark rooms. I knew how they took men and broke their spirit just enough to brainwash them into thinking they were part of a brotherhood. A family of sorts.

A family of sick murderers and women beaters.

They were weak men.

Each and every last one of them hanging on the promises of strength, power, and wealth.

All by the hands of men like my father and Bain's. Judge Stallard, too.

"And Gemma?" I finally asked as I undug my nails from the leather seat.

"Now that is a mystery I have yet to unfold. But if she's been living with a man like Judge Stallard for most of her life..." He flipped a page forward and scanned something. "At least from a young age, given what I can find... But if she's been living with a man capable of sending people to the Covens, I can't even imagine the things she has seen or heard." He shut the file. "I think she may have been born there."

My brows were crowded. "Where? The Covens?"

"There or maybe at the group home. I suspect that a girl at the group home got pregnant, or was pregnant, and Anne took care of the baby." He raised a brow. "Well...babies, in this case."

"What?" I asked hesitantly.

"Oh, yes. She didn't tell you? Gemma has a twin brother."

What?

"Where is he?"

My uncle gave me a look. "I don't know. There's no record of him. I looked into it after Gemma let it slip. Everything about her is very hush. I can hardly find anything."

My stomach bottomed out.

I had a feeling I knew exactly where her brother was.

And I was wondering if, deep down, Gemma did too.

CHAPTER FORTY-TWO

ISAIAH

My blood still rushed as I sat in the dining hall, waiting for Gemma to appear for breakfast. I had texted her ten minutes ago.

Me: *You're losing track of time in the art room. It's time for breakfast.*

She texted back within a minute.

Gemma: Cleaning up now. Thanks.

My fingers flew over the screen as my leg bounced under the table that Gemma and I had been shoved under less than forty-eight hours ago.

Me: *Cade will walk with you.*

Her reply came another minute later.

Gemma: *Did you send Cade to spy on me?*

I laughed under my breath as I slipped my phone back into my pocket after messaging Cade that he needed to walk with her. Gemma called it spying. I called it protection. Same difference.

My eyes glanced down to the rich wood that her bare ass

was on Saturday night with my finger deep inside her. Just thinking about it made the itch of concern and anger lessen in my bloodstream, but each time I looked over at Bain with his cropped-to-the-scalp haircut and hardened features, I grew tense. My father had yet to answer a single question I'd thrown at him after Saturday. In fact, I'd heard nothing from him except for the few curse words on the other end of the phone after I'd told him all about Bain's little adventure. Typically, I wouldn't care. I'd feed him the intel and then push him out of my head until he called me again. But now that Gemma was involved, and I knew that our family was tied to hers in some way, I wanted to know more. I needed to know more. I could blame the need-to-know feeling burning inside of me on the fact that I was soon to take over my father's entire gun-trafficking business, but that wasn't why I cared. Not even in the slightest. I could lie to him, or even the rest of the Rebels, but to myself? There was no chance. Gemma's sweet little confession was burning a hole in my brain. *I'm running from my uncle.* Why? What had he done to her, and how could I make him pay?

The thought was there, the minor dip in my rationality that allowed me to wonder what would happen if I made Judge Stallard disappear. I wasn't my father, but his blood ran through my veins. That evil part lived inside of me underneath years of staying in control of myself. I didn't let it out often, but would I for Gemma? Would she be able to stay at St. Mary's if her uncle vanished? *No.* Even if something unfortunate happened to Judge Stallard, which would be totally fucking risky if my uncle was correct with the assumption that he had a healthy relationship with the police force, Gemma and I *still* couldn't be anything. She wouldn't be brought into this life. Not a chance.

I unglued my tongue from the roof of my mouth as the doors of the dining hall swung open, and Sloane walked in, then Mercedes, and then Gemma beside her. Cade soon followed, keeping enough distance behind her that it didn't raise attention but just close enough that Bain's left eye twitched. My attention pulled from him and then immediately went to Gemma's bare legs and then right back up to her cute little heart-shaped face that I hadn't seen since Saturday night.

I hadn't seen her at all yesterday, and I was almost certain it had to do with what we'd done right here in this very spot.

We'd texted a few times, but she'd said she was getting caught up on homework and then having a movie night with Sloane. Apparently, Sloane had said I was taking too much of her time with *"tutoring."* She starred the word *tutoring* in the text, as if we were doing something other than studying in the deep, dark library...all alone.

When our eyes collided, it felt like the room shrunk. The walls caved in, and it was as if all the air was whooshed from my lungs and plowed straight into hers. The slight curve of her lips caught my eye, and I felt mine doing the same.

Jesus Christ. My uncle was totally fucking right. I did care for her. It took me by surprise because I had never let myself even consider the fact that I could feel anything but attraction for someone—so quickly, too. Gemma had grabbed my walls, and with the snap of her finger, they were down.

"I have never seen you look at someone like that in my entire eighteen years of existence," Shiner bemused. "You're scaring the entire student population."

I slowly shifted my attention to him as he held a piece of bacon in the air.

"How am I scaring the student population?"

Brantley grunted from the other side of me. "Because you look like you're in love."

I whipped my head over to him with a set jaw. I wanted to

snap. Recognizing something like that out loud landed on too many ears. It was a slap to my face, and he knew why.

"Don't say shit like that." I flexed my jaw.

"I said it for a reason, Isaiah." He went back to his breakfast, downplaying the intensity of our conversation. "Wake up. That's what I'm here for. To tell you to wake the fuck up."

Cade slipped into the seat beside me. "Thought that was my job. We all know I'm the favorite."

Brantley flicked his eyes up to him over the brim of his cup. "You can't be trusted with this anymore. You've been on both sides of the coin. After Jou—"

"Do not say her fucking name." The dining hall grew quiet, and I shifted my gaze back and forth between my two best friends. Shiner caught my eye across the table and sent a silent warning, as if I didn't see what was unfolding right in front of me. It wasn't unusual for us to argue from time to time, and even though I was technically Brantley and Cade's leader in and outside of St. Mary's, I usually let them hash it out themselves. Aggression faded when you hit shit. At least for people like us.

An annoyed sigh came from my mouth as I placed my hands on the table, watching Cade and Brantley glare at one another. The rest of the dining hall was pretending not to watch, but their attention eventually flickered over to us, one by one. "Guys…" I warned, seeing that a few SMC members were in the dining hall, grabbing breakfast along with some other teachers who had the pleasure of breakfast duty.

The sway of a chestnut-colored ponytail caught my eye, and three girls who were completely unaware of the fight seconds from happening began to walk past us, and my arm lashed out, and I snagged Gemma by the waist.

Her breath hitched, and she whipped her head down to mine, those bright eyes widening.

"Sit with us," I demanded, my voice a little harsher than

usual. "I have some questions on my homework that I think I need my tutor for."

Gemma's soft voice pulled Brantley and Cade's attention. "Um...there are no seats."

I looked to Cade, and his shoulders lowered with the crack of his neck. *Welcome back, fuckwad.* "You can have my seat." He began to scoot down after nodding to a few lacrosse players. They quickly stood up and moved down the bench too, making room.

Sloane rolled her eyes. "I don't want to sit beside you, Cade." She glanced at Mercedes who was fiddling with a curly piece of hair. "Will you sit beside Cade so I don't accidentally stab him with my fork?"

Shiner threw his head back and laughed, trying to lighten the mood, but we all knew that Sloane's insult was like pouring salt in Cade's wound, especially after the spat with Brantley.

Mercedes gave her a look that could only be described as sad and said, "Sure, Sloane." She slid in first, and then Sloane, although Sloane acted like she would rather lick the floor than sit down beside us, and then Gemma went to move next.

Once they had their trays in front of them, Gemma snuck a tentative peek up at me. "What did you need help with, Isaiah?"

Nothing. Not a single thing. My fingers drummed against the hard slab of wood of the table so loudly that Gemma looked down at them. A devilish smirk curved itself on my lips, and I couldn't stop myself from completely veering from anything homework related. "This is a nice table, isn't it?"

Gemma's brows pinched, and her pouty mouth that I couldn't stop glancing at straightened. "That's what you wanted to talk about? The tab—" Her gaze popped up once more, her ponytail swishing with the motion. Her cheeks blushed deeply, and I winked, which only caused her already red face to deepen.

"Why is the table nice?" Mercedes asked, glancing from Gemma to me and then to the rest of our group.

Brantley sighed disapprovingly as he threw his napkin onto his tray. I hadn't told them about what we did on the table, but Brantley wasn't dense. He knew something had happened by the tone of my voice, no doubt.

"Why *is* that table nice, Isaiah?" My entire spine stiffened as Bain's voice came to a screeching halt at my backside. My head slowly rose from Brantley's wadded up napkin, and I locked eyes with him as he slowly put his glass of orange juice down. "Is this where you and Gemma ran off to the other night after...you know. Did you fuck her here too?"

Was he insinuating that he knew we'd followed him? That didn't sit well with me. Not at all.

My chest began tightening as my fist clenched on top of the table. I couldn't even look Gemma in the face because I honestly didn't want to see the utter embarrassment and shame that would be there. It would only strengthen the immediate rage that was billowing in my body. I also did not want her to see the anger that was surfacing. I knew for a fact that the Rebels could feel it. In fact, given my reputation, the entire school was probably waiting for me to wrap my hand around Bain's neck and slam him to the ground.

Bain and I had never physically fought before, and the only reason for that was because of my father's instructions, but hearing Gemma's name roll off his tongue sent me to a dark place.

It was likely the fact that he'd already threatened her once and had that photo of her in his room, plus everything I'd just found out about her, that was mixing things in my head and twisting them in unfathomable ways, but either way, I was going to throttle him across the fucking room. Consequences no longer lived in my head. I'd quickly snapped my fingers and banished them right the fuck out.

For a split second, my thoughts went to my mother. I thought about how my father let down his guard once and caused a chain reaction of hurt and despair. I thought about how someone as equally as fucked up as my father thought they could harm the woman he claimed to love because of something he'd done. They had misjudged his love for her, but that didn't deter my father from revenge. An act of betrayal against him was forbidden in his world.

But make no mistake. We may have been blood, but I would never stand by as someone disrespected Gemma like that. This had nothing to do with the fact that Bain was disrespecting me in front of all of St. Mary's and everything to do with the fact that he was disrespecting her.

Bain's voice came back into earshot, and I cracked my knuckles with my back still to him. "Wait a second. She still has that virgin vibe to her. All sunshiny and cute as fuck. I mean, if Isaiah won't fuck the virgin out of you, then I will gladly do it for him."

That's it.

Something snapped inside of me, and every last thought fizzled right out of my head and evaporated into thin air.

My hand tapped the table twice before I stood up. It was so quiet in the dining hall you could hear a pin drop. I could feel the eyes on us. Even the SMC's. But my target was Bain and only Bain.

"Isaiah," Brantley's warning came into contact with my ears, as did the screeching of the bench as he pushed away from the table, but I still stalked around and glared at Bain who had his chin raised high like some sort of almighty king.

That title actually suited him.

Kings were often insufferable, weak men with too much confidence.

I thought Bain needed to be taken down a few levels, maybe be reminded that he wasn't a king—not in this school and not in our future line of business.

"You think you can talk to her like that?" Something cold came down over my body as I shut the entire dining hall out. It was just me and Bain, like a cord full of burning, red-hot anger connecting us together. He inched closer to me with a grin so smug on his face I felt myself mirror it. "In front of me?"

Bain's smile widened. A twitch under his eye caught my attention. He was just as riled up as I was. "You act like you're someone of importance, Rebel."

I chuckled, and it was menacing. So menacing that I hardly believed it had come from me. I prowled closer to him, stalking my prey like a lion would its next meal. "I'm certain you know just how important I am, Bain. Don't *fuck* with me."

He knew. He knew who I was. There was no doubt about it, and that meant he knew just how lethal I could be if I let myself. Flashes of gun fire and fists that didn't belong to me crowded my vision, but I pushed the past away, focusing on him.

"Isaiah." I felt a hand clamp down on my shoulder, and I quickly brushed it off.

There were too many emotions coursing through my veins, sparking the need to expose all my pent-up anger and resentment. I hated my life. I hated my father. I hated Jacobi. I hated most things, in all honesty. But then a voice flickered in the back of my head, making me pause for a split second. *Jack. Jack and Gemma. All of your friends,* it whispered. *You don't hate them.*

Bain's lips tightened as he took another step toward me. "You don't scare me, Isaiah. Do you want to know why?"

My fist ached as I planted my feet, and the very second I

wound my arm back, ready to punch the smug, arrogant, disrespectful piece of shit in the face, a faint swish of warm-brown hair caught my eye, and then two soft hands wrapped themselves around my cheeks.

Gemma.

CHAPTER FORTY-THREE

GEMMA

His jaw was like chiseled stone beneath my palms. The feeling was almost jarring as I stood there on tip-toes in the center of the dining hall with every single person staring at me.

"No," I demanded, bouncing my eyes back and forth between his. They were darker than they normally were. They weren't their typical airy, light-blue color that I was used to. Instead, they were dark and troubled, and it made my heart crazy.

Once his clenched fist dropped, he instantly wrapped his hands around my wrists. It took everything I had inside of me not to pull my fingers off his face and pull the sleeves of my school blazer down, but I fought it. Isaiah's hands were large enough that they could wrap around my dainty joints twice if he wanted. No one would see the pink scars.

His words were muffled with a coarseness that rubbed me raw. "He's disrespecting you. I don't like it."

My head shook very briefly. "Maybe. But he's also baiting you. And I don't like it."

I didn't like it. In fact, it didn't bother me in the slightest that Bain was pointing out that I was a virgin in front of the entire school. That insult, which I was well aware—even with my inexperience—*was* an insult to most, didn't even skim the skin. What bothered me was that Bain was causing a reaction in Isaiah, which gave him pure satisfaction. He wanted Isaiah to snap, and he knew very well that messing with me would cause just that.

Isaiah's spine straightened, and I felt mine do it too. Bain had begun laughing from behind me, and Isaiah's glare turned murderous. His eyes narrowed; his cheekbones sharpened. I squeezed his face with my hands until he dropped his gaze down to mine again. "Remember the plan, Isaiah. You are on probation. He knows that. He's trying to get you expelled. You are smarter than this."

His body seemed to relax just a little. "How do you know how smart I am, Good Girl?"

There it was. My nickname. That hopefully meant I was bringing him back down to the present.

I pushed myself closer to him, not caring who was watching. "Are there members of the SMC in here? Watching what's unfolding?"

His jaw wiggled beneath my hands. "Yes."

A smile graced my mouth as I whispered so close to his, "What a perfect opportunity to show them that the bad boy of St. Mary's is actually taming his wildly hot temper for once. Show them that you deserve to stay here. Prove to them that you've changed."

Isaiah's hands left my wrists, and I made no move to look to see if my blazer had crept below the shiny, jagged skin. Once he grabbed my waist, the tension in his muscles seemed to lessen. "You think my temper is hot?"

I let out a light laugh as he put his forehead on mine. For a second there, it was like he and I were shielded together in a room that had nothing but thick walls of stone surrounding us. It was just us. "I knew that would distract you."

Isaiah chuckled as he showed off his white teeth. "I don't think I give you enough credit. The good-girl act is cute and all, but you are a lot more devious than I thought." His lips brushed over my ear. "You're a damn good partner in crime."

Excitement and pride flared in me for a moment before I placed my feet back onto the solid ground and unwrapped my hands from his face. I pulled away from him just enough so I could grab onto his hand and begin leading him out of the dining hall, leaving just about everyone in there with their jaws slacked. As soon as we were passing by Bain, not close enough to where they could get into another tiff but just enough so Bain could hear my icy words as they protruded through the air, I leaned in. "I wouldn't say I'm devious, Isaiah. But I am smart enough to see through people pretty damn well." I said the last part just as I locked onto Bain. His gaze sharpened, and I knew he was angry that his little plan hadn't worked. He was using me against Isaiah, and to be quite frank, I was done with people acting like I had been put on this earth for their own personal gain.

The longer I was away from Richard and his subjective ways of living, the more I felt myself forming into who I was supposed to be. The shattered, submissive girl I had been molded into was slowly slipping right out of his grip. I wasn't stupid enough to act like that in front of him, or during our Monday night phone calls, but in front of Bain? Not a chance. Bain needed to see that I wasn't a little chess piece in his game.

Just as the dining hall doors swung closed behind us, I felt the rest of Isaiah's tension dissipate. The fury had washed off of him, and in its place was the Isaiah that I'd spent Saturday night with. The one that made me laugh and feel all sorts of things I wasn't used to.

Isaiah brought our clasped hands up to his lips and gave my hand a quick kiss. "Thank you." We stopped walking when we reached the hallway that split into two: one hallway led to the library, and the other led to the classrooms. The door behind us pushed open, and dread filled me at the thought of it being Bain, but when I heard Brantley's voice, I let out a trapped breath.

"Are you fucking out of your mind?" He appeared in front of us just as Shiner and Cade walked through the door too. "Were you really about to lose it on him? Your father would—"

Isaiah unclasped our hands and placed his on his hips angrily. The corded muscles along his forearms flexed, and I wondered where his blazer was. "I honestly don't give a fuck about my father."

"No," Cade said, shooting him a look of pity. "But you do care about Jack. Or did you for—"

"Of course I didn't fucking forget." Isaiah's chest rose and fell in swift movements. His anger was back within a flash. "But fuck, I am so sick of this." His hands had fallen onto the top of his head, and he pulled on the thick strands as I stood back and wondered who Jack was.

Brantley glanced down at me, and his set jaw loosened for a second. "You're lucky Gemma jumped in front of you before you managed to take a swing at him."

Shiner chuckled. "Girl has balls, that's for sure. I tried to tell her to stay back because we've all seen that look in your eye before."

"You were in a different mindset, man."

A different mindset? I knew all about being in a different mindset. Physically in the present but pulled to the past was kind of my specialty.

My voice was more of a whisper as I stood in front of the four very tall, strong, intimidating boys who rightly owned their title of ruling the student body. For goodness' sake, people made room for them in the hallway, and I wasn't even sure that they were aware they did it. My peers were like a school of fish. Each and every last one of them in their maroon uniforms, parting the way as one as the Rebels strode over the glossy floor. All except Bain and a few of his friends. They weren't intimidated in the slightest. "I...I just didn't want him to get in trouble. Isaiah is on probation, and I'm pretty sure fighting on school grounds is enough for expulsion, right?"

"Right." Cade pointed to me before glancing back at Isaiah. "And then Jack would be fucked."

Who was Jack? My face fell as the door swung open again behind us. My spine straightened when I saw Sloane cradling her wrist tightly to her body with Mr. Fishers, the PE teacher, looking grimmer than the Grim Reaper himself as he walked beside her.

"What happened?" I asked, running over to her.

Mr. Fishers answered for Sloane, scowling over at Isaiah and the rest of the Rebels. "Sloane took it upon herself to punch Bain in the face after you all stalked out of the dining hall." My mouth fell open in surprise as I grabbed Sloane's hand, inspecting it. Her delicate knuckles were as bright as her pink cheeks.

She let out a feral sound. "Bain is a jerk. He deserved to be punched! He was making sexual remarks about Gemma and also trying to get Isaiah in trouble by picking a fight with him. Yet, *I'm* the one in trouble?! You're dragging *me* to the headmaster's office?"

"That doesn't seem fair," Cade said, noticeably glowering at Mr. Fishers.

Brantley crossed his arms. "Agreed. Did you even ask

Sloane why she had assaulted Bain? Seems kind of sexist to drag her to the headmaster's office without even asking."

I gently pushed Sloane's hand back up to her chest and let her cradle it again. "It's true," I began. "What Sloane had said, I mean. Bain was insinuating that I was a virgin and saying very disrespectful things to me, all while prodding Isaiah to do something so he'd get expelled from St. Mary's. It's no secret that Isaiah is on probation with the SMC. In fact, I'm tutoring him in the evenings, which I'm sure you and the rest of the faculty are aware of, so he can raise his grades in addition to improving his behavior. Bain was being an instigator for the mere fun of it." I and the rest of the Rebels knew that Bain wasn't doing it for fun, but Mr. Fishers didn't need to know that.

"Well..." Mr. Fishers began to stutter as he took in the information I'd fed him. He glanced over to the Rebels and then back to Sloane. "Maybe...you can just do detention with me this evening instead of going to the headmaster. You cannot go unpunished. I do not take physical altercations lightly." He glanced at Isaiah. "Although, I am glad there wasn't a bigger one that I needed to jump into. Thank you for that, Mr. Underwood. Or should I thank Gemma?"

Isaiah grunted an acknowledgement, but that was all. The bell rung just as soon as Mr. Fishers gave Sloane details on her detention and then directed her to the nurse for ice. She brushed him off with an eye roll as students began piling out of the dining hall. Each and every one of them was searching for us like we held the world's greatest treasure in our hands. Mercedes ran over with her mouth gaping, and just as Sloane was filling her in, Bain stepped through the heavy oak doors with blood smeared along his upper lip. Dots of red were sprinkled over his white collar, and I smiled.

I actually smiled.

"Better luck next time," I quietly said as he walked past.

His smile was cold, and it should have chilled me right to the bone, but it didn't because Isaiah's glare, along with the rest of the Rebels', heated up the entire school. When I caught Isaiah staring at me once Bain was down the hall, a wry grin appeared.

I smashed my lips together so I wouldn't smile back at him and then turned to Sloane and Mercedes as we shuffled to class. "Are you sure you don't want ice, Sloane?"

"I'm okay," she answered, flexing her fingers. "I think."

"I can't believe you punched him," Mercedes laughed as she began to hand Sloane and me our books that we'd left behind. "I almost fell out of my chair when you walked over to him."

Sloane's brows pinched together as I snagged her books and held them with my own. "He needed to shut up. No one talks about my friends like that."

"Maybe we should call you girls the Rebel-ettes. Or Rebel-ritas?" Shiner plopped his arm over Sloane's shoulder with entirely too much amusement. He snagged her hand and inspected it as we all walked down the hall. I snuck a timid glance up to Isaiah, and our eyes caught, right along with my breath. How did he manage to do that? How did he manage to take my breath away so quickly?

Before I was able to look away, he snagged me around the waist and pulled me into his side, whispering into my ear, "I think I'm rubbing off on you."

"How so?" I asked, trying to pull my books back that he'd somehow grabbed with just one of his hands.

"I caught your sly remark to Bain. Both of them." His light chuckle vibrated my ear, and my face flamed, remembering what we'd done two nights ago. My body remembered much quicker than my mind. Things heated, something pulled, a slight jolt raced down my back. "And don't think I didn't notice how you avoided me all day yesterday. What was up with that?"

Heat landed on my head. "What? I wasn't avoiding you."

"Your cheeks tell me a different response." There was a light catch to his tone, and I knew he was entertained.

Our friends were up ahead of us, Shiner's arm still draped over Sloane's as her black hair swayed back and forth. I sighed, thankful no one else was listening to our conversation. "Fine. Maybe I was."

He froze for a second before stepping back in pace with me. "Why?"

The heat started at my scalp again, but this time, it continued down to the rest of my body. Why had I avoided him? It wasn't because I'd spent most of the day trying to dig up information on the psychiatric hospital, or because I had a paper to write. It was because there was the smallest part of me that felt ashamed and guilty—and confused.

I liked Isaiah. No matter how many times I told myself not to like him and not to get attached to him, I felt myself clinging to him like he was a reason to stay at this school. My stomach dipped when he popped into my head, his smile from across the room made my own lips curve, and he had made things go haywire in my body that didn't exactly disappear quickly after we'd parted ways Saturday.

I was confused about how much Isaiah had taken up space in my mind, and I was a little ashamed. I was supposed to be focusing on my plan to leave St. Mary's and finding my brother. My heart shuttered with agony each and every time Tobias crossed my mind, which was practically every time I glanced in the mirror, but with Isaiah near, the pain wasn't as unbearable. The stress wasn't as intense.

Isaiah was making me question things like leaving, and that was something that made vomit hit the back of my throat. It was absurd to think that I could actually stay here and keep away from Richard. My eighteenth birthday was soon approaching, and the social worker who dug up things Richard wanted to hide would no longer have an obligation to me. His sick plans would come to light if I didn't slip away unnoticed.

I was too lost in my thoughts to even realize that Isaiah and I had finished walking down the hall. We were somehow already standing outside of my first class, and he'd given Sloane back her books at some point while still holding mine tightly in his grasp.

His strong brow line deepened as he peered down at me. "Did I cross a line Saturday night?" His eyes shut briefly, then his thick black lashes fluttered back open as he shook his head. "I mean, of course I did. I shouldn't have taken you with me. It was dangerous and—"

I placed my hand on his chest. I could feel his heart racing beneath my fingertips. It was...unusual to see him flustered, but he was. His words were too fast; his eyes were darty. The steel arches of his cheeks were a little flushed too. "Saturday was one of the best nights of my life."

Isaiah's mouth clamped shut as shock rolled over his features. I think it may have rolled over mine too. What was I saying?

This. This was why I avoided him. Things were...too much. I wasn't acting like myself when he was near. I was impulsive and careless. I was caught up in him. His eyes. His breathing. Everything. And I wanted his hands back on me. I did. I really did.

"This is why I avoided you," I mumbled, putting my hands on my books and taking them out of his grip. "When you and I are together, I can't quite see the big picture anymore, and it scares me." I glanced away for a second, locking onto one of the oil paintings hanging on the hallway wall. "You scare me... And it has nothing to do with us running for our lives Saturday."

His head slanted as his features softened. "I scare you?"

I nodded as a tiny cut seemed to slice over my heart. I'd never see Isaiah again after I left. I may never feel *this* again, whatever it was. I was excited every time I walked into the dining hall or into the library for tutoring. I anticipated his text in the morning when I'd spent too long in the art room. Even earlier, as I stared over at Bain as he taunted Isaiah, I felt something that I'd never really felt before—I felt protective. I wanted to smash Bain's face onto the floor for messing with him. And then I felt gratitude and love for Sloane as she stuck up for me, right there along with Isaiah. They cared about me. I had people here that actually cared about me and not in the manipulated and twisted way that Richard did. It had been a long time since I'd felt anything but loss and fear.

Isaiah huffed out a breath, running his hand through his perfectly messy hair. The hallway was beginning to empty, and he'd be late for class if he didn't leave now. "You have no idea, do you?" he asked, peering down at me with an awed look in his eye. His hand clamped on my chin, and his thumb brushed over my lip, making my body tighten in the most delicious of ways. "*You* scare *me,* Gemma Richardson. You scare the shit out of me."

The late bell rang out over our heads, but neither one of us stepped away. I blinked once, ping-ponging my eyes back and forth to his. "How do I scare you?"

He swallowed roughly; his thumb laid still on my lip. "Because I'm afraid I'm going to ask you to stay when you try to leave with that fake ID and money."

My heart thudded to the ground, and my knees buckled. My eyes widened. "Don't." I took a step back and stared at the floor. "My only option is to run." The words felt like acid over my tongue, and my mind began to protest them the second they were out. *Is it my only option?* I knew what he was feeling, though. I felt it too. A tie between us. Some type of pull that was resisting as I said the words.

I didn't want to leave. There, I said it.

St. Mary's was like a safe house for me. I was relaxed here. I was becoming myself. *Living. Feeling.* And I was happy. I was happier here than I'd ever been before. If he asked me to stay, it would make it that much harder to leave.

"Is it, though?" he asked, halting my thoughts right there. "Is it your only option?"

"Yes." It pained me to say it; it truly did.

His hands found their way around my cheeks as he lifted my face up to his. His expression was pained, and a small little crease dug in between his eyebrows. A single wave of his hair graced his forehead. "The way you're looking at me right now almost kills me." His lips formed a straight line. "Your eyes are glossy."

My heart beat like a drum inside my chest. I was looking this way because I was conflicted. I had too many emotions piling in that I'd forced away for so long. The resentment, the fear, the loneliness, the uncontrollable need for love and safety and hunger for someone's help.

"What can I do for you? Let me help you." It was as if he'd read my mind.

I glanced away as footsteps began to come down the hall. I knew I needed to open the door that sat behind my back and go to class, but I couldn't move. I was stuck. My mouth was glued shut even though there were screams for help pounding inside my head.

Eventually, I opened my mouth, knowing very well that we needed to take a step away from one another. I was becoming too attached. Too lenient. "You are helping me, Isaiah. You're giving me a way out."

He shook his head angrily, dropping his hands. "No. I'm

giving you a way to run." His jaw tensed as he sliced his eyes to the teacher that was walking down the hall. "Tell me what he's done, and I'll make him pay."

Fear flashed within as I knew very well who he was referring to. "I don't want you anywhere near my uncle." I hardly recognized my voice. It attributed strength, and my determination to keep him far away from anything even coming close to Richard was unsparing. It surprised me.

"I am not afraid of Judge Stallard," he said point-blank, features unmoving.

"You should be."

A throat was cleared, and Isaiah and I ended our conversation abruptly, which I was more than thankful for. "Gemma, if you'll head into class, I'll be right behind you." Mr. Hobbs raised an eyebrow at Isaiah as he backed away from me.

Isaiah's expression told me that he didn't think the conversation was over between us, but it was.

———

LATER THAT DAY, Sloane and I sat on the bleachers with the sun dipping behind the clouds every so often, watching the boys at lacrosse. My sketchbook sat in between my knees, and the phone Isaiah had given me was clenched in my fingers as I revisited the Covenant Psychiatric Hospital's website again.

"You and Isaiah were a hot subject matter on the blog today," she started before tearing into a bag of Twizzlers. We were both still in our school uniforms, but I suddenly wished we would have changed, because now that we were nearing November, the weather was drastically getting colder, day by day.

"We were?" I asked, glancing at the side of her face.

She nodded, eyes still on the field. "No need to pull it up on your phone. The blog is already down." Sloane ripped some of the red rope candy from the pack and handed it to me. I glanced at it with suspicion but ate it anyway, and I almost moaned at how good it tasted.

"The blog is already down?"

"Yep." She laughed. "It seems every time you're featured on it, it gets taken down immediately."

I swallowed the last of my Twizzler, and Sloane put another one in my hand. I smiled. "What did the blog say?"

Someone yelled from below during the boys' practice, and I was pretty certain it was Mica. He was jogging with his stick and laughing at something, his bright-white smile so contrasting to his rich skin. Sloane shifted beside me, but I kept my eyes on the field. "It was just talking about how you were able to save Bain from an epic beating, and...it questioned your *friendship* and tutoring obligations with Isaiah. Oh, and there was some speculation as to why Bain and Isaiah hate each other so much." She paused before asking, "Why *do* they hate each other so much? Do you know?"

I stilled for a split second, not really knowing what to say. "Something that happened in the past, I think."

"Interesting. So you and Isaiah don't talk about that kind of stuff during tutoring? Or when he *claimed* you the other night, which by the way, I'm still not forgetting that you have yet to fill me in on what you did for the rest of the night. You two were long gone by the time the party lights came back on."

I opened my mouth, but she cut me off. "And do not tell me you two were studying. I'm not stupid. Isaiah is probably making you keep secrets..." She let out a sad laugh. "Those Rebels have too many secrets. And they're arrogant about it too."

I eyed her from the corner of my eye. "Why do you hate them so much?"

Sloane's fingers clamped onto the Twizzler bag, and I instantly felt bad for calling her out, but Sloane was sort of a closed book. Anytime Mercedes or I would ask her a question that had some substance, she was quick to change the subject. It wasn't obvious, but I was observant when I needed to be.

"I don't hate *them*. I only hate Cade."

"But why?" I asked, now fully seated toward her. I put my phone down, and she looked up at me briefly. Her eyes were troubled, and without knowledge of even doing so, I found my hand on her knee. "You're right, Sloane," I said, whispering even though no one was even close enough to hear us. "Isaiah does have secrets. But everyone does." I took a deep breath. "You can trust me with yours—if you want to, I mean." The conversation was beginning to make my skin itch. I wasn't sure if I was saying the right things to her or if she knew I was being genuine. And how fair was it for her to tell me her secrets, but for me to keep mine?

Her hand fell on top of mine. "I know that." Her pink lips tugged down. "I just feel..." She looked back out to the lacrosse field, and I followed. I immediately caught Isaiah's stare, and my heart flip-flopped. How does he make me react from so far away?

Sloane cut back in. "I don't want to put anything else on your shoulders. You are already..."

"Already what?"

"Troubled. I can just...tell that you're troubled with something." She looked at my covered wrist, and I shamefully pulled my hand away from her leg, but she was right.

"I am," I agreed, pushing back on my anxiety harder than it pushed on me. My fingers clasped my journal, and I almost wanted to just give it to Sloane to show her just how troubled

I was. But I didn't. Instead, I pulled myself back up and smiled. "If I wasn't messed up, I wouldn't be at St. Mary's, right? Wasn't it you that said we were all a little fucked up?"

Her features relaxed, and she laughed. "I did say that. It should be the school motto."

I laughed too before watching Isaiah run down the field with his stick in hand. "They should put it on the pamphlets."

She laughed, but it faded quickly. Her voice was shaky and not at all like the confident girl I knew as my roommate. "I hate Cade because he's part of the reason why Journey is gone."

"Journey was your last roommate, right?"

She sighed, pulling another Twizzler out. "Yeah, we were close. She and Cade were starting to…" She nibbled on her lip. "Date, I guess? I don't know. It was weird. Super intense. Kind of secretive. Kind of like you and Isaiah."

I said nothing, even though I wanted to deny that something was going on with me and Isaiah. Everyone assumed there was something going on with us after Saturday night, which was his plan all along. Some assumed we'd had sex and that I was just *another notch on his bed post,* whatever that meant. Some whispered that we were dating. No one ever said anything directly to me, though—aside from Sloane and Mercedes, of course. I didn't know what to tell them, and I had been too occupied with fighting with myself for most of the day on Sunday, debating whether it had actually meant something to him or not, to tell them anything. But instead of denying it right now, with Sloane staring out onto the field, looking conflicted, I stayed silent as she continued.

"I don't know the full story. Cade said he doesn't know either. But…" Sloane's head turned toward mine. Her eyes were muddied and wet, and my stomach dropped at the hurt that flashed within them. "Isaiah had found her…Cade came right after. They found her with her wrists split wide open, Gemma. She had tried to kill herself."

I gasped, and my hand latched onto hers. I squeezed tight as a chill wracked through me. I wasn't expecting that to come out of her mouth. Her eyes had dipped to my wrists again, and within the blink of an eye, I made sense of her question the other night.

"That's why you asked if I was hurting myself."

She nodded and worked a small swallow down her throat.

My shoulders fell, and I looked her dead in the face. "You don't have to worry about that with me, Sloane. I'm not suicidal."

"Then why do you cover your wrists?" Her voice was wobbly, and I squeezed her hand again. A part of my wall cracked, and I felt the rip down to my very stomach.

I looked down at Isaiah again for a split second and saw his eyes on me. *Trust*, a voice whispered in the back of my head. Trust. Did I trust these people? Did I trust Isaiah? And Sloane? Mercedes? The headmaster?

On shaky legs, I stood up, still holding Sloane's hand. I was half glad Mercedes had to retake a test today so I didn't have two sets of eyes on me when I gave another piece of myself up to someone I wasn't entirely sure I trusted.

But how could I learn to trust someone if I didn't give them a chance?

"What are we doing?" Sloane asked as I pulled her behind the bleachers. A few groups of students eyed us as we rushed away. I mostly knew all the faces that surrounded me now, especially since a lot of them seemed to track my every move when I was with Isaiah, but other than that, no one really messed with me—well...except for Bain. But that, too, was because of Isaiah.

"Showing you why I cover my wrists."

I spun Sloane around so quickly her plaid skirt fluttered

upward. She said nothing, though. She kept her pink lips crushed, and her face was a blank canvas as she waited for me to spill.

"Can I trust you?" I asked, one hand on my sleeve. "This is not something I have shown anyone. Ever."

She gave me a look. "Like...ever?"

"Never," I confirmed. Her brows puckered, and a slight breeze wafted around us.

I pushed my sleeve up, letting the cool air coat my hidden skin, and waited for her reaction.

Sloane's mouth went slack. "What...what are those?"

"They're scars." One on top of the other. Over and over again.

Sloane didn't even ask before she grabbed a hold of my arm and jerked me closer to her. Her eyes widened as she turned my wrist and saw that the pink shiny skin wrapped all around my tiny joint. "Scars from what, Gemma?"

I jerked my hand back and shoved my sleeve down. Anxiety clawed at my throat, and my stomach revolted. I didn't know how to answer her, so I was as vaguely truthful as I could be without lying.

"The past," I said, grabbing a hold of her hand and bringing us back over to the bleachers. "I broke the rules." A knife twisted in my stomach. "And I was punished."

"Oh my God." The words were no more than a breath of air, but they packed a punch so hard my chest caved.

"I'm not suicidal," I whispered, glancing back at my phone to busy myself. I was hot all of a sudden. Sweat coated my back. Nerves tingled along my skin. I couldn't believe I'd shown someone my scars. The only other person who knew about them was the one person who shared the same defective skin. *Tobias*.

"I hope whoever caused those scars is six feet under ground."

The harshness of her words didn't cause a single flinch in my body, because I'd hoped for that on more than one occasion. And maybe that made me just as messed up as Richard was. Or maybe that thought directly stemmed from the fucked-up girl that I was because of everything I'd been through.

But Richard wasn't dead.

And that was something that did make me flinch.

"Gemma?" I stiffened as the headmaster's voice cut through my thoughts. His face appeared through the foggy mist seconds later. "Your uncle called. He wants to have his chat with you earlier this evening. Which works out perfectly. Now you don't have to miss out on the annual pep rally bonfire to kick-start the rival game in Temple on Thursday."

Sloane mumbled under her breath, annoyed that she had to miss out because of her detention with Mr. Fishers.

I nodded at Headmaster Ellison who stood just below the bleachers with his hands in his pockets. "Oh, um, okay," I said before smiling briefly at Sloane. "I'll see you back in our room later."

She nodded as her eyes snapped down to my covered wrists before I began walking down the bleacher steps. The pounding of my shoes against the metal was just as loud as my heart when the headmaster spoke again. "He's waiting patiently to talk with you, so let's get there quickly. I fear that if you're a second too long, he'll show up."

Confusion and a leeriness filled me. "Why wouldn't you want him to show up?"

The warm air from the school hit my face as the headmaster and I walked through the doors. Students eyed us, as usual, some giving the headmaster a high five as they walked past. It was a weird dynamic he had with the students. He was professional while talking to other teachers, and especially Richard, but he was so friendly when it came to the students. Like he actually cared for them.

Headmaster Ellison hummed, thinking over my question. "Well, I guess because I feel that St. Mary's is good for you, and I think if he sees that you're flourishing here, he'll rip you away."

He'd rip me away right now if given the choice.

We were almost to his office when I let myself ask the question, "And why wouldn't you want him to rip me away? Why does that matter to you?"

He sliced his green eyes to mine, and the intense color of them struck a chord with me. My heart skipped a beat as I stared into them, feeling that same sense of familiarity in their depths that I'd felt the first day here. "Because my students matter to me, and I know more about you than you think, Gemma."

I paused as anxiety bubbled in my stomach.

His hand rested on my arm for the briefest of seconds before he pulled away. "That isn't meant to scare you. There is no hidden threat in my statement." A shaky breath clamored from my mouth as we walked into his office. He ushered for me to sit down near the foot of his desk, as always. "Though, I do know you wrecked my car."

Another shaky breath whooshed out of my mouth as it flung open. *How could I forget that I wrecked his car?* Deep down, I knew it was because I was so blinded by what had happened after I'd hit the stone wall. Truthfully, the only thing on my mind was Isaiah and his talented fingers that I couldn't stop myself from staring at today during art. "I... I..." *Deny it!* One look at the headmaster's glittering expression told me that I didn't need to deny it, that there was no point. If he had only guessed that I had wrecked it and was fishing for information, I just gave him the truth right there by not rejecting the accusation right after it came out of his mouth. "Did Isaiah tell you that?"

Suddenly, my heart began to beat harder. Surely Isaiah didn't tell his uncle I had wrecked the car. But what if he did because the headmaster assumed it was him? Or the SMC? Would he throw me under the bus to save himself? There was a reason Isaiah had to stay here, and I had a big feeling it had to do with someone named Jack. I hadn't asked Isaiah who Cade was referring to earlier today, but I saw how Isaiah's shoulders had tensed.

"Isaiah said he wrecked it. But I know how my nephew drives. He doesn't wreck."

My mouth formed an *O*. I could feel the muscles along my lips pinch. *So he didn't throw me under the bus; he tried to save me from it.* I said nothing to the headmaster as I let that sink in. He was staring at me intently, and I had no idea what to even say. Did I apologize? Did I beg him not to tell Richard? *Oh my God. What if he told Richard?* The floor was like water under my feet, and the chair felt like it was seconds from falling in.

"I did wreck your car." I clasped my hands together and felt my head dropping. "And I'm sorry." *What if he tells Richard? Shit.*

"Gemma," the headmaster said, voice a little softer than usual. "I feel like this is a step in the right direction."

"What?" I slowly brought my head up.

A cheesy smile broke out along his face. It was the kind of smile that I would assume a dad to have after saying a silly joke to his teenage daughter. Not that I would have any idea what that would look like, but it just seemed...genuine. In fact, my own mouth wanted to rise at the sight of it. Part of me wished the headmaster was my father. I didn't think much about my own dad. I never knew him, and my mom had disappeared at such a young age that I never even had a chance to ask about him. Tobias once asked Richard about him, and he was locked up for days in the basement. We never dared ask again.

"You didn't lie to me. You admitted wrecking my car." I shifted uncomfortably as I noticed he was still smiling. How could he be smiling when I wrecked his car? "You trusted me enough to tell me the truth. You didn't ask me not to tell your uncle—which I won't, by the way. But that's a step in the right direction, don't you think?"

Was I beginning to trust him?

I pulled at the hem of my skirt nervously. "I guess you're right." I paused. "I'm sorry about your car. I...don't know how to drive."

He laughed. "I can see that."

I bit my lip before asking the question that was nagging me. "Is Isaiah in trouble? For taking me with him?"

Just as he shook his head and relief pooled in my belly, the phone on his desk rang. I jerked upright as my stomach flipped.

"I'm betting that's Ric—my uncle," I said, correcting myself. I leaned closer to the phone. He nodded as he turned it toward me before standing up and rounding his desk.

"You can stay," I blurted, gripping the arm of the chair. The teeniest, tiniest smile found its way to my mouth. "I know you listen through the door anyway."

The headmaster looked surprised at first, and I let myself laugh softly.

"Well..." he said as the ringing continued. "Okay then."

Then, he plopped himself back down onto the chair just as Richard's voice hit my ear.

"Hello, Gemma. I've missed you."

Wish I could say the same.

CHAPTER FORTY-FOUR

ISAIAH

THE FIRE CRACKLED and popped every few seconds as my teammates surrounded it. The glow flickered across all of our team lacrosse shirts, making the white color appear orange with its burning hue. My eyes fell to every single person that circled the team, locking onto Bain for good measure and then scanning the crowd once more for Gemma. *Where was she?*

"Looking for someone in particular?" Brantley grunted, running a hand over his short hair. "A petite, brown-haired girl who has you wrapped around her dainty little *talented* finger?"

I snapped my gaze to him. "What do you know about her talented fingers?" A burning bolt of jealousy flung to my bones before I dug my shoes into the foliage underneath my soles. *Get a fucking grip, Isaiah.*

He chuckled, looking back out to the fire. "I was referring to her artistic abilities...but it's good to know that our little chat earlier didn't help get your mind out of the fucking gutter."

Cade laughed from behind us. "Been there, done that. It won't help, Brantley. Once you're sucked in, you're fucking done for."

"Will you two shut the fuck up, please?" I popped my neck to the side, irritated that I was at the center of their conversation. I was even more irritated that I knew they were right. Both of them. Brantley had pulled me aside after lunch, gripped me by the neck, and brought his forehead down to mine. If it weren't for our friendship, I probably would have swept him off his feet and choked him out, but his eyes burned with such an intensity that I actually waited to hear his reasoning. He was reminding me of my vow. The one I took when I first stepped foot in this school and had girls clinging to my side every single hour of every single day. I could touch, kiss, fuck, but emotions stayed out of it. Always. I made that clear to everyone when the claiming parties started. The claimings were supposed to be anonymous anyway, but some knew who I was, even in the dark, and they thought they could continue the charade well into the next day. *Not happening.*

Brantley and Cade knew of my reasoning: because of my mother, because of my life, because of my future. They made that same vow.

And it was all fine until I kissed Gemma.

She wasn't the type of girl you kissed and forgot, and she wasn't the type of girl you only touched once.

Cade knew how I was feeling. He had felt it with Journey, and just like Brantley was doing now, we all warned him to knock the shit off. It didn't work. And even though Journey was gone, I knew he still felt her deep inside his bones. He carried around the burden every single fucking day. That was probably why he tossed girls out three seconds after fucking them without an ounce of dignity in his tone.

I knew after today in the dining hall, when Gemma seemed to bring me back down to earth, that I wouldn't let her go easily. When she left St. Mary's with the money and fake ID I promised her, she was going to have to truly disappear, because if not, I might just try and bring her back. And it ate away at me that I didn't know more about why she was running. *What had he fucking done to her?*

"What exactly is your plan, Isaiah?" That came from Cade as he tipped back his Solo cup full of St. Mary's punch. I snatched it from his hand and lifted it to my nose, smelling the Bacardi.

"Did you lace the punch?" I glanced behind me and saw Coach talking with Mrs. Graves a few feet away from the punch table. "You better hope to God Coach doesn't catch you drinking that shit the night before a game."

Cade smirked. "I laced *my* punch. No one else's."

"Rude," Shiner snarled, walking up behind us. "Share, fucker."

Cade tipped his head over his shoulder and turned his back on the chaperones. He pulled out his flask next as I scanned the crowd once more for Gemma. A knot began to settle in between my shoulder blades.

"Bain's right there. You can relax." Brantley's voice was low, but I heard the slight uptick of annoyance in it. "What has your dad said about Saturday? Anything?"

"No," I snapped. "I don't know how he expects me to take over when I'm on a need-to-know basis with him."

Shiner smacked his lips after downing his cup of spiked punch. "Damn, that's good." If I weren't on probation, I'd have some too. The burn would surely soothe the coolness of anger pumping throughout my body this evening. I was still irritated that Bain had almost gotten to me earlier. He knew it, too, by the way he kept grinning at me over the fire like a smug fuck.

Cade threw his cup into the fire, and the flames erupted, causing an outburst from a group of girls nearby. He winked before turning to me. "I didn't know you wanted on better terms with him. You're usually avoiding his calls."

"Yeah, well, that was before I realized Gemma was connected."

The three of them nearly broke their necks looking over at me. Our tight group became a little tighter around bundles of students. "What do you mean? Like more connected than Bain fucking with her to get to you?"

I sighed, still keeping an eye on Bain as he wrapped his large arm around one of the girls who he often fucked. "Remember what I told you on Saturday? About Bain dropping guns at the Covens to some man?" They didn't answer, but they didn't need to. "It was Gemma's uncle."

"What?" Brantley's eyebrows raised to his hairline. "Did she see him? Did she point him out?"

I clenched my jaw. "No. But she did recognize the Covens."

"Are you fucking serious?" Cade dipped his head in low. "What does that mean? For her? Surely she hasn't been there."

I shook my head, glancing back at Bain over the sea of people. To be honest, I never used to mind these bonfires to celebrate our biggest rival games, but now that it was running into my tutoring time with Gemma, I found them to be annoying and fruitless. "There is a lot more to her than you guys know." I met all three of their hard gazes, and Brantley swore under his breath.

"There's more to you and her than we know, is what you mean."

Shiner straightened his back, growing serious. "You've fucked her, haven't you?"

"No." But I wanted to. Virgin or not. *Fuck, she was a virgin...right?*

He laughed loudly as he scanned the crowd for what I assumed to be his next smash. Shiner was notorious for snagging a willing participant during the bonfires and fucking her against a tree deep in the forest. "And you're already *this* into her? Interesting..." He paused before looking dumbfounded and mumbling under his breath, "I don't get it."

Cade sighed. "You're already so into her that you're going back on your own morals. You're dragging her into a life that you swore you wouldn't bring anyone into."

"Like the life you wouldn't bring Journey into?"

The muscles along Cade's temple popped as he kept his profile to me. Silence passed through the four of us as we gathered our thoughts. I was growing even more annoyed that Gemma still hadn't shown up. Maybe she was in the art room? Unease settled in, even as Bain stood across the pep rally, clearly not anywhere near her. I scanned the crowd, gazing over the small embers floating into the darkened sky, and sighed. "I am into her. I feel fucked up in the head. I'm possessive of her, protective, even more so now that I've gotten a small glimpse into her life, which by the way, I'm pretty sure is fucked up."

Cade nodded. "She's guarded. There's a reason for that."

"Gemma isn't staying around for long, so this thing between us, whatever the fuck it is—"

"You mean the whole tutoring shit on the front to save your ass but kissing her so possessively at the claiming that everyone cummed in their pants?" Shiner interrupted.

I ignored him as I continued. "As I was saying... This... thing between us won't last. She knows that. I know that. We're both just..." I wasn't even sure what to say. A female had never messed with my head before. I'd never even let someone get close enough.

"Fucked," Cade answered, still locked onto the roaring fire. "You're both fucked. Take it from me, Isaiah. Even if you deny it, you'll be completely fucking destroyed in the aftermath. I see the way you look at her."

The words went unspoken after that. And he was right. I did want to deny it. We all swore that we'd never fall for someone. The reasons were different for me, Cade, and Brantley than they were for Shiner, who was more guarded than most, but we all took the same damn oath one night after the claimings had started. Our lives weren't normal, and we fucking recognized that. Being tied down to someone only ended in two ways, and neither of them were good. I knew that first hand. *So why the fuck couldn't I get my shit straight?*

"It's..." Fuck.

"I know," Cade answered. "I know."

Right before Shiner stepped away, he patted me on the back. "We've got your back—and hers. Won't let anything happen to her as long as she's here."

"I don't approve of this. At all," Brantley ground out. "But we will not have a fucking repeat of Journey. We were caught off guard last time." He leaned forward and shot a look to Cade, which was warranted because Cade had kept her a secret, and if we'd known they were sneaking around, we'd have been able to have a better grasp on things. "And we will not be caught off guard this time. Especially with Bain fucking around. He's already sketchy with the roundabouts he does late at night. And after today, he's on my fucking shit list."

I barked out a laugh as I slid my attention to Bain. "My father says he's untouchable, but fuck me if I'm losing sight of that."

As if I needed a sign from above, my phone vibrated, and

Jack's name flashed on the screen. *Right.* I had more at stake than I liked to let on. "It's Jack. Keep an eye on Bain, at least until Gemma gets here. He wants me to call him."

"She's right there." Cade pointed his head up just as my uncle was walking her toward us. My finger swiped at Jack's message as Gemma smiled at something he'd said. Her perfect, pretty lips curved slightly as my uncle departed, and a breeze wafted around the fire. My breath caught the second our eyes met from across the grassy area, and Cade was right.

I was fucked.

CHAPTER FORTY-FIVE

GEMMA

THE SECOND THE headmaster left me standing in the middle of a rowdy bonfire, I frantically began searching the crowd for Mercedes, since Sloane was in detention, but then I stopped and froze. Isaiah's piercing stare snagged through the fiery flames. Embers danced throughout the wind, floating up to the sky before fading to black. The leaves crunched underneath my shoes, and it was the only indication that I was moving toward him instead of finding Mercedes.

What was I doing?

His eyes flared brighter as his lips tipped. The smallest dimple appeared on his right cheek, and it wasn't a dimple that I saw often. It really never came out unless we were alone in the library, pretending to be busy as he jabbed me with sly remarks and cocky comebacks to my chiding about doing his homework. He may not need actual tutoring, but he did need a little push to do the assignments.

"Hey," he said as he held his phone in his grip. I didn't

think he'd moved even an inch in the time it took me to walk over to him.

"Hi," I squeaked before clearing my throat.

"What took you so long?" Isaiah glanced behind me, phone still resting in his hand. "I was beginning to get worried."

Something tender poked my heart as Isaiah took another step toward me. "Worried you'll flunk without your tutor?" I grinned.

"That's not at all why I was worried." His gaze jolted down to my mouth, and my light and airy attitude was replaced with something much more intense and jarring.

I glanced out to the fire, briefly looking at some of our classmates, who were all dressed in St. Mary's lacrosse apparel instead of their school uniforms like me, before landing on Bain. His body was angled toward Isaiah and me, but he wasn't looking. A pretty, fair-haired girl was wrapped around his side with her head resting on his shoulder, and I wondered what she saw in such an untrustworthy person.

Isaiah stepped beside me, his phone screen bright as he texted someone. I only glanced at his screen for a moment before looking out at the fire again and explaining where I was. "I was checking in with my uncle. That's why I was late."

Out of the corner of my eye, I watched as Isaiah's shoulders stiffened. He was wearing a white St. Mary's lacrosse shirt that fit snugly around the wide berth of his shoulders, and it really did nothing but accentuate the tense way his muscles locked. I leaned forward some and saw that Brantley was also staring out into the fire, but his jaw was rocking back and forth like a ticking time bomb. That wasn't really unusual. Brantley always seemed a little on edge, but both of them? After I mentioned that I was checking in with my uncle? That was something that caught my attention. They were skilled with keeping a hold on their body language; the shift was barely noticeable. But Sloane's assumptions were correct: the Rebels had secrets. It was all part of their allure.

"That's right," Isaiah said seconds later. "It's Monday."

"Yep," I replied, pushing the thought of Richard and his phone call clear out of my head. It wasn't a lengthy conversation. A few hidden threats thrown in when he'd asked how my classes were. He reminded me that my birthday was soon approaching—as if I could forget—and that was about it. The only decent part of the conversation was that he didn't make me call him *Daddy* this time, which was a relief because, although I knew Headmaster Ellison had heard me say it last time, it would have been extremely awkward to say it in front of him, and I wasn't so sure he'd let it slide. He'd ask questions. Questions I wouldn't have answered.

"And how was that?" Isaiah asked. My skin grew warm, and it had nothing to do with the fact that the fire was growing larger and larger. I took a step back, leaves crunching under my shoe again. Isaiah matched my steps, staying in stride with me.

"It was fine."

He chuckled sarcastically. "Look me in the eye and say that."

Slowly, I turned my head and met his intense stare. His chin was raised, that same chin that looked as if it were made from granite, and his eyes gleamed so intently it was like he was trying to reach inside and pull all my secrets out, one by one. I searched his face long and hard before lying again. "It was fine."

His cheek twitched. "And here I thought good girls didn't lie."

A laugh tumbled out of my mouth as I turned back to the fire. I didn't understand how he could make me smile after having thoughts of Richard in my head, but here we were. If only I could take him with me when I left. Maybe then I'd be able to sleep without shit haunting me.

Isaiah's phone vibrated in his hand again as a small smile played on his lips. There was laughter in the air, mixed with the scent of burnt wood, and I felt as if my chest cracked open with light. Isaiah was glancing down to his phone with a hint of smile still there as I turned my head away from him, realizing right then how lucky I was to be standing there underneath the stars and moon with a ginormous school at my back that held a sense of safety so large I could hardly even fathom it.

I felt safe here.

I hadn't felt safe since Tobias left. I hadn't even really felt safe before then either.

It wouldn't last forever, but each day here felt a little more like home, and that made me feel warm. Even if it was only for a second.

"Jack?" Isaiah's voice cut through the happiness churning through my blood, and just like that, it was gone. When I turned toward him again, I saw the blood drain from his face. The healthy glow of his cheeks that were full of innocent laughter seconds ago was no longer there. Instead, it was an ashen gray with shadows of pure panic etching the curves.

"Isaiah?" I asked, not even realizing I'd reached out and placed my hand on his arm. "Are you—" The words died before I could finish. Terror pinched in between his brows as his eyes dipped to mine. "I need my uncle."

I didn't question him. I quickly swept around and found Headmaster Ellison standing with a few other teachers near a table that held some drinks. He was mid-sentence when I interjected myself, trying to appear calm on the outside, but I was twisted on the inside. I'd seen that look before. That look of dread and unease. I'd seen it in the mirror one too many times. I was right there beside Isaiah, feeling what he was feeling.

Only I had no idea *why* he was feeling it.

"Gemma?"

"Isaiah needs you. Now."

His shoulders straightened as he excused himself from the faculty who eyed me with suspicion. As soon as we were out of earshot, he snapped his attention down to me. "What's wrong?"

"I'm not sure. But I think it has something to do with Jack."

He paused for a moment before cursing under his breath. I wanted to ask who Jack was, but I didn't. Instead, we walked in stride. I had a feeling the headmaster was trying to act like he had everything under control in front of me, but he was actually sweating. The heat radiated from his body, and he frantically searched the bonfire for Isaiah.

"Where is he?"

My head snapped back and forth as I began to panic. "He was righ—" My gaze snagged onto Brantley who very subtly nodded his head toward the forest. I wasn't sure what the secrecy was about, but I was sure there was a reason.

I nodded, tapping the headmaster's arm before taking off down the grassy hill. He followed behind me a few seconds later, after Brantley had shouted something about winning their upcoming game, garnering everyone's attention. I wasn't sure if that diversion was planned, but with what I knew, I only had to assume. The headmaster following a female student down to the dark forest probably didn't look too good on the outside—at least not with the way the rumor mill liked to stir up gossip at St. Mary's. I could already practically see the blog post tomorrow morning.

"Jack? What's going on? I can't hear you."

The crunching and snapping of leaves and twigs pulled me

farther into the forest with the headmaster at my heels. A few branches sliced my bare thighs, and I scolded myself again for not changing after class today. Goosebumps raced along my exposed skin the second I was away from the fire, and when I heard even more panic in Isaiah's tone, I shivered.

Something was wrong. Something way bigger than just Bain sneaking off in the middle of the night.

Headmaster Ellison grabbed a hold of my arm as I tripped over a tree stump. "Let me help you."

His grip wasn't firm, but it did hold me in place as we continued to walk. "Isaiah?" he shouted as we both looked through the foggy mist that crowded the forest. It was hard to get my eyes to adjust, but I saw Isaiah's tall dark form up ahead, and I dashed forward, letting my arm fall and getting there before the headmaster.

"Get into the closet and lock it." Isaiah's eyes found mine, their glossiness hitting me right in the chest. His shoulders relaxed for a moment before he squeezed the bridge of his nose and shut his eyes.

"Isaiah? What's wrong?" The headmaster whooshed up beside me, glancing down and landing on my thigh that had a slight sting to it. Our gazes collided, but I shook my head. I was fine. Isaiah wasn't.

"Put it on speaker."

Isaiah stilled, looking over at me, but soon the phone was face up in his shaky hand as a small voice filtered through the other side. "I was already in the clo-closet! She found me, so I ran, and I can hear her looking for me again."

Headmaster Ellison cursed. "Where the hell is Mary, Isaiah?"

"I don't know! Fuck, I don't know! Cade already called her. She didn't answer. I'm afraid Mom did something to her. Jack said the nurses stepped out, and I'm not sure where anyone is! He's alone."

Isaiah seemed to be straddling the line between being terrified and angry. His shoulders were bunched, and the veins along his arms were bulging as he gripped the phone tightly, but his voice didn't sound like him. He sounded broken, and confused, and maybe even a little vulnerable. I wanted to take a step toward him and let him know that he wasn't alone. But I didn't because the tiny, hiccupping sobs on the other end of the phone *was* alone. And that seemed to cause a whole lot of terror for the headmaster and Isaiah both.

"Okay, calm down, Isaiah." Headmaster Ellison stepped forward and tried to take the phone out of Isaiah's hand, but the murderous glare shot his way had him putting his hands up instead. The headmaster ran a hand through his unkempt hair as he looked down to the phone. "Jack? It's Uncle Tate."

"Un-uncle…Tate? It's…Mom. She thinks—" A loud bang sounded on the other end, and I stepped forward as my hand flew to my mouth.

Isaiah's eyes clenched tighter as choppy words left his lips. "She doesn't know it's him. She's saying shit that he doesn't need to hear about that night. I think she's trying to hurt him."

The headmaster pulled on the ends of his hair and snatched the phone out of Isaiah's hands quickly. Isaiah stepped forward as Headmaster Ellison snapped toward me, "Calm him down." Then, he began talking on the phone. "Jack. Listen to me very closely, okay? We're going to play a game."

Isaiah's eyes gleamed with anger as his fists clenched, and I knew what that look meant. It was the same look he had when he almost hit Bain. It was the same look Richard got when he used to snatch Tobias up and keep him for days.

Before I knew what I was doing, I was leaping forward and putting myself between the headmaster and him. Both of my hands fell to his arms, and I peered up into his face. "Isaiah, stop." His jaw was set as he stared behind me. "If you want to keep Jack safe, you need to let your uncle help."

Isaiah's chest was heaving as I put my hand on his chest. The beating of his heart was thunderous against my palm, and my tight belly clenched. "Take a deep breath. Jack needs you to stay calm. Trust me when I tell you that kids can sense terror from a mile away. You stay calm, he stays calm." His steely gaze shot to mine, and the muscles along his face still held a tightness to them that I wasn't sure would ever soften again. "Just breathe and listen."

A rough swallow worked itself down his throat as his nostrils flared. Hot, seedy breath left his mouth and floated around me as I nodded. *There you go.* The headmaster's voice broke through our heavy embrace as we just stayed put. "That's right, Jack. Good job. Take your hand and run it along the side of the wall. Do you feel the little ledge?"

"Ye..yeah! I do!" Jack's voice was less fearful and more excited now.

Headmaster Ellison's chest caved as he put his fist to it. "Good! Push on it with those strong muscles I know you have. I bet you're stronger than Isaiah."

A few seconds passed as Isaiah's labored breathing lessened. My hand was still pressed to his chest, and although his strong heart was still beating wildly, I knew he wasn't going to jump over me and attack his uncle to get the phone back, so I began lowering it. My breath hitched when Isaiah's palm clamped over my hand, keeping it pressed to his body.

"I did it!" Jack rushed out.

"Climb in there. Quick. It's a cool secret tunnel."

Isaiah's gaze switched over to his uncle as confusion covered his face.

"I'm in here," Jack said, sounding more relieved than ever. "Now what?"

The headmaster slowly swung back around, his eyes landing on us. He stepped over a few broken twigs as he rubbed his hand over his forehead. "I'm coming to get you."

"What?" Isaiah's hand fell from mine as he stepped toward him. "But Dad—"

"I know, but until we get ahold of Mary or your mother's nurses, we have no other option."

Just then, Cade came jogging through the wooded area with his phone pressed to his ear. "Mary is there now. She said your father told her she could have the night off. That he would be there all night."

A sarcastic, crass laugh echoed out of Isaiah's mouth as he gripped the back of his neck. "I'm going to fucking kill him."

The headmaster grabbed the phone from Cade's hand and now held both of them out in front of him on speaker. He began talking to both Jack and the woman, Mary, about the situation and how Mary could find him. "Yeah, you know the secret passages from the library to the kitchen? That's where he is. I would find Beth first. Where are the nurses?"

"She locked them out. I found them out front when I pulled up. They're with me. They'll get Beth. I'll grab Jack."

The headmaster and I latched onto each other for a brief moment, and I wasn't sure how I understood what he was telling me, but I did. I felt a sense of understanding between us. It was a strange mix of bitter familiarity that had Tobias' face flashing through my head. *I missed him*. I swallowed as I pulled myself away and came back into the conversation with Isaiah and Cade, ready to de-escalate his rising anger again.

"What's the fucking point?" Isaiah shouted, crossing his arms angrily. "The entire fucking reason I am here, listening to his bullshit and doing his bidding—and for fuck's sake, taking over the family business—is to keep Jack safe. But fuck. He can't even keep his end of the deal? He can't even be bothered to stay at home for one night with his nine-year-old son to make sure he stays away from..." Pain radiated off Isaiah's face so intensely I felt a slight burn in my chest. "From..."

"I know, Isaiah," Cade said, stepping toward him.

"No!" he shouted, his hands running through his hair as his narrowed gaze locked onto him. "You don't. She's a fucking monster, Cade. That night...ruined her. The blood you saw? It all came from her head. It messed her up. She doesn't even recognize us half the time. Neither one of them can be trusted with their own flesh and blood, and fuck, she was the only person who could! Jesus, I had to basically bribe my own fucking father to keep his nine-year-old son safe!"

I stepped forward. "Flesh and blood have nothing to do with it."

Cade's and Isaiah's gazes both shot over to me so quickly I flinched. We all just stood there staring at each other with nothing but the breeze from the tall pine trees wafting around us. I swallowed back the unease wrapping around my body like a twisted vine and raised my chin. "Some people just aren't good people. They don't understand right from wrong. They're twisted and"—I glanced around the forest, not wanting to see the expressions on their faces as I continued on—"and maybe it stems from a fucked-up child-hood, or maybe they're too power hungry and controlling to see that they're causing pain, or maybe they *like* to cause pain, or..." I wrapped my arms around my body. "Or maybe it's an illness, a disease, or...whatever it is, it has nothing to do with flesh and blood. Some people are just...sick. And trust me when I say there is no point in trying to understand it."

Cade stepped forward, the light of the moon peeking through the limbs of the nearest tree over his face. "Sounds like you speak from experience, Gemma."

I shifted my attention and saw Isaiah standing there with

his arms down by his sides, staring directly at me, looking no less than completely defeated. "That's because I am."

Before anyone could say anything else, footsteps approached, and the headmaster appeared with both phones clasped in his hands. His gaze bounced from me, to Cade, and then to Isaiah. "He's with Mary. He's fine."

Isaiah's eyes were like shards of sparkling glass as they landed on his uncle. "He's not fine. No child should go through that."

The headmaster nodded. "I agree. Just like a child shouldn't have to hear their sibling running for their life on the other end of the phone."

My stomach lurched. Something hit me right then as I stared at Isaiah and all his beautiful brokenness and vulnerability that he tried so desperately to hide behind strength and anger. He was really good at hiding it, too. But now I knew that I wasn't the only one with a hidden past that had so much depth that not even an empty abyss could hold it. I wasn't the only one entering adulthood without being unscathed. I wasn't the only one who didn't have a typical, normal childhood. Sure, our childhoods were different, but that didn't mean they weren't just as messed up.

I had been sheltered from the outside world and its monsters, having my own vile one at home, but Isaiah was the opposite. He wasn't sheltered. In fact, I was pretty sure that he'd lived a thousand lives compared to me, and each one of them had something more dangerous than the last.

His shaky, anger-ridden voice cut through the sleepy forest. "I'm not a child. I'm the furthest fucking thing from a child."

The headmaster placed his hands on his hips and garnered all of our attention as his eyes flung from each of us. "None of you are." He glanced at Isaiah first. "Not you with your childhood surrounded by guns, violence, abandonment, fear…" He trailed off before he moved to Cade. "And the same goes for you. Especially with all that you've lost." Then, he landed on me, and I took a step back, wanting to move farther into the dark, wooded area so no one would see me. "And you... From the very moment you stepped foot in my office, I knew."

My heart raced, my breathing so loud I was certain they could all hear the choppy breaths as they climbed from my lungs. "You knew what?"

"That you've been through hell and that you don't plan to go back."

I gulped back emotion, frustrated that he was reading me so easily. I didn't understand. I didn't understand anything anymore. I didn't understand the headmaster for starters. He was so contradicting at times. And did Isaiah tell him of my plans? Did he tell him about our deal? Did he put it together that I was planning on running? That I would soon disappear from St. Mary's all together? Surely not, because wouldn't that go back on him? For not watching over his students closely enough? Did I even want to put someone through that spectacle? Richard would want someone to blame other than himself, and Headmaster Ellison's head would be on the line.

Up ahead, students roared with cheers as a whistle blew. I could see the very faint glow of the fire from the hillside as Cade started to head toward it. He called over his shoulder, "As much as I'd like to stick around and talk about how fucked up we all are, I'm going to get back to the bonfire before Coach flips his shit that Isaiah and I are missing."

Isaiah made no move to leave. Instead, he was staring at his uncle with so much vile that I shivered in my spot.

"I want to kill him." The hate in Isaiah's words rooted me to the forest floor. The muscles along his temples flickered within their shadows. "Same goes for Cade's father, and Brantley's, and fuck, maybe even Jacobi for leaving me high and dry." The headmaster said nothing, and his face was expressionless. Even with the thick darkness that laid around us, I could see that he was calm and collected. Isaiah's gaze shot to mine for a fleeting second before he was glaring back at his uncle. "I want to kill Judge Stallard, too."

My stomach rolled as the name left his lips. How did Richard even end up in this conversation? How did *I* even end up in this conversation?

The headmaster stepped forward and gripped Isaiah's head within his hands. Isaiah's brow line deepened. "You will kill no one, Isaiah. No matter how badly they fucking deserve it."

My lips parted as Isaiah flung his uncle's hands off his face. "And who's going to stop me?"

The headmaster briefly caught my eye before staring at Isaiah directly in the face. He took his pointer finger and pushed it onto Isaiah's hard chest. "You. You're going to stop you. Because you are not your father." He swallowed roughly. "Remember who you are."

Isaiah's head slanted, peeling his glare away. "And how do you know that, Uncle Tate? Maybe I am just as bad as him, because I feel the darkness. I feel that automatic pull to fucking destroy those who deserve it. Starting with Bain."

A faint, choppy laugh left the headmaster. "I know it because your father would *never* give up his wants for someone else. Not like you are doing for Jack. Not like you will do for those that you love. And he doesn't destroy people who deserve it, Isaiah. He destroys innocent people who stand in his way. You know this."

They stared at each other for so long I began to feel uncomfortable. Uncomfortable because I felt like I was intruding. Uncomfortable because whatever they were talking about went much deeper than what was at the surface, and I wasn't sure Isaiah even wanted me around to hear such things.

To see such things. I knew I wouldn't if I were him. If I were digging up something from my dark and twisted life, I wouldn't want anyone to hear it.

Another whistle blew, and we all heard Isaiah's name come from someone's mouth. He sighed as his head dropped.

The headmaster took a step back. "You two go somewhere for the evening. Go to the library. The art room. Somewhere away from here. I don't want you around Bain tonight."

Isaiah gave him a look, but the headmaster shook his head. "I will handle it. I'll tell Coach that your lovely tutor here"—he gestured to me—"is helping you study for a test tomorrow. He wouldn't want his best player getting expelled by the SMC for not raising those grades now, would he?"

"And what about Bain?" Isaiah asked, clearly annoyed that his uncle was banning him from the bonfire. "I'm sure Cade and Brantley will let you know if something seems off. They've always done so in the past, yes?"

Isaiah went to say something, but I took a step forward, snagging his attention. Something flickered across his face, and his shoulders lowered a fraction. "Okay."

The headmaster started to back away, and his lips lifted just a fraction as he threw Isaiah's phone toward him. "Take the night off from Isaiah Underwood, nephew. You deserve it."

Before the headmaster got too far away, Isaiah shouted, "And Jack is good? You talked to him?"

"I talked to both him and Mary. They're together. She has him. Now go be teenagers." He paused. "But...be good." He flipped back around and called over his shoulder. "And don't take my car."

Isaiah grunted under his breath with his back toward me. My lips begged to twitch into a smile, which was so absurd given all that had just happened a few moments ago. From Isaiah's little brother...to the headmaster calling out me,

Isaiah, and Cade on the fact that we had less-than-stellar upbringings...to the emotional conversation between Isaiah and his uncle. It was all so much, yet here I was, wanting to smile. *Don't take my car.* I think I liked the headmaster.

Isaiah's hands found his waist as his head dropped to the ground. He was still facing away from me, and the ridges of his back were hard and tense. I'd bet if his shirt was off, I'd be able to count each muscle along his shoulders.

Taking one step toward him, I said, "Your uncle is...unusual."

A sharp laugh left Isaiah's mouth as his head popped up. He caught a glimpse of me over his shoulder and then began to turn around. "That's what you have to say after all that you just witnessed? That my uncle is...unusual?"

I shrugged, wrapping my arms around my torso. There was a nip in the air, and while I had been warmed by the fire up on the hill, I was definitely chilly without it. "He's just..." A soft laugh floated out of my mouth. "I can't figure him out."

Isaiah and I were only a few feet apart now, standing in the middle of a circle of pine trees that went so high they looked as if they touched the stars. Silvery moonlight cascaded over our heads, and when our eyes caught, I knew the light moment was fleeting. "What are you thinking right now?" He looked away, showing off that flawless skin of his. "I'm honestly afraid to even know."

I chewed on my lip, my eyes burning a hole through his high cheekbone before taking another step toward him. "I'm thinking I want to know more about Jack."

Isaiah's head whipped toward me so fast I felt the strands of his hair fly past my face. "You want to know more about my brother?"

Lifting a shoulder, I smiled shyly. "He seems important to you."

"He is." Silence stretched around us. The faint sound of the bonfire caught my attention, along with the chanting of the forest, but before long, Isaiah's hands dropped, and he began walking farther into the wooded area with me following after him.

The farther we walked, the further the silence stretched. The trees grew more crowded, and the branches and twigs were messier, and they would have slashed at my bare legs, but Isaiah was always quick to move them out the way so I could move by easily. We were still walking when he finally broke the silence. "I've never told anyone about Jack."

My brows furrowed as I tucked a strand of hair behind my ear so I could see him better out of the corner of my eye. "Why not?"

"Because I keep those that I love close to me, and I love him the most."

Isaiah stopped walking and tilted his head up past the trees. I did the same, and a short gasp left my lips. The tall, looming trees that were crowding us during our short walk were no longer blocking the light of the night sky. A million little stars twinkled and sparkled above our heads as if they were putting a show on for us. "That's...beautiful."

His voice was rough. "Agreed." I turned away from the stars and caught Isaiah staring directly at me. My heart jolted as if it had reached up and touched one of the stars in the sky. Heat warmed my cheeks as I quickly glanced away.

Isaiah moved past me a few yards and rested his back along one of the thick tree stumps, kicking a leg up behind him as he crossed his arms over his chest. I stayed in the same spot, too nervous and consumed by the heat creeping into every little crevice of my body to do much more.

"The only people who know about Jack are the Rebels and, of course, my uncle." I opened my mouth to tell him that he didn't need to tell me anything, but he stopped me. "He's nine. Looks just like me, only with a goofy smile and the world's most hideous fucking glasses. He looks like Harry Potter."

I took a small step toward him. "Who's Harry Potter?"

Dark hair flopped on his head as he jerked. "Tell me you're kidding."

Now it was my turn to cross my arms over my chest as I shot him a disapproving stare. "I already told you I had a sheltered childhood."

He kicked off of the tree. "We must rectify this immediately." He paused before pointing at me. "And if you tell anyone I'm a Harry Potter junkie, I'll tell them just how much you like sitting bareass on the tables in the dining hall."

My mouth flung open. "You wouldn't!"

His brow flicked upward as if challenging me, and I rolled my eyes.

"Whatever. I won't tell anyone." I breezed past him and took his spot on the tree, resting my back against it. "But there's no need to threaten me. You could have just told me not to tell anyone, and I wouldn't have."

A sly smile curved on his face. "I know, but then I wouldn't get to see you blush."

"It's too dark to see me blush."

"Not true." He pointed a finger up to the stars and moon gleaming over us, and I clamped my lips together.

"Back to Jack," I reminded him, still feeling the heat simmer in my cheeks.

"There's not much more to tell that you didn't already hear. Jack is my little brother, and he's really the only thing I've ever loved, besides my older brother who..."

Wait. He had an older brother too?

He sighed, running a hand through his hair again. Talking about his older brother was obviously difficult for him. "I don't talk to my older brother anymore. But Jack...I'm really all he has."

I nodded gently as I empathized with a child who I'd never met and probably never would. My brother was all I had, too, as a child. I bet Jack missed him so much. "He's lucky to have you."

"He was until my father sent me here. Now he's alone."

I shook my head but stopped myself as earlier thoughts washed away my previous question. "Is that why you're so adamant about staying here? At St. Mary's?" I jolted forward as puzzle pieces clicked together. Cade had mentioned Jack earlier when Isaiah and I had stepped out of the dining hall after he'd almost lost it. "You're protecting him." My sentence came out in a whisper as my throat began to close up. "Did... did your father threaten your brother? To keep you here to watch Bain?"

That was absurd. Right? Parents didn't do things like that to their children. Did they? My earlier statement had filtered in. *It had nothing to do with flesh and blood...some people are just bad.* I'd always had the thought that Richard was so mean to Tobias and me because we weren't his real family. That he could punish us in such inconceivable ways because he didn't hold that unconditional amount of love that parents were supposed to have for their children. Richard raised us. He was the only parental figure that we had, but he didn't see us as his children. Or even as his niece and nephew.

I wasn't a mother, so I couldn't understand the concept of unconditional love, and the memories of my own mother were so blurry that I couldn't be sure, but I was pretty certain that parents were supposed to protect and love their children above all else. I'd lived with a real-life example of that. Anne, Richard's mother, had loved him even when he hit her and put her down. She had loved him even knowing his plans for me. She had loved him even through his many, many faults.

That was a prime example of unconditional love, but it was apparent that not all parents were like that. I was right earlier. Flesh and blood had nothing to do with it. *Some people were just bad.*

"Yes. That's why I can't get expelled. He's using my little brother as leverage."

Isaiah's answer startled me. I jumped, scratching the back of my thighs against the tree bark.

Shock rippled through me again, and I wasn't even sure why. I knew bad people existed in the world, just like I knew that not all children had a loving home. All the love I had growing up was a fake rendition of such, and you didn't break the things you loved.

"I'm..." I stepped forward just as Isaiah's eyes swung to mine. His head was low, and his vulnerability pulled at the strings inside my chest. "I'm so sorry."

"You are the last person who should say sorry. You're helping me with my probation. You're helping me keep Jack safe, in a way."

Part of me wanted to tell him to forget about our deal. That he didn't have to give me money or a fake ID. I didn't want anything in return if it meant helping him. It was as if I was seeing Isaiah Underwood, St. Mary's bad boy, for the first time. I saw him in a different way now. I saw his vulnerabilities, and to me, that meant everything. It made him real.

Of course I didn't tell him not to pay me or give me what he promised, because that would be insane given all that I had on the line too, but I wanted to. I wanted him to know that I wasn't only in this because of our deal but that I would help him with anything.

St. Mary's had it all wrong. Isaiah wasn't this almighty, arrogant, ruler-of-the-school bad boy.

No.

Isaiah was *good.* And protective. And loyal.

CHAPTER FORTY-SIX

GEMMA

ISAIAH and I had been standing silently in the empty forest for entirely too long. Goosebumps continued to rise over my flesh as I wracked my head for something to say to him. For something other than the annoying and unneeded apology that kept trying to escape my mouth.

I knew I had nothing to say sorry for. That whatever else laid behind those icy depths of his wasn't my fault and likely had nothing to do with me, but I was still sorry. I was sorry that he was in a constant battle between keeping his brother safe and losing sight of himself. That had to have weighed heavily on him. It had to. Just like it weighed on me that I was in a constant battle of getting as far away from Richard as possible or getting close enough to him to find out where Tobias was. One made me feel selfish, but the other was like signing my own death certificate.

"Do you want to go back up to the bonfire?"

Moving my attention from the twigs and leaves underneath my shoes, I found Isaiah standing only a few feet away from me. His brows were raised to his hairline as he waited for my answer, and I found myself shaking my head no.

There was a glint of gloss on Isaiah's bottom lip, like he'd recently licked it, and I felt myself pushing my back further into the tree that I was leaning on.

"Well, then what do you want to do? Go back up to the school? Go to the library to pretend we're studying, even when we both know that's total bullshit? Take my uncle's car for a test drive?" He waggled his eyebrows. "I can teach you how to drive."

An abrupt laugh flew out of my mouth. "Absolutely not."

His lip curved until we both snapped to the left as a branch broke. The rustling of leaves quickly followed, and my heart flew up to my throat. The options were honestly endless as to what could have made such noises in the middle of the night, trapped inside a dark forest.

Isaiah was in front of me so quickly that I didn't even have time to register the fact that he'd moved. His body covered mine as his hand clamped over my mouth. I breathed in and out of my nose, smelling pine and his earthy cologne, as fear crowded my thoughts, and shadows began to dance in the distance. Isaiah's forehead slowly fell to mine as he whispered, "Relax. It's probably nothing."

Relax? It could be a bear! Or...or someone from the SMC wondering what he and I were doing sneaking away from the bonfire! Or...or Bain! Not that I would be too concerned if Bain showed up. I knew that I was safe with Isaiah. He wouldn't let anything happen to me.

Another twig snapped in the other direction, and we both turned our heads to see if anything appeared. I glanced up to the stars and moon again as it acted as a spotlight over our bodies, and Isaiah nodded, catching what I was saying. He dropped his hand from my mouth and intertwined our fingers before pulling me a little farther into the forest. We walked slowly so we didn't make too much noise and then nestled in between two more trees that had better coverage. Our hands stayed joined together as my pulse drummed behind my skin. I tried to shake off the unease slithering over my shoulder as I was quickly reminded of the last time I was running through a wooded area. I could almost feel the sharp stabbings of twigs puncturing my legs as I ran as fast I could from Richard.

"Gemma, relax." Isaiah squeezed my hand a few times as I took a deep breath through my nose. "There's nothing to be afraid of. I won't let anything happen to you."

I squeezed his hand back, feeling a slight flutter in my belly. "I know that. I'm not afraid."

He pulled me in a little closer to him, our bodies colliding. "Are you sure about that? You're breathing like..." A quiet chuckle left his rumbling chest. "Never mind."

I felt myself relax against him until we heard some more rustling. Isaiah's hands cupped my waist as he looked over my head, and I peeked around. My brows crowded as I watched something move, and then came a loud smack and a giggle. *Who was that?*

"*Fucking Shiner,*" Isaiah mumbled, flipping me around so my back was pressed to his front as we faced the noises. Isaiah's warmth grew closer as his breath floated over my ear. "Shiner's known for bringing girls out here during the bonfires. I should've known."

And as if on cue, Shiner said, "You like that, baby? I've always heard you like it a little dirty."

My eyes widened as Isaiah began shaking behind me with laughter. Certainly they couldn't be doing stuff...out here? Right?

"What..." My eyes squinted as I watched through the swaying grass and tree limbs as two dark shadows moved languidly with one another. "What are they...wait. Are they...?"

The taller shadow, who I assumed was Shiner, put his hands on the smaller shadow's shoulders and pushed her down below his waist. My brow furrowed even more as I took in her moving figure and the noises that came with it. It sounded like a hiss of an animal followed by Shiner mumbling, "*Fuck yes*." His head tipped back, showing off his long neck and the side of his straight nose. When I scanned my eyes down to where the girl was, my breathing quickened even more than before. The movement of her head in between the small openings of the branches had my cheeks flushing so quickly I felt the burn.

Isaiah pulled me back a little bit, whispering into my ear. "Did that answer your question?" There was something flirty in his voice, but I couldn't even process it. I was too focused on what was going on in front of me.

My mouth parted as I kept my eyes glued to the girl whose head was bobbing below Shiner's waist, and all of a sudden, things were twisting and curling inside my stomach. His hand quickly fell to her hair, and I pulled back as he began thrusting his hips toward her.

"Is..." I couldn't stop staring. My eyes were glued to them, in awe. It was a world I wasn't familiar with, like dipping a toe inside an ice-cold pool before quickly darting away again. Did I even want to keep looking? Should we leave? Wasn't this...private?

Isaiah's hand splayed over my stomach as he pulled my hair off my shoulder, letting the thick strands fall behind my back. "There are all kinds of places we hook up around here, Gem. Not just the dining hall." He teased me, and I felt his chest rumble against my back. "So, yes. To answer the question that never left your lips. They are hooking up."

A zip of lightning rushed down my spine and pulled at my insides. A ragged breath left my lips as I whispered, "Oh."

Isaiah paused from behind me as I continued staring at Shiner's quickly moving hips. His tempo was getting faster, and I knew I should have looked away. He had come here with a girl to be alone. Not to be spied on by me with curiosity.

"Do you want to go back up to the bonfire? Is this making you...uncomfortable?"

Isaiah's hand stayed glued to my front as his breath grazed over the sensitive skin that laid on my neck. I found myself moving my head to the side for more. I wasn't even sure why I did it, other than that I enjoyed the feeling of sparks flying over my skin.

"No," I answered quietly.

"No?" I looked down to Isaiah's hand that was still laying over my stomach. He was moving his finger, barely notice-able, but I was too hyper-aware to not notice. Did he even know he'd begun rubbing a circle over the fabric of my skirt? Just below my belly button? Did he know how tightly things were coiled there? *This felt so wrong. But so good.*

I shook my head, my neck still craned to the side as his quick breaths filtered over my flushed skin. "No. I... I'm..." I licked my bottom lip, focusing back on the forbidden sounds I was hearing.

"You're what?"

"Curious," I answered quickly. "I'm curious."

I heard Isaiah swallow from behind me, the roughness of it making my heart skip a beat. His finger was still moving in slow, lazy circles, but at some point, his hand had somehow traveled to the side of my hip.

"You're curious?"

My insides spiked with fire as Shiner pulled the girl up and crashed his mouth to hers. *Whoa.* This was intense, and I was hungry to see what else they'd do. It was such a forbidden, dark thing for me to watch. But I needed to know more. I needed to see just what I'd been missing out on while being locked away in a basement for someone else's sick desires. My head tipped to glance at Isaiah for a quick second. It was dark now that we were tucked away behind two trees, but I still found my way to his eyes. "What was she doing? Just a second ago?"

I turned away as I saw the sly grin slide onto his face. "She was giving him a blow job." My brows furrowed. *A blow job? What exactly was that?* I stayed quiet as I began thinking over the words until Isaiah answered my silent question with a tone that made me clench my legs

"She was sucking him..." Isaiah's hand clamped harder onto my hip. "With her mouth."

The shock flew from the very bottom of my belly. "Oh." My attention went right back to Isaiah's hand that had suddenly begun wandering over my hip gracefully and inching underneath my shirt *just* enough to drive me freaking crazy. The pad of his finger against my skin felt like tiny little fires flying throughout my blood. "And...that feels good? When she does that?"

He huffed, his hot, seedy breath touching me like hot coals. "Yes."

I nodded, taking in the new knowledge. My eyes traveled back through the jagged limbs of the forest as I locked onto Shiner and his partner again. My pulse skyrocketed as he quickly picked the girl up, wrapping her legs around his waist. He moved quickly, thrusting them farther into the wooded area and pushing her back up against a tree. It was too dark to see her face, but I could see the way her long hair flew back into the darkness. I could hear her breathy moans as Shiner did something to her that was likely similar to what Isaiah had done to me the other night.

"Gemma," Isaiah whispered again, pulling me flush with his body. "We should go back up to the bonfire."

Disappointment flooded my chest. "Yeah. You're right."

Neither one of us moved. Instead, Isaiah's finger began working even faster. The long finger that was barely moving against my belly was swiping so low that it dipped beneath the waistband of my skirt and touched my panties. I felt the thundering beat of his heart as my head leaned back onto his hard planes. His earthy cologne sent my senses into overdrive along with the sounds of the couple several yards away from us.

"Didn't—" I gasped as Isaiah's other hand gripped even harder onto my hip, steadying me in place. "Didn't the head-master tell us to be normal teenagers tonight?"

"*Mmhm.*" His rushed whisper awakened something deep inside of me. It took everything I had to keep my feet planted firmly to the ground instead of swinging around and pushing my lips to his. Because that was what my body was telling me to do. It was telling me to kiss him. To touch him. To let him touch me.

"Is this..." I gasped as his lips touched the side of my neck. "Normal? To sneak away from a school bonfire to—"

"To do dirty, dirty things?"

"Ye...yeah." Isaiah pulled me even harder into him with one hand, steadying me so our bodies were flushed together so tightly not even a breath could float in between us.

"We need to go back up to the school, Gemma." The roughness in his tone and beating of his heart told me that he was lying. That he wanted to stay here just as badly as I did. I also wanted to take his hand and push it farther south where the bundle of nerves was. It was an erratic thought that was driven purely from something that had been brought to life by him on Saturday night.

"Do you want to go back?" I asked, watching with hazy

eyes as Shiner rocked his hips forward into a girl that was all but screaming out his name. *"Oh my God, Shiner. Don't stop."*

"Fuck no," Isaiah answered, gripping me so tightly I was likely to have bruises tomorrow. The hand that was swiping back and forth over the top of my panties stilled.

"Then why did you suggest we go back?"

"Because I can't keep my fucking hands off you." Isaiah's nose grazed the side of my jaw so slowly and tediously that I began to throb in places I didn't know I could. There was a sudden pull in my belly that made my stomach dip with his admission. "You're standing here, panting, with my hands on you, watching something so fucking *dirty* with an innocence that I want to taint so badly." His lips gently touched the side of my mouth, and my hand clamped onto his wrist that was so close to where I wanted it. "I'm not a decent person, Gemma. I've seen bad shit. Bad shit that I didn't put a stop to, but fuck...you're good, and I'm not going to ruin you. I've already crossed the line and—"

"And I want you to touch me, Isaiah. So do it." If I wasn't in overdrive from everything else I was feeling, I would have been in shock at my demand. "If anything, just for tonight."

He growled as his teeth nipped my ear. I gasped aloud, my back curving. I felt a heat cling to my skin so quickly that I wished the trees would waft a breeze over us to cool me down.

"Don't say things like that to me." His heavy breath clamored over my skin as he flung me around to meet his dark stare. "I feel out of control around you. I honestly don't know if I can even go slow with you and treat you the way that you deserve." Isaiah's palms wrapped around my face as his fingers dove into my hair. "And you have to understand something, Gemma." His mouth was so close to touching mine that I could almost taste him on my tongue. I licked my lips, and he somehow pulled me even closer. "You are leaving. I am stay-ing. This won't last."

"I know that."

He shook his head, pushing our bodies flush. I could feel a hardness lay between us, and I knew what it was. Only this time, it didn't scare me. "You don't understand. I'm not going to want to let you go. Especially if we keep this up. Things are different with you."

There was a slight knock in my heart that understood his words. I already felt that way. I already didn't want to leave St. Mary's, but it was absolutely vital that I did.

My shaky hands dropped to Isaiah's waist as I moved my head just a fraction closer to his. *Can't we just pretend we're normal? Just for the night? Like we're two teenagers who don't have a load of baggage at their feet?*

I didn't say this aloud, but it was *so* easy to forget who I was with him. To forget that guarded girl who was terrified for the future if she stayed just a moment too long at this school. It was so easy to just *lose* myself when, in reality, I should have been finding myself. But there were no fearful thoughts, no hold-backs, nothing. I just *felt* when I was with him. I let my mind, heart, and body all come together as one for the first time, and maybe that was how it was supposed to be.

Isaiah didn't say anything as he peered down at me. I was pretty sure that Shiner and the girl had left, because I didn't hear a single thing except for my own heartbeat and Isaiah's labored breathing.

"Once I acknowledge that I'm willingly crossing this line, *again*, it's going to be hard for me to go back, Gemma. I fucking can't. I feel wildly possessive over you, and that should scare the fuck out of you."

"So possessive that when it's time to let me go, you won't?" My heart raced up my throat, holding me hostage to the answer that I needed him to give me. *Please just give me this. Just for the night.*

His answer was sharp. "No. Because although I am possessive, I am also protective, and getting away from me is in your best interest. And that has nothing to do with the real reason you're leaving."

I stayed quiet for a few moments. My fingers rested along the hem of his t-shirt as his hands dropped from the sides of my face and ran down the length of my arms so slowly I shivered.

His gulp drew my attention to his mouth as the question floated out. "So what will it be? Do we go back up to the bonfire and stop this before it becomes something more? Or do you want to stay here?"

"Here," I said, gripping his shirt within my hands. "I want to stay right here. With you. We don't even have to discuss it tomorrow. It can just be for tonight."

Isaiah didn't respond. Instead, his hands moved quickly, and his fingers dug into my thighs, hoisting me up to meet his middle. His mouth descended onto mine, and the kiss rocked me. It was rough, our teeth clanking, his tongue diving forward and licking up my innocence like he'd starve without it. My head was dizzy, and I wasn't sure if it was because he had swung us around and stomped through the forest, or if it was a reaction to what his mouth was doing. Either way, I loved it. I loved every single bit of it.

He pulled away when we reached a different area in the forest. I glanced up and saw the opening of the stars and moon again, and I knew we were back to where we started.

"The things I could do to you are endless, Good Girl."

Excitement flooded me as my teeth sunk down into my lip. Anticipation rushed in as Isaiah's eyes traveled down to my middle that was pushed up against him with my legs wrapped around his back. Our gazes collided for only a second before his mouth was back on mine, licking and exploring so tediously that I couldn't think of anything *but* him. I felt him everywhere. His hands roamed, running the length of my body as I pushed myself further onto his hardness. *It felt so good.* He grunted as his hands slapped over my waist, hoisting me away from him as he lowered my shaky legs to the forest floor. Sticks crunched underneath his weight as he erased all the space between us, tipping my head back so it rested along the rough bark of the tree. With the stars and moon above our heads, I could see the look in his eye. That icy blue burned brighter as his thumb rubbed over my bottom lip. "I'm starving." *What? Right now?*

My breaths were rushed, and they grew even choppier as Isaiah held me around my ribcage, right underneath my bra. His hands traveled slowly over my curves as he began to lower to one knee. I peered down at him, slack-jawed, completely and utterly confused. "What.. What..." I gulped as one of his warm palms gripped the inside of my thigh.

His breath coated my skin as he ran a finger up and down my thigh. "When I first saw you walk into the bonfire, I wondered why you hadn't changed out of your uniform before coming." He chuckled before landing the softest, sweetest kiss on the skin right above my knee. Everything grew hot, and I was pretty certain the ground moved. "But I'm really fucking glad you didn't."

I swallowed again, glancing up at the stars before bringing my attention to him hovering right in front of the part of my body that held so much tension I thought I might combust. "Why?"

"Because it's easier for me to do this." The finger that had been running up and down my thigh started at the base of my knee as he slowly trailed it up farther and farther, disappearing underneath my skirt. Our eyes caught, and my stomach tightened. "Do you trust me, Gemma?"

I nodded quickly, clenching my teeth as I forced myself to stay still. He watched me with lazy eyes as I responded to his finger lightly touching me over my underwear. My lips parted as he pressed his thumb slightly into my most tingly part. "I want to taste you."

I pushed myself back into the rough bark. *Wait, what?* Isaiah's arm wrapped around the crook of my back for a second, pulling me closer to his mouth. "No, that's not true." Then both of his hands gripped me again as he made a noise that sent me into complete overdrive. "I fucking *need* to taste you."

"I...I've never done that."

Isaiah shut his eyes and whispered, "Good," before his head disappeared, and my mouth flung open. I didn't know what to expect, but I didn't have time to consider it because the warm heat from his mouth closed in on me, and my hips bucked toward him all on their own. Isaiah's hands traveled up higher, and I felt the rough way he hooked his fingers into the thin cotton, pulling them down to my ankles and flinging them somewhere into the forest. I couldn't even care that my underwear was long gone, because all of a sudden, I was in a frenzy. His mouth was hot as he kissed my center again, licking and sucking as his fingers dug into my soft skin.

I couldn't speak. I couldn't move. I was completely and utterly focused on the way that my body was bundling and curling and throbbing.

My attention was pulled away for a brief second as Isaiah's fingers let up from one of my legs only to prop my calf up onto his shoulder. He popped out of my skirt for a second and peered up at me with a wild and untamed look on his face. "I will never fucking be satisfied again after this. I hope you know that."

He mumbled something that sounded like, "*Only tonight*," but I couldn't ask him to clarify because he'd dipped under-

neath my skirt again and sucked me into his mouth so possessively I cried out. My head tipped backward, and my hands
wrapped around the rough bark of the tree stump behind me.
Isaiah pushed my legs apart even farther, and I was blinded.
My eyes shut; my body sagged. The way his warm mouth felt
as he kissed me all around was too much. It was as if he was
marking me, and I liked it. I felt the shift of his finger as he
ran it over my slick seam. The feeling left me breathless, and
I burned for more. I needed more. I said that, too.

"Isaiah, more." My hips rocked, and he growled, his finger
finding my center as I cried out.

"Anything for you," he whispered before sucking me and
licking up everything I had to offer. The feeling started to
make things tingle, my toes curled against the bottom of my
shoes, and my fingers dug into the bark of the tree so fiercely
I thought they might be cut. "*Fuck*," he said between licks.

I couldn't stop spinning. The trees swayed, the breeze
blew over us, and the second Isaiah curled his finger and
pushed farther into me, I felt the rush. The mind-blowing,
soul-shattering, so-bright-the-stars-didn't-even-match rush. I
cried out, not even realizing until later that the sound had
come from me. Isaiah sucked and licked as I rode out the
most amazing feeling I had ever felt until I was left breathless
and sated. At some point, my leg had been lowered to the
ground, and a jolt went through me, making Isaiah's eyes
grow dark. He crowded my space as soon as he was off his
knees, wrapping his arm around my waist and pulling me into
his body. I felt his hardness in between us, and my head began
to dip down to look at it pressed against my belly, but he
caught my chin and shook his head.

"I don't trust myself."

My brows crowded, still unable to even form words. My
insides felt like jelly, and my heart was hardly back to normal.
I still felt the desire flooding through my veins, though. That

momentary silence that Isaiah had just given to me was enough to wash every last worrisome thought from my head. He had no idea what he'd just given me.

I went to look down again, eager to give him something back, even if I had no idea what to give, but his grip on my chin grew tighter. "If you so much as look down there, I will rip the rest of your clothes off and fuck you right here, Gemma, and that's...too much, too fast. That'll definitely be crossing the line."

My face flamed, almost embarrassed that I found his words so...*inviting*. Did I want that? The answer was simple. *Yes*. I did. And surprisingly enough, it didn't even scare me. It should have, but it didn't. Just like it should have scared me when Isaiah said he felt possessive over me, but I kind of felt that way about him too. I had a sudden rush of anger earlier that St. Mary's had labeled him as such an arrogant, heartless person. That the SMC was giving him so much trouble when they really had no idea what he was up against. What he had been tasked to do. I felt...protective. I'd never felt protective over someone. Not even Tobias. Tobias was always protecting me, not the other way around.

Isaiah gave me a piece of himself earlier. He was completely and utterly bare as his hurt and anger came out in full waves over his little brother. He trusted me enough to talk freely in front of me with his uncle over something so personal.

And there was a hidden part of me that wanted to give him something back.

Especially now.

CHAPTER FORTY-SEVEN

ISAIAH

THE LAST COUPLE of days had been nothing less than torture.

After the bonfire on Monday, and what followed after, all I thought about was putting my mouth on Gemma. Every inch of her skin. I wanted to corrupt her even further. I wanted to get down on my knees, rest them on the dirt-covered floor of the forest, and tongue-fuck her over and over again.

But instead, after I'd handed her back her underwear that I'd found laying several feet from us, I took her right up to her room because she kept giving me those fuck-me eyes that I knew she wasn't even fully aware of, and if we had stayed put, all alone in that wooded area, I would've fucked her. I knew what would have eventually happened, and it just...couldn't. Not yet. Probably not ever.

When I went back to my room after pulling myself from the girls' hall, I lay on my bed, waiting for Cade to let me know if Bain had been up to anything during the bonfire, and thought over her words very carefully: *Just for tonight.*

Deep down, I knew there would be more nights. *There had to be, right?*

It was inevitable because we both seemed to lose sight of the future when we were together. Fears and worries became distorted.

In fact, my future looked a lot like her, and just before I shut my eyes after still tasting her on my tongue, I told myself *no*. I told myself that little word over and over again, and it was fine until I saw her the next day.

She didn't shy away from looking at me like I had suspected she would.

She didn't avoid me.

In fact, during art, when she'd shifted to stand, pulling her journal tightly to her chest, she peeked over her shoulder at me, showcasing her innocent yet *very* inviting smile, and my dick hardened.

If Bain hadn't *wandered* off last night—just to go in fucking circles again—then during our up-close-and-personal tutoring session, where Gemma's leg kept brushing along mine after she scolded me for pushing aside my English 4 paper, I would have kissed her. I would have done a lot more than kiss her.

And when I told her I had to go, because of Bain, I saw a flash of something cross her features.

She was disappointed. It was subtle, but I saw it.

She didn't want our tutoring session to end.

She didn't want the lingering touches to fade.

She didn't want to keep beating around the bush about what had happened Monday, even if there was a shyness to her too.

I was doing my part in crossing back over the line, because her words sat very quietly in the back of my head. *Just for tonight.* They sat along with the Rebels' warnings and my dreadful future, but looking at her all day and remembering what I had felt when I touched her *really* fucking weighed on me.

Just like it was weighing on me that she kept lifting her head to peek at me over her laptop.

I wouldn't get to tutor with her tomorrow night.

It was the big rival away game.

I usually enjoyed away games because I didn't have to worry too much about Bain. I always had it covered. But being in Temple tomorrow meant that I wouldn't get to see warmth rise to Gemma's cheeks when our eyes would catch. I wouldn't get to watch her nibble on her lip as her gaze lingered on my mouth from across this fucking table. I wouldn't get to argue with myself about whether I should cross the line again or sit here and try to decipher if she wanted to cross it too.

She continued to glance up at me every few minutes, and each time I'd catch her, my core grew hot. Her typing was more furious, but instead of listening to the chanting of regret going on in the back of my head, I stared at her. I was minutes, maybe even seconds from flipping the table over and saying to hell with it all when her fingers finally stopped typing, and she slammed the laptop closed.

"I want to show you something."

The next thing I knew, she was standing up, still sporting that goddamn schoolgirl uniform, and placing her hand in mine. The softness of her palm felt sacred in mine. Like I didn't even deserve to be touching her. It felt as if it were grounding me to something that didn't even come close to reality as we left the library and headed toward the hallway.

I suddenly had a feeling of unworthiness go through me over the fact that, on Monday, after I'd completely lost my cool in front of her and threatened to kill my father, she didn't look at me differently. In fact, she looked at me more intently now. Like she understood.

And I had tried to give her an out before dipping my head between her legs. I tried to push her into going back to the school and to the bonfire, but she fought hard to stay with me, to show me that she wasn't judging and that she wasn't afraid. That spoke volumes about her. It truly did. And maybe that was why I'd been able to keep myself on a leash the last two days. Maybe I knew, deep down, it was going to be extremely difficult to let her go, because in the end, I would have to let her go. No matter what.

"Where are we going?" I asked, catching up with her just enough that she could still pull me in the direction that she wanted to go. The library doors were shut, and the hallway was dark since it was after curfew.

Her flushed cheeks made an appearance again as a soft smile covered her mouth. "You'll see."

I didn't show my skepticism as I continued to walk with her. I pulled my phone out once to see if I had any missed texts, but there was nothing there, which meant Bain wasn't being sly tonight. I didn't even have a text from Jack. We'd briefly texted yesterday when I checked in to make sure he was okay after the whole *running-from-our-mother* thing, but I hadn't heard from him since. I made a mental note to call my father tomorrow on my way to the game and demand to know where the fuck he was. I would have called him Monday night after I left Gemma, but I knew I needed to wait until the anger subsided all the way before I did that. What I really wanted to do was throat-punch him for leaving Jack alone without Mary as our mother had an episode.

"Isaiah?" Gemma's sweet voice tore my attention away. "Are you okay?" Her doe-like eyes punched me in the core as she looked down at our hands. I quickly let her hand go, pulling my throbbing one closer to my body.

"Fuck, I'm sorry." Anger simmered beneath the surface, right below guilt. "Did I hurt your hand?"

She surprised me again when she reached out and rested her palm against mine, intertwining our fingers. "Are *you* okay? What were you thinking about?"

I let a heavy breath leave my chest as we stayed in the same spot, right in front of the art room. "Nothing. And I'm more okay right now than I ever have been." And that was true.

Gemma seemed to think over my answer for a minute before nodding, her shiny hair swaying off her shoulders. "Me too." Then, she turned on her heel, opened the art room door, glanced down to both ends of the hallway, and slipped us inside.

The smell of paint and clay filled my senses, and it honestly pissed me off a little because, up until now, all I could smell was her. I glanced down to her legs, remembering how she tasted the other night. The thought was never really far from my mind. The second I would taste anything sweet from the dining hall, I thought of her. If anyone else got a taste of her like I did, they'd never ever be the same.

Gemma's hand left mine as the door latched behind us. She made no move to turn the light on. Instead, she walked over to the supply closet, the same one I had pulled her into on her first day of school, and glanced over her shoulder. "I'll be right back."

I nodded and watched her disappear before sitting on the end of Mrs. Fitz's desk, who would likely scold me if she saw me sitting here, but most of the teachers were gone for the night, unless they had duty.

After a few long seconds, Gemma came back out of the supply closet, holding something in her hand.

"What's this?"

Her soft expression caught mine, and there was a quick jab to my chest. "I want to show you something."

Her guard was up. I could tell that much. Her chestnut

hair swayed in front of her face, catching the slight silvery gleam of the moon through the window. Her small hands trembled as she fiddled with the piece of paper.

"Gem?" I asked, taking a step toward her. "Whatever you're about to show me, you don't have to."

Her green eyes struck another chord with me. "I *want* to show you." Her fingers swiped back and forth as she gulped. Gemma and I were close enough now that I could smell her shampoo again, and the strangest feeling flew through me as I stared at her. My stomach knotted, and my chest felt warm. Before I had a chance to say anything, Gemma flipped the paper around and angled it toward me. Her lower lip trembled as I tore my eyes away from her face and glanced down to what she felt so strongly about that it caused her to nearly cry.

Without even knowing I had done it, I grabbed onto her hands that were clenched onto the pale paper. A spark flew from our fingers, and I knew she felt it too. My finger slowly rubbed over hers as my eyes finally adjusted to take in the piece of art that I assumed she'd drawn.

It was fucking amazing. The detail was astounding. So astounding that I couldn't tear my attention away. My head dipped further, a piece of dark hair falling into my eyes as I flicked my head to make it disappear. The boy that stared back at me looked to be a little younger than us. Closer to Jack's age. He had a strong jaw and eyes that were too famil-iar. There was a faint line of freckles over the straight nose, and the shadows under his eyes were so haunting I was forced to swallow before talking.

"Who is this?" I asked, finally getting a grip and looking back at Gemma. Her bottom lip, the same one that I desper-ately wanted to suck on, was pulled into her mouth. When our eyes collided, I knew right then who it was. It was her brother. Her twin.

Her tone was shaky as she pulled the paper back to her chest. "I have a brother too."

Of course, I knew this information from my uncle, but I didn't want Gemma to know that. She was being honest with me and giving up one of her secrets, and I'd fucking treasure it.

"A twin."

"A twin?" I asked, sitting back on the desk and giving her the space she was seeking.

She flipped her small frame around, plopping the paper down onto the opposite desk from me. "Yes. His name is Tobias."

The question clawed at me, as did the answer that I was certain she wasn't even aware of. At least not at the surface. "And where is he? Why isn't he here too?"

Gemma slowly spun back around, the green in her eyes glittering with unshed tears, and I almost flew off the desk to wrap my arms around her out of an instinct I wasn't even aware I had. "I don't know. I haven't seen him in four years." Four years? If he was at the Covens for that long...*fuck*. My hand clenched in my lap, and I hoped that Gemma couldn't sense the dread in my posture. Before I could say anything, she spoke again. "I know he's okay, though. I know he's still alive."

That caught my attention. I stayed locked on her, watching the way she fiddled with the hem of her skirt. "How do you know that? Have you talked to him?"

"No." The tremble in her tone cut me. "I think..." She shrugged. "I don't know how to explain it. I just know he's alive. Call it a twin thing, I guess." A small smile appeared, but it left just as quickly.

I thought for a moment, continuing to stare at her as her eyes bounced all over the room. Things were starting to make sense. Now I understood why she was so desperate to leave

St. Mary's, if not for the fact that her uncle was a piece of shit. "Is that why you're leaving? To find him?"

I truly hoped not. Because if she had a hunch that he was at the Covens, and she walked in there without hesitation? They wouldn't give her back.

A shaky breath floated around me as her eyes grew glossier. A mix of anger and fear and—shit—I think hurt etched all over her delicate features, and it felt like my flesh was being pulled from my bones. If she cried, I would rip apart every building, every person, every last living thing on this earth until I could make her tears disappear. I'd tear down the Covens, brick by brick, person by person, to find her brother if that made her happy. If that meant she could stay.

She can't stay, Isaiah.

I pushed the voice out of my head and stood up on two confident feet. I strode over to her quickly, grabbing onto her warm cheeks that I hoped would stay free of tears. I was ready to tell her every last thought I'd just had. That I'd do anything to make her smile, to make the light come back in her eyes that completely messed with my head, but she clenched her eyes shut as she grabbed onto my wrists. "I don't want to talk about him anymore." Her head shook, and my stomach thudded to the ground. It was strange. I'd never felt like this in my entire fucking eighteen years of existence, but I felt the connection. Her feelings were palpable—the pain, the fear. I felt it inside, and it was tearing me apart. I didn't like it. I didn't like that she had this effect on me. And I especially didn't like that I couldn't seem to make her problems disappear. Her voice hitched, and I was suddenly snared within her. "I just wanted to give you a small piece of myself like you did to me. I wanted you to know that you aren't alone in what you feel. Life doesn't seem to be easy for us."

"No, it doesn't," I confirmed, my fingers weaving into her

soft hair. My blood was beginning to run hot again, and I couldn't stop staring at her lips. Passion was licking over every last nerve, and all I wanted to do was consume her. All of her. Her mind, body, soul, and even her heart. Gemma-fucking-Richardson just became the center of my world. And she had no idea. Our lips drew closer, and she peered up at me. "I want to take your problems and make them mine, Gemma." *I shouldn't have said that. What was I doing?*

Her fingers dug into my skin, and if only she knew that that made me want to lay her flat on the desk she was currently leaning against to claim her. "No," she snapped. "I didn't tell you this to make my problems yours. I just..."

"Wanted to give me a piece of yourself."

She nodded, pushing her body closer to mine and resting her forehead on my chest. I was certain she could hear the racing of my heart, the way the muscle ricocheted off the hard planes of my ribs, trying to climb its way out of my body and into hers. "You could, you know. Give me all your troubles," I said, dropping my hands from her hair and wrapping them around her to clutch her close. *To hell with the fucking future.* "If you want me to solve your problems, I fucking will, Gemma. Don't tempt me."

A small, light laugh floated from her mouth. "Some problems only have one solution, and you're already on your way to helping me with that."

That wasn't true. I knew what the problem was. Or part of it. And I was ready to snap Judge Stallard in half and throw his body into the Pacific Ocean.

Gemma and I stood together in the dark art room, intertwined in each other for so long my arms grew numb. I had no intention of moving, but my phone vibrated in my pocket, and reality came crashing back in like a tornado. Gemma pulled apart from me as I wiggled my phone out and read the screen.

"Is everything okay?" she asked, glancing down to the brightness.

I sighed. "Yeah. It was just Cade, letting me know that Bain had left his room, but apparently, he is in Bethany's."

"The blonde who can't seem to keep her hands off him?" She looked disgusted, and I laughed out loud.

"Keeping tabs on Bain now, are we?"

Another glimpse of a smile peeked on her flushed face, and I couldn't even help the rise of my lips. "Just trying to help out when I can. He likes to stare at me, so I stare right back."

I recognized the annoyance poking at my brain as I released a growl. I didn't want to talk about Bain. In fact, I didn't want to talk about anything dealing with the reality of either of our lives, because I knew it would make me want to step away.

"I have an idea," I said, dropping her arms and slowly striding over to the supply closet before giving her a coy smirk over my shoulder.

She crossed her arms slowly after tucking a strand of hair behind her ear. "An idea?"

I nodded before disappearing behind the door and then coming back out again with a box of charcoal and a thick piece of paper tucked under my arm. Her eyes narrowed as her thick eyelashes brushed against her cheek. "What are you doing?"

"Tutoring?"

This time, Gemma was the one to hop up onto Mrs. Fitz's desk, letting her legs dangle below her. *She was perfect.* "And that requires art supplies? Am I suddenly tutoring you in art now?"

I paused, holding the paper out before walking over to an easel and dragging it across the floor to set it up in front of me. "If that'll make you feel better, then yeah. This can be an art lesson."

Gemma fought a smile, sucking her lips into her mouth for a second. "Okay."

Warmth washed over me, just like it always did when I was with her, and up until she had walked into St. Mary's, I hadn't even realized I was so cold on the inside. So...disconnected from life. She was doing something to me. "Okay," I repeated, surprised she went along with it. I walked over to her, standing just a few inches away before quickly grabbing her by the hips. A soft breath flew from her as her eyes widened. "First," I started, pulling her ass toward me so her middle would connect with mine for a brief, antagonizing second. "Don't look at me like that."

"Lik-like what?" She peered up at me all innocent-like, but I saw the fire brewing as I flicked the desk light on. The same damn fire I'd been fanning over the last two days.

"Like you want me to dip my head between your thighs again." *Because I would. I fucking would.*

She blinked a few times, the skin of her legs burning a hole through the sides of my jeans. "And second," I whispered, pushing her hair behind her shoulder. "I need to pose you so I can draw you."

A huge smile broke out on her face, and it was like a swift punch to my core. "You're going to pose me? Can you even draw, Isaiah?"

I cocked a brow as I ran my hands down her thighs slowly, enjoying the way her smooth legs felt against my palms. "What a discouraging thing to hear coming from my very educated tutor."

A loud laugh left her, and it tilted the room on its side.

"You don't do that enough."

"Do what?" she asked.

"Laugh." I licked my lip, gripping her behind her waist

now and slowly lowering her to her back on top of the desk. "And I've gotta say, it might be the best sound I've ever fucking heard." *Next to her little moans of pleasure, of course.*

Gemma glanced away as her cheeks raised. "Who knew Isaiah Underwood was such a sweet talker?"

I hummed, gently gripping her chin and tilting it toward my easel. "If only you could hear the thoughts in my head."

The roll of her eyes made me grin as I made my way back over to the paper and charcoal. Gemma lay flat on the teacher's desk with the soft glow of the lamp caressing her body as she sighed. "Really? You want me to lie like this? Flat on my back...staring at you?"

If only she knew how mind-fuckingly hot she looked *just* like that. I roamed my eyes over her amused face. The small smile playing at her lips was so damn innocent it *almost* made me feel guilty for the sexual thoughts in my head. She sat up a little, placing her elbow on the desk with her head in her palm. "This is silly."

"I don't think it is when you're smiling at me like that." I winked, and she sighed softly.

"Okay, fine. But as someone who draws often, how about I lie like this? I am your tutor, after all." Gemma adjusted herself on the desk after taking off her school blazer to leave only her white blouse. She was half lying on her side and half lying on her back. Then, she slowly rested the back of her head down and tilted her delicate chin toward me, her brown locks swaying out from behind her shoulders, circling her heart-shaped face so perfectly all I could do was stare. Her eyes. The bright green of them somehow vibrant in a hazy room. The perfect tip of her nose and sculpted lips that didn't need even a fraction of color on them to stand out. My eyes slid past her chin and over the hollow part of her neck, the dip nearly begging me to graze my teeth over it.

My dick was growing harder as I continued to gaze over

her curves and the two perfect-sized mounds that I lingered on for far too long before Gemma shifted nervously. I darted my eyes away, knowing very well she had caught me staring.

"Okay, let's get started, shall we?" Gemma giggled at me, and I peeked up over the canvas. "No laughing, or it'll mess me up."

She laughed again. "I can't wait to see what this looks like when you're done. I hope my tutoring skills are up to par."

"Shh," I hushed through a smile. "I'm...creating."

Her lips rolled together, holding back a laugh, as she softened her posture some.

Several minutes passed by as I sketched her on the thick paper with entirely too much charcoal smeared over it. I had no idea what I was doing, and it had nothing to do with the fact that I was totally distracted by Gemma and the smallest of dips over her body. Halfway through staring at her, I decided to just draw a stick figure to make her laugh again, but when I looked up at her once more, her eyes were closed, and all the breath was sucked from my lungs. *Beautiful*.

Her tiny chest was rising and falling slowly, her leg that was twisted to the side had fallen more relaxed, and her hand that was sitting nicely over her hip was sprawled out as her eyes remained closed. Gemma was so damn beautiful that it stole my breath. I couldn't stop looking at her. And I meant, *really* look at her. Not a fleeting glance, not a quick look down at her lips before I had to take a step back so I didn't accidentally kiss her in front of the faculty. No. I mean truly stare at her without any holdbacks. It was world-stopping. She wasn't just hot or someone I'd like to fuck because I was attracted to her...she was more. She radiated beauty, and it honestly made me feel a little uneasy.

Was this what Cade felt when he saw Journey? If so, I regretted every single thing I'd ever said to him about the situation. Everything.

Placing the charcoal down on the easel, I wiped my hands on my pants and started toward her. It was nearing midnight, everyone likely tucked away in their beds since curfew had started hours ago. Cade had texted once more that Bain had gone back to his room and that his roommate had confirmed that he was asleep in his bed—not that I cared at the moment. I was having an even harder time staying on task than usual. Some of that had to do with the brown-haired girl lying in front of me, and some of that had to do with the anger still simmering over my father leaving Jack. What was the point in it all if my father wasn't staying true to his word? If he wasn't watching over Jack like we'd bargained for? I was still so angry about Monday.

Looking down at Gemma once more, feeling the anger drain, I silently cursed because I knew the night needed to come to an end. We both needed to get back to our rooms before the duty teacher became suspicious over our tutoring session lasting this late if we had a little run-in walking back to our rooms. But the longer I stared at her, the more blood rushed to my dick. *Don't do it. Don't cross the line again.*

Just as my hand shot out to wake her, listening to the faint sound of rational thinking in the back of my head, she twitched, rooting me in place. Her head flopped to the side, falling slowly before her eyes squinted as if she were flinching. I waited as my hand stayed stretched out. A few pieces of hair stuck to the side of her face, and that was when I realized that her hairline had a bead of sweat covering it.

Her breathing had picked up as I moved closer to her, and she grew tense. The soft way her hand was lying just a few moments ago sprung open fast, and my spine stiffened. She jostled a little bit, and I wasn't sure what was going on, but I reached out to steady her, to wake her up, but then all of a sudden, Gemma started to pull at her wrists. Both of them, back and forth her hands would move. The left would rub the right, and the right would rub the left. She made a little whimper as I took the last step over to her, and then I froze as she pushed her white sleeves up, the button on the side of the uniform top popping from her aggressively pulling and tugging, and that was when I caught sight of something.

What the hell was that?

My eyes stayed glued to the pink, raised skin circling her wrists. I wanted to pin her hands to the desk to inspect them further, wondering what they were, but another noise came from her, and it snapped me out of my confusion. I reached for her. One of my arms went underneath her legs, and the other went underneath the small of her back. One second she was lying on the hard surface, and the next she was crashing onto my chest as I slid down the front of the desk and cradled her in my arms. Her eyes sprung open, her hand ruffling my shirt tightly in a firm grip.

"You're okay," I said, pulling her in tighter. "You fell asleep."

Her head snapped down to her wrists, and I watched as her expression went from confused to mortified. Her eyes grew wide, her cheeks hollowing out. She knew I saw what she had been hiding, and her entire body tensed.

There was a hot burn that whipped through me. I was angry over the fact that I'd just now noticed her wrists. The pieces clicked together, and I was infuriated that I hadn't thought to question the way she pulled her sleeves down when I grew too close or the reason why she was in her school uniform most of the time, and if not, she was wearing long sleeves. I remembered being frustrated over the fact that she was wearing a sweater at the last claiming, because I wanted to see more of her skin like the rest of the girls. *Shit. What were those?*

Gemma moved to get off my lap, and I pulled her in closer. "No." My words were as cold as I felt on the inside.

"Don't you dare climb off me." Her shoulders sagged, her chest heaving with ragged breath that did nothing but spin shit up in me that shouldn't have been spinning.

I felt the shift of Gemma's head over my chest, and I peered down at her, catching the look in her eye. I wasn't sure what she was thinking, but I planned to demolish every last negative thought in her head. "Don't try to hide from me. I saw them, and even though it's ripping me to pieces not knowing what you were dreaming about so intently that you felt the need to scratch at those scars, I won't ask."

Gemma sucked in a shaky breath and swallowed. I leaned in close, my lips touching the softness of her ear. "But if I find out who put those there, I will fucking kill them. I promise."

And for once, I didn't even care that saying those dark words made me sound just like my father. I was beginning to see that there was no limit I wouldn't go to for her, and that in itself was a total game changer.

CHAPTER FORTY-EIGHT

GEMMA

I WANTED TO KISS HIM. I wanted to kiss him and drink in his promise like it was the only thing that would keep me alive, which was fitting because, with Richard still breathing, death wasn't such a distant thought.

Isaiah's hands were planted firmly on my body, and they were doing nothing but enticing me further. It was the way he said it. The way he looked down at me like he wanted to burn the world to ash instead of looking at me with pity or asking questions that I wasn't ready to answer.

My body was humming. I was angry and desperate in my nightmare—the same one that had been reoccurring since Monday after my phone call with Richard, and maybe even because of what Isaiah and I had done during the bonfire. There was the nagging voice in the back of my head that told me it was wrong that I had let Isaiah do things to me that I knew Richard would kill him for. Even kill me for. If he knew that Isaiah had even touched me with the tip of his finger, he would lose it, just like he had lost it on my mother when a man had looked at her for too long.

I remembered that.

It was one of the only memories I had left of her.

Why did the bad memories always stick out more than the good? I never understood that, and to be honest, it really wasn't fair.

My body was wound up. Like I was seconds from exploding. The nightmares always felt so damn real, and I was usually left shaking afterwards, but being in Isaiah's arms was doing something else to me. Something that was so much bigger and scarier.

The room was warm around us, the moon still streaming through the window behind the desk as the warm glow from the lamp fell upon our heads. Isaiah's thick eyelashes were lowered as he took in my face, his grip on me only growing tighter as his words soothed the goosebumps on my skin.

"Did my promise scare you, Gemma?" The roughness of his voice was like a match lighting me on the inside. It didn't scare me at all. In fact, it...it was *hot*. And I didn't care if that was wrong. "Does it scare you when I say things like that? Because if there is anything I'm willing to give up my humanity for, it may be you."

My heart skipped as his admission floated around me. The drop in my stomach turned to intense fluttering, and I couldn't stop myself from falling. I felt it. I felt the fall as if I had been pushed over the ledge of a tall cliff.

Isaiah.

I felt things for him that I'd never be able to put into words. He was putting me together but tearing me apart in the same breath. I knew, deep down, I needed to put space between us, because the more we were together in these intense and personal moments, the closer I grew to him. I was becoming attached. I couldn't stop the push and pull I was feeling. I couldn't stop as I gripped his shirt tighter and flipped around in his arms, pressing my lips so forcefully against his that he stilled.

But then his hands clamped to my torso, just beneath my breasts, and he pulled me so I was straddling his lap. His long legs stretched out in front of him as I wrapped my hands around his face and moved my mouth over his as if I knew what I was doing.

In reality, I had no idea, but my body seemed to know what to do. There was an instinct buried deep within that was finally crawling out of the darkest parts of my body and allowing me to feel the desire and passion that we sparked to life every time we touched. I felt out of control. *Wild.*

"Fuck, Gemma," he mumbled against my mouth as his hands roamed up my back and into my hair. I felt him beneath me, growing harder and harder, and it felt so good to move above him. To rock myself against him. I didn't understand how it could feel so good, but it did. Even with clothes on. "Gem," he rasped, pulling my face from his. "You've gotta stop."

"No." I shoved his hands away from my cheeks and brought our lips together again, pushing against him once more. His hand flew underneath my blouse, the same piece of clothing that had betrayed me moments ago during sleep as it showed Isaiah the one thing I hid from everyone. *I knew I should have kept my blazer on.* "I want you to just..." I pulled back, and his hand stilled just beneath the bottom of my bra. "Take it. Take it all. Just for the night." There they were again—those four little words that I kept throwing around but ignoring seconds later. *Just for the night.* I had to say it to remind myself that Isaiah and I would never be a long-lasting thing.

His tongue jolted out and licked his lip. "Take what, baby? What do you want me to take? 'Cause I'll take it. Fuck,

Gemma." Isaiah's throat bobbed, and his cheeks grew slightly pink. "I think I would do anything for you."

A ghost of a smile washed over my face. "Take *me*." I wanted to give myself to him. I wanted to cross over that line, because if by any chance Richard got me back in his care, at least he wouldn't be the one to do it. I would have the tiniest bit of control left, even if, in reality, it wouldn't stop him from ruining me all together.

Isaiah's nostrils flared as he clenched his eyes. "Gemma, you cannot say things like that to me, because I want nothing more than to drive my cock into your wet little pussy and make you mine. My hold on myself is slipping faster and faster, and you can't possibly want that. I'm...*fuck*." The more he talked, the more frustrated he sounded. "I'm not the one that should do this! It'll mean too much."

My hands fell to Isaiah's shoulders as I scooted forward, causing a breath to rock out of his mouth. His forehead came down and rested on my chest, his fast breathing hot against my blouse. "Please, Isaiah." My voice was strong, and it felt *so* damn good to take control of something and choose what *I* wanted. Because in the end, this was my choice. Even if Richard didn't think it was. Maybe I was moving too fast, but it wasn't like this exact moment, the moment where I lost every ounce of my innocence, hadn't been whispered into my ear while being at someone else's mercy. I knew the time would come that I would lose my virginity, and I wasn't sure I would have a choice in the matter. But I did right now. "If you don't do this...someone else will. And I need it to be you. Let me have the choice."

That was all it took. It was like a rubber band being snapped throughout the empty room. Isaiah climbed to his feet, wrapping my legs around his waist as he pushed the rest of the contents of Mrs. Fitz's desk to the floor. Pencils flew, the lamp shattered on the floor, and papers swayed softly through the air.

My back was flat against the cool wood as Isaiah hovered over me, spreading my legs so slowly they trembled.

"Are you sure?" He peered down at me, looking so dark and dangerous. The promises I could see lurking behind his hooded eyes made my toes curl. "And this will be the last time I ask you, because if I don't touch you in the next few seconds, I will need to remove myself from this fucking room."

My hand stretched between us as I pulled the collar of his shirt toward me. His middle met up with mine, and desire raced to every part of my body.

"I'm sure," I whispered, and his lips were back. He sucked my bottom lip into his mouth, tugging on it, and I arched my back as his hands went up my skirt, gripping me by the hips and pulling me even closer. A soft sound left me as Isaiah peered down with a look so hot I was left panting. His eyes were lustful, his cheeks flushed and his chest heaving. He looked like he wanted me, and I *loved* how that made me feel.

His fingers left my hips, and cool air hit my legs as his hands came out from underneath my skirt. They landed on the front of my shirt, and Isaiah watched me closely as he popped each button through its rightful hole until my shirt was wide open and my bra was exposed.

Normally, anxiety would have been holding me back, and I'd have been terrified that someone was about to see me bare. The only times I'd ever been naked, other than showering, were the few times Richard *really* upped my punishments and left me cold in the basement, without a single layer of clothing, but this was so different. Isaiah's gaze drank over my skin, his eyes scorching my flesh as he pushed my shirt off my shoulders and down my arms. My plain, white bra was all that stood between his eyes and my breasts, and when his finger traced over the thin delicate strap over my shoulder, I shuddered.

"I've never seen something so goddamn perfect in my life." Isaiah's mouth descended over the thin cotton straps, and he pulled them down, one by one, with his teeth. The scrapes against my skin had me withering underneath him, and I had never been more wound up than I was now. I needed him to touch me. I needed him to ease the bundle of nerves that were coiling in my lower stomach that I was beginning to recognize. And I needed to get lost again. I wanted that feeling that he gave me the other day. I wanted that feeling he gave me hours ago in the forest.

"Isaiah," I whimpered.

The sound of him unclasping my bra shot through the room, and I held back a gasp. "Patience, Gemma. We have to go slow, or it'll hurt you."

My brow furrowed as he stared down at me, pulling my bra from my body and dropping it to the floor. His lips parted, and there was a big part of me that wanted to hide, but his expression changed that feeling in me within moments.

"*Shit*." His head dipped down, and I felt the warm, wet touch of his mouth over my nipple, and at first, it surprised me, but after a second, I was gasping for air and enjoying it. It felt...amazing.

"Isaiah," I said again, this time even more desperate. His licks and kisses branded my body as he worked his way over both my breasts, my nipples tightening just as quickly as my center. I couldn't believe how good it felt. How lost I became in his touch. I couldn't fathom letting Richard do this—and he wanted to. He wanted to touch and lick and keep me all to himself, like my mother.

"Oh my God," I whispered, and he popped his head up just before his kiss touched my hip bone.

His smirk was devilish, but the look in his eye told me that he was just as infatuated as I was. That he was just as lost as me. "We have to go slow. You have to be ready." His head tilted in the most predatory way I'd ever seen. *Whoa.* "Unless…" His lone finger trailed up the side of my leg, and it tingled all the way to my toes. I opened myself to him even with the small amount of nerves that were there in the back of my mind, and he hissed, slipping past my underwear and running the pad of his thumb over my opening. His eyes clenched as he threw his head back. "It was like you were made for me." His head came back down, and my cheeks flushed. "And only me."

I gulped as I watched him rip off his shirt. I awed over each curve of his chest and abdomen. I knew that he was fitter than most due to lacrosse. I'd watched him play several times, and each flick of his stick showed a thick band of muscles that liked to tease me, but seeing him without his shirt was mesmerizing. There were dips and valleys of hard muscle, and without even realizing it, my hand slipped out from the desk, and I slowly ran my finger over each hard ab. Once I got to the bottom, just above the hem of his pants, his hand gripped mine, and he squeezed it. *He was the beautiful one.* My heart crawled up my throat as something intimate was shared between us. Something that couldn't be described in words. Only actions.

Isaiah took a step back from me, and I sat up from the desk slowly. My long hair fell down in waves behind me, caressing the bareness of my back. The beating of my heart grew as I scooted myself to the very edge and reached my shaky fingers out in front of me. We held eyes the entire time. His baby blues collided with mine. The button of his jeans was slowly pushed through the hole, and my fingers trembled as I pulled the zipper down. Isaiah's stare darkened as the pad of my finger touched over his boxers, and once I pushed the rest of his jeans down to the ground, he stepped out of them and hooked his fingers into the waistband.

I knew what awaited me. I'd felt a man before. But never like this. I'd never come face to face. I'd never actually been *intimate* with someone. I'd never wanted to see. But it was all different with Isaiah. I was hungry to make him lose himself in me like I'd done on Monday when he had pushed me up against that tree. I was eager to do this with him. To have this moment with him.

Our gazes collided as Isaiah pushed his boxers down. I heard the soft fabric hit the floor, and slowly, so slowly, it felt like time had actually stopped. I pushed my hand out and dropped my head.

My heart slowed as I waited for fear, or anxiety, or even surprise, but the only thing I felt was heat. He was hard and long, and my escaped breath propelled me to touch him, to feel him in my hands, to make him come undone, and to please him. I wanted him to feel good. I wanted to drive him crazy. I wanted to do what that girl did in the forest. I wanted Isaiah to want me. Hearing his sharp inhale of breath when I finally reached out and ran my finger around his hardness gave me an incredible amount of confidence. I shot a quick peek up to him, and his jaw was set, and his eyes were pinned on mine.

"Am I...doing it right?" I looked away shyly. "I'm not sur—"

Isaiah's hand came down on mine, and he wrapped my fingers around the thick base. He was warm, and I licked my lips. It was a little intimidating but fascinating, too. "You can't really do it wrong." He paused, taking our joined hands and rubbing them over the length of him. "I'm convinced you can't do anything wrong, Gemma."

Isaiah's hand left mine once I got the hang of touching him. My grip grew a little tighter, and I watched as he grew thicker. His head flung backward, and the muscles along his neck were defined through the shadows of the room. After a few more seconds, he grabbed my hand and held it firmly. His breath was coming in short spurts, his large chest expanding quickly. "You have no idea how wild you drive me."

Isaiah's head dropped back down, and he locked onto my lips. He took my hands and placed them directly onto the desk, the cool wood washing away the heat along my palm that I had felt seconds before. Once I was firmly seated, he leaned into my personal space, his legs brushing against the insides of mine, and he grabbed the back of my skirt and lowered the zipper. "Lift up," he said, breathing down into my personal space. I pushed myself up, hovering for just a moment before he rushed my skirt and panties down past my legs and over my ankles before depositing them to the floor with his clothes.

Another bout of cool air covered my skin, but it didn't last long as Isaiah crowded me once more. His fingers splayed over my hips, and my head fell into his chest. It only took one swipe of his finger over my middle for me to buck my hips forward and for him to catch me in the process.

"Lie back, baby," he whispered softly, pushing me gently so I was lying back on the desk again. My hair fanned out around me as he hovered over me, pulling me just a few inches closer to him so my legs were dangling all the way off the desk. He reached down for a split second, and I heard the crinkling of a wrapper before he popped back up and gripped my legs. He drove his gaze into me with a firm jaw. "I should stop this right here and right now, but I fucking can't."

I swallowed the nerves and licked my lips. "Please don't stop. I need this."

He gritted his teeth. "This might hurt for a second." His

mouth was right above mine, and I had to force myself to lie back so I wouldn't kiss him. "But I promise you, I will make you feel good. Just like on Monday. Do you trust me?"

There was absolutely no hesitation on my part. I nodded quickly as he ran a finger over the side of my face. His hand gripped my chin, and his mouth covered mine, taking away any thought I may have had. His tongue swept over every inch of my mouth, making me spin, before I felt him at my center. He pushed in slowly and paused, pushing up on his forearms to glance down at me. "You okay?"

I swallowed and nodded as his finger trailed past my neck and down my chest. Isaiah had one of his hands gripping my hip and the other moved over to my left breast. He shot me a sexy grin before lowering his head and kissing the tight bud, causing a rush to sweep over my body. I inhaled sharply, meeting him with a small thrust. A pinch of pain came from below as he pulled up and shot me a look. "Careful. Trust me when I say we need to go slow. You're tight, and I have every intention of taking care of you"—his stare grew hooded as he pushed in a little further—"and making you come so hard you'll never be the same."

His words were a little dirty, and it did nothing but make me sweat. I nodded sharply as he came down and crushed his lips to mine again, and this time, the sweetness from earlier was a little more bitter. Our kisses turned urgent, and my breasts pushed up and met his naked chest. A grumble of a sound rumbled out of him and echoed over my mouth, and that was when I felt the fullness of him. He'd pushed in even more, and our middles met. I felt him everywhere. In every inch of my body. In every space inside my head. We stayed like that for a few seconds, his forehead pressed to mine, a bead of sweat running over the perfect curve of his cheek. I moved first, curving my hips up to his for a moment to test the waters. I couldn't believe it was happening. I couldn't believe that somehow Isaiah and I had ended up like...*this*. It was nothing I'd ever expected, and it seemed to happen so quickly, but I was ready. I hadn't known I was ready, but I was. Every interaction I'd had with him from the very beginning felt different. Like we were connected somehow. My body seemed to twist in certain ways when he looked at me from across the hall. And maybe, deep down, my soul begged for him to mend mine. Because that was what it felt like. It felt like Isaiah was taking my deepest scars that laid ever so painfully over my soul, and he was healing them. He was replacing the bad with the good. He was giving me the light, showing me that there was so much more out there than what I'd been given.

"Gemma, goddamnit." Isaiah pulled up, and his hands flew to my hips. His fingers dug into the skin, and I loved it. *I loved it so much.* I felt alive. He could rip me apart, and I would still feel myself piecing together. "I have to go slow, or I'll hurt you. You need to adjust to me."

I wiggled myself under him again, feeling something click into place. I was ready to take what he was giving. I was freeing myself, letting loose to enjoy what I was feeling. My hands found his biceps, and I gripped them hard as I pushed closer to him. His eyes grew frantic, and his mouth opened and then closed. "That doesn't hurt?" he asked, moving my hips slowly before he began pushing farther into me.

"No," I rushed out, arching my back. "My body wants this, Isaiah. It wants you." It did. My body knew what was right and what was wrong. And this? This was right. It felt too good to be wrong.

"Fuck." His mouth fell to mine again, our teeth clanking together. His hips started to move as his arm came around my lower back to steady me. My hair was woven between his fingers as he dug his palm through the strands, and we were in a frenzy. My hips fell apart, his body moving over mine in the most scandalous of ways. "I'm already about to come. You're..." He leaned in and pulled my lip with his teeth, and I whimpered as I felt my body tensing beneath his. "You're so wet and hot, and tight, and fuck me if I'll ever be able to live without this." His hand left mine, and he pushed it in between us. I felt the pad of his thumb rub over me, and I wanted to keep watching him. I wanted to watch his eyes roam over my body like I was the most fascinating thing he'd ever seen, but it was too much. His skin against mine. The fulfillment I felt with him inside me. The way my body pulled and pushed and sang. I moved underneath him, finding the best way to ride how he was filling me, and then I felt it. I felt the wind up. I felt my body twist and curve. The heat started at my head, and all it took was one little movement from my hips and his mouth over my breast, and I was falling. I was falling fast. Isaiah mumbled a curse as he lifted from my tightened nipple and his teeth grazed my neck before he sucked on the skin, and I saw stars.

I felt everything break and come back together again. The wave of pleasure and nothing else was like a drug. It felt so good. He felt so good. Even more so when he stilled above me, making a noise that I would take with me when I left and replay on my loneliest nights. And that was how we stayed. We stayed like that for so long the sweat dried on our skin.

I couldn't move. I couldn't even look at him. I just lay there, completely and utterly sated and...content. I'd never felt so worshiped or...loved. That was the only way I could describe it. Loved. I knew nothing about love, but I felt emotion bubbling up. The realness of it. The raw feeling of a mutual connection.

Eventually, Isaiah pulled out of me. I knew it because I felt the sting and soreness come in crashing waves. But I still couldn't form sentences. I was too afraid of what I would say. My eyes opened briefly as I saw Isaiah hovering over me with a wet paper towel that he must have grabbed from the sink in the clean-up corner of the room. "I'm just going to clean you up. Is that okay?"

I smiled softly and nodded. The cool water felt good against my middle as he wiped me gently, and it made me want to reach out to him and hug him. Isaiah was so much more than what was at the surface. I kept my lips sealed, still too afraid I would say something that would be wrong, and my eyes were so incredibly droopy. They closed a few times as I lay on the desk as Isaiah ran the paper towel over me. My clothes came next, the feel of my panties sliding up my legs slowly then my skirt. The straps of my bra went over my shoulders, and Isaiah pulled me up by my hand, clicking it into place.

When I finally snuck a glance at him as he was buttoning some of my buttons, I saw that he was dressed—well, sort of. His pants were still undone at the waist, but he had his shirt on. When I managed to meet his face, he was staring down at me, expressionless. The blues of his eyes were soft, his mouth relaxed. His hands slowly came up, and he cupped the sides of my cheeks, and my heart was suddenly back to life. It raced as we silently said things neither of us wanted to say aloud.

We knew this was bigger than anything we'd ever felt before.

At least I did.

His thumb brushed over the arch of my cheek, and he shook his head slowly. "What am I going to do now, Gemma?"

My voice broke as I tried to speak words, but I ended up coming up empty-handed. Instead, I shrugged, knowing what he was referring to. There was no future for us. At least none that I could see.

I didn't know what this meant. Or if it meant anything at

all. Nothing was changing. Richard was still a threat. Tobias was still missing, and I was determined to find him. It wasn't like Isaiah could come with me, and it wasn't like he didn't have his own problems to deal with. He'd already told me once before that we'd crash and burn, and I was beginning to see that he was right.

CHAPTER FORTY-NINE

ISAIAH

MY BACK ACHED. It hurt so fucking bad it felt like I'd slept at a nintey-degree angle all night. But I was warm. I was warm, and there was something so peaceful about the way I felt. Why did I feel so content? The first thing I'd always felt when I woke up in the morning was irritation and anger because I wasn't in my childhood bedroom but rather in a dorm room at St. Mary's, acting as an errand boy for my father. But this was different. There was a bright light flashing in my eyes, causing my brows to crowd, and then I felt a slap on my head, and my eyes immediately opened. *Who the fuc—*

Cade's big brown eyes drove into mine, and I saw two things I'd only seen a handful of times: panic and anger. "Get the fuck up, now," he seethed out in a whisper.

"Not sure who you think you're talking to," I snapped before feeling a shift in my lap. It took me a moment to figure out my surroundings, but then I glanced down and saw the peaceful side of Gemma's face with a piece of brown hair over her eyes. I almost moved to brush it away before Cade spoke again.

"Isaiah, get the fuck up. Now. Get into the closet. Mrs. Fitz is seconds from walking in, and if she finds..." The words stalled out in the air as I sprung to my feet.

Fuck.

After Gemma and I...I couldn't even put a word on what we'd done last night because it was so much more than a fuck...we didn't talk. Not much, anyway. I got us dressed, and she seemed to be in a daze, and I felt the same. There were things I was feeling that were so unknown to me that I knew I needed to keep my mouth shut. So, instead of saying anything or discussing the fact that I took her virginity, I wrapped her up in my arms and sat on the floor against Mrs. Fitz's desk. I kissed the top of her head as I ran my hand over her arm, and eventually, her breathing evened out, and she fell asleep.

I fell asleep too, but not before I took her arm and pushed her sleeve up, inspecting the marks around her wrist. That was the last thing I remembered before this moment right here as I rushed us to the supply closet with Cade right at my back.

"What's going on?" Gemma's sleepy voice hit me right in the chest, and I hated that I couldn't see her face in the dark.

"You two are playing with fucking fire," Cade whispered, but I heard the bite in his tone. "Mrs. Fitz is on the fucking SMC, Isaiah. What do you think she'd do if she found you two half asleep in here when, number one, it's obvious you've been here all night, fucking on her desk. And two, you're on probation! Don't you remember that all this bullshit with Gemma is to keep you here? The tutoring? Getting your grades up? She's your cover for the nights you're out past curfew! You can say goodbye to that if they know you two are fucking. Of course she'd lie for you and say you two were tutoring when you were actually sneaking out of St. Mary's. They aren't stupid. In fact, I'm surprised they even believe your act in the first place."

"Cade, back the fuck up." My blood was pulsing through my veins as fast as the rapids. Gemma stilled against my chest as Cade's hoarse whisper grew stern, and it was most likely because what he was saying was right. We were stupid to fall asleep in here. But with Gemma, my mind became messy. Things didn't seem so urgent and testy. I forgot that we had a plan. I forgot about everything the second I touched her. "Don't you think I know all of this? My number one priority is to stay at St. Mary's so my father doesn't ship Jack off just to be the biggest fucking dick in the world. I understand why I'm here. I know what my future holds."

"That isn't your only priority anymore, Isaiah. And you fucking know it." He scoffed as I saw the light underneath the door shine through. Gemma sucked in a breath, and I ran my hands down her arms. Cade leaned in close and whispered, "It's a good fucking thing you have me now, isn't it? Or you'd be trying to explain to Mrs. Fitz why you and Gemma are in the art room at six in the morning, half undressed. It's obvious you two were not studying, unless you two take human anatomy very seriously."

I clenched my teeth, angry with myself that I let us get into this situation. Cade was right. My priority wasn't just with Jack anymore but with Gemma, too. I didn't quite know what I was going to do with any of the knowledge I'd learnt of her this far, but protecting her was high up on that list, and us getting caught like *this* would bring shit down on both of our shoulders. I was sure of it.

The three of us stood quietly as we heard Mrs. Fitz shuffle around, getting ready for her day. We were lucky no one had alerted a teacher that we were missing last night. I wondered what Sloane was thinking since Gemma was her roommate, but I had to hope she wasn't stupid enough to go to someone other than my uncle if she were concerned. Sloane was observant, and she knew much more about the Rebels and me than she let on. After all, she was Journey's roommate.

"How the hell did you even know we were here?" I asked in a whisper so low Cade had to lean into Gemma and me to hear.

Cade held up a finger that I was barely able to see in the darkness of the supply closet. He pulled out his phone, the screen giving way to some light before he turned it in our direction.

A cold hand wrapped around my throat and squeezed as I looked at the newest blog post on Mary's Murmurs. "What the fuck," I muttered, snatching the phone out of his grip. Gemma's hand went up to her mouth. There, staring back at us, was a clear-as-fucking-day photo of Gemma curled up in my arms with her shirt half undone and my pants clearly unbuckled. Her hair was a sexy mess, and it was obvious that she'd been thoroughly fucked, not only by our appearance but by the slightly bruised hickey on her neck.

I quickly pulled the phone up, and my cool hand landed on Gemma's warm skin. I pushed her hair off her shoulders as she tilted her head, and sure enough, there was a mark on her neck. I had fucking marked her. Fuck, when did I do that? Was it my subconscious that came out of hiding when I was buried inside of her?

"Jesus Christ," I growled, nearly snapping the phone in half. I shoved it into Cade's hand and seethed under my breath. "That was taken no less than a few hours ago."

He quickly put it back in his pocket and leaned in close. "It popped up twenty minutes ago. After the last blog post, I signed up to get an alert when they went live again so we wouldn't have any more surprises. Once I realized you weren't in bed, I jumped out and banged on Mica's door. He was able to get in there and take the post down, but Bain is missing from his room, so my guess is the photo came from him."

I silently belittled myself for falling asleep with Gemma. If my phone wasn't currently dead in my pocket from my night spent in the art room, I would have seen that photo— or better yet, the photo wouldn't have been taken in the first place.

It didn't surprise me that Bain was missing this morning. He'd been snapping photos of Gemma and shoving them into his little hiding spot in his room, which was why I didn't want her alone. And surprisingly enough, I wasn't nearly as upset that we were on the blog as much as I was over the fact that he'd seen her with her shirt unbuttoned and in my arms. I didn't like that he was spying on us, just like I was spying on him.

That started a whole new chain reaction in my head concerning Bain. Things were beginning to stand out, and I had a feeling that there was a reason behind every one of Bain's moves. Pushing that thought aside for the moment, I brought Gemma's soft palm into mine and rubbed my finger over her delicate skin. *What was she thinking?*

"So what's the plan? How do we get out of here without Mrs. Fitz seeing us? Usually, I wouldn't care but—"

"But you're on probation, and I cannot, under any circumstances, get in trouble and get sent home," Gemma's voice broke through Cade's and my testosterone-filled circle. We both shifted uncomfortably. "Please tell me you have a plan, Cade."

The whites of his teeth stood out, and I rolled my eyes. "Of course I do, Good Girl. I told you I had your back, didn't I?"

"So?" I whispered just before I heard the classroom door slam open. Shiner's voice came through, and my lips twitched. I was damn lucky to have the Rebels on my side.

Shiner didn't have the same bleak future that Cade, Brantley, and I had, but at least he had our backs nonetheless.

Mrs. Fitz's voice faded as she followed Shiner out of the room, and then we all quickly darted out of the supply closet and rushed through the classroom. Before we stepped into the empty hallway, I ran back to the trash can and grabbed my used condom and shoved it into my pocket. Gemma's journal was half underneath Mrs. Fitz's desk, so I snagged that, too. Cade sighed annoyingly, and when I caught Gemma's eye, her cheeks filled with blood before she snatched her journal and brought it to her chest. I winked at her, even if it was whole-heartedly inappropriate at the time. Her lips curved before she turned around and followed Cade.

"Now what?" Gemma asked as we rounded the bend in the hallway. Her hand found mine again, and a feeling of satisfaction came over me. I really fucking liked that she still wanted to hold my hand. I didn't think she regretted me taking her virginity, but I was afraid she'd pull away like the last time we had pushed the limits.

Brantley came out of nowhere, slipping beside us and striding down the hallway as if he'd been here the entire time. Gemma paused for a second before catching up.

"We need a 24-hour watch on Bain. He cannot be fucking trusted. What a bastard. He's trying so goddamn hard to get you kicked out of here, Isaiah."

That wasn't all he was up to, but I didn't say that in front of Gemma. Instead, I brushed him off and shrugged. "We'll talk later. I still need to talk with my father. I'll keep you two updated."

"Gemma!" A girly voice filled the hallway, and Gemma's shoulders nearly fell to the floor at the sight of Sloane. She rushed over and grabbed Gemma right out of my grasp. I huffed as she began pulling her toward the south wing girls' restroom with a uniform and Gemma's bookbag in hand.

I glanced at Brantley, and he shrugged. "She came to me, looking for Gemma. Figured we could use her help in getting you two out undetected." He shifted to Cade, and then they both turned toward me. "What are you doing, bro? You're being..."

"I know," I snapped, looking at Gemma and Sloane once more. Sloane was giving her a disapproving look as she ran her finger over her neck, right over the spot that I'd sucked on as I came inside her warm walls earlier in the night. Heat went to my groin before I heard an annoyed sigh.

"For fuck's sake." Brantley stalked off, leaving me staring at Gemma like she was the only goddamn thing that I cared about on this earth. I was in over my head.

Before I knew what I was doing, I stalked over to her and pulled her out of Sloane's arms. The hallway was quiet. The only eyes were Cade's and Sloane's, but I didn't care if the entire school was watching. I wanted them to know she was mine. Only this time, it wasn't for show. I might not have even cared if the SMC had formed a circle around us. I would still grab her just as fiercely, and I'd still tip her head up to meet me halfway.

"What are you doing?" she asked, eyes bouncing back and forth.

"I don't have many choices, Gemma." I dipped in close. "But right now, I'm choosing you before I can't any longer." Then, my lips fell to hers, and everything else ceased to exist. She was willing, too. Her mouth parted, and her tongue moved against mine. I pulled her into my body, crushing us together. Kissing her was like a gift. Or maybe it was a punishment.

Either way, I didn't care. I'd kiss her every day until I no longer could. And then, I'd find a way to keep her. I'd find her one way or another and make her mine again.

CHAPTER FIFTY

GEMMA

"Oh my God." That was the seventh time Sloane had said that in the last thirty seconds. I'd started counting after the third time. "I knew there was more going on than that one kiss and some lame tutoring sessions." Sloane handed me a new pair of underwear and a freshly cleaned bra, and I turned around to put them on. She glanced at my wrists once before quickly moving past that and focusing on Isaiah's kiss. "I cannot believe you and..." She swooped up my uniform and threw it into my backpack, handing me a new one. "Did you want to have sex with him? Did you want him to take your virginity? Did he even know he was taking it?!"

Sloane kept asking me questions, but I couldn't answer her. Every time I would open my mouth, she'd ask another question. It wasn't until she took out her makeup and started covering up my hickey that I finally answered her. "Yes," I said, feeling my stomach dip as I thought back to last night. Butterflies filled me up, and I had to fight to keep my feet on the ground. I was so twisted around all things Isaiah that there wasn't much room for anything else in my head. It was...him. And only him. "I did want to have sex with him, and yes, he knew that he was taking my virginity. The entire school knew I was a virgin, because of Bain, remember? I didn't exactly deny it."

Sloane blew minty breath out of her mouth so fast that it tickled the hair on my neck. She dabbed some more makeup on the sponge thing and got back to work. We were both tucked back into a stall in the girls' restroom, and I knew the morning bell would ring soon. "I'm just surprised."

"Surprised?" I asked, buttoning up the rest of my blouse before pulling on my maroon blazer. "That he would have sex with me?"

Her hand stilled, and she looked me dead in the eye. "No. Not at all." She glanced away. "It's no secret that Isaiah isn't a virgin. He's definitely made himself known in that department." My cheeks burned, and I bit my lip. It didn't even cross my mind last night that he was much more experienced than I was, but it was obvious. He knew how to make my body succumb better than I did. "It's just different with you. From the moment you walked into this school, he's been different."

I bit my cheek as she pushed my hair over my shoulders and ran her fingers down the strands. "Or maybe he's just finally showing who he really is."

She hummed under her breath, handing me my now-zipped backpack. "True, and it's no surprise that it took you to get it out of him." Her cheek lifted. "You're pretty great when you let people in. You know that, right?"

A closed-lip smile fell to my face as she opened the stall door just as the morning bell was ringing.

"He seems consumed by you. Like you are the center of every room you're in. His eyes gravitate toward you. It's not evident to most, but I can see it. I see the way he looks at you. It's the same way Cade used to look at Journey. Like he's afraid you're going to slip through his fingers at the last second or something." *That's because I will, and he knows it.*

Sloane paused before placing her hand on the restroom door. She glanced over her shoulder, and her smile turned down into a frown. "And that's why you need to be careful, Gemma. I don't know why you two seem to be keeping so many secrets, but that's exactly what got Journey a one-way ticket out of this school."

I nodded, and she intertwined her arm with mine as we began walking toward our classes. Just before the hall was swarmed with wandering eyes and the clanking of shoes against the tiled floor, she whispered into my ear. "Just know you can always come to me, okay? I'm here for you, no matter what. Secrets or not."

I nodded, shooting her a smile that was actually genuine.

———

SLOANE AND I both missed breakfast this morning and rushed straight to our first period. It was likely all in my head, but I felt like everyone knew what Isaiah and I had done last night. I felt different, but I knew it was in a good way, because any time I would feel the twinge between my legs, my stomach would flutter, and I'd have to bite my lip to keep myself from smiling.

I wasn't sure what this meant for us. I didn't think either of us knew. The only thing I did know for certain was that I was half-dreading the moment our tutoring ended. Whenever the SMC decided Isaiah's grades were better and his behavior had improved, gaining their trust back, he'd be taken off probation, and he would no longer be dangling over the edge. Which meant that I would no longer need to tutor him, which would also mean I would no longer be a cover for him if he was caught in the hall after hours, coming back from following Bain. I wasn't sure how that would affect him when it was all said and done. What if he got caught sneaking out after I was gone? And what was going to happen when he handed me payment for our deal? Would I leave without telling him goodbye? Would it be easier that way?

My stomach ached at the thought, so I quickly pushed it aside as I sat down at the art table for class. *No. I wouldn't go there right now.* I peeked behind me only to see Cade and Brantley sitting at the table that they shared, but no Isaiah. When Cade caught me staring, he winked at me, and I shot him a tight smile and quickly turned around and opened up a clean page in my journal and began sketching with my pencil.

The room was loud and chaotic, and my head was no better. Everything was jumbled, and I was antsy. Antsy to see Isaiah. Antsy to be alone with him again. Antsy for the future.

Just as Mrs. Fitz walked in and began shuffling things around on her desk—the same one I was on last night—the room grew quiet. I began lowering my pencil when I felt the shift in the air. The corners of my lips curved, and I closed my journal.

Two smoldering blue eyes were staring directly at me, and the way he walked into the room, commanding everyone's attention, had my heart galloping. His long lean legs in his dark pants, the white dress shirt unbuttoned at the top along with his tie hanging loosely around his neck. The tan of his skin caught my attention, and my mouth went dry, remembering just how hot it felt rubbing against mine last night. I couldn't believe the way my body reacted to him. I couldn't believe what he'd done to me and how mind-numbing it was.

He was in front of me within seconds, pulling out the chair as it screeched along the tiled floor. Mrs. Fitz looked up and shot him a look.

"That's not your seat, Mr. Underwood."

Isaiah gave her the warmest smile I'd ever seen. "I know Mrs. Fitz, but during my last tutoring session with Gemma, she was teaching me a little about the components of drawing. Would it be okay if I sat beside her so we could resume our lesson? I'm not sure how many more tutoring sessions we will have since my grades are drastically improving."

What was he doing? I watched Mrs. Fitz's disapproving glare soften. She looked over to me and then back at Isaiah, placing the backs of her hands on her full hips. "I suppose that's fine. Gemma is doing a wonderful job tutoring you. I'm very glad she is helping you. The SMC is impressed with your overall change, Isaiah. We just discussed it Monday night during the bonfire."

I jumped as Isaiah's hand swiftly fell to my bare thigh underneath the table. I swore my leg caught on fire. My shoulders flew back, and I fought to keep my breathing in check. I snuck a peek at him, and he was looking straight ahead, completely unaffected.

"I'm glad to hear that. Tutoring with Gemma has been nothing less than a godsend." There was a slight shift in his tone, and my brow furrowed as he erased some of the space between us, pushing his hand up higher on my leg. Was he serious right now? I almost pushed it away, but I enjoyed it a little too much. "Oh, and Mrs. Fitz? I meant to tell you how nice your desk looks today. Did you reorganize it?"

I snapped my head straight ahead and clamped my legs shut. My hand grabbed onto his, and I squeezed the life out of it, causing his shoulders to shake for a moment. I was pretty sure I heard Cade snicker from behind, and I threw a glare over my shoulder at him too.

Embarrassment flooded me as I remembered everything flying off her desk last night, but then came the laughter. My own lips started to tremble, and I hated myself for finding it so funny. It could have been catastrophic if Mrs. Fitz had found Isaiah and me half-asleep with our clothes undone. He might have gotten expelled, and Richard would have found out. We were being so careless, but part of me loved taking that risk with him. I liked breaking the rules.

Mrs. Fitz scoffed as she looked over at her desk, and I slowly shook my head, knowing that Isaiah could see me. "The strangest thing happened. I walked in here this morning, and all of my things were completely scattered on the floor. Nash had walked in before breakfast and asked if I had seen the raccoon that had somehow gotten loose in the school. Apparently, it came in here and dismantled things!" She gave a little laugh, and a few of our classmates began murmuring.

A raccoon? Really? That was what Shiner had told her? And she believed that? I thought for a moment... Shiner *could* be very persuasive. Or at least that was what he thought, anyway.

"Is that so?" Isaiah's thumb began rubbing circles on the inside of my leg, and even though my hand was still clamped over his, I let him. I felt the rush of warmth. He whispered down into my ear. "Now that would have been a good headline for Mary's Murmurs, yeah?"

I snuck another peek over at him as he peered down at me. His thick lashes were full of life along with the chiseled smile on his face. We both knew what was on Mary's Murmurs this morning, and I was beyond thankful that Cade had gotten it shut down before anyone had seen it—except the one person who had put it on there, which was likely Bain.

But why was Bain sneaking out of bed in the middle of the night and taking pictures of Isaiah and me? That was beyond creepy. Was it just to get Isaiah expelled?

"Stop worrying about it," Isaiah whispered just as Mrs.

Fitz started to gather the rest of the supplies for class. "I'll take care of Bain." I went to nod, but the rest of Isaiah's sentence stunned me. "And I'll take care of you, too."

My chest locked as I turned fully toward him. The amusement that was there seconds ago was replaced with a steep determination, and the tick of his jaw had my heart thumping louder than I wanted. He raised his brows, and I briefly nodded, turning back to focus on the rest of class.

CHAPTER FIFTY-ONE

ISAIAH

THE FINAL BELL had echoed in the hall fifteen minutes ago, and all of our lacrosse gear was already being loaded onto the one bus that St. Mary's owned. My jersey was resting along my tense shoulders as I waited for Gemma to come around the bend in the hallway.

It was torturous not slamming my mouth to hers every chance I saw her today. Every time I turned around, a member from the SMC seemed to be near, and although I had every intention of kissing and touching her every second I could, I had to remember that if I needed an excuse as to why I was out of my room after curfew, I needed to use Gemma as my scapegoat. If they knew things had shifted for us, it was unlikely they'd believe our tutoring gig, and I was so fucking close to being off probation that I couldn't risk it. I'd save the touching for behind closed doors and hidden nooks in the school.

The thought made me feel wrong. A girl like her didn't deserve to be shoved into closets and kissed behind stacks in the library. It probably made her feel like my dirty little secret, and although that was what she had to be—for now—it didn't sit right with me. She was so much better than that, and I wanted everyone in this fucking school, even the teachers, to know she was mine.

After everything she'd learned Monday and seeing me lose myself to anger and resentment, she still stood there, accepting me. She felt for me. I could see it. It was like we had some tangible connection that made me stop in my tracks. I was so fucked up over her that I had myself coming up with crazy reasons to explain why we were so drawn to one another. Had we been soul-mates in another life? Was she a past lover reincarnated to become just that again? Why couldn't I breathe when she was near? Why couldn't I stop searching for her within every room I stepped into? Was I just *that* afraid she'd leave without saying goodbye?

I didn't even want to think of the moment that was soon approaching. I wouldn't stop her from leaving. I knew it was the only logical thing to do, not only because of the shit I had going on but for her too. That was another thing added to my shoulders. *What did he do to her?*

Gemma's need to keep her secrets close was understandable. I understood. How could I not? I was the same way. But that didn't lessen the need to know. That didn't take away the burning stake that was driven into my chest every time I'd come up with a scenario in my head as to why she was running.

I had every intention of finding out what was really going on, whether she was gone or not.

"There she is." Cade nodded down toward the end of the hall and stepped away near the side door of the east wing. Coach would be wondering where we were if we didn't get out there soon, and the last thing I wanted was a fucking search party for his star players, only to find me with Gemma.

Her soft voice floated down the hall with as much sweetness as a mouthful of sugar. "I can definitely study with you in a few. I don't have to tutor tonight because of the big lacrosse game. Isaiah won't be back until late, so I'm free."

Another voice. "Oh, thank God. Do you want me to just meet you in your room? Or mine?"

"Just come to my room. I'll let Sloane know. She won't mind!"

"Awesome! Thanks so much, Gemma."

"You're welcome!" I could hear the smile in Gemma's tone, and it gave me an unwelcome fluttering in my core. My hand shot out at the last second, and I grabbed onto her arm.

A high-pitched squeal echoed in the tiny crook underneath the stairs, and when the swirl of brown hair settled, I locked onto two big green eyes.

"Isaiah!" A gasp came next as I pushed her small frame against the stone wall gently. "You scared me. I thought you were Bain."

My lip lifted. "Disappointed?"

A half-roll of her eyes deepened my smile. "Quite the opposite. What are you doing? I thought you had an away game."

I took a step closer to her, nestling my knee in its rightful spot between her legs. My fingers intertwined with one of hers, and I brought our joined hands up above her head, resting them against the cool wall of our haunted boarding school. "I do," I said, leaning in close. "But honestly the thought of getting on that bus with twenty sweaty guys is already bad enough without going an entire day without touching you." *What was I doing? This was not why I came to see her.*

A rush of pink swept over Gemma's face, and I loved it. I

loved every shade of red on her skin. She blushed so much. "You've gone eighteen years without touching me. What's one more day?"

I shrugged. "After last night, I don't really intend to find out." My lips closed in on hers, and she paused before opening her mouth and letting me kiss her. I deepened the kiss, completely unable to stop myself, and she fucking loved it. Her tongue jolted into my mouth, exploring like she'd done the night before when her walls seemed to shatter. I dropped her hand and gripped her tightly to my body, trying like hell to reel myself in before I was even more late for the bus.

I broke away just as Gemma's hands started to creep up my jersey. "Fuck, this was not what I had intended to do when I pulled you in here."

Her breaths were soft and fast. Her warm hands were still on my tense abs. "Did...did you need something else?"

I shook my head slowly, peering down at our touching chests and her inviting lips. I glanced away before I kissed her again. The girl was a drug. Intoxicating. Every bit of her innocence nearly begged me to destroy it. *You did destroy it, last night, on Mrs. Fitz's desk.* "Not really. I just wanted to remind you that you need to stay in your room tonight. With me and the rest of the Rebels at the game, Bain will be free, and he is unpredictable at this point."

A tiny smile appeared. "You could have just texted me that. Remember? You gave me a phone."

My finger brushed the side of her cheek as I pushed a stray piece of hair behind her ear. Her little hands cupped me around my stomach, and I fought the shiver that worked itself down my back. "I know." There was a small amount of vulnerability seeping in with my next words. "But I wanted to see you. Every time I turned around today, it seemed like someone was watching us."

She nodded in agreement, sucking her bottom lip in

between her white teeth, and I *felt* my pupils dilate. My chest grew tight as I pushed up along her body, and I felt the war brewing inside of me. A strangled growl crawled out of the deepest parts of my soul, and Gemma paused.

"What's wrong?"

What was wrong? I felt crazed. That was what was wrong. The need to touch her and feel her and kiss every inch of her skin was driving me fucking mad. The rational part of me needed to shove her away, close down my emotions, and get back the numb Isaiah. But that part of me lost. That part of me lost the second I looked into her innocent eyes and perfect bow-shaped lips.

My hands found the small of her back, and my lips brushed over hers before I moved to the side of her neck where I'd left my mark. "Everything feels wrong when I'm not touching you," I whispered before kissing her neck gently. "And that's a troubling thought, Gemma." A soft breath left her, and that was all it took for my temptation to take over. I didn't care if I was late to lacrosse. I didn't care about anything except fueling the fire I felt when I was with her. Gemma had changed me, and I couldn't change back. She was the one thing that I'd get on my knees for, and when the time came, I would look for her. I'd look for her, and I'd find her, and I'd bring her back to me because what I was feeling right now eclipsed the dark future that was clawing at my back like a fucking hellhound. I'd find a way to make my life mine with her by my side. I was through giving my father the choice to dictate me.

"It's like that for me too. I *like* your hands on me." Gemma's sultry tone had me rubbing my growing dick over her pussy that was so close to being completely bare in her uniform. My finger skimmed the outside of her panties as I thrusted my hips upward, catching that plump lip in between my teeth as she gripped onto my shoulders. I was so damn hungry for her that I felt like I'd die if I didn't get a taste. Just one. *Go slow.* I was going too fast, too soon. Gemma wasn't like the girls I was used to. She wasn't experienced, but fuck me if she didn't act like she was.

"Do you like when my hands do this?" I asked, dipping my finger inside of her. Her eyes caught mine, and it was pure euphoria. Seeing her pleasured was life changing. *Fuck, she was already wet.*

She nodded vigorously, her hair sticking to her forehead. "It feels..." Her eyes closed as she rested her head back onto the wall, letting me play with her body all tucked away in a dark corner of the school. I lied earlier. I liked having her to myself. She could be my dirty little secret. No one needed to know what she looked like when I touched her or graced her lips with mine. *No. She was mine.* "I like how you make me feel, Isaiah. I can't stop thinking about it. I've been thinking about it since that night you pulled me into the linen closet and rubbed a finger over my hip."

A whimper left her, and I kept my mouth shut because I felt the same, so much so I couldn't put it into words. My finger pumped in a few more times, and I watched her hand come up and touch her breast, and I had to shut my eyes from whipping my dick out and sinking it into her. If it were anyone else, I wouldn't care to go slow, but I had *just* taken her virginity last night. *God damn, don't fuck it up.* Her wetness coated my finger, and I couldn't control myself. Dirty things started to spew from my mouth into her ear as I ran my thumb against her swollen clit.

"You are the dirtiest good girl I've ever met, Gemma." I sucked her earlobe into my mouth, and she cried out. "I can't wait to do things to you that will have you screaming my fucking name."

Her hips moved back and forth, and her words were ragged. "Like—like what?"

A deep chuckle rumbled out, and she started to move faster against my finger as I added in another. She moaned, and my dick was so hard I almost took my other hand to rub one out.

"Dude, hurry the fuck up," Cade called out. "I'm heading to the bus. I'll tell Coach you're right behind me. You've got two minutes."

Two minutes? No problem.

Shock flew from Gemma's mouth in a fast breath, but I placed my lips on hers, drowning out Cade. It took her a second to relax, but when she started to move her hips again, I pulled back and hovered over her ear. "I'll taste you while you taste me." My blood pumped as Gemma's breathing grew faster. "I'll make you come from that, and then I'll make you come again as I finger-fuck you like this."

A soft moan came from her, and she began tightening around my finger. I grabbed her thigh that was clamped down to my hip and pushed it open wide, letting cool air brush over her sensitive skin. *God, this was so fucking hot.*

"And then I'll fuck your face until we're both seconds from coming and flip you around and sink deep inside your tight little pussy so I can feel you clamp down on me and watch your beautiful face fill with pleasure."

"Ahh," Gemma's cry was muffled as I swallowed her moan. Her nails dug into my jersey, and her hips thrust against my finger one more time before she came undone. My mouth kept moving over hers as I relished in her taste long after she was done orgasming. I couldn't stop kissing her.

"Fuck, Gemma," I said, finally pulling back. "That was fucking hot." My finger slowly left her middle, and a wicked part of me wanted to pop it into my mouth and suck on it. I didn't, though, because was she ready for that? Was I ready to show her what I was capable of? I was hardly hanging on by a thread. I was fucking crazed on the inside.

"I didn't know I could feel like this. I..." she whispered, all doe-eyed and dazed. She was beautiful. So beautiful my chest ached. "I didn't know this was what it was like."

I shook my head, pushing her hair away from her flushed face. "It isn't always like this, Gemma." Her eyes flicked to mine. "There's something different with you. With us. When we touch..." I glanced away, wading through the thoughts that were clouding my vision and making me want to keep her tucked away in this school forever for my own personal gain. When I glanced back at her, the guilt came crashing back, and I knew that we were fucking doomed. I'd seen her shield slip down a few times and watched as the innocence she held so delicately in her hands was washed away by me. Was it wrong? Was she letting her guard down only for me to destroy her in the end? Only for *her* to destroy *me* in the end?

I lowered her leg and straightened her skirt, feeling the truth burn the back of my throat. "I feel like every time I touch you I'm stripping you of your innocence. I'm taking away something that you should have with someone else." *I feel like I'm ruining you.*

Her chin tipped upward, and a determined look came over her face. That fiery girl was back, and I'd missed her. Her hands bunched up into my jersey, and she pulled me closer to her, surprising me. "Don't look so guilty. I want you to take all of my innocence, Isaiah. I want *you* to have it. And no one else."

There was a moment right there, as she said those words, that I felt like I was holding the entire world in my hands. And maybe I was. But the moment was fleeting as something bright caught my eye. Our intimate moment was cut in half as I snapped my head over to the left, just past the break in the tiny crook I'd pulled Gemma into. The air turned to ice.

I quickly turned my back to the flash that caught my eye and bent down to kiss the tip of Gemma's nose. "I'll take whatever you want to give me. But for now, go to your room so I'm not tempted to lose my spot on the lacrosse team for staying here with you." Gemma smiled shyly at me, and I winked. "I'll text you when we're back later. Just to let you know."

Just before she started to walk away, I pulled her back by her arm gently. "Stay in your room, and if you go to the dining hall for dinner, take someone with you. Like Sloane. Don't walk the halls alone, got it?"

Her brows dropped for a moment. "But what if Bain sneaks out while you guys are all gone? Who will follow him to tell your dad what he's doing?"

My hand tightened a fraction as her blazer bunched in my fingers. She shouldn't have been worrying about this, and she looked awfully concerned over it. "I have it covered...and don't even think about it."

Her lips pursed. "Think about what?"

I raised an eyebrow as my hand dropped. I knew what she was thinking, and she was absolutely crazy if she thought I'd allow her to follow him for me *or* my father.

Her mouth twitched, and she sighed. "Just trying to help you. If you need me to do anything, just text me."

What I needed was for her to stay in her room all night long. "I'll text you when I'm back." I quickly bent down and kissed her lips again. "Go the long way back to your room, okay?"

I could tell she wanted to ask me why, but instead, she nodded and turned around, heading in that direction.

I waited underneath the stairwell until Gemma had disappeared, and then I whipped around, knowing very well that it had been more than the two minutes that Cade said I had. Lacrosse could wait, and I wouldn't give two fucks if Coach wanted my balls for being late. I'd gladly lose my spot on the team if it meant catching Bain alone without watchful eyes.

I walked over to the side door that Cade had darted out of minutes ago, pushed it open as if I were leaving, and then slammed it shut. Silence filled the long hallway, and I glanced at the tiny crook that Gemma and I were tucked away in and then to every spot that could have had a visual on us. One small area behind the corner of a classroom snagged my attention, and I slowly strode over on light feet and listened again.

My heart had slowed, and my ears were sharp. My fingers hung loose by my side, and the second I felt a shift in the air, I reached my hand out and connected with bare flesh. "Drop the fucking camera, Bain."

His crazed eyes turned to slits as his face began turning red. His free hand came up out of instinctual panic, and he clamped onto my wrist, digging his nails into my skin. I turned my head and let out a laugh. Did he really think a little cut to my skin would lessen my grip on his throat? Did he have any idea who I was or what I'd fucking seen? My father used to wrap both his hands around my neck until I saw stars, and he taught me to do the same.

Bain's face began turning a shade of purple as I pushed him further up against the stone casing. The panic I saw turned to calculation as he figured out how to get out of my grip. His elbow raised above my arm, and just before he could connect, I let go and flicked my own up to knock the camera out of his free hand. Black pieces scattered all around the floor, along with the Polaroid photos of me with my hand up Gemma's skirt. The photos skittered along the black-and-white tile, standing out like knives in the middle of a goddamn gun fight.

Bain was gasping for air as I bent down and snatched them with my hand, feeling my pulse drum so violently that I could feel it behind my eyes. The side door opened, and I knew it was Cade, coming to get me. He was beside me within seconds and had Bain pinned to the wall. Not that Bain was putting up a fight. A coy grin covered his face as he glanced at the photo in my hands.

"She's quite the moaner, isn't she?" Red covered my vision, and the hold on my resolve slipped through my fingers just as fast as the photo fell to the ground.

His blood splattered on the wall as my fist connected with his cheek. One slice of his skin wasn't nearly enough to calm my anger, but when I met Cade's eye, he was giving me that look that made me pause.

Think, Isaiah. Fucking think.

Bain's laughter was sinister, and my head turned away as I reeled in my irrational behavior and tried like hell to think of the bigger plan. I needed to be smarter. I needed to be the man I was meant to be and not the man my father wanted. But fuck, I was tempted lately.

Cade grunted as Bain forcefully bucked his head back and nearly connected with his nose. "I swear to God, I will fuck you up, Bain."

He laughed, the noise echoing throughout the empty hallway. "Neither one of you will fuck me up. There's too much on the line."

Taking a step forward, I leveled him with a glare. "Looks to me like I just stepped over that line."

"Oooh. There he is. The Huntsman's flesh and blood that everyone fears. The prodigal son. The one that is supposedly going to *end* the war of arms trafficking in the west." Bain threw his head back again and laughed harder as I stood with my arms down by my side and zero expression on my face.

"You mean the war that you're setting up? The war that your father plans to win?" I took another step closer and breathed down on him with as much distaste as I could possibly feel in my body. Bain had no fucking idea that I was one step ahead of him. Cade didn't know either. No one did.

This was something I had to handle on my own. Keeping my secrets close—that was what I did.

Or maybe I just held them close because I knew that the future I was currently choosing for myself and my younger brother may have made me just as bad as my father. I knew Cade and Brantley stood behind me, and they backed my decisions, but when it came to their futures too, would they be so willing to stand beside me if it meant that the people they loved could possibly be caught in the web?

Bain struggled against Cade's hold once more, and although Cade was stronger than he appeared, Bain was just as muscular. He was stocky and knew how to use his body weight, just like me. "You think I don't know what you're up to, Bain, but I fucking do." Something dark began to stir in my blood as I glanced down to the photo of me and Gemma again, and before I knew it, I was spitting in his face and getting as close as I could without risking the chance of him headbutting me like he'd tried to do to Cade. "Take another fucking photo of Gemma, and I swear to God, I will rip your fucking eyeballs out of your head."

There was a slight twitch in his eye as his lips forced out another haughty smile. "You won't touch me."

"Fucking try me." All bets were off when he included Gemma in this little game of ours. Of our fathers'. I wanted to believe that Gemma had nothing to do with this war of weaponry that was brewing and setting up the next line of gun traffickers, but after seeing Judge Stallard with Bain at the Covens, it would have been naive of me to think otherwise. I didn't believe in coincidences.

Bain's voice lowered as the side door slammed open. "Jack's life is on the line, Isaiah. You won't do a damn thing because you know he'll be the one to suffer. Your father is even sicker than mine."

My cheek lifted, and I could sense that Cade was

confused by my reaction. Bain wasn't nearly as good at masking his emotions as he thought, because I could see the confusion brewing in him too. "You mistake me for someone who's selfless, Bain." I laughed as I bent down and swooped up the rest of the photos of Gemma and tucked them into my pocket. "Think again, errand boy. You may be on your father's payroll, but I'm sure as fuck not on mine, no matter the threats he sends my way."

"Boys!" Coach's raspy voice echoed throughout the hall as Cade and I began walking toward the door. He stood there with his maroon polo on and tobacco half hanging out of his mouth, even though tobacco wasn't tolerated on school premises. "Get your asses on the bus now. We're 'bout to be late to Temple, and for fuck's sake, Isaiah...wipe the blood off your knuckles. You're on probation, and this team will be damned if you get expelled."

Cade snorted as we briskly walked out the door with Coach following, leaving Bain with his broken camera on the floor of St. Mary's.

As soon as we were seated on the bus with Brantley and Shiner sitting directly across from us, Cade dropped his voice. "What the fuck was that?"

I leaned back onto the sticky vinyl backing of the seat and stretched my legs out as far as I could, glancing out the window at the high, castle-like dome of St. Mary's. "Bain's been playing us this whole time."

"What do you mean?" Brantley demanded, his face a mask of determination.

I craned my neck toward him. "Do you really think a guy like Bain doesn't know we're following him when he leaves? Do you really think he doesn't know about the fucking trackers we put on his cars? He probably already knows there's one on the G-wagon. From the very second he knew who I was, he changed his path. He's starting a war between his father and mine."

"We already knew there was a war brewing," Cade noted.

I shook my head, glancing back out to the school and wondering why Gemma's uncle, Judge Stallard, seemed to be in the middle of all of this. I wasn't positive if his part was large or small, but what I did know was that Gemma needed to leave now more than ever. Especially if her uncle was more than just a vessel in between two opposing sides. "Bain wanted me to see the deal at the Covens. He knew I'd tell my father that his father was moving into our territory."

Brantley slumped back into his seat. "Therefore, you kick-started things by telling him what you'd seen."

I nodded again.

Silence passed as the rest of the team chatted around us. Shiner sighed and pulled his headphones on, drowning out our conversation out of respect or maybe annoyance that he wasn't as big of a part of it as we were.

Cade glanced over at me. "So now what?"

"Now?" I asked, raising my brows. "Now we decide which side of the war we want to be on."

CHAPTER FIFTY-TWO

GEMMA

Trust was such a fickle thing. It was delicate too. Easily broken, but not easily mended. I'd trusted before, and it was a fleeting entity. Trust was volatile. Someone could take the trust they gave you and become unpredictable with it. I was jaded with the term, and the flip in my stomach when I thought about trusting someone made me queasy, but I was nearly there with Isaiah.

And I thought he was there with me too. I knew things about him that others didn't. He shared Jack with me, even in such a small way, but he trusted me enough to tell me about his little brother and the threat of his father. I didn't take that information lightly, which was exactly why I was doing this alone.

I just hoped that it didn't ruin the little trust that we had in each other as of late. He trusted me when I'd told him I would stay in my room all night. And when he'd said it, and I agreed, the idea was just barely a seed sprouting in the back of my head.

Now it was full on blooming, and with each step that I took toward the side door of St. Mary's, well past curfew, another seedling sprouted.

The hallway was quiet and motionless. Sloane had fallen asleep early tonight, which was to my benefit, and either she thought the guys were already back and that I was sneaking out to see Isaiah, or she didn't wake up, because I had no missed texts besides the one from Isaiah that said they were on their way back to the school from Temple.

My heart pounded as my foot hit the pebbled stone beneath my shoes, and the cool moisture from the night air hit my warm cheeks. The hood was pulled up over my head, and the feeling of someone lurking behind me made the hairs on the back of my neck stand erect.

Bain wasn't leaving the school tonight. I knew that because of his conversation earlier in the evening. I called it fate. It was like a stronger force had aligned all the stars and put me in the perfect spot to overhear his phone conversation at dinner, bringing me to my current decision. He had been tucked away in the same little corner that Isaiah had pulled me into earlier to do things to me that made me blush at the mere thought, chuckling into the phone.

"The Rebels took my keys for the night. Or sent someone to do their dirty work."

The other person on the phone rumbled out a grumpy laugh, and it echoed along the stone walls. He must have been on speaker. *"Do they not assume you have a spare? They truly do think you're a fucking idiot, don't they?"*

Bain snorted. *"I'm sure they searched high and low for the spare. Little did they know, it's in the fucking electrical box at the warehouse."* He laughed menacingly before sighing. *"It doesn't matter. It's not like I'm leaving tonight anyway. Who's doing the run tonight?"*

I left the conversation shortly after, feeling my heart

thrash inside from the eavesdropping. It was like listening to Richard on the phone inside his office all over again. The fear of being caught made every nerve in my body fizzle out every single time.

After glancing back behind me a thousand times, sweat lining my hairline, I watched as St. Mary's disappeared in the distance, and I retraced the same route that Isaiah and I had taken. It wasn't difficult to find the warehouse, as there wasn't much more around St. Mary's other than long winding roads and a few streetlights here and there for good measure. My breath fanned out in front of my face from the chill in the air, and my pace picked up when I eventually saw the rickety metal shack up above. The closer I got to it, the more my blood raced. Adrenaline filled me up as I breathed heavily. I kept pushing Isaiah out of my head, knowing he would be upset with me if he knew what I was doing, and there was a little bit of shame and guilt that came with that, but my curiosity was coming in like rolling thunder. *The Covenant Psychiatric Hospital.* I had to know. I had to know why it was so familiar. I needed to know why the hospital was so clear inside my memories that I'd managed to draw it before Isaiah even took me there.

There was nothing on the website that made me think twice, but each and every time I saw that drawing, something pulled at my chest. Something urgent. And there was a nagging thought in the back of my head that said, *What if Tobias was there?* What if it was some weird twin telepathy thing going on?

I sighed, pushing my hair away from my face. There was only one way to find out, and I knew that Isaiah wouldn't take me with him again. It was too dangerous last time, and he regretted taking me in the first place. And I wasn't going to bring him with me or ask him to take me back. Not only would that open up a lot of questions that I wasn't ready to answer yet, but Isaiah had more on the line than I thought.

I wouldn't put him in a position that could extradite him to expulsion. If the SMC somehow found out that I'd snuck out, then that was on me. But if Isaiah was with me, and we were caught off school grounds, *not* tutoring like we were supposed to be? He'd be done for. Expelled just like that. And I didn't want him to cover for me, and I had a big feeling that he would try to.

And if I were being honest, being on my own, making choices for myself—even if I was breaking the rules—felt empowering. Like I was climbing the ladder that I'd been forced to hold for someone else all my life, finally reaching that top rung. Good girls who listen to others and follow all the rules never rise to the top, so I was done being good. I was done being forced to the bottom and doing what I was supposed to do for someone else's benefit.

I needed answers, and I was going to find them one way or another.

The second my hand landed on Bain's spare keys shoved inside the electric box off to the side of the warehouse door —just like he'd said—I was filled with intoxicating pride.

I was doing this.

I slid inside Bain's car with my heart pumping blood to every inch of my body so viciously that my skin singed with anticipation. I really hoped that Isaiah's little driving lesson was enough for me to get to the Covenant Psychiatric Hospital and back without wrecking into any stone walls like last time.

The car came to life as I turned the key and pressed my shaky foot on the brake. I took my time figuring out the seat, wiggling my fingers over the steering wheel, and looking in the rearview mirror every three seconds, hoping to God

Bain's beady eyes didn't pop up in full rage that I was taking his car for a spin, but no one appeared.

It was just me and the open road.

After a few seconds of pushing my foot on the accelerator and jerking the brake once or twice, I was on my way.

I followed the directions I'd written down, knowing my phone didn't work without St. Mary's Wi-Fi, and before I knew it, the curvy roads and blurred white lines gave way to the looming building, and I was there. My head jolted forward as I slammed on the brakes, and my parking job was completely off, but I'd made it.

The sign was flickering ominously, the P in Psychiatric brighter than the rest, and every once in a while, the only letters that were lit spelled the word Coven, but I had made it. Chills raced over my arms, goosebumps rising as I stepped one foot out of the car. I jumped at the sound of my door slamming, even though I was the one who'd done it. I was on edge, and that was probably a good thing.

That meant I wasn't stupid enough to walk into a random place and think I would make it back out. If this place meant something to me in my subconscious, it likely wasn't something good.

Damp leaves smooshed beneath my shoes as I traveled through a small wooded area, careful to keep hidden. It was pitch black outside, and the flickering light of the sign grew dimmer as I rounded the building that I could barely see through the limbs. My breathing was labored, and I could hear my heartbeat in my ears. I stood beside a tree, placing my hand on the rough bark and staring at the small opening that showed the building, and waited for something to happen. Would my subconscious take over and take me back to the time that I'd first seen this building? Would I remember something that I'd suppressed long ago? Would the beating of my heart ever calm enough for me to walk to the side door and peer inside? What exactly was on the other side of that door? Tobias?

The pain I'd constantly pushed down was surfacing. The hole in my heart grew deeper, and the sting of my brother being gone for the last four years was cutting away at me the longer I stood beside the tree. If he was in there, I'd figure out a way to get him back. Just because it was a psychiatric hospital didn't mean that my brother was mentally ill. He was as sane as ever the last time I'd seen him. Back then, I thought he might have been sick. Or maybe delusional. With everything he was spouting off to me and how he had gripped me tightly by the shoulders and begged me to survive, telling me not believe anything Richard said, was alarming. He had acted erratically, and it had scared me. But now I knew that Tobias was telling the truth. He was right.

Why weren't any memories coming back to me? I grunted in frustration, anger and annoyance beginning to force my feet forward. I didn't see anything but the door in front of me, and the closer I got, the more frantic I became. It was a black door with a green awning overhead. My eyes ping-ponged between the two, and when I found myself underneath the tattered green fabric, I found my eyes rising and locking onto it.

This. I remembered this. Only, it wasn't tattered the first time I'd seen it. And the green wasn't as faded.

Why have I been here? I clenched my eyes, bringing my hands up and underneath the hood of my black jacket, fisting at my hair. *Remember, Gemma!*

Just as I started to sort through the dark memories, digging my heels into the hard surface below my feet, I jerked, shooting my eyes open. A hand wrapped around my bicep, and I was swung around violently and thrown up against the door. My head banged off the back of it, and I cried out, fear nearly choking me to death.

I gulped back a scream when I peered up into a man's face who was glaring down at me with sick pleasure in his dark eyes. "And what is a good girl like you doing in a place like this?"

His grip grew tighter, his fingers pulling the fabric of my jacket. My heart climbed to my throat, and I felt the blood drain from my face. *What the hell did I get myself into?* The puffs of air were barely making it out of my chest as panic started to surface. The beady look on his face grew with satisfaction as my body began to shake. He smiled, and my stomach fell. "Where is Bain? Huh?" He dipped his face closer to me, and I smelled the cigar scent lingering on his tongue. Just like Richard. "Where is he, you stupid little bitch?" His arm rose quickly, and before I could duck, the back of his hand landed on my cheek, and I cried out in pain. I blinked a few times, trying to steady my vision, but the trees in front of me swayed even more. "Did he send you to make the sales?"

"What?" The word came out slowly, and I tried to snap myself out of the lull I was in. My head pounded. The throbbing was there at my temples, making me wince, but I dug down as deep as I possibly could and stared at one thing in front of me, steadying my gaze. *You've been in worse places, Gemma. You are strong.* I swallowed as his lip snarled. "Bain isn't with me. I came here on my own."

Regret began to poke at the thick wall I shot up from the second I made the decision to come here. I shouldn't have. It was a mistake. It was apparent that I hadn't learned my lesson with Richard. My plan had holes in it, and I convinced myself that fate was leading me here for a reason, but I was wrong. Fate had tricked me. My plan wasn't concise, and I knew better. I knew better than to jump into action and feed the stupid impulses without a solid freaking plan, and here I was. Caught.

I'm going to end up in that fucking basement again.

No. No, I wasn't.

I leveled my chin and tried to yank my arm out from his grip. "I stole his car."

He snorted, clearly not believing me. I watched as his tongue ran over his white teeth. The man was tall, taller than Richard and slimmer too. He wore a nice black suit that screamed prestige, and his black hair was gelled back to perfection. On the outside, he looked like he could have been a nice businessman in a fancy office somewhere in the city, but I knew better than most that looks could be deceiving. It was the handsome ones that were the sickest. They thought they were untouchable, and that made them unpredictably dangerous.

"*You* stole his car?"

I nodded, ignoring the throb behind my eyes.

"So then that means you know him?"

I said nothing, and his eyes flared. He pushed me up against the door again, and I whimpered as my head hit it once more. *Shit.* What did he want from me? It was obvious he thought Bain had been here. Did he see his car? Had he been following me? "So you say Bain isn't here?" He chuckled, and my stomach convulsed. He was amused, and I had no idea why. "So he didn't bring along his little piece of ass with him on a run? To show her how manly he was? How rich he could get off a few gun sales? In my *fucking* territory!" I jumped as his voice bellowed around me. "Tell me..." He creeped in closer, and I felt his hot, angry breath over my face. My entire body began to shake as the familiar feeling of panic crept over my skin like a slithering snake. "Does he fuck you while he holds those precious guns too? To show you how *dangerous* he can be?" He threw his head back and laughed loudly. It was the only noise I could hear. The forest sounds were gone. Even the buzzing of the light above our heads had vanished. "I'll show him how dangerous *I* can be. This is my area. Not theirs."

Suddenly, I was jerked to my knees as his hand pushed on my head, gripping my hair in his tight fist. The concrete scraped my skin even through my jeans, and I bit my lip to keep from crying. *This was not happening. This was not Richard. I didn't have chains around my wrists. I could run.*

"I'm going to fuck your pretty little mouth and film the entire fucking thing. Then, I'll fuck you until you bleed, and you can take it back to Bain and show him what I'm capable of. He touches my things? Well, I touch his."

My eyes grew wide, and just as I was about to scream from the panic clawing right out of my chest, a voice boomed from behind.

"Dad."

I froze. My heart stopped beating.

The grip on my hair tightened, and I pushed my head up to meet his hand to ease the pain. "Isaiah. How nice of you to show up."

Isaiah. Isaiah was here. And the man who had a tight grip on me, threatening to do horrific things to me just like Richard, was his father. *Holy shit.*

A small amount of relief seeped in through the fear and panic. It was fine. Isaiah was here. He'd tell his father that I wasn't Bain's girlfriend or whatever he thought I was to Bain. He'd tell him that Bain would be glad that he was doing this to me. That it wouldn't even affect Bain at all, and then he'd let me go.

When Isaiah's dad flung me up to my feet by pulling my hair, I fought a yelp and locked onto Isaiah. He spared me a fleeting glance and then looked back at his father with nothing but boredom across his features. *Wait.* I sliced my gaze to Cade and Brantley who were a few feet away, and neither one of them would look at me.

What the hell was going on? Why wouldn't they look at me? Surely they weren't *that* upset that I had left the school. It was a mistake, but... *Never trust, Gemma.* Tobias' voice cut through, and it made me angry. It was okay to trust the right people, and I trusted Isaiah. He would get me out of his father's grip, and it would be fine.

I swallowed past the emotional lump that was sitting nice and still in the back of my throat and leveled my chin, even if it did make my scalp hurt.

Isaiah crossed his arms over his chest, still sporting his lacrosse jersey that had grass stains and mud all over it. "What are you doing here? Isn't this my job?"

His father chuckled, but it was full of cynicism. "You can't do your job right. I got the alert from the tracker. I thought you said you had tonight handled."

Isaiah raised his arms. "I'm here, aren't I? And where is Bain?" Isaiah looked around sarcastically, the moonlight hitting right over the arches of his cheek. "Nowhere to be seen, yeah? That's because he's back at the fucking school." He took a step forward, still unable to look me in the eye. "You say I can't do my job right? Let me ask you this? Where's Jack? Hopefully not all alone with your shell of a wife, like Monday."

Isaiah's words struck a nerve with his father. My hair was pulled, and I was standing on my tiptoes now, trying to ease the pain. "Then who is this? She was driving Bain's car. Are you sure he's back at St. Mary's?" his father asked, full of sarcasm. "I bet he's out here right now, watching me touch something that's his."

I paused. My body seemed to stop functioning. Blood didn't rush. My heart didn't pound. I just stood...and waited. I waited for Isaiah to jump in and make his father let me go.

Isaiah moved his dark gaze over to me so slowly that I almost screamed out his name. I waited for that connection, that small dip in his exterior to show me that he had everything handled and that he'd protect me and take care of me like he'd promised, even if I hadn't responded to his admission earlier. But then he moved his attention back to his father and shrugged.

"Just another piece of fresh ass, I suppose."

The pain. The betrayal. The complete and utter shock from what had left his mouth had my feet touching back down to the concrete even with the pulling of my hair. I blinked once. And then twice. I stared at him, begging myself to scream and kick and demand he give me back what I'd given him. But I couldn't. I just stood there in shock.

Another piece of fresh ass?

"Oh yeah?" his father said, looking over at me. I couldn't even meet his sick gaze. Instead, I stared at Isaiah. Dumbfounded. *I trusted him.* Had he been playing me this entire time? Confusion swept me off my feet so quickly I hardly heard his father ask, "And how was she? I'm sure she was yours first. Otherwise, Bain wouldn't have wanted her."

Isaiah smirked, and it drove a knife into my back. "It was like fucking an angel. Nice and pure."

His father laughed, and I felt the first tear roll down my cheek and land on the concrete below. My knees buckled, and I wanted to feel rage and hate and lash out. But I didn't. What I felt was so much worse. It numbed everything but the pain.

But that numbness was gone as soon as I heard the next words come out of Isaiah's mouth. "I say we get back to the lesson that you were talking about. He touches our things... we touch his right back."

Isaiah's father breathed out a sigh of relief. "Finally comin' around to this lifestyle, aren't ya?" My face burned with his heated look on the side of my face. "And all it took was a pretty little thing like this to make you submit. I'll keep that in mind."

And then I was pushed forward into a pack of untrustworthy fucking wolves.

TO BE CONTINUED

Isaiah and Gemma

Bad Boys Never Fall, book two, is now live! You can find it here: sjsylvis.com

Bad Boys Never Fall Blurb:

Isaiah:

We were destined to burn from the second I laid eyes on her.

Within every dark corner of St. Mary's Boarding School, watchful eyes tracked our every move. My guilty conscience whispered unjust excuses in my ear anytime we touched. Our futures suddenly became unclear, and the already blurred lines became blurrier.

A past we didn't know existed turned our walls of self-preservation to rubble. The truth was suddenly revealed, and our plan went up in flames.

Gemma thought I was the one letting her fall into the ashes. But little did she know, I was there to watch her rise.

Bad Boys Never fall is book two in the St. Mary's Duet and concludes Gemma & Isaiah's story. Bad Boys Never Fall is intended for readers 18+ and deals with subjects that some may find triggering.

AFTERWORD

What a wild ride, am I right? This has been the most difficult book I have ever written but it had nothing to do with the characters and their hearts. The plots twists (that are soon to come) and the revelations throughout this duet made my head spin on more than one occasion. I distinctly remember sitting down at my desk to write with 15 pieces of paper scattered around me full of notes regarding this plot! I hope you have fallen in love with the St. Mary's gang and are super excited for book two! I promise you that your questions will be answered and you'll learn of everything that is really happening with Gemma and Isaiah. They have been my favorite couple to write thus far. Isaiah Underwood is the perfect mix of hero and villain. He's hot, authoritative, but *man* does he have a good heart or what? & Gemma, poor Gemma. The things you're about to learn are jaw-dropping! Here's to book two, my friends! Buckle up. It's just as wild as book one!!

XO.

ALSO BY SJ SYLVIS

English Prep Series

All the Little Lies

All the Little Secrets

All the Little Truths

St. Mary's Series

Good Girls Never Rise

Bad Boys Never Fall

Standalones

Three Summers

Yours Truly, Cammie

Chasing Ivy

Falling for Fallon

Truth

All of SJ Sylvis' books are FREE in Kindle Unlimited!

ABOUT THE AUTHOR

S.J. Sylvis is a romance author who is best known for her angsty new adult romances and romantic comedies. She currently resides in Arizona with her husband, two small kiddos, and dog. She is obsessed with coffee, becomes easily attached to fictional characters, and spends most of her evenings buried in a book!

sjsylvis.com

ACKNOWLEDGMENTS

As always, I would like to mention my *amazing* family for making me smile daily and for always supporting me. I love you forever and ever. <3

To my author friends (I can't list you all. I would feel too bad if I accidentally left someone out, so you know who you are!!)--where would I be without you? To our daily voice messages, shares, likes, encouraging words, and writing sprints—I love you all SO much and I am so grateful for your friendship. Here's to many more books!

To my Betas (Andrea, Danah, Emma, & Megan)—Thank you SO much for helping me with plot holes, confusing scenes, and for reminding me that I need to flip imposter syndrome the bird. You four helped me in ways you don't even realize. xo.

To my Editor, Jenn, Thank you for always making my work shine. I would not be where I am without you! xo.

To my Proofer/PA, I honestly have no idea where I would be without you, Mary! Thank you for reminding me to do the things that I forget about, for picking up my slack, and for everything else. xo.

To my Cover Designer/person who keeps me sane—Danah, thank you for everything and for making the St. Mary's covers AMAZING. xo.

Laura, you are so much more than just an author friend. I love you and your friendship! Thank you for helping me with anything I throw your way! xo.

To my readers, bloggers, ARC readers, tiktokers, anyone who helps spread the word about my books—*WOW*. You are the reason I can make this writing gig an actual career. Without your support, reviews, & shares, I wouldn't be where I am today. Thank you so incredibly much for everything you do. It does not go unnoticed.

Xo,

SJ

Lightning Source UK Ltd.
Milton Keynes UK
UKHW010713300123
416172UK00004B/276